D0437324

Blood Relations

ALSO BY JOHN A. PEAK

Spare Change

Blood Relations

JOHN A. PEAK

ST. MARTIN'S PRESS
NEW YORK

A THOMAS DUNNE BOOK.
An imprint of St. Martin's Press.

Design by Nancy Resnick

Library of Congress Cataloging-in-Publication Data

Peak, John A.
    Blood relations   /   John Peak.
        p.   cm.
    "A Thomas Dunne book."
    ISBN 0-312-15182-9
    I. Title.
  PS3566.E157B57   1997
  813'.54—dc21   97-8804
                                        CIP

First Edition: July 1997

10 9 8 7 6 5 4 3 2 1

For Dad,
who can still trim the wings of a fly
at a hundred yards.

Blood Relations

ONE

To Robert MacDonald the old-fashioned rotary phone in the kitchen sounded more like a fast clicking noise than a proper ringing sound. It forced him out of his comfortable chair in the living room and made him walk all the way to the bedroom to retrieve his hearing aid from on top of his dresser, left there as a matter of habit when he changed out of his police uniform.

He was vaguely irritated because the only calls he usually got were from people who started out, "How are you this evening?" which was his cue to hang up. People that knew Robert knew better than to use the telephone for social calls. He did, however, take calls for his son, Kevin, who was a normal twenty-year-old and operated out of the other room at the end of the hall.

What Robert remembered later was that as he came back up the hall, the persistent ringing changed his irritation to alarm.

"Hi, Mac, Bill Farrela." They had patched Bill through from a car phone and his voice sounded hollow. Farrela was a fifteen-year veteran who had worked with MacDonald off and on. He was a good inspector and, if they patched him through, he was in a hurry.

1

"Yeah, Bill, what's up?"

"Mac, there's a problem with Terry." Terry was Robert's oldest son, another cop. Farrela paused, then said, "I'm outside Terry's apartment. Can you come over?" His voice was almost casual, but not quite.

Robert couldn't catch his breath for a moment, the receiver pushing into his hearing aid until his ear hurt.

"Yeah, sure . . . What . . . ?"

"I need to talk to you over here, okay? I'm sending a car for you."

Robert squeezed the phone. No way could he wait for a car to be sent. "No, I can drive over. Be there in ten minutes." He looked automatically at his wrist but he had taken off his watch. The kitchen clock said 11:30. Robert felt the blood leave his head, nausea rising fast. Farrela was Homicide now, wasn't he?

"Okay, buddy. See you in ten minutes."

Robert snatched his gun belt off the dresser, struggling with the buckle because his hands were shaking and nothing was working right. He grabbed his jacket and raced for the front door, at the last second skidding to a halt as he thought to leave a note by the phone for Kevin.

That done, he tried to slow himself down. He hadn't been told anything yet. Terry's place wasn't far. On Jackson Avenue, he tore recklessly around a station wagon that was all but stopped in the lane in front of him, skidding to make the curve on the other side. He caught himself once more, forced himself to slow down, to make his turn now off the main street, heading over the canal on a small bridge into a dark neighborhood, a residential street bordered by huge live oaks that made the streetlamps all but useless.

A block away from Terry's street he could see the reflection of emergency-vehicle flashers on the tops of the houses up ahead of him. He came around the last curve and confronted three double-parked black-and-whites. One of the cruisers had its blue and red flashers going, the lights whirling maniacally. Robert saw light spilling from Terry's open garage door onto the darkened sidewalk.

He stopped his car in the middle of the street and watched, his mouth hanging partly open. An ambulance approached from the opposite direction. One of the black-and-whites had to move to let it back up to the garage door. Robert pulled to the curb, got out slowly and locked his car, his heart skipping about every third beat. He stood still, trying not to think, because now he knew for sure. The ambulance had not been code three. The overhead light bar had been turned off and there had been no siren. There was no hurry, no medical emergency. It was already too late.

Robert walked slowly toward the house, his hands stuffed in his jacket pockets. The scene before him was printing itself on his unthinking mind, an etching on blank silver plate; the ambulance, the police, the scattering of spectators, the garbled sound coming through one-sided on his hearing aid. The ambulance driver finished his backing maneuver short of the sidewalk without going over it into the garage. Now Robert even knew where Terry was.

As he approached the light he saw Farrela with his back to him, talking to somebody, from the coroner's office by the look of the surgical gloves he wore. Several uniformed cops were walking around, trying to step gingerly through the area that had been secured with yellow "Keep Out—Police Line" tape, an area they shouldn't have been in under any circumstances, but they went into anyway because they were as curious as the people across the street.

Robert saw the huge silhouette of James Phillips. Jimbo stepped over the tape, looking at the floor of the garage. Jimbo was Terry's partner now, wasn't he? Robert thought. It was hard to say because Terry changed partners so often, but Robert thought that was right, that Jimbo was the current one. So what were they doing here? Jimbo, all 235 pounds of him, was in uniform, obviously on duty, but looking around like he had just arrived himself. Robert saw Farrela turn and say something and Jimbo responded and walked toward the detective.

Robert stopped just short of the yellow-tape line, outside the sphere of businesslike activity where the photographer, lab technicians and then the paramedics went through their routines. A bearded young paramedic was unlimbering a portable gurney while his partner, a short young woman with a tousled mass of blond curls, tugged a yellow tarpaulin out of the back of the ambulance and turned to go back into the garage, taking her time, craning her neck to listen to the conversation from the coroner's deputy. Robert forced himself to step up to where he could see, then looked over and saw Terry's body.

The side of the back of his head was missing, the curvature of the skull vacated, leaving a cavity filled with red, creamy, gelatinous matter. The face was still, swollen, the eyes half-open, the mouth slack. It didn't even look familiar. The tarpaulin went over the body and the head, leaving the shoes exposed.

The coroner's deputy was a chubby, self-important Northerner, bald shiny head over plastic-framed glasses. He pointed to the body that they had covered. "Now, just wait a minute. Don't you move a goddamn thing until we get the pictures. You know better than that." The paramedics looked at each other but didn't say anything. They left the tarpaulin where it was and waited, lounging against the rear bumper of their ambulance.

The shoes were a pair of brown loafers that Terry had worn for many years. They were scuffed, the heels worn down, drops of old faded white paint on the edge of the soles. They were old enough that they were as comfortable as house shoes and Terry had worn them all the time at home when he had lived with Robert and Kevin. He had even had those loafers

4

two years ago when his mother was still alive and they all lived in the house. Robert had often picked those same shoes up off the kitchen floor at the house and tossed them with a satisfying double thump into Terry's room. Even now, they didn't have any indication of death on them. The shoes identified Terry better than the bizarre parody of his face. The bloody contents of his head had sprayed in a widening path across the floor to the garage entrance from where he must have been standing when the gun went off, but it had not touched the shoes.

Robert stood, hands in pockets, and let the crime-scene business go on in front of him without really seeing it. He had done it any number of times himself in the past: securing the scene, looking for evidence without disturbing anything until the inspector had a chance to see it where it lay, the body just another inert object to be stepped over, catalogued, and described. Robert stared at the shoes, thinking that he needed to cover them, like he had when Terry's feet had stuck out from under the bedcovers as a child.

At a sign from the coroner's deputy, the paramedics worked at getting the lifeless body into a zippered bag. Robert wanted to help them, but made himself stay back, watching as they loaded it onto the gurney, belting it in place. They would take care of him. This was how they were supposed to do it, the proper order of things to be done.

Bill Farrela said something and Jimbo shook his head, adamantly. Jimbo's voice continued to get louder. "Jesus H. Christ! He got so bad last week we wound up sticking him in the fucking hospital. Last two nights in a row, he didn't even call in was the only thing we knew, but I'm telling you, the way this asshole was . . ." Jimbo stopped and stared at Robert, his mouth slowly forming a small, silent "O." His face turned a deep red, flushing all the way from his huge neck to his hairline so that his eyes looked shiny and bright under the single heavy line of his eyebrows. Robert looked away from him, his eyes unfocused, wandering aimlessly over the walls of the garage. There were droplets of blood in a pattern around the track that the garage door came down in, on the wall inside the garage and presumably on the inside of the door when it was down. In the corner, where the floor would have met the door, there was a fragment of what would be parietal bone about three inches long and two inches across. Robert stared at it, focused on it until Farrela was suddenly right in front of him, blocking his view.

"Oh, man. Bad fuckin' break, Mac. Jesus, I'm sorry." Farrela was standing with his hands on Robert's shoulders. He was an inch or two taller than Robert but he bent his head over so that he could peer up into the older man's face. "I'm sorry, Mac."

He seemed to be asking for some kind of response. Robert started to say something but it stuck. He cleared his throat and tried again.

"What . . . what . . . ?"

"I don't know. I really don't. The guy that lives upstairs found him." Farrela took a deep breath and looked around. His eyes looked a little frightened when he focused on the spray pattern, the skull fragment. He put one arm around Robert's shoulders and tried to turn him away but Robert didn't move. He didn't resist but he stood still, staring at the gurney quietly, his hands still in his jacket pockets.

The deputy coroner pushed the gurney farther into the garage to get it out of his way, then started to lower the garage door. He glared at Farrela. "Excuse me, do you mind? The inspector stepped back onto the sidewalk and this time phys-ically pulled Robert out with him, letting the door close, seal-ing the garage interior from their view. In the bottom corner of the door there was a spot of light coming from a perfectly round little hole. Farrela squatted in front of it and peered, pro-fessionally engaged. He banged on the garage door with the flat of his hand.

"Hey, you getting a picture of this? Dr. Bundy, you see this down here?"

The doctor's voice was muffled, coming from inside the garage. "That's why we closed the door, Einstein."

"Well, be sure you get a couple from out here, too. Try not to overexpose 'em again, okay?"

From inside they could hear Bundy's voice, rising in anger. "Hey! Hey, don't open that door until we're finished here! Officer!"

The door rose, Jimbo bent double to get out and then closed the door behind him again with a careless shove. Standing, he looked down at Robert, opened his mouth, but then didn't say anything. He glanced over at Farrela, the top of whose head was about level with Jimbo's nose, and then both of them looked at MacDonald. Robert hadn't moved at all; beside Jimbo he looked almost diminutive, with his hands in his pockets, staring at the blank outside of the garage door, his face grave, almost glassy-eyed, but otherwise wooden, not showing anything. Jimbo stood next to him silently, his thumbs hooked into the front of his utility belt, his head bowed, waiting for those inside to finish.

Farrela coughed discreetly. "I called Dr. Williams at home. He's going to come down to the morgue to meet the ambulance." Kermit Williams was the county coroner. Farrela cleared his throat again. "Mac?" He stared at Robert, trying to tell if he had been heard.

Robert looked at him mildly, his face a long mask. "Okay, Bill. Thanks."

The garage door jerked up in front of them and the light from inside glared suddenly in their faces. The two paramedics were grinning, laughing at some private joke between themselves. They pushed the gurney ahead of them out of the garage to the rear of the ambulance, snapped its legs up into their folded position and then shoved it, strapped-down bag and all, onto its rack inside. The driver with the blond curls strolled past the cops toward the front, throwing her head back to look up into the night sky before opening the door. The bearded one closed and locked the rear doors, unaware that Robert had approached his elbow and stood there. The paramedic was still chuckling to himself when he turned the other way, away from Robert, and headed for the front of the ambulance.

Jimbo caught up to him quickly. "This is the father."

The paramedic stopped, looked up at Jimbo, then quickly looked over his shoulder at Robert, the humor dissolving from his face. "You are?" He didn't need an answer. "Sorry, I didn't see you. You want to ride with us?"

Robert nodded. "Yeah, thanks." He went to the passenger-side door and stood there, holding it politely, waiting for the paramedic to get in. The paramedic took hold of his elbow and gently moved him up the step. The blonde looked at him questioningly from behind the wheel.

"This is Mr. MacDonald." The one with the beard opened his eyes wide and raised his eyebrows.

She got it. "Oh. Pleased to meet you, Mr. MacDonald. You might as well go with us, huh? You need to call anybody else to meet you there? We can get the dispatcher to do that if you want."

"Sergeant MacDonald's another cop." Jimbo's head loomed in the open window on the passenger side. He looked at Robert. "Hey, Mac! I'll meet you over there and give you a ride back, okay?"

Robert nodded politely. "Yeah, okay, thanks."

Jimbo looked undecided. "Well . . . all right then, see you there."

Robert sat quietly between the two paramedics and stared through the windshield. The blonde started the engine and with some energy threaded her way back to Jackson Avenue.

She turned onto the all-but-deserted street and sped down the center lane, headed for downtown. She glanced at Robert. "So, what station do you work out of? I don't remember seeing you before."

He didn't answer, but she wasn't offended. "Sergeant Mac-Donald? Where do you work, normally?"

"Pardon?"

"What station do you work out of?"

"I . . . I work out at the range. I'm the range officer."

"Now, that's a job I think I'd like. You're probably outside almost all the time, huh? Don't you just use the indoor range when it's raining?"

He didn't answer, staring through the windshield. He was listening as best he could to the back of the ambulance, listening for any indication that the gurney might have slipped or the bag come loose from it somehow. He saw that the traffic lights had switched from their normal cycle to flashing—amber on Jackson, the through street, red on the cross streets. He suddenly noticed that it had been raining although he couldn't say when that might have been. The streets were wet and the flashing lights at the intersections made long vacant amber reflections, turning the street yellow then black then yellow again. It seemed to him that nobody was out at this time of night and apparently the Department of Public Works had made it official. Odd that so many arrests were made at about this time.

With a start he remembered something and looked at the bearded paramedic next to him. "Did you pick up that piece of bone?"

The paramedic stared at him. "Yeah. Yeah, it's in the bag with him. He's all there."

Robert seemed satisfied with that answer and went back to staring through the windshield. The ambulance swung off Jackson onto the ambulance drive to Kettering Memorial

County Hospital, continued past the emergency room bays to the back of the hospital and stopped next to a ramp leading to a set of closed double doors.

Robert stood to one side while they unloaded the gurney, then followed them up the ramp. They wheeled into a broad hallway and past a glass door with gold lettering: "Kermit Williams, M.D., Coroner, In and For the County of Forrest, State of Texas." Through the glass he could see that the lights were on in the office area in the back. The bearded paramedic stopped outside the door and looked in, leaning through the open door, standing on one leg as though eager to keep moving down the hall. "Hello! Anybody home?" When he didn't get an answer right away he turned back to Robert. "You know your way around in there? Dr. Williams is around somewhere, I can see his light; so why don't you just wait in here for him, okay?"

Robert stood for a minute in the unlit reception area. In fact, in his thirty-six-year career he had only been in here about three times. He didn't like the place. He didn't like the fact that when you went into the county coroner's office you were met by a standard bureaucratic counter with the standard bureaucratic forms as though you were there to take out a permit to sell hot dogs on the street. He groped behind the counter until he found the button that released the gate separating the public area from the clerical bay and the doors leading back to the inner offices. He could see that the light was on in the coroner's office, so he went in and sat down across from the empty desk.

It had started raining again. The window behind the doctor's chair had a ground-level view of the parking lot in back of the hospital and Robert could see the rain slanting under brilliant arc lights. Those lights had been put in at the insistence of some of the hospital employees. Robert knew all about that because this had been his beat when the dispute came up and the employees, a loose group of lab technicians, janitorial and dietetic staff had asked him to come to a meeting that they called in the cafeteria. They wanted him to tell the director what he found when he had arrested a juvenile out there in the dark with a gun and a five-inch knife in his pockets. That had been more than twenty years ago. Terry would have been in kindergarten then. Robert had a quick mental image of the back of the five-year-old, dressed in a miniature blue-jean jacket.

The wind changed direction and the rain drove in a solid wall against the coroner's window, the squall setting up eddies and currents on the vertical surface, rolling off in turbulent sheets and piling up on the window ledge at the bottom before pouring off onto the ground. Lightning flickered behind the all but opaque sheet of water and immediately the thunder crashed loudly, shaking the building, it was so close. Off in the distance, barely audible through his hearing aid, Robert heard shrieks and loud, nervous laughter.

On impulse Robert turned his head and looked out across the dark clerical bay to the backlit door to the corridor. It was just opening, Jimbo coming through. He stopped in the reception area and shook the rain off his hat, saw Robert watching him and grinned sheepishly. "Be glad you're not on patrol anymore, old man. This is a fuckin' cloudburst." He made his way past the secretarial stations, stopped and stared around at the walls.

"I never been here before. This what this guy calls art?" Jimbo was staring at mounted photographs, haphazardly stuck on the acoustical tile walls with drawing pins, pictures of blood splatters photographed under poor conditions and sometimes with a shaky hand. Red circles had been drawn on some of the photographs to illustrate a forensic point. Jimbo stood in the doorway and looked at the photographs on the walls, then at the rain beating on the window. Farrela came in, followed by the tall, loose-jointed figure of Dr. Kermit Williams. The coroner was about fifty-two years old with

11

thick, dark brown hair, salted with gray and cut like a conservative Boy Scout's. He looked more like one of the local soybean or cotton farmers than he did a doctor.

He gave Robert a subdued smile as he stuck out his hand. "Hello, Mac. Good to see you again. I'm sorry about your boy, I really am."

Robert hadn't formed any response to that yet, so he just nodded mutely and shook the doctor's hand, embarrassed, unable to meet his eyes.

Dr. Williams knew all about these meetings. He smiled compassionately. "I haven't been out to your range for a couple of months. I need to get out there pretty soon and have you shoot a seven millimeter into a tub of lard for me." He laughed as though he had told a joke. Turning to Farrela, he explained, "Sometimes we try to set up these demonstrations of what a bullet does as it tracks through something. You take these plastic tubs of lard you can get in the supermarket and the stuff pretty well holds its shape if you shoot it dead center. Sometimes we use a bar of soap or something like that. I get Mac to shoot it for me so we don't waste so many tubs. I know he's going to hit it where I want." He grinned at Robert. "How's your rifle team doing?" He turned around without waiting for him to answer. "Bill, you're on the P.D.'s rifle team, aren't you?"

Farrela shook his head. "No. Shit, I'm never gonna be that good. Jimbo's been shooting with them, though."

"No way! They let me go practice with 'em, sometimes, but I'm not good enough to get into a match." Jimbo was looking up close at one of the photographs. "This a case here in Martin?"

Dr. Williams shook his head. "That's in Fort Worth. They asked me to see if I could help." In spite of the circumstances of this meeting he couldn't help showing a little pride that he had been called in by the big-city guys to help them with something that they couldn't handle. Not that Martin was that small—three hundred thousand was a respectable size—but the doctor was never very far from reminding you that he had

12

gone to school and worked for a time in California in a *real* big city before his wife convinced him to come back here to be nearer her people.

Williams took his seat behind the desk and looked steadily at Robert. "What can I do for you, Mac? What would you like to know? I just took a brief look at him, so anything I tell you, I might change my mind about after a full postmortem, but I'll try to answer any questions you have."

"Thanks . . . I'm not sure . . ." Robert stared past the doctor at the rain still coming down in the parking lot. Lightning flickered, high up in the cloud layer. Robert was having trouble thinking. "Well, how long was it? How long was he there?"

Williams nodded as though that was the question that he had expected first. "I'd say he's been dead about two days." He looked at MacDonald, waiting for the next question, but he could see that Robert's face was all but vacant. The coroner spoke quietly, almost academically. "There were no signs of external trauma except for one gunshot wound to the head. It looked to me like there was a powder ring on the entrance wound, so the gun barrel was probably in contact with the scalp when it was fired. It was a .38 caliber. That's about all I know, right now." He hesitated, watching Robert. Finally, he looked at Farrela. "You said you haven't found the gun?"

Bill shook his head. He was leaning against the wall, hands in pockets, staring at the floor. He looked up at the coroner, avoiding having to look at Robert. "We'll find it. It's there somewhere; we just haven't turned it up yet."

"It wasn't a suicide." Robert said it quietly, but with finality, as though he had been thinking about that and rejected the possibility already.

Farrela looked back at the floor and the doctor studied his hands. When Jimbo heard the long silence behind him he turned around. "Well . . . probably nobody can say one way or the other, yet, huh?" The coroner continued to look at his hands.

Finally the doctor leaned forward, looking at Robert again, trying to make eye contact. "Mac, he . . . Terry was involved in another investigation. You're going to have to find out about this sooner or later, I guess. There was a young woman that was killed in a . . . I don't know, some kind of scuffle at a protest or something—"

Jimbo broke in. "I know about that. That was a fuckin' street riot, that wasn't any protest. . . ." He saw Farrela glaring at him and stopped.

Williams studied Robert to see if he was following what he was saying. "See, in my inquest it looks like this girl got hit by a cop. It may have been accidental, but we're pretty sure that a cop is what we were looking for and, probably, it was Terry." He glanced at Farrela. "That's right, isn't it? You guys in Homicide had it pretty well pinned down?"

Bill was looking down, studying his shoes. He glanced at Robert and saw him staring back intently, listening to every word. Farrela sighed. "Nobody could make an absolutely positive ID, but from the other stuff, what the cops saw and where everybody was, it had to be Terry. We were . . . to us there wasn't any doubt he was the one."

"But you couldn't prove that!" Robert's voice was suddenly harsh, loud in contrast with the soft, civilized voices of the others, trying to explain things to him so rationally. "I can tell by the way you're telling it. What you're telling me, you can't prove it!"

Williams sighed and leaned back in his desk chair, almost slumping. "Mac, we're just trying to tell you how it looks, okay? They were getting ready to bring departmental charges against Terry because of this thing, weren't they?" He tossed the question to Farrela.

Bill shook his head, looking at the floor again. "I don't know. That's IAD that does that and, and they don't tell me shit."

"Well, it was my understanding that they were going to

charge Terry with excessive force. They were bringing an administrative action, at least, to fire him. I don't think anybody had made up their mind about charging him in criminal court with manslaughter yet, but no matter how you look at it he was in a hell of a lot of trouble."

"He didn't shoot himself." Robert glared at him.

Dr. Williams sighed. "Well, maybe you're right. I just thought you'd want to know how it looks now, that's all. I've known you a long time, Mac. I didn't want to keep anything back."

"Terry wouldn't have shot himself."

Williams looked from Farrela to Jimbo. "Maybe not. We don't really have much information, yet . . ."

Robert was on his feet, furious, unable to control himself. "These goddamn killers! Goddamn murderers!" He could see the shock on the doctor's face, and he knew in a corner of his mind that he was acting in a way that was alien to what they expected from him, but he couldn't stop it. He was shouting, his voice cracking. "Goddamn killers get away with this all the time, don't they? Goddamn every one of 'em!" He turned away suddenly and when he bumped into the chair he had been sitting in he kicked it, clattering, against the door. Dr. Williams watched him silently. Jimbo and Farrela didn't move, carefully ignoring any impulse to look at him.

After a moment Robert reached down, picked the chair up, and stood it on its legs again. Farrela, who was closest to him, watched to see if he might be ready to throw it. He didn't. It seemed like all the fight had gone out of him. He brought the chair back and put it carefully in front of the doctor's desk. "I'm sorry. . . . I guess I . . ." He held on to the back of the chair, looking down at it so they couldn't see his face.

Williams sat forward, started to get up, but then thought better of it. "Mac, don't apologize. Here, come on, sit back down, you don't owe anybody an apology. You want me to prescribe something for you? Something to help you to sleep maybe?"

Robert looked up at him, his face dry, eyes hard. "No, I don't need anything like that." His face softened as he looked around at Jimbo, who was staring at him like he had never seen him before. "I guess I got some bourbon or something."

"Okay, that'll be all right. You call me, though, if you need anything."

Robert stood; a blank uncomprehending expression on his face as though he had lost the thread of the conversation. Jimbo stepped up to him. "Come on, I'll give you a ride."

Robert nodded silently and walked out of the coroner's office, leaving the doctor sitting, looking at his hands, and Farrela, leaning against the wall, studying his shoes. He walked out into the rain and it felt good, hitting him suddenly in the face, cold and harsh. Jimbo bent down, holding on to his hat with one hand to keep the water from getting in his eyes and trotted to the driver's side of the patrol car. Robert walked around to the passenger side and got in without any hurry, showing no urgency.

He wiped his hand over his face and then sat staring through the windshield as he had on the way over, staring ahead and seeing little. He could hear water running in the canal next to Jackson Avenue and knew that if he could hear it, it must be running pretty high. He lost the thread of that thought and heard Jimbo clearing his throat. He realized that Jimbo had asked him something.

"What?"

"Is anybody at home? I mean, is there going to be anybody . . ."

"Yeah, I still got one boy at home."

Jimbo seemed to think that over. "Why don't I just take you there? You could go get your car tomorrow, huh? It'd be just as easy . . ."

"That's okay. If you don't mind, I'll just pick up my car."

"Sure, okay." He turned into the residential neighborhood. "If you want, I can check with you tomorrow. You gonna have to make . . . you know, make the arrangements and everything."

"Appreciate the offer. I think we can probably manage, okay."

"Well, call me if you need anything, all right?"

Robert might not have heard. He rode the last couple of blocks in silence, staring through the windshield, seeing nothing until they were almost to Terry's address. He pointed to the side. "That's my Bronco, right there."

Jimbo braked the patrol car to a stop and waited while Robert unlocked his car and then turned around. Jimbo rolled down the passenger side window to see what he wanted to say. Robert put his face down in the window, looking through it directly at Jimbo. The dim light from the instruments showed that his face was drawn but hard-eyed. He looked at Jimbo as though he had challenged him.

"I am going to find the son of a bitch that did this."

TWO

Robert only owned one suit but it was a nice one. It was charcoal gray, a summer-weight wool, with subtle herringbone pinstripes that you couldn't even distinguish ten feet away. It was Lorraine's selection. She had taken him to Rafael's, a men's clothing store that he couldn't remember ever being in before although she insisted that he had been there when she picked out the boys' last suits. He had gone with her because she had been after him for years to replace his last one and because he intended to go with her to the church she had been attending without him for twenty-five years. The boys knew then that she didn't have long.

He hadn't had it on in the two years since her funeral and now, after their oldest son's, he took off the jacket and hung it carefully in the closet. He paused and, having thought about Lorraine, straightened the shoulders on the hanger. Then he turned and unexpectedly saw himself in the huge mirror behind the double dresser that had been jam-packed and overflowing when it had been Lorraine's exclusively but now held all of his clothes with half the drawers empty. He looked at himself because he so seldom saw that image in a tie and it surprised him that he looked nice, dressed up. Lorraine would have approved. His short hair was thick as a shoe brush and had gone almost completely white. He had been five-foot-eight when he was younger but now was a little shorter than that. He'd had broad meaty shoulders and heavily muscled arms and legs, too, the Scotsman clearly present in his generation. The frame was still there, but the weight had settled a bit. His eyes were deep sky blue and, this morning anyway, a little bloodshot.

His police star was mounted on a leather case with a belt clip, and the holster he had worn this morning was a little one with a belt clip too, for wearing on dressier occasions. It exactly fit a Colt Cobra, a gun Robert considered just about worthless because of the two-inch barrel. An officer in the Martin P.D. was required to wear a weapon all the time, though, and the little Cobra was as unobtrusive as you could get. Robert had given an identical gun and holster to Terry when he had graduated from the Academy.

Instead of immediately changing clothes, Robert sat on the foot of the bed and regarded his reflection in the mirror. He couldn't fathom how in the hell Farrela was still convinced that it was a suicide when he hadn't found the goddamn weapon. What did he think, that Terry shot himself in the head and then hid the gun?

He could hear Kevin moving around in the next room, probably changing into his standard jeans and sweatshirt. He had about four of each and they were all identical so he could launder some and nobody would suspect that he owned a change of clothes. Part of the student image, Robert supposed, part of chasing women as though he was afraid the supply wouldn't last.

Robert got up and walked to his son's doorway. He had to step over several cardboard cartons in the hall, boxes still packed from their move although that had been two years ago. "Want to go out and get some lunch?"

"Can't, gotta get over to campus." Kevin was just tying his running shoes. He glanced up at his father and hesitated. "Well, sure, why not? It's not that late, huh?"

They went to Ivy's, a restaurant that specialized in catfish, fried chicken and skillfully defrosted vegetables. Ivy's was the preferred spot in Martin for the after-church crowd on Sundays. Lorraine had dragged them there often although she was the only one that attended church after Kevin and Terry got big enough to object. Robert and Kevin took the same booth they had occupied with Terry after her funeral. Then, Kevin had been cracking jokes, sneaking sips from his father's beer, making no effort to conceal how relieved they all were. Lorraine had been a long time dying and now that it was over they could talk about how she had been before and start trying to forget what she was like at the last, an insensate, contracted being connected to machinery that even breathed for her. Terry had sat there, moody as always, brooding. Robert had decided that he wasn't necessarily grieving; he was always like that.

This time, it was different. Now they were down to two, and Robert couldn't shake off the feeling that they were waiting for somebody else to join them. It seemed as though two was too small a number to be his whole family.

So this time it was Robert who was brooding. Not the soulful, intense brooding of a young man like Terry but the restrained, unwilling endurance of someone who is trying to be normal and can't quite do it.

There had been about thirty-five people at the funeral. Almost all of the competition rifle team was there and the others were mostly older cops who were friends and acquaintances of Robert's, not Terry's. Robert had vaguely recognized two young men who solemnly shook his hand, members of Terry's high-school class. There was a young woman that Robert didn't know at all who had kept a tight grip on a tiny child's hand. Robert assumed that she was with one of the former classmates.

Only a few of these people had thought it necessary to follow to the Episcopal Cemetery where Terry was buried next to his mother. Farrela had come, walking and talking quietly to Dr. Williams, who never went to funerals. Although they tried not to act like it, neither of them had wanted to talk to Robert. Jimbo had hovered around like an oversized Mafioso in a navy double-breasted suit that he must have paid a fortune for to have it tailored to fit him.

The others that came were gray-haired or bald, granite-jawed lifetime policemen like Robert. He was grateful to them. Unlike any other town within a hundred miles, Martin was a Catholic stronghold and most of these old-timers were Irish former altar boys. They would have known all about Terry's reputation, his problems and his presumptive cause of death, but they had come anyway, showing as much courage in the face of social and ecclesiastical acceptability as they would have under fire, wearing the same grim faces.

"You care if I order a beer?" Kevin was looking at him like he was about to laugh.

Robert had to reorient himself quickly because there would be a waitress there soon. "You're not old enough."

"Hey, Dad, I do it all the time." Now he was laughing. Robert wasn't sure if he was serious or putting him on.

"You mean people serve you liquor?"

"Sure. Hey, I'm six-four, who's gonna ask for ID?"

"That's against the law. They could lose their license."

"Dad, can you imagine yourself coming into this place and asking to see my ID at lunchtime in the middle of the week? Can you picture yourself doing that?"

Robert grinned. He hadn't asked to see anybody's ID ever, that he could remember, unless they were driving a car or had given him some other reason.

"What'll it be, Sarge?" The waitress was a part owner of the place. She was tall and stringy and knew just about all the policemen that came in there. "Anything from the bar?" She handed out the menus.

"No, thanks."

"I'll have a Bud."

"One Bud." She turned on her heel and disappeared in the direction of the bar. Robert watched her, then looked at his son in amazement.

Kevin shrugged. "Never know, do you?"

Robert gave him a halfhearted grin and studied the menu. It was just for something to look at. He never ordered anything but steak in this place, not really trusting them to get anything else right, including the specialties. He could feel Kevin watching him.

Robert thought that it was good that Kevin seemed to be in such good spirits, although he was dubious about how genuine that joking attitude was. Kevin was hardly ever at their apartment because he practically lived at the English Department at State. He had settled on an English major in the middle of his freshman year. He had always been a reader, so it wasn't much of a surprise, but it was his friendship with the people that, as far as Robert could tell, really mattered. Kevin had told him it was a small department, about 140 majors, in all levels, and only a dozen faculty members with tenure. Everybody knew everybody else and made the department office their headquarters at school. Robert guessed that it was to these friends that Kevin unburdened himself, let down the laughing facade, if that's what it was, and confided how he really felt about things.

"So, how you doing, Dad?"

"Oh, I'm doing all right. How about you?"

"Pretty shitty, same as you."

Robert nodded, trying to stare at the menu, but then made himself look up at his son. Kevin had deep circles under his eyes. It was easy to miss them because he kept laughing or at least grinning if you looked at him directly.

Kevin studied the menu. "You gotta let me take you to Firenzo's. There's two or three decent restaurants in this town, Dad and Ivy's isn't one of 'em. Next payday you can loan me the money and I'll take you to a decent restaurant."

"Okay, that suits me."

"See, Dad, the problem is you don't like to cook and you don't like to eat out. You could be facing a serious question of starvation, here."

"Oh, I guess I won't starve."

There was a pause while they both studied the useless menus. Kevin finally laid his down and looked off in the direction the waitress had gone. "They kind of run together, don't they?"

"What?"

"The funerals, burials, all that."

Robert took a long look at his son. "I guess so. I hadn't really thought of it like that, but you're right."

"Yeah, I was just beginning to think that Mom died a long time ago. You know, just a couple of years, but long enough that it wasn't a big deal. Now all of a sudden it's like it was yesterday and here we are, doing it again."

Robert thought about what he ought to say. He wasn't good at this. Kevin needed the kind of help that Lorraine would have found natural, somebody to comfort him, make him feel it was all right. Robert didn't know how to start.

The waitress put the beer and a glass in front of Kevin and waited for their orders. Kevin looked up and grinned at her. When they'd ordered he looked at his father and then off at the waitress's retreating back. "I just never thought about Terry shooting himself."

Robert frowned. "I guess . . ."

"I mean, now it seems pretty obvious, how he must have

been feeling, but I didn't realize . . . I didn't know it was that bad."

Robert crossed his arms and leaned on them, his elbows on the table. "He didn't commit suicide, if that's what you're talking about."

"I know you don't think so, Dad, but he did."

"You been talking to Farrela."

Kevin looked at him directly, for once not smiling. "Sure, I talked to him a couple of times. That has to be what happened, Dad. I know they didn't find a gun, but Farrela says that kind of thing happens all the time."

"What kind of thing?"

"Oh, just some piece of the puzzle that doesn't fit. Terry was there for a couple of days. Maybe the guy upstairs took it, or somebody else was going to burglarize the place and just happened to find it. . . ."

"That is pure speculation."

"Sure it is. The point is, the gun is either there or it's not. If it's not in the garage somewhere, where they just haven't seen it, then any number of things could have happened to it. Terry had his wallet, the keys to his car were in his pocket and the car right there. It doesn't make any more sense to think somebody broke in and killed him."

"You're just saying they don't know why somebody might have done it."

"No, Dad. That's not what I'm saying." Kevin leaned close so he could be sure of being heard without making their conversation general entertainment for the whole restaurant. "Dad, he was in a hell of a lot of trouble."

Robert pulled back away from him. "I know, they told me all about that."

Kevin took a breath as though he was going to say more, make some kind of statement, but then stopped himself. He looked down at the table for a minute, then looked up at his father, again seemed about to say something, but at the last second changed his mind.

Robert anticipated him. "I know, he was in a lot of trouble."

"Dad, you don't know . . . That's right, a hell of a lot of trouble."

"What do you mean? What did Farrela tell you that I don't know?"

"I just said it wrong. Farrela told me that he was going to be fired, that they thought he might have killed Melody Arneson."

"Who?"

"Melody Arneson." Kevin flushed and looked away. "She was a student, that's how I know her name. She got killed and they think . . . They were sure that Terry was the one that did it, hit her with his riot stick." He frowned, working the label off the beer bottle, leaving little scraps of paper all over the tabletop. "At least that's what they told me."

"You knew her?"

"This girl? Well . . . kinda. Another English major, you know. I'd seen her around." The bottle slipped out of his fingers and he just caught it before it dumped the entire contents on the tablecloth. He took a deep drink out of it, set it down and crossed his arms on the table, a taller, thinner image of his father.

"What else did they tell you?"

"Didn't you talk to Farrela, too?"

"Yeah, but not very much."

"Well . . . They told me that Terry was out of control, swinging his nightstick at everybody and later this girl was down on the street in the same area. I guess they have a witness or two say a cop hit her, although there was supposed to be a lot of fighting going on. . . ."

"What does that mean? A lot of fighting . . ."

"Jesus Christ, Dad." He had raised his voice more than he meant to. He looked around sheepishly, but nobody was paying any attention. "It was in the paper, all over television, everything. You must have seen it. Somebody was getting arrested or some goddamn thing, some other people interfered and then there was this big crowd gathered and . . ." He looked at his father, almost pleading. "You must have heard about all that."

"Well, yeah, I just didn't know Terry was there. I didn't know that until after Farrela started talking about it."

"Yeah, well . . . I didn't . . . well, that's what they told me, anyway." Kevin was ripping the remainder of the label off the bottle. He finished it, then tipped up the naked bottle and drained it. "Anyway, I guess, from what they tell me, they were going to prosecute him; I don't know."

Their food arrived and they had to move their elbows so the plates could be set in front of them, but they ignored them, except to stare at the food for someplace to look other than at each other.

Robert looked up to make sure the waitress was out of hearing. "I can't see Terry doing anything like that."

Kevin had picked up his fork, turning it distractedly in his hand. He put it down in disgust. "Come on, Dad. Terry always was a bully."

"Terry never hurt you in all the time you were growing . . ."

"Not to me, to everybody else. I got to admit he was great to me. He was my protector at school, but he was a goddamn bully to everybody else. Half the people that knew him in school must have groaned out loud when they heard he became a policeman. He used to beat up kids for no reason at all. I'm not putting you on, Dad, even when he was in high school, when everybody else was outgrowing the macho fighting stuff, he would lose his temper and knock the shit out of somebody for almost no reason at all."

Robert nodded, staring down at his plate. "He took it hard when your mother got sick. It was hard on him at that age . . ."

Kevin stared at him, then looked away. "Dad, I'm talking about a long time before Mom got sick. I mean when he was still in high school, for Christ sake."

"Everything all right here?" They both started. The waitress stood over them, smiling brightly. "Need anything else? More coffee?"

Robert recovered. "Yeah, more coffee, thanks."

"Is everything all right? You're not eating."

Kevin grinned at her. "Just telling stories." He picked up his knife and fork and plunged into the catfish in front of him with a show of appetite. When she was gone he put the utensils down and leaned forward on his arms again. "Dad, I really and truly don't want to be saying anything bad about Terry right now, but the fact is that he could be one mean son of a bitch. Why you thought he should be a cop is one thing I never . . ."

"Me? I never said I wanted him to be a cop. I never encouraged that at all!"

"Well, he sure as shit didn't do it for me or Mom."

"Okay, keep your voice down." Robert picked up his knife and stared at the steak without seeing it. He glanced up at his son, who was sitting there staring vacantly at the beer bottle and the little pile of paper scraps as though wondering how they got there. Robert looked around, but nobody was paying any attention. "Kevin, look . . . I just don't think they've looked at this very well yet. It doesn't make any sense to me that they could just automatically jump to a conclusion like that. . . ."

Kevin's eyes swept over the restaurant, but he leaned his face close to his father's hearing aid again. Robert was startled at the intensity of his voice, the angry urgency of it. "Dad, you're wrong! You just got to let this drop. For God's sake just let it go." He licked his lips and swallowed, looked around as though for someplace to go, but then turned his face back suddenly to look right at his father, close up. "It's all over, Dad. Just let it drop."

THREE

Bill Farrela and his partner Edward Goldman both looked miserable. They acted as though it was their relative's case they were working on and not MacDonald's. Robert was maintaining a determinedly calm composure that came off looking like a wooden mask in the face of the mess in front of him. Farrela looked at Goldman. "I guess we better wait for the photographer."

Goldman nodded quickly, then looked at Robert, explaining, "Absolutely have to." He looked at the debris on the floor, the filthy windows, his partner—anything but Robert. They had, just moments before, broken the seal on Terry's apartment door and opened it for the first time since his death. No one had gone in there when they discovered the body and investigated the garage because there had been no reason to think there was anything in the apartment to look at. Now they had a warrant to look for Terry's guns and try to account for all of them that they knew about. Presumably, he'd had a .38 caliber Smith & Wesson service revolver and the .38 caliber Colt that Robert had given him, so they wanted to see if they were both still there.

What they found when they opened the door, though, was a garbage dump. Robert stood just inside and tried to imagine what this place had looked like when he had last been in here. He couldn't. It had only been eighteen months, but things that happened two weeks ago seemed remote now.

There was a sizable living room that the front door opened directly into. It was full of sunlight from two large undraped windows, but not much else. Terry had acquired a second-hand recliner that Robert hadn't seen before and in front of that was a small, relatively new television on a straight-backed wooden chair. There was a mostly full, plastic, half-gallon-sized bottle of very cheap vodka sitting on the floor next to the recliner.

There were no rugs on the floor and here and there the old wax was scorched where someone had ground out a cigarette by stepping on it as though he were outside on a sidewalk. A few items of dirty laundry, including at least part of one police uniform, were scattered in a long loose pattern from the recliner to the hallway that led to the rest of the apartment. Robert was aware that he was hearing a noise that he couldn't identify until Goldman walked around in front of the television, looked at the screen and turned it off. He saw Goldman look up and focus on a corner of the room behind Robert, behind where the front door had opened when they came in. Robert turned and saw that he was staring at an AK-47, apparently loaded with a long, curved, vicious-looking clip, leaning in the corner where Terry could reach it easily as he answered the door.

Neither Farrela nor Goldman wanted to say anything in front of Robert, but he could see them looking at each other from time to time as though this mess confirmed something that they had talked about earlier. Robert tried hard to see it with a policeman's eyes, taking in facts, making as few judgments as possible, but he couldn't do it. He wasn't an inspector and he hadn't even investigated anything as a patrolman in at least six years, maybe more like ten. It might not have been so bad with just Farrela here. Robert considered him a friend, but Goldman, he barely knew and seeing this mess of his son's was painfully embarrassing. He knew it was making it virtually impossible for him to sort out what he was looking at, to make some connection, if there was one, between the mess and the circumstances of the death.

Robert was not invited in here as a policeman but as the next of kin, the presumed heir, the obligatory formal witness, watching to make sure that the cops didn't take anything. If, after Photography was done, they wanted to remove property as evidence, Robert would have to be there to sign the tag; not because it helped establish chain of custody but to cover the cops' asses. It made Robert an outsider to the two cops that were there, strictly on business. It was ironic that Robert was the only one in uniform. He was wearing a blue police jump-suit with an embroidered name tag and his star pinned on the front, a regular utility belt, and his weapon. The other two could have been furniture dealers if there had been any furniture to look at.

Goldman was getting to where he couldn't stand the silence, a small indication that he might have some sympathy. He looked at Robert. "You already been at work? What time you guys open for business out at the range?"

"Academy class comes in at nine-thirty, but I'm usually there at eight if anybody needs to come in and qualify." Robert was grateful to talk about anything else.

Goldman nodded. "Yeah, I think I'm due in a couple a months. I could hardly hit shit last year, had to come out there four times, remember?"

Robert thought he remembered. "That happens to a lotta guys. Come on out on your time off and get in some practice, makes it easier."

"Maybe you could give me some pointers, huh?"

"Sure, no problem." He decided that Goldman was all right.

The photographer pushed open the door and looked around. "Good, this must be the place, huh? You guys waiting for me?"

Farrela was irritated. "For about twenty minutes."

"Sorry. They didn't tell me I was supposed to cover this until this morning and I was already heading downtown to . . ."

"That's okay. Let's just get this done so we can start looking under things, okay?"

"Yeah, sure. Just take me a minute to set up."

The photographer looked like he was about nineteen, probably a college student working part-time. Robert knew that there was a policeman assigned to take pictures like this but when they wanted something done right they had somebody like this kid on call, presumably an expert no matter how young he looked to the old man. He was carrying two cameras on straps around his neck and had a blue canvas bag with lenses and his other accessories.

Farrela walked into the hallway and looked around. The hall was only a few feet long. To his right there was the bathroom and, straight ahead, a single bedroom. Facing the bathroom door was the open doorway to the kitchen. There was more laundry in the bathroom, underwear and socks scattered in the hall and on the floor of the bedroom. Robert had come up behind him and Farrela glanced at him over his shoulder. "Must have had a lot a clothes." He tried to grin.

Farrela stepped into the darkened bedroom and switched on the light. There were two big windows in here, too, but Terry had tacked army blankets over both of them. Not very elegant as drapes, but Robert had also worked the graveyard shift in his time and knew that the motivation for this, at least, was normal. There was a king-size bed that occupied almost the whole room, no sheets but a sleeping bag wadded up on top of it. There were balls made of crushed cigarette packs on the floor and on top of the small dresser. Parts of uniforms, T-shirts, towels and even some socks hung on every conceivable knob or projection. There was an empty Early Times bottle on the dresser and another one of the oversized plastic vodka jugs in the corner of the room next to the closet.

Terry's utility belt with all its equipment, including the service revolver, hung precariously on the corner of the closet door. They could see clothes in a heap on the closet floor as though he had got that far with them in an attempt to organize and then gave it up. The only things hanging in there were two uniform shirts, no pants, and the civilian suit that Terry had got at about the same time that Robert got his.

There was an open blue spiral notebook on the bed next to a pillow with no pillowcase. They could see writing on the page from where they stood in the doorway. Farrela looked over MacDonald's head to exchange a knowing glance with Goldman as if to say, "What'd I tell you; there's the note."

Robert pushed past him and reached for the notebook without thinking. Farrela called out to him. "Don't touch it yet, Mac. Let that guy take his pictures first, okay?"

Robert stopped and leaned over the bed, bracing himself with his hands on the mattress to read the writing. He tried to adjust his glasses, tilting his head up and down to look through both lenses of his bifocals, a deep frown on his face.

"Is it a note?" Goldman came up behind him and although obviously impatient, courteously waited for Robert to read it first. Robert squinted at the page as if trying to make out the writing. He finally backed off the bed. He saw Farrela staring at him but could only shake his head. "I don't know." Farrela grabbed up the notebook. He turned the page, looked at the next page and then the next, then went back to the place where it had been open.

Goldman crowded up next to him and stared at it, too, both of them puzzled. Goldman shook his head, turned around and walked off into the kitchen. Farrela looked at Robert and frowned. "This is just gibberish. It's nonsense, Mac."

Robert didn't respond. Farrela put the notebook back

where they had found it. "Doesn't make any sense to you either, does it?"

"No."

The photographer, working his way through the apartment, finished in the bathroom, came into the bedroom and looked around. Farrela went into the kitchen to get out of his way, indicating for Robert to follow. Robert was feeling stunned, unable to make any sense out of what he was seeing or any kind of contribution to what they were doing.

There was no indication that anyone had ever cooked in the kitchen. There was a pizza box with half a pizza on the counter next to the sink, fast-food wrappers and cartons were scattered on the counter and the floor. There was a large green garbage bag in the corner of the kitchen next to the back door. It seemed to be mostly full of empty cartons, a few more vodka bottles and beer cans. Staring at it, Robert wondered what period of time that bag represented.

Farrela sat in a chair across the kitchen table from Robert. "Look, Mac, let me tell you something. You're the expert on guns and shooting and stuff like that and I'm the expert on this kind of shit, okay?"

Robert waited for him to go on.

Farrela crossed his arms on the table and looked Robert in the eye. "I don't know if we gonna find that other .38 in here or not. Even if we do, it doesn't prove that he didn't have another one, right?" He paused for an acknowledgment, but Robert just waited. Farrela sighed again. "I bet you didn't know about that assault rifle, huh? Did he tell you about that?"

"He knew I wouldn't have recommended anything like that . . ."

"Wouldn't have recommended? Hell, you would have told him it was a piece of shit! It isn't good for a goddamn thing except killing people at close quarters and that's what you would have told him. Am I right?"

There was a pause. "Sure."

"Okay." Farrela softened his voice. "Okay, so we're gonna look around up here and see what we can find and then we're gonna go through the garage again. Just once more, thoroughly, to see if there might just be some corner we didn't get a good look at before, all right?"

"All right."

"Now, Mac, if we don't find the gun, we don't find the gun. That's all, understand?"

Robert looked at him.

"Mac, what you got to understand is that there's always something missing, something that doesn't make any sense. If you can look at this like any other case, there's always pieces of evidence that we can't find or that we find but they won't fit. Once I investigated a case, a lady fell while she was running to catch a bus. She cracked open her head and died. Now, we were looking at it to see if maybe the bus driver had something to do with it. You know, maybe she was trying to get on and he just pulled away and caused her to fall or she was banging on the door to get in and the bus moved out and knocked her over or something. Anyway, we had four independent witnesses that saw this thing happen. One was on the bus and three of 'em were at different places on the street or the sidewalk. They had little inconsistencies that didn't make any difference, like they all thought she had on a different-colored coat, but on the important parts they all said the same goddamn thing. The lady never even reached the bus. They all said she was running flat out to get to it, but she tripped and fell before she got there. She never even touched the fuckin' bus. The trouble is, she hit on the back of her head. Now you tell me how somebody running as hard as they can straight ahead can fall and hit the back of their fuckin' head. I don't know. I never will know how she did it, but that's by God what she did."

Robert watched him for a moment, thinking. His voice was emotionless. "So what?"

34

Farrela sighed. "So, I don't know."

The photographer came into the kitchen and looked around, ready to take aim and shoot if they'd just get out of the way. Farrela stood. "Okay, let's start at the front door, work back and see what the fuck we can find. Then we can talk about it." He turned to the photographer. "When you get through in here stick around, okay? We might need you to get some more if we turn anything up, okay?"

The kid grinned. "Sure. I'm on an hourly plus the pictures."

"Good for you."

The kid quit grinning and concentrated on his cameras.

For the next two hours they turned the apartment inside out. Robert stayed back out of the way and watched while Farrela and Goldman searched the place like they were looking for evidence on the biggest dope dealer they had ever busted. They were slow and methodical, taking each little area of the apartment as they came to it, carefully removing whatever was there, looking, then going down to the next layer. Every few minutes, it seemed, they came across another vodka bottle or more beer cans.

They found *TV Guide*s from the last six months, a couple of police training manuals, some fishing line (although Robert had never known Terry to go fishing since he was about ten years old), a set of brass knuckles with a T-bar to fit into the palm up against the heel of the hand. They found two gold neck chains that nobody had ever seen Terry wear and put these carefully in Robert's hand along with Terry's checkbook, bank statements and bills. There was an old pocket watch and a fair supply of pornography that probably had to have come from Dallas. They found some ammunition for the AK-47 and some .38 caliber, police issue, probably. They didn't find the Colt or any other guns.

When they finished with the apartment they went back down to the garage and went through that. Farrela had Terry's keys so they started by going through the car. It could be towed to the police lot and searched there by people that could take it apart and look better, but they did what they could. Nothing in it but more beer cans and fast-food wrappers.

The floor of the garage had been cleaned and there were some particularly well-scrubbed spots. The hole in the garage door was still there. The walls of the garage consisted of bare studs with concrete block behind; nowhere to hide anything. They examined the floor with a strong light to see if there were any chips or scratches to indicate where something hard might have fallen, but didn't see anything conclusive. They searched everywhere for a hole, a crack, somewhere that a reflexive jerk of the hand might have thrown a small gun, but there wasn't anything. Nothing.

When they finished they went back upstairs and dumped the pizza in a plastic bag to get rid of it. Otherwise, they left things as they were. Robert even put the gold chains back where they had found them.

Farrela locked the garage door and then stood before it, staring at the driveway for a minute. Finally, he looked up at Robert. "I doubt we're gonna find any more evidence than we got right now. We'll follow up anything we can come up with after we finish talking to the neighbors, but that's probably gonna be it." He looked back down at the pavement. None of them started to go to their cars.

Goldman looked at Robert and then at his partner. "Doesn't seem like anybody broke in. No signs of a struggle."

Farrela glanced at him and then away. "No, there was a hell of a struggle. But there was just the one guy."

FOUR

Double that whiskey with a draft beer, back."

The bartender nodded and poured without looking at Greg. It was Greg's friend, the man on the stool on his right, who stared at him.

"Hey, Greg, you ain't going to get rowdy, are you? Just 'cause I brought you your paycheck?" He grinned. The man on the stool was wearing a grease-stained work uniform shirt, white with gray pinstripes and an embroidered name patch that said "Lee Vail." Lee was pudgy, with blunt, grease-blackened hands, and short enough, even sitting on a barstool, that he had to look up to see Greg's face.

Greg tossed off the double whiskey and picked up the beer without looking at anybody. He was studying the mug as though he could read from it. He had to shift his weight and hop once to turn sideways, leaning with one cheek on the barstool instead of sitting on it, his right leg extending rigidly down, encased from hip to toe in plaster. His jeans were slit to accommodate the cast's bulk and tied at the bottom to keep the loose ends from flapping when he tried to walk.

"Hey, Greg. You think you going to drink enough to dance

on the table? 'Cause they got to get a reinforced table for you, if you think you might want to get up and dance with that rock on your leg." Vail laughed at his own joke but the laughter died when Greg did not respond. The bartender shook his head as he picked up Lee's beer bottle, checked the level in it and set it back down.

Greg continued to look in the beer mug. "Thanks for bringing me my paycheck."

"That's all right. It's nice to know somebody that don't need it to the point he can wait two or three months to pick it up." He peered at his friend's face. "Greg, are you all right? You hardly even said hello."

Greg's face was already red, the lined, sunken cheeks glowing, feverish. His eyes were shiny and bloodshot, nearly hidden under the bill of a Texas Rangers baseball cap. He was lean, with a sharp nose that crooked in the middle like the beak of a hawk. An old scar, a memento from a retaining ring off a truck tire, curved down across the lower part of his face and fell off the side of his chin. He looked around the room, searching it quickly, then looked down and closed his eyes as he took a long drink from the mug.

"Hey, Greg, you ain't taking any pills for your leg, are you?"

Greg held up the mug to indicate the nature of his medication and took another drink. It was already three-quarters gone.

"No, I mean, you ain't taking any painkiller pills, too, are you?"

"No." Greg looked around and his eyes settled on a table that was being vacated. "Help me over there, will you?"

"Sure, Greg. Here, just lean on my shoulder and move slow so you don't trip on nothing." Greg leaned heavily on his friend's shoulder, tried to hop to keep his weight off the injured leg and made an uncoordinated mess out of the whole effort of movement. He stopped and balanced, then deliberately stepped off, putting his weight on the cast and gimping the final two strides to the table. He leaned on the back of the chair for a moment before he turned it around and sat in it. His face was definitely sweaty now. "I need another round." He leaned back and hooked a twenty out of his jeans pocket.

"I don't know, Greg. You sure that's a walking cast?" Lee turned and looked over the tables. There were a few other workingmen, casually watching the injured man, not wanting to stare. Lee caught the eye of the waitress and waved her over to their table.

"Alice, this is my boss, Greg."

Alice grinned and looked down at him. "Hi." When Greg didn't respond she looked at Lee. "Your boss?"

"Well, he was, up to a while ago. What you think, Greg? Any chance you coming back?"

"How about getting me another round of the same?" He held out the bill.

"Sure, hon." Alice grabbed the twenty and peered under the bill of Greg's cap. All she could see clearly were the beaked nose and the scar. She drew back involuntarily. "What you drinkin', hon?"

"Bartender knows."

"Okay, hon. Be right back."

"Hey, Greg?" Lee tried to get a look at Greg's face in the shadow. He couldn't tell if Greg heard him at all. "Greg, you was about to get a prize or something, some kind of bonus, I think, because you hadn't missed a day of work in ten years on account of illness. Not one sick day in ten years before this, did you know that?" He ducked his head, still trying to see under the cap. "I talked to Mildred, in payroll?"

"I missed work before."

"Yeah, but she said it was just things like . . . days when you did something for . . . you know, for family, for school or something, and so those were administrative or vacation days or something, but not sick days."

"I didn't take no vacation."

"No, the days were counted as administrative days, like when I had to go to court for my kid. . . . You know what I'm talking about?"

"Oh. Yeah, I know."

"So according to payroll, you hadn't missed a day in ten years."

"Twenty-one."

"What?"

"Never took off a sick day for twenty-one years."

"Rickenhauer's Cadillac only been there for ten."

"Yeah, but I been working for longer than ten years. It was Anderson's before, and I worked eleven years straight before they folded."

"Yeah . . . so . . ." Lee gestured with both palms up, trying to get Greg to fill in the blanks. "Why didn't you, at least, call in? I mean, a few days, even a couple a weeks they would have just chalked it off to grief or something, but now, it's been a couple a months, hasn't it?"

"That's my business."

Lee bobbed his head up and down as though Greg had made a reasonable argument. "Yeah . . . okay. What about your friends, though? You got a lotta friends and we ain't heard nothing from you, can't get you on the phone."

"How'd you hurt your leg?" Alice put the glass with the double whiskey and the beer bottle in front of Greg and dumped the change on the table next to it.

"I got shot."

"What?"

Greg tipped his head back so that light finally hit his face. His eyes were shining and he grinned like a maniac in a cartoon, his mouth distorted on one side by the scar. It held down the corner of his mouth on that side and gave him a lopsided look as he watched Alice take another step back. "Got shot by a bad man."

"Why don't you just say it's none of my business?"

40

"You brought me the drinks, that wouldn't be nice." He knocked back the double and reached for the beer. He stopped his hand, then shoved a five toward her. "Here, let me buy you one of whatever you're drinking, too."

Alice hesitated, not sure how to take him, intrigued but a little afraid of him. She looked at Lee. "Is he always like that?"

"Like what? Listen, honey, my wife is going to be coming in that door any second. If you didn't look so good, I'd ask you to join us, but . . ."

"Well, la-di-da!" Alice rotated her head with irritation, then turned on one high heel and went back toward the bar.

"How *did* you break your leg?"

"I got shot."

"Yeah, right. Hey, look, you want me to tell 'em you got hurt? I could tell 'em you got hurt and maybe when you're ready they'd talk to you about coming back to work."

"Maybe it's too late for that."

"What, are you kidding? You the only foreman we ever had. I tell, you, Greg. Marty James is a good mechanic but he ain't no foreman. I bet they'd still talk to you."

"Maybe it's too late. I don't know."

"I'll talk to Rickenhauer for you. I can't stand the guy, either, but sometimes he's not so bad. What d'ya think?"

"I don't know. I might still have something else to do. I'm not sure, yet." He was already halfway through the second beer.

"You working someplace else?" Lee bent over the table, trying to look under the cap again. "You got another job? Where?"

Greg wiped one hand over his face. "Get me another round, okay?"

"You're going through that awful fast."

"I'll get it myself." He started to try to get up, so Lee put a hand on his shoulder.

"Okay, I'll get it. Just sit still a minute."

Lee's wife got to the table before he got back. She was small, dark hair curled around a pale face, overdressed for this bar in a cheap blue suit. She looked pretty. "Greg, where you been?"

"Hi, Cindy."

"Where have you been? What did you do to your leg?"

"It's a long story."

Lee set down the drinks. "He's got another job already."

Cindy looked up at her husband, then at the glass of amber liquid and the beer bottle. "Which one's mine?"

"I'll get you a gin and tonic."

Greg picked up the glass of whiskey, drained it and reached for the beer.

"You been keeping up with him?"

"I had one beer, but I'm getting drunk just watching him."

"Okay, gin and tonic." She turned back to Greg, but he had pulled the bill of his cap even lower so she couldn't see his face except for the end of the scar on his jaw. "You got another job? Where? They got any openings that Lee could fit into?"

"Not another job. I just said I might still have something else to do. It's a long story."

"Greg. Look at me, Greg, you're not listening."

"I can hear you."

"I know, but you're not listening." She looked at him and her face looked mournful, sad, in sympathy with him. "What's it been, now? Six weeks? Two months, since . . . ?"

"No, now, you just stay away from that." His voice was harsh and Cindy flinched, her face going from mournful concern to fear to anger in a second.

Greg was repentant. "I don't mean it like that. I just can't . . ."

"No, it's all right, Greg. I won't say anything about . . ." She shook her head as though with the effort to stop that train of thought. Then she seemed determined to push on. "Look,

Greg? You just got to pull yourself together. You got to go on back to work."

Greg looked up, tipped his head back to see her, then pushed the cap back on his head. He tried to lean forward on his elbows but the cast dug into his hip and he had to lean back again. He looked at Cindy and she flinched again. His look was hard and resentful, then softened, for her benefit, but just a little. "What for?"

"I don't know. You just have to, that's all. You're not yourself."

Greg looked at her a long time as though trying to figure out what she was saying. He leaned a little toward her. "There just ain't any point. It won't come straight."

"What won't?"

"Nothing will. No matter how I try to look at it, I can't see any point. Nothing worked out, you know?"

"Well, sure, you must think that sometimes, but . . ."

"No, wait, I take it back." He looked at her and then back down at the table. "There is one good thing. I found my little brother."

"I didn't know you had a little brother."

"Just about forgot about him, myself, I guess. He ain't really so little. Matter of fact, my little brother . . . he's a great big guy." Greg looked up at her again and started to chuckle. His expression was milder, a hopeful look, almost. "I ain't decided yet, but, probably, I could get another job, all right."

"Of course you could. If you don't want to go back to Rickenhauer's, you could probably . . ."

"I wouldn't go back there. I dragged my ass over there too long, already, getting up ever day and dragging . . ." He shook his head, losing his train of thought. "Man!" He shook his head again. "You get up ever day, work all that overtime like that 'cause you got to—there was a reason for it, you know?"

"Yes, of course, I know."

"Then, all of a sudden, you got no reason anymore and there's nothing that you got to do at all." He made an effort to lean toward her in spite of the awkwardness of the cast; his voice dropped to a whisper. "See, I guess I never thought about it when I was just going to work ever day. You know? I wasn't thinking ever day, 'there's a reason for this.' I just did it and didn't think about having to have a reason until all of a sudden there wasn't one anymore. All of a sudden. Then you wake up and, damn! You don't have any reason to . . ." His voice dropped down until he was almost muttering to himself. "But maybe then you got to do some *wicked, bad, awful* thing . . ." She flinched again and his voice hesitated. He straightened and then his voice sounded almost normal. ". . . but there's nothing that you have to do, anymore, that is the right thing, the thing you thought so long was what you was supposed to do."

"Greg, you are scaring me. Do you know you aren't making any sense?"

"Yeah."

"Did you hear what I said?"

"Yeah, I feel better now."

Lee sat down next to his wife and pushed a glass toward her. He looked from her face to Greg's. "Greg?"

"Shit. I guess I forgot how to drink."

Cindy started to touch his arm, then held her hand back. "It's all right, Greg. We're your friends, right? I mean, it's all right with us." Her husband nodded solemnly, not sure what the conversation was about.

"Anyway, I turned out bad." Greg stared at his mug, then looked up, a sudden idea. "Except then I did find my brother. Been a long time since I seen him, last."

Cindy nodded, encouraging him. "You hadn't seen him in a long time?"

"Yeah, 'cause I thought he was bad. Hell, turned out I'm

worse than he ever was, except that just . . . it's only like a final thing, you know?"

Cindy frowned, glanced at her husband as though to verify that he was hearing the same thing, then leaned toward Greg and kept her voice low. "Greg. You are not making sense, do you understand?"

Greg raised his voice, cutting her off. "Ain't none of it ever made any sense. To hell with it, anyway." With a convulsive effort, he lurched to his feet and stood a moment, mastering his balance on the cast. Then he deliberately stepped off toward the door. Lee and Cindy were after him in a second, trying to help him, one on either side. He raised his arms to ward them off.

"I'm all right now. I can walk. Can't hardly feel it, now."

Lee nodded. "I bet."

"Lee can drive you home. You can't drive like that."

"Sure, I can." He got into the passenger side of his car and slid across the seat, dragging the cast after him so that it stuck out across the hump of the transmission. He started the engine and demonstrated his dexterity with one foot going from the brake to the gas pedal and back.

Cindy threw her hands in the air. "All right. Fine! Be that way!"

"I'll go to my brother's."

"Is that whose car this is?"

"No, I just bought it. Cheap, but I got it running pretty good."

"Then what are you going to do at your brother's?"

For a moment, the question stopped him. "I don't really know. It's all done now, anyway, so far as I know." He shook his head, trying to clear it. "I shouldn't drink." He looked up at Cindy, suddenly grinning, his face twisted until she couldn't tell if he was grinning or getting ready to cry. "I forgot how to drink, even. Just get to running off at the mouth . . ."

Cindy bent over to look at him closely. "It's all right, I told you that."

Greg shook his head again. "Well, no, it's not all right. It's just that . . ."

"Hey, Greg?" Lee was leaning in at him through the passenger window. "You wanta come over to our place? Get some supper? You can sleep on the sofa if you want. It's nice; it's real comfortable."

"Got to get out to my brother's place. If there's any more I got to do, I can get him to help, maybe." He grinned up at Cindy and his face under the baseball cap glowed with fever and sweat.

Cindy looked at her husband across the top of the car. "I have never seen him like this, have you?"

Lee shrugged his shoulders. "Hunh-uh."

"Greg, you should not be driving."

"Yeah. You right, come to think of it. Regular menace, ain't I?" He grinned up at her, then started the car forward.

FIVE

Robert opened his eyes and listened, lying very still in his bed in the dark. He had been dreaming about dogs. The dream had been so real he thought that he could still hear the bassoon baying, echoing off a distant hill. He realized that listening was a futile effort without his hearing aid. He reached to the bedside table, found the glasses that he kept there because they had a small hearing aid built into the earpiece and put them on, lying on his back so that he could hear. It was raining outside, a drumming, soaking rain with hardly any wind at all. Still not fully awake, he listened, hope gradually drowned out by the steady, relentless beating of the rain on the roof.

The memory of the dog's baying faded, sinking into the black well that he seemed to live in now when he was awake.

He wondered why he dreamed about the dogs, of hounds bawling in the Missouri Ozark hills. That sound was from a long time ago, before everything else, before he had ever heard of Martin, before the war in North Africa, even before going off to school and meeting Lorraine. But suddenly there it was, projected in the front of his memory—a small, nearly smokeless fire was the center of an irregular wheel formed by the bodies of boys extending out from it like spokes. With their feet near the fire they could see each other across it to talk. They were coon hunting: talking quietly, not too seriously, listening to the dogs in the distance and trying to identify them by their voices and, by their pitch and urgency, tell what they were doing. If the dogs managed to tree the coon, the boys would have to get up and, mostly without light, trek off across country to catch up and either shoot it or let it go depending on whether the dogs had hurt it or not.

Their faces were indistinct but in his mind's eye the boys themselves were clear. Michael, Angus, Peter and Robert. They were all within a year of being the same age and all, including Robert, pure ridge-runners: lean and hard-bodied, full of wild reckless humor that could sometimes spill over into passionate, adolescent violence, supremely confident that they knew it all yet innocent of the most rudimentary knowledge of how things worked. They thought Lyndon-Lure and Forsyth were cities, places you could sneak off to where only about a quarter of the population knew all your relatives.

Once, when they were sixteen, they had gone all the way to Springfield on a lark, convinced that they could make money selling four one-gallon jars of homemade whiskey that Angus had picked up in trade for a shotgun with a split chamber. When they had finally struck a deal with what appeared to be the entire basketball team of a Springfield high school, their customers couldn't come up with the cash and they had to fight it out. They lost the fight and the whiskey. Robert had to sit, wrapped in a blanket in the backseat of Michael's father's car, nursing a broken nose while Michael, Angus and Peter rinsed out his blood-soaked clothes in a park creek. Then they had held the duck cotton trousers and white collarless shirt out of the car windows all the way home to try to dry them out. They were friends and allies for life.

They had been briefly famous in the county because Angus shot the windshield out of a game warden's car while the warden was driving it. The sheriff finally had to let all four go because nobody would say who had done it. The warden was not a local man and was a stickler about hunting deer out of season, even if you were on your own land. He had finally been transferred to another county for his health and the boys got most of the credit.

Robert hadn't seen any of them since he had left home in 1938. After all the intervening years, he knew he had changed considerably from the way he had looked as one of the boys sprawled around that camp. He had heard that Michael Whitcomb died on an atoll in the Pacific and Angus Gill succumbed to appendicitis in some army camp before he even went overseas. Peter MacBride had not gone anywhere because of his missing toes from a hunting accident. After the war he was going to write Peter, but before he knew it five years had passed and it would have been awkward. He had been meaning to contact Peter for forty years but he hadn't done it and now he had to admit that he never would.

Lorraine had been the correspondent for the family. She was from Springfield and didn't know any of his people. He met her when he managed to get in two years of college. She was in his freshman math class, Lorraine Perkins then, taller than him and bird-like, with delicate hands. She had big, lively eyes and he had told her they were like lanterns. Ten years later she had become a little stout, and ten years after that she was definitely rotund, but her eyes had always stayed the same.

Robert sat up suddenly and rubbed his face with both hands, knocking off his glasses, shutting out the sound of the rain. He didn't know why he had started to think about all those people from so long ago. All of them were dead. Now Angus and Michael had been dead for more than forty-five years and Lorraine, two. For Lorraine, now it had been two years and three months and something.

So, why in the hell was he dreaming about fox hunting?

Robert had been a good hunter back then. But hunting was generally a solitary thing, waiting for the deer . . . Fox hunting was about the only kind they did as a group since none of them were too excited about shooting birds over the dogs. They didn't have that kind of dog, any of them. He wished that he could talk to them now, the other boys. His family was almost all gone now, and the other boys had been gone so long that he was surprised that he even thought about them. It must have been the dream. He wished . . . He shook his head.

Robert found his glasses on the bed covers, lay back on his pillow and put them on, careful to insert the hearing aid so that he could hear in the dark. Lorraine might have known what to do now. Anything to do with his own boys, The Boys, as they always referred to them, she knew more about than he did. She was closer to them, knew them better, her judgment solid no matter how he had argued sometimes that she was being emotional. He had to smile, because he hadn't thought about that for a long time. If they argued about the boys, he always lost. Lorraine always knew; her judgment, if not perfect, then was as close to it as he could have reasonably asked or expected.

In the last, what was it? Two years, three years before she got sick? Something like that. For something like three years Lorraine had been virtually their only contact with Terry, the oldest. Lorraine, without knowing what it was about, had given Robert bad advice about that. She had said to let it alone, let Terry take his own time and get over whatever grievance he thought he had. To Lorraine anything was preferable to the open hostility that broke out whenever Robert tried to approach Terry directly. Even living in the same house, Robert had hardly exchanged ten words with his older son in all that time before the need for direct communication because of Lorraine's disease had changed that somewhat. In that sense she was still the cause if not the conduit for any contact they had right up to the time of her death. But now she was dead, too.

He tried not to think, any more, about the last part of Lorraine's life; the cancer that had come, it seemed from somewhere else, and engulfed them all. It had taken so long to happen that at first, after she died, that was all that he thought about: the suffering, the drugs, the machinery in their house that fed her and finally even breathed for her. It had gone on and on, the nurses coming and going and the three male members of the household sitting in turn around the clock, watching and waiting and finally, after she hadn't spoken for months, all three of them secretly hoping that it wouldn't be too much longer. The city's health insurance plan wouldn't cover the home care and Lorraine hated the hospital, wanting to be home, not expecting it to last much longer when she asked for it.

He'd had to sell the house without telling her. The boys' college money had gone, too. In spite of himself, in spite of all of his good intentions, he had lost track of his sons. He had wanted to make a point of talking to her every single day, whether she could understand it or not. He had meant to take a little time every day to tell her what was going on with the boys. But he couldn't do it. His mind had been filled to the point of distraction with the details and sheer hard work of her final illness. All of his time and energy had gone into arranging nursing coverage, talking to the doctors who didn't seem to want to do any more than wash their hands of it once she was out of the hospital, trying to keep ahead of the bills.

During that final eight weeks after Lorraine went into a coma and Robert realized that she was already gone, there hadn't been any time to mourn or grieve. It wasn't until after it was all over and Terry got his own place and Kevin started college, when most of Robert's off-duty time was spent alone, that he began, gradually, to remember Lorraine the way she had been before she got sick. It was a delayed grief and maybe it was easier for the delay.

He would be sitting alone reading the paper, eating his solitary dinner, when he would abruptly look up to tell her something about what he was reading. Then he would see where he was, the apartment empty. He would have to sit there, still, listening and watching for the breeze in the hall, the shift of light through the window that had made him think that she was there when of course—of course he knew it—she hadn't been there at all.

Even if there hadn't been the strain between him and Terry, there just had been nothing at all of himself left over for the boys. No question that they had needed him and, to his own mind, no doubt that he had failed them both because he had run out of energy, interest, stamina, whatever it was. He hadn't even seen what was happening to them. Kevin, finally, seemed to have come through it okay on his own. But all Robert knew about Terry was that he had abruptly moved out after they buried his mother. He was old enough, it was time for that in the natural order of things so there had been no need to explain. If Lorraine had not been sick, Terry would have had his own place before. And, Robert had to admit, Terry's move had relieved the strain on them both. Now, whether he was willing or not, Robert had to think about it because the fact was that he didn't know anything about Terry. He had given up on him. Not consciously, maybe, not admitting it at the time, certainly, but he had given up because he hadn't tried to stay in touch, to breach that seething wall that Terry had surrounded himself with. Maybe he couldn't have done it, but by God he wished now that he had tried.

Lying there, alone in the bed, Robert stared at the ceiling, seeing it in the dark, hearing the hard rain on the roof. He tried to make himself focus on that, on the immediate sensations, the concrete sounds and sights in front of him in the dark. He couldn't do it. The whole history was chasing him, washing up at him, merciless, relentless. Terry, when he got those cowboy boots. There was a first baseman's mitt that cost a fortune that Terry had lost at the second or third practice after Robert gave it to him. He couldn't afford it, but Robert had replaced the mitt immediately because he couldn't stand to see the boy's grief, the parent's anger at his carelessness evaporating instantly when he saw the pain of loss in the child's face as he fearfully explained what had happened, that small suffering face suddenly in front of him in the dark.

Robert jerked upright in bed and looked at the clock. It was 5:10. He threw the covers back and turned on the light, hurrying so that he could catch Mallen at work and talk to him at the station. David Mallen had been Terry's last watch commander.

"Jesus Christ, Mac. I had no more idea than anybody else it might go this far. Honest to God, at first I thought I could just get him an experienced Field Training Officer or something." Sergeant David Mallen was forty-seven years old, and a veteran of every imaginable kind of police action. He looked around on the top of his desk, hoping something there would demand his immediate attention and get him out of this conversation. He seemed to realize what he was doing and leaned back in his chair to give Robert his full attention. Robert was sitting in a visitor's chair holding a ceramic mug filled with coffee from Mallen's own private Norelco that he kept behind his desk on a low table, out of sight of the troops.

Robert looked down at the mug in his hands. It had little cartoon pigs all over it, obviously a gift from somebody, that had probably been funny at first. Robert looked at the little pigs to avoid seeming to confront Mallen. There didn't seem to be any good way to explain that Mallen probably knew more about Terry's last six months alive than he, the father, did. Mallen seemed to think that he was being accused of something.

Robert looked up at him, trying to seem as sincere as he felt. "What do you mean? What did you need a particular kind of FTO for?"

Mallen sighed, profoundly uncomfortable. "Mac, I don't know how to tell you about all this, you know? I mean, what difference does it make now?"

MacDonald sat forward in the chair, his elbows on the arms, holding the mug in both hands and looking at it. "Why don't you just tell me like you told Homicide? I don't mean to . . ." He looked up and half smiled. "I'm not trying to give you a bad time, David, I just need to hear it from you, that's all."

Mallen waved off the explanation. "I know. Shit, I guess I'd want the same damn thing." He stared at the ceiling for a minute, trying to come up with the right words. "Terry was real weird. I'm sorry, but that's the honest-to-God truth, Mac. I don't know how Bert let him get through but I'm telling you, he didn't do me any favors."

Bert Carlione was the commander at the Police Academy. He had been four years behind Robert but had passed him in rank years ago. Bert was a superb marksman, specializing in pistols and had been one of the original members of the competition team when he and Robert and four others had turned it into a serious, prize-winning force. They had traveled over most of the South together, competing against other police departments and bringing home a trunkful of trophies over the years. Nobody needed to explain to Robert how Bert would have let Terry do just about anything and still would not have washed him out of the Academy.

Mallen went on, "We got two guys out of that same class. The other one was Neil Frasier and he said Terry was much worse lately. I guess, at the Academy he had a reputation for a bad temper, and mostly kept to himself. But he got much worse, Mac, just in the time he was here at Southern. Shit, I couldn't get anybody to work with him."

Robert could see that Mallen didn't want to continue and

wouldn't unless he kept reassuring him. "Why didn't they want to work with him?" Robert had been a patrolman long enough to know what the reasons would be, but he had to hear it.

"Listen, I stuck Terry with Art Kennedy when Art's partner was off on vacation and they lasted one shift. I mean, one fucking shift. Sure, some guys just don't get along, but usually they'll give each other at least a couple a weeks, especially if it's temporary like that, but Art came in here the morning after the first shift he had to work with Terry and just said, 'This isn't going to work out,' just like that. Now, Mac, you know Kennedy, he gets along with anybody."

"Did he say why?"

"Hell no. You know how these guys are, the sergeant gets paid to figure all this shit out, not them. They wouldn't rat on a partner if he was fucking the shotgun in the backseat. Only thing Art would tell me was that Terry was real quiet most of the time and then he would just pop off. I mean, he would all of a sudden be so pissed off about some little trivial thing that he was ready to start screaming or shooting or something."

MacDonald looked back down at the mug in his hands, at the cold coffee. Yes, he could picture Terry doing that.

Mallen lowered the tone of his voice. He changed it so that he sounded more sympathetic, more consciously aware of what this must sound like to the father. "See, but then a whole week would go by with no problems at all except he was so quiet and I'd think, what the hell, maybe the guy was having a bad day."

"But you didn't really think that was it." Robert looked up at Mallen's face, looking at him directly, one sergeant to another.

"C'mon, Mac, you been around long enough. You were the sergeant in this same goddamn desk, right?"

"You think he shouldn't have been a police officer." It wasn't a question.

Mallen stared at him, a hard look in his eye. "No, I absolutely did not." He stopped although he was clearly ready to say more. He changed his tone again, giving Robert his sympathy, as though in spite of himself. "Look, Mac, I didn't think Terry was really a bad kid. I thought . . . well, after everything, I just wish I had tried to get him some kind of counseling or something. That's a hell of a thing to think about afterwards, but I'll admit it to you. That's what I wish I'd a been thinking about instead of just going after him so hard. You being his father, I know his career must have meant a lot to him."

They could hear good-natured shouting and laughter from the change of shifts going on outside the office. Mallen would be ready to brief the next sergeant and take off, himself, but he didn't act impatient.

Robert decided he better get to the rest of what he wanted to cover. "David, I heard Terry was in trouble."

Mallen sighed and shook his head. "I would have got the investigation this week sometime so I could rubber-stamp it and send it on to the captain. Understand, I didn't want to save Terry's job for him, but even if I had wanted to, I don't think I could have."

Robert looked up from the mug. "From what I heard I didn't think the evidence against him was all that much."

Mallen snorted. "Yeah, shit, just a little negligent homicide."

"I mean, you didn't really have direct evidence that it was Terry, did you?"

Mallen thought for a minute. "Listen, Mac, that investigation's over now as far as I'm concerned. Jimbo was the one that was there; you wanta talk to him about it yourself? I heard his voice out there."

Jimbo seemed to have anticipated this conversation. He didn't look surprised when Mallen summoned him into the office and he saw Robert sitting there. If anything, Jimbo seemed to be relieved that he was going to get it over with. The only thing he seemed genuinely uncomfortable about was sitting in the sergeant's chair while they talked.

"Listen, Mac, I'll tell you everything I told Homicide. If I think of something else, I'll even tell you that. Okay?"

"I'd appreciate it."

"Okay." Jimbo leaned on his elbows on the desk top. He was wearing a cut-off sweatshirt and his arms looked huge. No matter how used to Jimbo he got, it always surprised Robert how big Jimbo's arms really were. As he looked down, thinking about what he was going to say, Jimbo inadvertently presented his tonsure-shaped bald spot to Robert's view. It made him more human somehow. "Did anybody tell you anything about this incident?"

"No. What you guys said in the coroner's office was the first I heard about any of it."

Jimbo nodded. "Figures." He looked up at Robert and took a deep breath as though he was about to plunge into a pool for a long swim. "Okay, we got this call, 'officer in trouble' and responded out to, I think it was Fourteenth and Campbell. Know where that is?"

"Sure." That was a middle-class black neighborhood that bordered the State College campus. It was not particularly known for trouble like some other parts of town, but it had a higher than average crime rate, and the police public relations with the citizens was not good.

"Okay. Well, I think we must have been the first unit that responded and when we got there Sheila Enderby was there with her partner, Danny Escobito and there were a whole lot of pissed-off people on the sidewalk. When we first pulled up this bottle hit on the hood of our car right in front of Terry. He was driving. He just got out of the car and I didn't pay much attention to him because I could see we were gonna need more than just our two cars there, okay?"

"Yeah." Robert could picture the scene clearly. Some minor

incident, a number of people misunderstanding what happened in the first place and then nobody listening anymore. All you could do was to try to restore order and get out without getting hit with anything or making matters worse.

"Anyway, I didn't see which way Terry went because I was calling in for some more bodies. Then, when I got out I could see that there was this bunch of kids; I mean like young teenagers, about twelve or thirteen years old, that were standing closest around the cops. So I ask 'em, 'What's goin' on,' you know, like they might tell me their side of it. Well, at first nobody would talk to me and then this kid got his nerve up and he yells at me, 'We weren't doin' nothin' and them cops come up and started harassing us.'

"So, I shrugged at him and said, 'You must've been doin' something, huh? Making too much noise?' See, it was about fifteen or twenty minutes after midnight.

"So then this other kid yells out 'a little noise, big deal, huh?' and I said, 'Well it's okay now, why don't you just go on home,' you know, hoping that was all there was to it because I could see these guys over on the sidewalk, these older guys, giving Danny a bad time and I figured there was going to be some kind of serious problem pretty soon. But the kid yells back, 'We can't, they got our stuff.' So then I looked at him, 'What stuff?' and he says, 'Our stereo stuff.'

"Then I see what the thing is about. They got this Safeway shopping cart full of speakers and a turntable and probably some more components. I can see they were probably pushing this cart down the center of the street and that's probably what started the whole thing when Sheila tried to check it out. Then, the next thing I see is Danny, looking pretty pissed off and he's cuffing this kid that can't be more than thirteen years old and then these guys on the sidewalk come running over and start trying to push Danny around and Sheila in the middle of the whole thing. Well, you got the picture, right? A big fuckin' mess over nothing."

MacDonald nodded, eyes closed. That was one thing that he did not miss about patrol: these situations that seemed to grow on their own with nobody left to blame until there you were, hip deep in shit just looking for somebody to arrest so you could have an excuse to get out of there. Somewhere, though, he had to get Jimbo to the point. "Where did this girl come from?"

"Well, see, that was later. We weren't a block away from the campus and with all the yelling and people throwing things and I guess about a half dozen patrol cars with all their lights on . . . anyway, a bunch of students started showing up. I think, to them, this was a great show except they took the kids' side, of course, and started yelling at us, too."

Jimbo paused and looked up at the ceiling. He seemed to be trying to picture how all this could have happened. He had told this story a number of times, to Internal Affairs and Homicide, but now here was his partner's father wanting to know. Jimbo was trying not just to relay the facts like a good witness, but to explain what happened to a friend, the father of one of the participants who happened to be another cop. It was a different kind of explanation. He took a deep breath. "I think . . . I think up to that point there had only been a couple of things that were actually thrown at us." He thought about that a moment. "There were a couple of bottles or cans just sort of lobbed in our direction. But it was after the students got there . . . when there was a lot more people in the crowd, a lot more bodies there yelling and getting excited . . . and somebody hit Sheila in the head or the side of the face and she was standing there all hunched over and bleeding so you couldn't tell how bad it was. I don't know what Terry had been doing because I guess I lost track of him because I was helping to wrestle this one guy down, I had hit him with my fist and . . . well, I looked up and there was Terry going after the crowd like a fuckin' Cossack or something. He was swinging in all directions with this big riot baton, trying to hit people in the head . . . Absolutely hog-wild. That's all you could call it was crazy, the way he was going after 'em."

He stopped and looked at MacDonald, but he was seeing the incident in his mind and Robert could tell without question that he was being as honest as he could about this. "It wasn't just being pissed. We were all more or less pissed. But Terry, it was like he was really trying to hurt somebody. Crazy. So I went after him and a couple other guys got ahold of him and we just put him in the patrol car, just stuck him in there and watched him until he got calmed down."

MacDonald waited for a moment and then prompted him. "What about the girl?"

"Yeah, I was just trying to think about that. See, I'm pretty sure I saw her. It was some time after we got Terry stashed in the car . . . I just can't remember how long it was, but some time after that I saw her on the ground and these other kids, other students, I guess, were trying to get her to stand up, trying to help her up.

"I remember that because up to then I didn't think anybody had been hurt. Even later, Sheila had this little cut that turned out it didn't amount to anything, and I didn't think anybody else had been hurt. But when I first saw this girl on the ground with the other students trying to help her I started to go over there to tell 'em to wait for an ambulance. I was thinking, 'Shit, Terry creamed one of 'em.' But as I was walking over, this other kid, a girl maybe eighteen or nineteen years old, was jumping in front of me yelling, 'Fuck you, pig! Fuck you, pig!' And it kind of shocked me. Stupid, huh? It was just that here was this nice-looking young girl, practically a child, really, long blond hair and nice clothes, and she was jumping up and down, almost spitting in my face."

"What about the girl on the ground?"

Jimbo looked at Robert and shook his head. "I don't know. I don't know what I was thinking about. Maybe . . . maybe I was just thinking about my own ass then. I mean here was this kid, hurt, and no matter what, these people were going to say the cops did it and who could miss describing me, right? Maybe that's what made me stop. See I was going over there and then this other kid was in my face and I just stopped. I looked at the students helping the girl that was on the ground and I just decided, 'What the hell. They'll take care of her.' "

He paused and looked at MacDonald, thinking about it. "But they didn't. From what I heard she could have been saved if she'd gone to the hospital, but those kids just took her back to the dorm and put her to bed."

Robert shook his head. "They're just kids. . . ."

"That's exactly what I mean. See, if she had internal injuries, which is what I heard, those kids wouldn't have known to look for any of that . . . you know, the signs to watch out for. If I could've or for that matter, if any of us could have gone over there and taken a look at her, we would have known to at least get her to a doctor, get her looked at . . ."

"Well, Jimbo . . ."

"Okay, well, I guess that's not the point, huh? I don't know what Homicide got in their investigation because, technically, I suppose I'm a suspect along with everybody else out there."

"But that's it, huh?"

"What's it?"

"As far as you know Terry was in trouble on that kind of evidence. You know anybody saw him hit this girl?"

"No . . ." Jimbo paused. "But that's not all they had on him. You don't know about any of the rest of it, huh?"

"Rest of it?"

"Shit, no wonder. I better tell you." Jimbo looked over Robert's head as though to see if anybody from the station was listening. He leaned forward on his elbows, ignoring the Sergeant's paperwork that he was wrinkling.

"Well, we come back here. We had two prisoners in the back of our car so we brought them in and I booked 'em on some bullshit that I'm sure got thrown out. Anyway, that took me a while and when I came back downstairs here's this fucking brawl goin' on right out there." He pointed to indicate right outside the Sergeant's office. "There's all this yelling goin' on and arms and legs are flying. I get up close and there's Terry on the goddamn floor with about three cops holding him down and swearing at him. I look over and there's David Mallen bent over, all twisted because he's trying to rub his back, the back of his rib cage where he's hurt. Then he turns around and it's obvious he's having trouble getting his breath, but he yells out, 'You asshole!' and I thought he was going to kick the shit out of Terry right there on the floor. But Mallen just barely restrains himself, maybe because there's all these other cops all over Terry and Mallen just can't see a spot to kick. Anyway, he's practically hopping up and down he's so pissed and can't do anything about it."

"Wait a minute, what happened?"

"Yeah, that's just exactly what I asked. It seems that some of the other guys had already told Mallen about Terry acting like a maniac, so Mallen was just laying for him to come through. When he sees Terry come charging in carrying his equipment like it's the end of the shift or something, he comes out and grabs him by the arm. Then Terry, who's carrying all this stuff, just spins around and swings that fucking baton at Mallen. Lucky for David that Terry had to drop all this other shit because that gave him time to see it coming and duck, but Terry still got him on the back. He didn't tell you about this?"

MacDonald shook his head. "Mallen? No, not a word."

"He's probably still embarrassed about it. Anyway, I walked up to see what the hell was going on and Judy Ramirez comes up behind me. You probably don't know her, she's another Q2 patrol officer been out here about a year, but Judy was pissed off. She looks at this pile of guys on the floor and she yells out, 'Now what did the sonofabitch do? He was just in the Ladies' room.' And everybody looks at Judy and she says, 'Walked in and stood there like a goddamn tourist, looking around.' Well, you can imagine, that kind of did it. Everybody thought about the same thing and somebody says, 'What were you doing, Judy?' and somebody else says, 'What happened, you get pissed off?' and somebody else: 'Did you have to wait until he got it out to say anything?' and 'Well, maybe she wanted to get a measurement first.' So Judy gives everybody the bird and starts laughing, too.

"But Mallen, he was still pissed off, of course. He was standing there staring down at Terry and then we looked down and Terry looked like . . . Well, like no expression at all, his face just blank. Then he says . . . I don't remember, but it was something like, 'Thought you were somebody else,' or some damn thing. But then he was looking at one of the guys holding him and it looked like he thought that was the guy he had hit."

"What are your talking about?"

"Mac, it was just real strange. It was eerie, enough to make the hair on the back of your neck stand up. It looked like he was hallucinating or something, I don't know."

"I don't understand. What was eerie?"

"Well . . . At first, it was like he was going to apologize to the wrong guy and then he looked like he didn't know anybody there. We could see he was calmed down again and when they let him up, he just acted like he could pick his stuff up off the floor and walk off, like nothing had happened."

"But he didn't."

"Oh, hell no. Mallen had him pee in a sample cup right in front of all of us in the hall and then made him sit there 'til the paramedics came."

"That's when he went to the hospital?"

"Yeah, but one more thing. While he was waiting, sitting out there in the hall in a chair, he was shaking all over. I mean really, really shaking like he was damn near frozen to death. The paramedic that looked at him before they took him off said he had a lump on his head, but I think he got that when they were taking him down here. I mean, I don't think he got hit out on the street and then started acting funny. I think he started acting weird and then got the lump on the head."

"What's the difference? I don't understand what you're talking about."

"Because that's the reason they didn't keep him in the hospital. They thought he had a mild concussion and got disoriented, so when he seemed relatively normal after a couple of days they just turned him loose. Just fuckin' let him go."

SIX

There were phone numbers scribbled in the margins and across the dates of the calendar printed on the back of Terry's checkbook. First, Robert had painstakingly gone through page after page of the check record without finding a single entry that stood out. If anything, Terry wrote fewer checks than most people since just about all of them were for payment of routine bills, month after month. An inordinate number of the others were made out to the neighborhood liquor store, but that didn't surprise Robert.

Finally, he had given up on the checks as a source of information and tried to decipher the phone numbers. Three of them he readily disposed of as being familiar police department numbers. Another turned out to be David Mallen's home number, which probably everybody at Southern Station was supposed to have written down somewhere. Three numbers were identified with individual's names. The first was Lawrence Pitts, the tenant upstairs from Terry's apartment and both of the other two were for a Camille Hamilton. Robert dialed one of them without having a clue if it was her work number or home phone. No answer. He dialed the other one. It turned out that it was the phone in the liquor store. Camille used to work there but hadn't for the last four months.

Finally, in the early evening, he got an answer at the other number. Robert explained to her who he was, that he had found her number in Terry's things and asked if she would mind talking to him.

There was a long pause. "I . . . I was at the funeral. I wanted to come up and introduce myself, but I had my little girl with me and she was starting to get antsy."

"Sure, I remember seeing you. Were you a friend of his?"

There was another long pause. "Mr. MacDonald, would you like to come over? I'm not working tomorrow so it's not too late for me if it's all right with you."

"Thank you, I'd appreciate the chance to talk . . ."

"Oh, wait a minute, you're a policeman, too, aren't you?"

Robert hesitated. "Yes, I am."

"What am I saying? I'm sorry, I just wasn't expecting to hear from you. Please, come on over. Do you have my address?"

Camille Hamilton's apartment was a second floor studio that she had crammed with about twice the amount of furniture it would comfortably hold. Robert guessed that she was about thirty. She had blond, coarse hair, dark at the roots, barely confined in a knot at the back of her neck. She wore thick wire-rimmed glasses that were slightly tinted, distorting her features behind them. She had a trace of a mustache on her upper lip that was damp with perspiration when she invited him to sit on a threadbare couch.

She had a glass of wine on a coffee table next to an ashtray with a cigarette burning in it. Robert sat and watched her light another one, apparently oblivious to what she was doing. She sat across the table from him and reached for her glass. She stopped. "I'm sorry, you want some wine?"

Robert thought there was something missing in the apartment, but he couldn't think what it was. "No, no thanks. I can't stay too long." He also thought it smelled funny.

"I was very sorry to hear about Terry. I saw it in the paper and I just . . . well, I was surprised, I guess."

"You must have known him for a while, huh?"

She frowned. "Just . . . I don't know, maybe six months or so. Why did you want to talk to me about him?"

The blunt question stopped Robert for a second. Finding her number on Terry's checkbook didn't seem like such a good reason now that she had asked. "Well, I don't really know any of Terry's friends outside the police department and he had your number. I just thought you might be able to tell me if you knew of anything he was worried about recently, anything he might have talked to you about."

"Mr. MacDonald, I went out with Terry exactly one time. It was after I left that job at the liquor store. . . ." She shook her head and looked down. She started to flick her cigarette in the ashtray, saw the one that was already burning in it, and stared from that one to the one in her hand, not really seeing either. "He called me a couple of times last month and we talked a little, but . . ." She shook her head again, her face drawn in concern. "Was it really suicide?"

"What makes you ask that?"

"Well, you're asking about what might have been bothering him."

Robert was vaguely irritated with himself for having put it like that. "I meant, was he having any problems with anybody that you knew about? Any arguments or fights or anything?"

"No, nothing I know of, anyway. I don't think he would have told me about something like that, anyway."

Robert watched her take another drink out of her glass of wine and then stub out both cigarettes in the ashtray, breaking them clumsily in the middle without getting them out. He knew that he wasn't smelling marijuana. He realized that he wouldn't recognize the smell of cocaine burning and took another look at her eyes. They were all but invisible behind the distorting lenses of her glasses.

"Do you know of anybody else that he might have talked to?"

"Pardon?" She looked up at him, blank-faced.

"You said you didn't think he would tell you, but is there someone else you can think of?"

"Oh, I don't know . . ." Camille lit another cigarette, still staring at the embers of the two that she had just tried to crush out. She seemed to make up her mind about something. "Mr. MacDonald, you didn't say so, but if you told me I was the only friend of Terry's that you could find, I would believe that." She blew smoke in an arc over her head.

"Why do you say that?"

"Your son . . . Terry was a very odd guy, to tell you the truth. He used to come in the store and buy booze about three or four times a week. Maybe not that often, but it seemed like it. He was always quiet and polite as far as I know, so I always spoke to him and even gave him my home phone. To tell you the truth, I think I gave it to him without him ever asking for it. I was the aggressor, you know?" She shook her head again, remembering. "But I wouldn't go out with him twice."

"What happened?"

"Well, nothing. I mean he didn't attack me or cause a big scene or anything, he just . . . I don't know, he was just inappropriate. It was almost like he didn't know how to talk to anybody. He acted like he was shy, but I didn't think that was it. I thought he was hostile. I thought he was about the angriest person I'd ever been out with and I just didn't want to be around him after that. No, that's not what I mean." She looked at Robert again. "I didn't mind being around him, I just didn't want to date him, and have that kind of relationship, you know?"

"Yeah, I think I know what you mean."

"I'm sorry, I guess that's not much help, huh?"

"I don't understand. He was angry about what?"

Camille shrugged and exhaled a huge cloud of smoke. "Hell, I don't know. Traffic, other people in line at the restaurant, the phase of the moon, who knows? See, he didn't start arguments or say much . . . he just glared all the time and breathed deep like he was going to say something and just barely stopped himself, does that make sense?"

It did to Robert, perfectly. He could picture Terry in a thousand situations that he had seen him in, gritting his teeth, seething, and then not saying anything. He didn't know when he had first seen it. He remembered Lorraine, a mock-scolding voice, "Terry! What in the world?" and Terry, sullen, turning away. "Nothing."

"Really, I'm making him sound just awful. I did consider him a friend, though."

"Sorry?" Robert wasn't thinking about this conversation at all.

"Well, I guess when I lost custody of my daughter I learned what it was like to really appreciate having a friend around and Terry . . . Terry could be very kind, too."

"How do you mean?"

Camille laughed suddenly and took a big gulp from her wineglass. "Oh, I didn't mean to laugh at the question. I was just remembering. I got myself in this stupid fix. Well, it wasn't really my fault. My ex is such a son of a bitch! Anyway, he was all pissed off even after he was the one that got custody and he was coming over here and calling me all the time."

"Who?"

"My ex-husband. Name's Frank Falzon. Anyway, that shit was calling me all the time and coming over in the middle of the night. . . ." She laughed again, remembering. "I got Terry to come over when I knew Frank was coming and Terry told him to bug off or he was going to break his fucking neck." She laughed again. "That's what he said; he goes, 'I'll break your fucking neck.' " Flexing her arms at her side, she giggled at her own imitation of Terry's demeanor. She looked at Robert. "Well, it was funnier if you'd seen it."

"You said his name is Frank Falzon?" Robert turned the hearing aid toward her to hear better.

Camille quit laughing. "Yeah, why?"

"So, would you say your ex-husband had a grudge against Terry?"

"I suppose . . ." She thought about the question. "Terry did commit suicide, didn't he?"

"Well, that's one theory, but there's a lot we don't know about yet."

"You think someone could have shot him? You're not thinking about Frank!"

"Why not?"

"Frank Falzon is about five-foot-six and weighs a hundred twenty-five pounds on a good day! He's a squirrel!"

"You don't have to be big to shoot a gun."

"Frank doesn't even own a gun."

Robert nodded. "I know of at least one that's missing."

Camille shook her head in disbelief. "Sorry. No, Mr. Mac-Donald. Frank is the wrong guy for that. He might threaten me because I'm his ex but if it came down to it he would be afraid to fight with me. I mean physically he's a squirrel and mentally, he's a rabbit."

"Would you mind giving me his address anyway? Just to check it out."

"He's in the book. You got to have a better suspect than that, though. I mean, I was surprised to hear Terry committed suicide. . . . It just didn't sound right, but this doesn't seem like a very good explanation to me."

"You don't think somebody could have killed him?"

Camille shrugged her shoulders. "No, I suppose that could have happened. Could have been suicide, too." She shook her head. "Could have been either one as far as I know. He could have gotten pissed off enough at the whole world or he could have gotten the world pissed at him, either one." She looked at Robert thoughtfully. "All I could say for sure was that Terry was not on good terms with the world."

SEVEN

"Hey, Greg? Greg, are we in some kind of trouble?"

"Like what?" Greg's voice was irritated, distracted. He was poring over a newspaper at a small Formica table in an otherwise nearly bare room.

"I don't know. I mean, it's okay if we are, 'cause . . . what the hell, you're my brother, right? But I just thought it might help if I knew what kind of trouble we might be in."

"Don't worry about it, Larry. You're not in trouble." He turned the page of the newspaper and carefully looked at each of the articles on the next page, searching.

Larry turned a chair around and straddled it, crossing his arms over the back. He took a pack of cigarettes out of his pocket and put it on the table in front of his brother with a lighter. "Maybe, trouble isn't what I mean. It's just that you seem like . . . like you was haunted or something. Like you was afraid or something." Greg lit a cigarette, inhaled deeply and blew out the smoke in a long cloud. Larry shrugged his shoulders. "I'm not complaining. 'Cause, you know, what the hell, right? I mean, I really, really don't mind. I just thought, maybe, if I knew what it was, I could be a help, you know? Maybe, if

I knew, then I could help you think of something or at least be alert for, you know, problems that might come up."

"Like what?" Greg didn't look up.

"Like somebody looking for you?"

Greg looked up from the paper and stared at Larry. He caught himself and turned back to the page. "Somebody been looking for me?"

"No, not that I know of." Larry's eyes suddenly got big with discovery. "See what I mean? You were kinda thinking that might happen, right?"

Greg stopped reading, leaned back in the chair and looked at his brother. Twice, he started to say something and then changed his mind. Larry's grin broadened.

Larry was a tall man to begin with but outweighed his older brother by a hundred pounds. He had long reddish-brown hair and a beard that seemed to grow more out of neglect than by any intention on the part of the owner to achieve an effect. Larry's freckled arms were thick and dirty, covered with a layer of gritty sweat since he'd just come in from work. He was seven years younger than Greg.

Larry tipped his head slyly. "See, I been thinking about it. You ain't even talked to me for ten years. You know that?"

Greg's face grew serious. "No . . ."

"I'm not kiddin'. I figured it out last night, it's been ten years."

"That couldn't be . . ."

"Look, Greg, it's okay. I know, I been the black sheep. I went to prison and you had a daughter to take care of and all. Hell, I'd a probably done the same thing."

"Look, I didn't . . ."

"Hey, it don't matter. You helped me out when you could; when I got out of jail, you gave me some money when you didn't really have any to spare, helped me to find a place. It's not your fault I ain't done better. It's just real tough to get anything but day work when you got a record and no good skills.

73

I mean, I never was much of a mechanic, like you. So what I done, I just did it to get by, you know? You probably think some of the stuff I do is real stupid, especially for a con, but it makes me a little money, enough to get by on, you know? And it don't really hurt anybody, what I do. I ain't robbing people."

Greg nodded. "Yeah, sure. I know that."

"Anyway, that ain't the point. The point is, I figured that check you gave me was probably your last paycheck. That was a lot of money for somebody like me, but I figure you ain't got any more coming in or you wouldn't be staying out here with me. It's either that or you're hiding from somebody. Am I right?" He grinned, wide-eyed.

Greg finally smiled and nodded his head. "Yeah, well, that's pretty close."

"See, the point of all this is, I'm trying to say you can stay here as long as you like. It ain't the Hilton but it's home and it's free and clear, fourteen acres."

"Really? I didn't know you bought it."

"Yeah, I did." Larry grinned and almost bounced up and down in the chair with delight. "I'm an honest-to-God property owner."

Greg leaned back in the chair and looked around approvingly.

Larry jumped up and gestured with his arms enthusiastically. "See, I been thinking for a long time I was gonna fix this place up, you know? There ain't a whole lot you can do with that trailer, but this part could be a lot nicer than it is now. It's just that when you're living by yourself there ain't a whole lot to get you going, to get you to do things. But if you was to decide you wanted to stay here after your leg heals, we could work on it together, you know? I mean, there's little things like them cabinets practically falling apart and the place needs paint but also we could replace the floors, work on getting the outside fixed up to where it looked nice and . . ."

Greg was grinning at his brother's enthusiasm. "Yeah, I know how to do that stuff . . . wiring and stuff . . ." His voice trailed off. He looked away, out the window where he could see a cottonwood tree and the blue sky behind it, a relief from the squalor inside the place. He rubbed a hand over his face and the grin was gone, replaced by a strained sadness and a look of deep fatigue. "I don't know. I just . . ." He lifted one hand as though to explain himself but then stopped.

"Hey, Greg. You want to tell me about it, fine. You don't want to talk about it, that's okay, too. I just would naturally be curious, but it don't really matter."

"I can't tell you."

"That's okay."

"I would, but . . ."

"No, it's okay."

"I got things I need to do . . ." Larry took a deep breath and looked at his brother, evaluating. "Actually, I probably don't actually have to . . . See, I'm just not sure because I'm going to get some more . . . some information in a few days . . ."

"Oh, yeah, I see. You're gonna find out if you might be in trouble, huh?"

"Well . . ." Greg stared out the kitchen window, thinking. He looked back at Larry. "I just can't tell you about it. I wish to hell I could, but . . ."

"No, it's all right."

"Well, see, I'll know the rest of it in a few days, I guess. I think that's going to be the end of it, but I'm not positive."

"Sure, I got it. You don't have to say another thing. I understand."

"But I actually do have some savings. I ain't broke . . . yet." He grinned.

"Expenses around here ain't much. If you want to split costs, that check you gave me can pay your share, for about three or four months—or more even. Tell you what. That was enough money to pay for whatever time it takes until you ready to go back to work or whatever you decide you want to do. Okay?"

"Well, Larry, that's nice of you . . ."

"No, it's a good deal for me, too. I'd like to have your company. We can catch up on all that time, you know?" Larry glanced around, looking at the mess, but not seeing all of it. His eyes stopped on the table. "I can get a subscription started on the paper. I can do that tomorrow; probably start the next day, coming every morning." He looked around again. "Besides, when you ready there's all this fixin' up I'd like to do."

Larry was so enthused, so innocently delighted, that Greg could only grin at him and nod. "Okay. All right. I could get started doing a few little things. It's just this damn leg . . ."

Larry nodded in sympathy. "Yeah. Must be about killing you, huh?"

EIGHT

Robert MacDonald took a breath, let out half of it, then held it. Almost without thinking about it, he tightened his grip, squeezing with his whole hand until the explosion rocked him backward. He didn't even blink. He raised his head and looked over the top of the sights as though he could make out the bullet hole in the target two hundred yards downrange without the aid of a scope. Then he nestled his cheek back down on the stock, snuggling into it, and closed his left eye again. The rear sight was a disk with a tiny round hole, a circle of light as he looked through it. The front sight was a broad flat blade with mud wings on either side of it that looked to him like a post between outcurving arches. He centered the post in the circle and focused exclusively on the small round black dot that was the bull's-eye, sitting solidly on top of the post. He breathed again, held it and squeezed until he felt the sudden, satisfying, thump of the stock against his shoulder.

This time, instead of raising his head and looking downrange, he glanced to his right to notice how far the spent brass cartridge went when it was ejected. He extricated his left hand with its stiff padded shooting glove from the front of the sling and laid the rifle on the shooting bench. The "bench" was a table with deep concavities cut into either side to accommodate either right or left-handers. There were six of them lined up as shooting stations down the firing line on the two-hundred-yard range, but this was the only one occupied on a Tuesday morning.

Deliberately, Robert avoided looking through his spotting scope until he had collected all five brass cases that he had just fired, wiped them carefully with his fingers and stuck them in the shooting block. Only then did he satisfy his curiosity and peer through the eyepiece of the scope. Three of the rounds formed a single L-shaped hole just inside the black bull's-eye to the right and slightly above center. The other two rounds were less than a half inch from this hole, one above it and the other below. Robert allowed himself a small satisfied smile and muttered, "Eight ring, two o'clock" as he would have called out to someone sighting in a weapon. He would wait and make the sight adjustments when he was ready to fire again.

Shooting was one thing that he could do with complete absorption, without having to think about anything else at all. During the time he allowed himself to do it he would not be thinking about Terry, official investigations, plans for the Academy class that afternoon or even lunch. He believed that there was no way to shoot accurately without concentration so complete that, for him, nothing existed outside the narrow cocoon that enclosed the shooting bench and extended, almost incidentally, through a narrow tube of sanctity to the target downrange. This world included his M1 Garand, a target rifle that was the envy of everyone else on the team. It was not the standard M1 carbine that you could get anywhere for 150 dollars. That one was a short, light weapon that he held in contempt. His was a Garand Match Grade that weighed nine pounds (you had to specify that the weight was without the standard bayonet) and had a full walnut stock. He had put on a modified rear sight which was allowed by the rules but the broad blade front sight was the key to using it in the "military" class in competition. Robert had rebuilt the firing mechanism until it pulled a sweet, smooth three pounds with no rough spots. It was his pride and the centerpiece of his private arsenal, which also included a 30.06 Springfield, "sporterized" and scope-mounted for another class of shooting and a 7 mm Mauser with a set trigger for another.

To go out shooting was, for Robert, a solitary, necessary condition for living, a reward for getting through the rest of it, a theological compromise where the truth of the universe could be encompassed in an effort to punch holes in paper with the precision of a drill press over a very long distance.

Robert estimated that there were fewer than two hundred men in the whole world that could do that task better with a high-powered rifle. But the idea of superiority, of competition, was secondary to him. If he had been more competitive, he thought, he might have been shooting for the Olympics or spending his time pursuing national meets, but that had never been the point. He honestly didn't care about that aspect of it, except that by participating in competitive matches he could get the time from his employer to shoot, to make a living and do what he wanted all at once. In that respect, he considered himself a very fortunate man.

For the past eight years he had been the Martin Police Department's range boss. On paper that job belonged to a lieutenant but no one could remember when the department had a soft enough budget to be able to put someone of that rank into the job. There were four hundred active duty officers in the department, down from an authorized but unfunded strength of nearly six hundred. Robert got his job initially because with his poor hearing he was a candidate for mandatory retirement. His captain, Bruce Kelly, had known him for twenty years and grabbed him for the range job as soon as he had the medical excuse to talk him out of patrol. Robert and Bruce were friends but that wasn't the primary reason Bruce wanted to keep him.

Kelly knew that MacDonald had come to work every single day he was scheduled since he signed up. MacDonald was just about the most reliable man he could have found and Kelly's judgment was vindicated as he watched this little section of his responsibility quit losing city property, steadily improve as a facility without any increase in budget and start winning awards in competition with other police rifle teams all over the South. The PR of this team was so good that Kelly's only regret was that they didn't have the money to send them farther to compete.

Robert had been a good patrolman, an unassuming man with enough strength to endure, without losing his humor, the petty daily insults that went with the job. He had a sense of fairness that gained the respect of the people who lived and worked in his area. In thirty-six years as a police officer he had never drawn his sidearm as an enforcement tool. He often told recruits his belief, which was not department policy, that you should never draw your weapon unless you intended to kill. He, personally, had never seen the need for it. That, however, did not keep him from becoming, long before the range job opened up for him, an unofficial expert in weapons. He could disassemble and repair almost any make of firearm and frequently performed gunsmithing favors for other cops. It was as natural to make him the range boss as it was to make Jimbo a patrolman.

At least once a week Robert left the police range as he had this morning to drive across the river to a private range run by Stuart Branson. Stuart was a retired warehouseman who had worked on Robert's beat twenty-five years ago. They had stayed friends in spite of the fact that Stuart was convinced that almost all cops were suspect. After he had retired Stuart tried raising horses, his first love, but found as had everyone else in the county that tried it, that he couldn't make any money. He turned a natural bluff at one end of his pasture into a backstop and gradually built up one of the finest shooting ranges anyone could ask for. Because of his friendship with Robert he allowed free use of the range for official police department functions which exclusively meant long-distance shooting by Robert's team members.

Robert was vaguely aware that someone had moved in on the shooting bench next to the one he was using. As was his habit, he ignored him, hoping to avoid having to put in his hearing aid and carry on a conversation. Finally, though, he became aware that the man was standing still and probably watching him so he took off his ear protectors and looked around. He was almost startled when he realized it was Bill Farrela, and that he had dumped a black plastic garbage bag on the bench. Robert was beginning to think that he would forever associate homicide detectives with garbage.

"Good morning, Mac."

"What are you doing way over here?" Robert fished a spare hearing aid out of his shirt pocket and plugged it in. He was wearing amber shooting glasses instead of the regular pair that had the aid built in so he wouldn't forget it.

Farrela grinned. "I'd like to say I had to find you right away, but the truth is, I wanted the excuse to get out for a drive." He quit grinning when Robert didn't respond to it. "That guy's story checks out. Frank Falzon was in Dallas all week before they found Terry."

"How do you know?"

Farrela barely kept from looking exasperated. "Because he was registered at a Holiday Inn except for one night when he stayed at a Motel 6 in Denton. His car, his driver's license, his credit card receipts. It all checks."

"You found out all that in two days?"

"Yeah, and it was a hell of a lot of trouble for nothing, Mac. Look, we never had any shortage of people that Terry had a run-in with. I just did all that because you were the one that came up with the fuckin' name."

Robert nodded and looked away. "Yeah, okay. Well, thanks for checking. I didn't mean that I didn't appreciate it, Bill."

Farrela tried grinning again and thumbed toward the bag. "Terry's stuff out of his locker. I guess we're through with it so I thought I might as well turn it over now."

MacDonald looked at the bag and nodded. He was not in the mood to have to get back into thinking about this right now. Almost immediately he felt a twinge of guilt. "Yeah, okay, appreciate it. You want to go through the inventory now?"

"Sure, if you're not too busy."

Again the twinge. "No, of course not."

Farrela turned around and spread the contents of the bag over the top of the bench. There was a uniform and an old pair of gym shoes that made up the bulk of the contents and the rest was the common accumulation of useless refuse saved by most people at their workplace. There was a package of chewing gum, half-gone, two disposable lighters, seven or eight pens and pencils and a spiral notebook. The notebook was the small, pocket-sized one that most policemen used to make notes on before writing their reports. This is what Farrela held up to MacDonald.

Robert frowned. "What's that?"

"Probably nothing, as far as I know, but I thought you ought to look at it."

MacDonald opened the front cover and was immediately struck by the recognition of his son's small, neat printing. It was the contrast between this and the drunken scrawling that they had found in his apartment that made an impression. There was nothing about the content of the writing, though, to be excited about. There were names, license numbers, physical characteristics, all routine stuff for a patrolman. The only thing unusual was that he hadn't torn out the pages and thrown them away yet. Robert looked up at Farrela.

Bill motioned with his head. "Look in the back."

MacDonald turned the notebook over in his hand and opened the back cover. The handwriting here was different. It was still Terry's printing, but it wasn't as neat, as though he had written it in a hurry. Starting on the first line of the last page there was a list of addresses without names. Each address was separated by a blank line from the one above and below it, deliberately kept as a list that continued for four pages, written into the book backward, turning the pages from left to right as though it were written in Japanese. The addresses were written in different inks, a few of them in pencil, as though they had been entered at different times. Robert looked up at the detective.

Farrela raised his eyebrows in interrogation. "Mean anything to you?"

Robert shook his head. "Not to me. I don't recognize any of 'em." Looking past Farrela's shoulder, he could see Eddie Goldman walking down toward them. He had bought three coffees from Stuart's snack bar and was carrying them awkwardly with two hands. The guy was trying too hard, Robert thought. He looked back at Farrela. "You check 'em out?"

The detective raised himself up with his hands to sit on the top of the shooting bench, with his feet on the stool provided to sit on. He looked over MacDonald's bench as though he had just come out here to talk about shooting. Finally, he seemed to make up his mind about something and looked back at Robert's face. "No, I didn't check 'em out." His thin face was lined, serious.

"Okay, so what are you going to do with it?" Robert indicated the list.

"Probably nothing, Mac. There's nothing there. It's a list of addresses, probably places he went to on patrol, that's all. I don't know why he would make a list like that, but I haven't got time to try to figure that out. I thought you might know; that's the only reason I brought it up."

Goldman came up with the coffee, spilling a little as he set the three Styrofoam cups on the bench. He had heard the last sentence and slowly fussed with the coffee, adding two packets of sugar to one of them without looking at Robert. There was a long silence and finally he looked up but not directly into Robert's face. "Coffee?"

Robert ignored him, watching Farrela closely. "Well, then, what's the next thing?"

"Next thing?"

"Yeah, what are you following up next?"

The two detectives exchanged a quick glance. Although Farrela took in his breath as though about to speak, he didn't seem to be able to find the words and just looked at the cup in his hand.

Goldman was thoughtfully stirring his coffee with one of Stuart's wooden sticks. "Unless you got an idea we haven't thought of, there doesn't seem like much to follow up."

"You mean you're just going to drop it?"

The detectives exchanged quick glances again. Farrela's voice was soft. "Mac, there's just nothing else to do here. We got no suspects, no leads, no indication of a homicide at all."

Robert turned the hearing aid toward him, his face showing his distress. Farrela raised his voice. "There's nothing else to investigate, Mac."

"You found the gun, then?"

Farrela shook his head, looking down at the ground. "No, we still haven't found the gun."

"Well, don't you think that's a little odd?"

"No, Mac. It's not odd at all. I told you he was there for two days. Anything could have happened to that gun. There's always something like . . ."

Goldman broke in. "Mac, we got thirty-two unsolved homicides in three years. We got sixteen of 'em so far this year and it's only October. Last night some guys on patrol picked up a car full of little turds from Los Angeles, all of 'em wearing blue bandannas for Christ's sake."

"So what? That's got nothing to do with this."

"You're wrong, Mac." Farrela seemed more determined. "Those guys are gang members, dope sellers. We are very busy."

"So Terry's just another unsolved homicide, is that it?"

"No. Terry is not an unsolved homicide." He looked directly at Robert. "It's not unsolved because it's a suicide. That's a closed case unless the coroner tells me different."

"Then what happened to the gun?"

"Forget the fuckin' gun!" Farrela stopped himself, stared again at the ground for a minute, then finally looked up. "Everything else says suicide, Mac. All the evidence points to that."

"You mean that lousy case you had where you think Terry might have accidentally hit a bystander that might have been the one that died later? You think Terry'd commit suicide over that?"

"Mac, there isn't the slightest doubt in my mind Terry was guilty of that. You're right, he wouldn't kill himself because of my investigation. He did it because he knew he was guilty." Farrela's face looked hard for a moment and then he looked away again. "I can't just ignore all the rest of the evidence because there's a missing piece, can I? Just . . . just give it a while. Give it some time and you'll agree with me. Promise." He held up one hand as though swearing or making a cowboys and Indians peace sign. He tried to smile.

Robert pulled the stool out from under the left-hander's side of his shooting bench and sat down. He was lower than the other two and when he looked from one face to the other he had the look of supplication. "You're just going to stop?"

Goldman looked at his coffee but Farrela looked Robert right in the eye. "Yeah, we're going to stop."

NINE

The woman's face loomed abruptly behind the screen, framed in the open front door of the house. It caught Robert by surprise because as he had crossed the porch he could see that the room on the other side of that screen was dark. At first he thought that the woman was enraged at something, possibly at being disturbed since she couldn't know who he was. He tried to smile but she had unsettled him and he was aware that it showed. "Hi. I'm Sergeant Robert MacDonald, Martin Police Department."

The woman stared at him without speaking, looking, if anything, more irate. She seemed to be about his age, white-haired, with a thin, wiry neck sticking gracelessly out of a cotton housedress. Her stiff hair had been brushed all in one direction so that the outline of her head was smooth on one side and stuck out, raggedly disheveled, on the other.

Robert tried again. "I'm sorry, I don't have your name. Do you live here?" It was almost dark but there was enough light that he could see her reasonably well. When again she didn't answer, he noticed her hands. They were arthritic, the fingers twisted sideways with large, painful-looking joints, her nails at least an inch long. He could see that she had not grown them that way on purpose. They were yellow and as unkempt as the rest of her. He began to suspect that he knew what the problem was. "I'm a policeman. Do you understand what I'm saying?"

She continued to stare, her expression basically unchanged, but he saw it differently. She was concentrating, trying to focus, not being combative. He could see that she didn't comprehend anything that he said.

"I didn't mean to disturb you. Is anyone else at home?" He said the last louder, speaking as much past her as to her. This was the fourth address from Terry's list that he had visited and he hadn't talked to anyone yet. The first two that he had tried were both bars and he hadn't gone in, thinking that he would go back if he couldn't find a residential address with someone home.

"Who's out there?" It was a man's voice coming from inside the house, somewhere back behind the room that Robert could see into.

Robert called over the woman's head, "Hello! Anybody else home?"

Finally, the woman moved, shaking her head slowly from side to side, staring balefully at Robert, wringing her hands. She said, "Oh, shit!" Robert smiled at her again.

The light came on in the hallway behind the room and a man entered and switched on a lamp near the door. He was older than the woman by at least ten years and stooped sideways from a scoliotic back. The man pushed the woman gently out of the way, holding on to her upper arm to keep her from losing her balance while he squinted myopically at Robert through the screen. "What can I do for you?"

The woman said, "Oh, shit!"

"I'm with the Martin Police Department."

"You're a cop?" His mouth opened with the effort of his squinting.

"Yes, sir, I am." Robert realized with some discomfort that he hadn't planned how he was going to explain this visit. He tried to improvise, knowing that he wasn't good at it. "I hope I have the right place. I wanted to follow up on a visit some officers made here . . . some cops were called out here before, right?"

"Yeah, there been cops here before. I didn't call, though. . . ."

"Oh, shit!"

The old man made an effort to straighten his crooked back. "She doesn't mean anything by that." He patted the woman on the arm. "Most of the time, she just can't get the right words out but she can say 'Oh, shit,' just fine. Always remembers those words." He changed his tone, peering at Robert through the screen. "What were you asking?"

"Well, I just wanted to follow up and make sure everything was all right."

The man looked Robert up and down, a serious, dignified expression forming on his face. "What makes you think it wouldn't be?"

"What?"

The man glanced over Robert's shoulder. "What made you think you needed to come back? I didn't call you before and I told those guys that came out . . ."

Robert raised a hand to stop him. "I just wanted to ask you about one of the cops that was here before. A tall, young cop?"

"You want to know about what?"

"Oh, shit!"

"One of the cops. A tall young cop with sort of sandy-colored hair if he had his hat off."

"Yeah, yeah, I remember that guy." The old man nodded his head and glanced over Robert's shoulder again. "There were two of 'em. We're talking about the tall one, right?"

"That's the one."

The man lowered his voice. "He tell you why they were called out here? That why you come back to check up?"

"Well . . ."

"Can I help you, mister?"

Robert jumped and looked behind him. There was a woman in her mid-forties, standing on the sidewalk at the bottom of the steps holding a bag of groceries. She was frowning at him, her eyes shifting to the old man in the doorway and back. She probably weighed two hundred pounds.

Robert reached for his ID. "I'm with the Martin Police Department."

"Goddamnit!" She came up the steps, stomping on each one. "Who called you this time? You got a warrant, mister?"

"Well, as a matter of fact, I don't. It's not really a matter that needs a warrant, though."

"You assholes don't have anything else to do, is that it?"

"Pardon?"

"Where the hell are you when somebody really needs a cop, huh? I'll tell you where you are, you're out at the Silver Dime having coffee. I went by there once and there was about ten cops in there, all of 'em drinking coffee on the taxpayer's money."

"I just wanted to stop by for a minute and ask you some questions about . . ."

"Screw that! You ain't got a warrant, you ain't gettin' any questions answered. Now just get outa here!" By this time she stood between Robert and the door.

"All right, lady, now just calm down. I have to ask you about one of the officers that was out here before, that's all."

"Oh, shit!"

"Shut the fuck up!" The younger woman screamed at the older one through the screen. Robert was startled at the violence in her voice and surprised again when she calmed down and turned back to him. "Well, okay, what do you want to know?" She casually opened the screen door, put the groceries down and pulled out a bag of M&Ms that she handed to the older woman. Then she rudely shoved the old couple out of the way and closed the wooden inner door on them. "Look, these old farts take up all my time and attention. I really don't have any time left over for you goddamn cops to keep coming around here."

"Ma'am, I am truly sorry to bother you. It's not a question of trying to harass you or anything. Actually, it's more of an ad-. ministrative problem with the police than it is an investigative matter. I was hoping you wouldn't mind helping, that's all."

The woman rummaged in her pocketbook while he was talking and came up with a pack of cigarettes. She shook one out and lit it, looking at Robert. "Yeah? Like what kind of problem?" She was interested.

"Well, there was a young officer that came out here to see you. A real tall young fellow, about six-four."

She grinned, her face full of malice. "You talkin' about Mac-Donald?"

"Yes, that one."

"Sure! I shoulda known that asshole would be in trouble." She laughed out loud. "I hope they cut off his balls! I told him next time he came around here, that's what I was going to do."

"Was he here more than once?"

"You kidding? Once was plenty for him! You see the report? They tell you what that motherfucker did?"

"Well, actually, no."

"The son of a bitch had me in handcuffs, that's what he did."

"What for?" Robert asked it as if he couldn't imagine anyone treating her that way.

"For nothing, that's what for! I got some . . ." She raised her voice to a shout. "Shitheaded busybody neighbors!" She lowered her voice again. "The shitheads called the cops just because they don't like me and this MacDonald asshole tried to arrest me on the word of that old loony in there."

Robert frowned and shook his head. "He didn't actually book you, though? He didn't take you downtown?"

"Oh, hell, no! His partner finally talked him out of it. I told him it was a good thing one of them had the sense God gave a goose or I would've made a formal complaint about it."

"But you didn't?"

The woman looked uncomfortable. "I telephoned it in but I never went down and filled out the paperwork. I probably should have. He damn near broke my arm." She threw the cigarette, still burning, off the end of the porch. "Look, I got stuff I got to do. You guys want me to make a formal complaint, I'll do it, but if you just keep that asshole away from me, that's all I want."

"Well, no problem there."

"Good! Just so I don't have to see him, I'm satisfied." She went into the house and closed the door in Robert's face with a triumphant flourish.

There didn't seem to be anything else to do so Robert went down the steps and slowly walked to his Bronco, parked at the curb. He started to put his key in the door and saw the notebook open to the list on the passenger seat. He wasn't following the list in order, but randomly going to addresses that seemed close together to save time. He didn't have any idea when Terry might have been to this place or what it had been about. He looked back at the front of the house, wondering about it, not sure what he should try to do next.

The front door opened and Robert tensed, dreading that the woman might have changed her mind and now wanted him to take a formal complaint against his own dead son. Instead, it was the man with the bent back. Robert watched him come out the screen door and close it carefully behind him to keep it from banging. Then he shuffled to the top of the steps and motioned to Robert to come to him.

When Robert reached him the man grabbed his arm and pointed down the steps. "You might as well be useful, huh?"

"Oh, sure. Just hang on."

"Don't worry, I will. Eyes gone all to hell. I can get up them steps okay, but I'm never very sure where I'm stepping, going down."

"You should have a railing put in."

The man snorted. "Right, a railing." He released Robert's arm when they reached the bottom step and kept walking, a slow shuffle toward the street. "I don't want her to see me talking to you, if I can avoid it." He had lowered his voice and Robert wasn't sure that he had heard him right.

Robert turned the hearing aid toward him. "Pardon?"

The man gestured away from the house. "Come on."

Robert walked next to him, walking slowly because the old man moved carefully, squinting at the sidewalk in front of him as he went. When they had gone about a hundred yards from the house the old man looked over his shoulder as though afraid he could be followed. He shook his head. "That's pretty nice of you guys to come back, but it won't be no help. I'd just as soon you didn't come around if that's all right. It just makes her mad."

"Makes who mad?"

"Bridget, my daughter." He walked a few more steps, thinking, then glanced at Robert. "It don't do no good, except to make her mad."

They were passing under a streetlamp and Robert was not surprised to see an old blue mark across the top of the man's forehead. He might have been taller when he was younger but the warp of his back bent him severely, his ribs showing through his T-shirt on the upper part of the curve of his back. Robert guessed there would be marks there, too.

The man stopped and looked back the way they had come. "I don't want to be gone too long. Evelyn . . . that's my wife . . . she gets upset if she can't find me and then Bridget gets mad again." He twisted his head around to look at Robert. "What did she say to that young cop?"

"Who? Bridget?"

"No, Evelyn." He stared back down the sidewalk. "Maybe he

didn't tell you about that. That young guy talked to Evelyn for about fifteen minutes when he was here. Evelyn can do that once in a while; talk to you, I mean. Most of the time she can't seem to find any words and just when you want to give up, she can do it all of a sudden. Never lasts too long, though." He grinned. When he lifted his head Robert could see a strong chin. The way the man stuck it out when he smiled, he must have been proud of that chin before it was tucked under by the kink in his spine. "Almost makes me wish I'd listened more twenty years ago, when I couldn't wait for her to shut up." He laughed, gently.

Robert smiled and nodded to show he understood. "She talked to Terry?"

"Yeah. That the young cop's name?"

"Terry MacDonald."

"Well, maybe you could give him a message for me."

Robert was rooted, immobile for a minute, his deception making him feel guilty, but seeing no point in telling this old man.

"If you see that young guy, you tell him never mind."

Robert looked back in the direction of the house. "Aren't you afraid for your safety? Don't you want us to do anything?"

The man laughed again, a soft melodic gentleness to his voice. "Well, sure, I get scared sometimes. But look at this. She goes to prison what we gonna do, huh? That's what I told his partner, Kennedy. I remembered that one's name because of the president. I told Kennedy it was better for us if they just turned Bridget loose and left her alone." He grinned sideways at Robert. "That young guy was so angry you couldn't talk to him." He looked back in the direction of the house and the smile faded. He looked at Robert. "It's not so bad most of the time. You tell him that, hear?"

"All right." The two of them started walking toward the house. When they got to the Bronco, Robert stopped and watched the man's laboring back as he shuffled away.

He stopped and turned to say something else and Robert went to him so he wouldn't have to retrace his steps. The man raised one hand to make a point. "You tell that young guy . . . Terry, was it?"

"Yes, Terry."

"You see him, you tell him we said 'thanks anyway.' You tell him that, all right?"

"All right."

"He was so mad and everything else going on, I didn't get a chance to say anything to him before and I don't know how to call him. But you tell him Evelyn and I appreciate . . . put it like that, tell him, 'Evelyn and I appreciated his concern.' And 'thanks anyway.' I want you to be sure and tell him like that, if you wouldn't mind."

TEN

Kermit Williams, M.D., liked to give the coroner's inquest hearings a little flair. County coroner was an elective position and Dr. Williams acted like a politician although he hadn't been challenged in the twelve years that he had been in office. He liked to hold public hearings, presiding like a judge and taking testimony from live witnesses, although the law didn't require that. His usual high point was a week or so after the testimony, giving the impression that in each case he had to give the matter very careful thought, when he would call a press conference in the form of another public session, another hearing on the inquest, to announce his verdict.

When he appeared at these pronouncements he was always carefully low-key and solemn, trying to avoid the appearance of grandstanding, but giving the public the information himself rather than issuing a dry report to be quoted without credit. In the case of *In Re Terrance MacDonald,* though, he dispensed with all of that except the pronouncement. He didn't hold public testimony, relying solely on the written police reports which, he ruled, were not to be made public for the protection of the privacy of the innocent people involved.

This was an unusual tack for him to take, but not entirely unexpected to any of the insiders in the investigation. On a Friday morning at ten o'clock he convened the final session of the inquiry.

Robert was notified by a telephone call from Dr. Williams's secretary two days in advance, a personal touch that he said he appreciated. If the coroner ruled that Terry's death was murder then Homicide would be obligated to keep going on their investigation until they could truthfully say that they had exhausted all possible leads. Robert arrived wearing his suit but he didn't bring Kevin. His second son arrived independently, deciding at the last minute to cut class to be there, showing up in his jeans and sweatshirt.

Williams used one of the grand jury rooms in the basement of City Hall. Even if it had been offered, he would not have used one of the regular courtrooms on the fourth floor because he liked the smaller scale of things downstairs. Instead of a judge's bench he had a small metal desk that he sat behind, while any spectators that cared to be there lounged in comfort in the padded swivel chairs provided for the grand jurors. This morning there were the beat reporters for Martin's two dailies and a young woman from one of the three local television stations, but no cameras.

Farrela did not attend but his boss, Captain Jerry Foster, was there. Foster was a fifty-year-old, 220-pound African-American who perpetually looked as though he was about to go to sleep. His eyelids drooped to half conceal large brown irises surrounded by red veins. He was reputed to be an athletic drinker, but a serious, no-nonsense cop. When Robert came in Foster turned around to see who it was, recognized the elder MacDonald and nodded solemnly.

Robert acknowledged the greeting with a nod of his own before turning his attention to Dr. Williams at the desk. The coroner had a distressingly thin folder in front of him and seemed to be reading it over one last time. Robert noticed that

Kevin, sitting next to him, was shaking. He looked up at his son's face and it was white. He wanted to pat him on the knee as he might have when he was small, to reassure him, but held back. He thought to himself that Kevin was making an extraordinary effort to be there, just for his sake. With some surprise, he realized that Kevin hadn't been indifferent when he had told him earlier that he wouldn't be able to make it. He just didn't want to hear the verdict any more than Robert did. But then he had come anyway. Robert was silently grateful. He had been beginning to think he was the only one on earth that gave a shit about this.

Dr. Williams looked at the clock high on the wall, then checked it against his watch. He looked around the room at the few people there and cleared his throat. "Well, I guess we'll start." He cleared his throat again. "In any death there are three possible verdicts: death by natural causes, death by misadventure, or homicide. Homicide can be death caused by the victim's own hand or death at the hand of another. In this case I have reviewed carefully all of the evidence, including the findings at autopsy which showed that the acute cause of death was a single gunshot wound to the head, which, by definition, is homicide. There are sworn statements by witnesses, including many police officers and there is physical evidence from the scene of the death and from the victim's place of residence. Based on all of the available evidence I find that in this case death was at the victim's own hand. Thank you, ladies and gentlemen, that's all I have to say." He returned the page from which he had been reading to the folder in front of him, closed it with finality, and started to rise to leave.

"Dr. Williams." Robert was on his feet without realizing that he was going to do it.

The coroner froze and looked at him, surprised. "Yes, Sergeant MacDonald." He tried a kindly smile.

"Doctor, I'm not sure I understand. Is your finding subject to . . . would new evidence make any difference?"

Williams frowned. The journalists were leaving, not in any particular hurry, unless it was to go outside, where they could have a cigarette. The doctor raised his voice for their benefit, although they didn't seem to care. "The coroner's verdict is always subject to review if there is any new evidence, but . . . Well, I'll leave it at that. It's always subject to be reopened for newly discovered evidence."

Robert nodded and looked down, suddenly self-conscious. "Thank you."

When the coroner left, Foster slowly rose to his feet and turned around to look at Robert. He gave Kevin a long, cool, level stare until he saw him fidget and look away. Then he stepped between the swivel chairs to where Robert was standing. "Hey, Mac. Sorry about this one."

"Well . . ." Robert nodded, but couldn't think of what to say. He looked down at a dark brown accordion folder in Foster's big hand. It was considerably thicker than the file that Williams had on the desk.

Foster held it up in front of him. "This is the Homicide file on Terry. It's confidential, understand?"

Robert nodded, started to say something but then stopped and waited.

Foster looked at Kevin. "You mind?"

Kevin jumped as if his foot had been stepped on. "Oh, no, of course not. Dad, I got to get back to school. I'll probably see you tonight, okay?"

"Have you met my son?"

"Yeah, I met him." Foster seemed to think twice about his callous treatment of Kevin. He held up the folder in front of him again. "This hasn't really got anything to do with you." He paused, looking at Kevin for a moment. "I guess your dad can tell you anything he thinks you ought to know, but it's confidential, police business."

Kevin blushed from his height and nodded vigorously. "No, sure, I understand. I'll . . . I'll see you later, Dad." He left in a hurry and Foster watched his back for just a moment before turning back to Robert.

The detective captain thought carefully about what he wanted to say. "Now this file is not supposed to be out of the department although I guess you don't have to be assigned to Homicide to have it. You can't take anything out of it, and you can't change anything in there, understand?"

Robert nodded silently.

Foster looked at him as though assessing whether he really understood. "Okay, now that means you can't make any copies, either. Understand?"

Robert looked at him, his eyes narrowed, one old veteran looking at another. "I understand."

"Okay. Now I got to get it back just like it is." He handed the accordion file to Robert. "And if you think you're about to come up with anything, you talk to Bill Farrela about it or bring it to me."

"All right." He held the folder in his hand, hefting it, feeling the weight. He looked back at Foster again. "Thanks."

Foster closed his jaw tightly, his mouth a thin line across the lower part of his face, and shook his head. He turned away without saying anything else and walked out.

ELEVEN

Farrela and Goldman had been reasonably thorough. Robert sat at his dining table with a flat, warm beer in front of him and read. Page after page, there was the same non-result. They had interviewed seven neighbors and all of them swore that they had seen and heard nothing to do with Terry MacDonald or anything that sounded even vaguely like a gunshot the week of the death.

There was a six-page transcript of a taped statement by the young man who lived upstairs from Terry and had found the body. He said that he opened the garage door after being away for three or four days, saw the body, and immediately called 911. He denied touching anything or seeing any gun.

There was a fourteen-page Report of Incident that mostly contained statements by other cops. In that part there was a meticulously detailed description of the physical surroundings in the garage, with an emphasis on the absence of any gun. Farrela described the interior of the apartment and the photographs supported his not-quite-stated view that it was the den of a madman. Farrela hadn't put it in those words, but that's what he said. Robert found it hard to fault his factual description of what the place looked like.

There was a separate memorandum, signed by both Farrela and Goldman, giving their unofficial opinions on the case. In careful, bureaucratic style they explained Terry's idiosyncrasies as they had been described to them by cops that had worked with Terry. They called him a misfit, an evil-tempered, unbalanced individual who never should have been in uniform. They made reference to a separate homicide investigation in which Terry was the prime suspect and speculated that he knew that disciplinary action was to be taken against him and probably knew that he was going to be terminated from the police department. Their opinion was that these facts were "sufficient motivation for suicide."

Robert stared at the paper in front of him without seeing it. It was not true. There was simply not enough there to convince someone to shoot himself in the head. He knew that as surely as he knew that he was sitting at his dining table.

He thought that what was true about the report was that Terry should not have been a police officer. Robert had been as surprised as anyone else when his son had graduated from the Academy. During the time that Terry was there Robert had expected daily to get a call from Bert Carlione to tell him that he was going to have to wash him out. Robert could not understand why Terry wanted to be a policeman in the first place and understood it less the more he tried to figure it out.

To Robert's mind Terry was the biggest failure of his life and he unconsciously groaned out loud thinking about it, leaning over the investigation file in front of him.

Terry hadn't spoken to him for two years until the necessity of dealing with his mother's final illness seemed to bring him out of it a little. Terry's normally quiet nature had concealed the depth of their estrangement from the rest of the family although, of course, they knew that something was wrong.

Robert thought, as he reached and passed his sixtieth year, that there were a number of things that he had basically done wrong. He might have chosen a career that had more financial reward than police work, he might have worked harder at the political tasks, the alliances and connections that it would have taken for him to make it to the rank of lieutenant and then captain. He had never been good at that kind of thing and Lorraine had laughed good-naturedly at his failure. She told him (and anyone else who thoughtlessly brought the subject up) that she depended on him to keep order, just like the public did, and that a neighborhood cop was all she wanted. To him those failures were small ones, things that would only bother him if he was down for some other reason.

In his mind he had truly stumbled only once. Just once, but it was enough to cost him his oldest son.

She was one of Lorraine's "church" friends, the wife of a partner in a women's clothing store who had to make trips to New York to buy stock, a nice man that Robert had met several times, but never really got to know. Her name was Suzanne Lynch and she was bright-eyed and energetic, a young forty years old at the time of their affair, with a tiny waist and small breasts that were taunting and inviting when her nipples stood erect.

She must have known that he was taken with her, staring at her when she visited his wife. But at first she had been no different from the many other women in his innocuous fantasy world, an inchoate stirring that was never in danger of consummation.

Then he had begun to notice that she stared back at him, smiled, and caught his eye when she could. They were signals that he could have failed to notice or just passed off as an over-the-hill wishful thought, but with her he hadn't. He thought about her, caught himself thinking of her at odd moments and felt the vague, deep rumblings of discontent, dissatisfaction, resentment that he had spent his entire adult life without the experience of a single woman other than his wife.

He became afraid of his own thoughts. He would try to imagine how he would feel if he knew that Lorraine had these yearnings for another man and only knew that he could not imagine such a catastrophic event in his orderly, correct life. He tried to force himself to imagine the horrible consequences of being caught, of being confronted by Lorraine with a truly guilty affair with another woman, but it was absurd. His aching longing for this woman had nothing to do with Lorraine. It didn't change his feelings for her except when he involuntarily, irrationally blamed her for keeping him back from it.

Then Suzanne would touch his arm as she passed him; once she put her hand flat on his chest and left it there, warm and thrilling as she talked to him, standing too close. He'd had an almost uncontrollable urge to wrap an arm around her and pull her body closer, pressing her up against him, and Lorraine was right in the same room.

Then, when her car was not working, she had come to see Lorraine in a cab. He offered to take her home, telling himself it was a favor he would do for any friend.

And so, finally, there was opportunity. Her driveway was long, concealed from the house and the neighbors by a high hedge. When he pulled his car up near the door he stopped and looked at her, but she made no move to get out and so he had turned off the headlights. She still sat, relaxed and facing him in the car seat, smiling in the faint glow from the street-lamp far behind them. He had shut off the engine and looked at her, almost boyish with excitement and, unsure of himself, asking himself if he was just going to let this chance go by. He had wondered, fleetingly, if she had done this before, decided in an instant that he didn't care and then that he did. She touched his hand. The barest, lightest touch that yanked him irrevocably into the cauldron.

Afterwards, for a time, he was amazed that he did not feel guilty. He was astonished at his own capacity for duplicity and illicit pleasure. He loved it. He reveled in the fact that he, Robert MacDonald, was fucking this desirable, wonderful woman, Suzanne.

When they stole their time together they conspired without mentioning what they were doing, without admitting that their plotting and scheming meant that they were doing something they both thought was wrong, both afraid that the other would decide to end it, stop taking the risk; Robert was afraid that it would end, wishing that it would, hopelessly at a distance from his own thoughts of who he was.

But the town wasn't big enough. Maybe the whole universe would not have been big enough to contain Robert's secret guilt, but the physical size of Martin was the mundane reality that almost guaranteed that they would be caught if it went on long enough.

Suzanne's husband was in town and so they had gone across the river to a motel, a small neat franchise with anonymous clerks where they thought they would be safe. Suzanne had come out of the room ahead of him and sat in his car. He had come out and the first thing he saw, as though the earth had paused in mid-rotation, was Terry sitting at a traffic light staring at him. Terry was a senior in high school, should have been in class. No, when he thought about it later it was after four and school had been out for an hour. For what must have been only seconds, but seemed like much longer, Terry sat in the strange car that Robert had never seen before and stared at him while traffic passed him as the light changed to green. Then he had accelerated and was gone.

Robert had expected calamity. He had expected to come home and find that the house was burned down or that it was empty, everyone moved out or that the locks had been changed and that he no longer lived there. Of course, none of that had happened. Terry never said a word. He never admitted that he had seen anything, and Robert never could bring himself to talk about it to him. What could he say?

"Sorry, kid. Someday you'll understand these things." Jesus, Robert didn't understand one thing about it himself, so what could he say to this quiet, strange boy? His oldest son became the keeper of Robert's chastity. Maybe, then he had failed twice: the first a failure of the flesh, the second a failure of the spirit. Because he hadn't known what to do or say, he had done and said nothing.

Robert knew all about policeman suicides. Everyone knew the numbers, the statistics, and he had seen a few friends join the numbers. People who had been good cops, cops who had worked hard, tried to intervene in the rise and ebb of human weakness, their belief in basic human goodness eroded by too many examples, too many experiences that taught them the worst lesson: that they had been wrong; that people were no good; and that ultimately, they wouldn't make any difference. That thought process wouldn't apply to a rookie like Terry, though, unless it was well developed before he became a cop, and then being a cop would have had very little to do with it at all.

Robert was startled out of his daydream by the sound of the front door. He glanced at the clock over the stove and saw that it was only 9:15, an early night for Kevin. Robert started putting the file back together.

Kevin didn't say anything when he stood in the doorway of the kitchen. Robert gave him a glance and continued to make sure that he had all the pages of the Report of Incident in order before sliding it back into one of the divisions of the accordion folder. Then he looked at Kevin again because the boy hadn't moved, hadn't gone to his room or come into the kitchen, but remained in the doorway, watching his father.

"What happened, the library go out of business?" Robert asked.

Kevin didn't reply. Instead, he went to the refrigerator and helped himself to a beer. He sat in the chair across from Robert, who finally looked at him closely. Kevin's face was white and scowling, deeply troubled about something, staring at the folder that Robert was just closing.

"Dad, we got to talk."

"Sure."

"It's about Terry, Dad. This investigation that they were doing on him before he killed himself."

"Well . . ." Robert started to argue with him about it, but from the look on his son's face he decided better. "All right, what about it?" He smiled at his son, trying to make him relax, not take it so seriously.

"I know something about that, Dad. I know about when Terry killed that girl."

Robert continued smiling, but he was puzzled. "What do you mean? Something you read, or . . ."

"David St. John was there, Dad." He started to take a drink out of the can of beer in his hand, then stopped and looked directly at his father. "In a sense, anyway, I was involved in it. Just . . . you know, in a sense."

"You were?" Robert stared at him. It hadn't occurred to him that Kevin might have been one of the students Jimbo had mentioned. Now he thought about it, knowing his son, it made sense, of course.

"Dad, I just got to tell you about this, okay?"

"Sure, I wish you would."

"I mean, I have to just get it all out without you saying anything, okay?"

Robert nodded, still thinking that Kevin was being overly dramatic.

"Okay. First of all I knew Melody Arneson, the girl. She was in the English Department so that's how I knew her." He took a deep breath and let it out. "The night it happened David St. John . . . you remember David?"

"Yeah, sure." Robert vaguely remembered meeting another

student that had a car and was a good friend of Kevin's, someone that he had mentioned several times, talking about school or somewhere he had to be.

"Well, David slept with Melody that night. He was up in her room in the dorm with her and later, after that, I saw them downstairs in the street."

"Wait a minute. Before, you said you just knew her. . . ."

"Dad, just let me say it. Okay? Just let me get it out."

"But if you really know about this, you should have talked to the investigators and . . ."

"Dad, I talked to Farrela and Goldman. Right here. At this table. Will you let me just tell you about it?"

"Sorry."

"Okay."

There was a long pause while Kevin struggled with his ideas, trying to decide how to put it. Finally, Robert couldn't stand it. "This was your friend's girlfriend?"

"No. No, not his . . . Dad, it was just a thing. Screwing some guy in her dorm room was not a big deal for Melody."

"A thing."

"I mean something that just kinda happened. I went over to the dorm in the first place because David was going to give me a ride home later and he lives there in the same dorm. . . . Okay. I couldn't find David because he had been up in Melody's room with her . . . her roommate was out of town or something, I don't know . . . and when all the noise started down on the street they went over to see what was going on. I never knew anything about that until it was pretty much over. I was just hanging around downstairs in the dorm because I was still hoping to get that ride. Anyway, David said Melody must have been pretty drunk because she'd been at this party with him before they went upstairs, and then she wanted to go to see what all the noise was about. There were people yelling and cop cars and stuff and it looked exciting. I don't know, something to see; something going on.

"Anyway, I went outside to take a look and I saw David bringing Melody back. There were a couple of other girls there from the dorm that were helping him sort of carry her but she fell down in the street outside the parking lot where I was. People were yelling and running around and Melody was on the ground and I saw her start puking. I ran over and I was sort of holding her up by the shoulders. I was worried about her getting it on her clothes. I was worried about her making a mess on her clothes, for Christ's sake. Anyway, David told me she'd been hit by this cop in the stomach and there were all these other people helping her and so I ran back in the dorm and called an ambulance. I gave my name when I called, and that's how Farrela knew to talk to me.

"After I called the ambulance I went back out in the parking lot and everybody was gone. The ambulance got there in about five minutes but I didn't know where they were then. I thought maybe they had taken her over to Student Health or something. I didn't know what the hell happened to her. I saw David later and that's when he told me they had just taken her up to her room. That's when he told me about Terry.

"Wait a minute. David knew Terry?"

"Let me just tell you what David said, please!"

"Sorry."

"Anyway, he said when he and Melody got over to where all the noise was, it looked pretty ugly. I mean there were cops all over the place and a lot of the students were yelling at 'em and throwing like cans and stuff.

"David said, all of a sudden there was this great big tall cop swinging this long riot club. When he described him, I knew it had to be Terry."

"How do you know if you didn't see it?"

"I know. Dad, they way he described him, tall skinny cop with sandy hair. Just the way he was so pissed off and swinging that big stick of his at anybody that couldn't get out of his way fast enough. There aren't two cops that look like that, that act like that. . . . It was Terry. I didn't have to see him, I knew.

"David told me he saw this tall cop swing at this one guy's head and he missed and the stick hit Melody right in the stomach and she fell down. He said the cop stopped and looked kind of shocked. I could just picture Terry doing that. One of his crazy rages . . ."

"Wait a minute. You told Farrela . . . ?"

"No. Dad, please."

"Okay."

Kevin sat and stared at the table a minute before he went on. "I told Farrela and Goldman most of the rest of it but I didn't tell 'em it was Terry and I didn't give 'em David's name. I told 'em some student I didn't know told me about it. Hell, I just lied.

"Anyway. When they put her to bed they thought she was mostly just drunk." Tears sprang from his face, rolled down his cheeks and dripped onto the tabletop. He made an effort to wipe them away with one hand and then stared at the table where they had been. "See, they just thought it was all the beer."

Robert nodded and got a handful of paper napkins from a drawer under the kitchen counter. "Sure. Well, that's what they would naturally think."

Kevin blew his nose on the paper napkins and swiped at his eyes with the back of his arm. "All they had to do was to wait for the goddamn ambulance."

"Well, now, that's got to be pretty hard to say . . ."

"No, Dad. Farrela showed me the autopsy report. She had a ruptured spleen. People don't die of a ruptured spleen if they get to a hospital. She was bleeding internally and they just put her to bed and left."

"You didn't know where they'd taken her. You couldn't have known, right?"

"Dad, that's not the point. I didn't tell Farrela and Goldman because I knew Terry had hit her. You see? These girls didn't know David so the cops didn't have his name. The girls said this guy helped take her up to her room and the cops had my name because of when I called for the ambulance. I just let 'em think it was me. I mean, I didn't want 'em to talk to David. I thought I was protecting Terry and shit! Terry, he was just . . . he was crazy, Dad. That's why he killed himself. He was really wacko, and he knew he'd killed this girl. Maybe if I'd just told 'em the truth, they might've gotten him some help, or . . ."

"Well . . ."

"No, Dad, you don't know how crazy he was. Years ago he thought he heard people living inside the walls. When we were little kids he told me . . ."

"Kevin, kids say things . . ."

"And when Mom thought he was mad at her for a long time . . ."

"Lorraine thought he was mad at her?"

"Or maybe it was you, I don't remember. Maybe it was you. It was just in his head. He really loved you, Dad, why else did he want to be a cop so bad? But he was pissed at everybody. I mean everybody, the whole goddamn world."

"What are you talking about?"

"I don't know." Kevin half laughed and wiped his face again with his hands. "I don't know what I'm talking about. I guess I just have to go back and tell those guys, those cops, that Terry was the one that hit her."

"They know that."

"They do, yeah, but not for sure."

"Kevin, it wouldn't do anybody any good. They don't have any other suspects that they might go after. You could be in very serious trouble."

"I could?"

"For giving false information."

"Oh." Kevin thought about that. He took a drink from the beer and then looked at his father.

110

Robert was sitting low in his chair. He suddenly glanced up at Kevin. "You know her family?"

"Who? Oh, Melody. No, I really just knew her because she was an English major and she was kind of fast and loose, a real hell-raiser for a freshman. I think her father was a mechanic or something. Wait, yeah, she said her father was the foreman at one of the big agencies downtown, in the repair department I guess." Kevin stopped talking and looked at his father. "What are you thinking?"

"I don't know." Robert rubbed his chin, looking off in the middle distance. He was wondering if they might feel better if they knew the whole story. It might be easier for the girl's family if they just knew. Knowing was better, he thought, even if it didn't do any good otherwise. But then there was the chance that they would charge Kevin. No, no point in putting him in jeopardy now.

Kevin had been absorbed in his own thoughts. When he spoke his voice was quiet. "You know what those guys thought? Farrela and Goldman. They had the autopsy and they knew that Melody had sex the night she died. They had talked to the two girls in the dorm and thought it was me that came up there with them to put her to bed . . . they thought I screwed her after she passed out. Maybe even after she was dead, I don't know. They actually thought that, Dad."

Robert picked up his beer, felt the warm can in his hand and took a long drink, anyway. Kevin was staring at the table, thinking about the cops accusing him of necrophilia. "That is sick."

Robert looked at him. "Well . . . cops see a lot."

Kevin looked up at him, struck by a new thought. "If Terry saw things like that, it couldn't have helped him any. I mean, that might be part of what made him do it." Kevin looked at his father, dry-eyed. "Dad, I should have tried to talk to him. It must have been ripping him apart to know that he actually killed that girl. It was an accident, but I know Terry would have just eaten his heart out about it. Maybe, if I'd tried to talk to him, he wouldn't have had to commit suicide."

"He didn't do it."

"Oh, Dad . . ."

"Where's the gun?"

TWELVE

Jimbo's face was bright red. "I told . . . eight . . . Bill Farrela . . . nine . . . I . . . ten . . . can't talk . . . eleven . . . twelve . . ." The barbell that Jimbo was curling, palms up, had a total of 125 pounds attached to it and when he set it back in the rack in front of him it clanked and seemed to make the rack settle into the gym floor. He walked in small circles, shaking his arms.

"You told Bill what?" Robert leaned against the rack and watched him.

"I think I remember one of 'em. One of those addresses. But look, I'm not even sure about that."

"Which one was it?" Robert studied the list of addresses in the back of Terry's notebook.

"Jesus, Mac, I don't know. I'd have to look again. Listen I got one more set to go and then I'm through with this, okay?"

"Sure, go ahead. I can wait. I'll get some coffee. Want some?"

Jimbo gave him a look that said that the answer should be obvious. "No thanks."

They were in the weight room at the Academy and eight

o'clock on a Wednesday morning was a good time to be there. The place was almost deserted. Jimbo Phillips preferred that time for his workouts because he hated to attract attention and if he came out there when the place was busy that's just what happened. Cadets would stop in the hall between classes just to stare in at him. Robert knew his workout schedule because he had tried to catch him at the end of his shift at Southern Station and missed him. Everybody at Southern knew that Jimbo hurried off three mornings a week without fail to get in his workout. Jimbo's expression was that he had to do it because otherwise, he would turn into a 235-pound can of Crisco.

Even before Jimbo was Terry's partner Robert had gotten to know him fairly well. When he first came into the department, five years ago, he was one of the few cops of his generation who wasn't a native of Martin. That and the sheer size of the man made him an object of curiosity. Before he became a policeman he had never even held a gun in his hands and he worked hard at learning everything he could about the one that was issued to him. The older cops, Robert and the others on the rifle team that were around the range on weekends, were glad to give him a hand.

Jimbo had played two years of football at the University of Florida before he dropped out of school. When he figured out that he wasn't going to have a starting assignment as a junior he had decided to take a year off and figure out what he was going to do since it seemed obvious that he wasn't going to be good enough to turn pro. He had drifted into Martin, in part because of a former teammate who was working as a licensed contractor and wanted to bring him into the business and in part because he was hopelessly chasing a young woman who was teaching school there.

Jimbo became a policeman because it seemed like steadier work. The pay and benefits were excellent and he liked the semi-jock atmosphere, with the locker rooms, uniforms and especially the sense of belonging to a team, in this case a small community, where it was "us against them." He had never had the slightest intention of being a career cop or, for that matter, of settling permanently in Martin, but he liked the city and liked the work.

Jimbo was not the biggest man in the Martin P. D., although he came close. His size was enough to intimidate most people he came in contact with, but, of course, that implied that they would have to have enough judgment left at the time he dealt with them for it to make any difference. That was frequently not the case. Instead of depending on his size to deal with problems he had learned to take advantage of his naturally open, friendly personality and take a genuine interest in other people's problems. This good nature, along with at least average intelligence, made him a very popular cop.

"So, which one seems familiar?" Robert had decided to take a vacation day so he could deal with the question of the list of addresses without being in any hurry. He had stopped to talk to one of the instructors when he got coffee in the faculty lounge and then come in the locker room to try to pin Jimbo down while he changed into his street clothes. Now, he was sitting on a bench, leaning forward, elbows on knees, holding the notebook in both hands and staring at it as though it might speak to him.

Jimbo pulled a sweatshirt on over his head and looked down at Robert. "I don't know. What's the difference?"

Robert looked up. "Maybe none. I got to start somewhere."

Jimbo sighed. "Mac, Homicide's already been all through that stuff. What are you doing?"

"Well, they're pretty busy . . ."

"You don't think they did a good job of it?"

"No, it's not that. I'm not being critical, I just want to be sure everything's covered, that's all."

"Yeah, but those guys are trained investigators. If there's anything there, they would've found it, don't you think?"

Jimbo rubbed his head vigorously with a towel and then dropped it on the bench. Robert looked up at him and seemed to struggle with how to answer the question.

"Okay, Mac, I was just asking. What do you think this list is?"

"I don't know. It could be a list of contacts that he had, people that he knew."

"Why wouldn't he have put the names with the addresses?"

"I don't know."

"I mean, what's the point of writing down a list of addresses? It doesn't make any more sense than . . ."

MacDonald looked at him, trying not to fill in the blanks, trying to keep from thinking that Jimbo thought Terry was crazy when he wrote this stuff, too, that the list was nothing. The list was all Robert had.

Jimbo shook his head and reached out his hand. "Let me see, maybe I can remember something." He sat down on the bench next to Robert and stared at the list. "I think, maybe this one on Washington. That's in Southern's district . . . Wait a minute. These all might be in Southern." He turned the pages, reading closely.

MacDonald grinned. "I haven't tried to plot all of 'em out yet with a map, but I think that's right. He could have been to all of these when he was on patrol. This is his working notebook, so that makes sense, right?"

"What makes sense?"

"That if these addresses are written in the back of the notebook he used when he was on patrol, that they'd be places he went to when he was working."

"So?"

"So, I don't know. Look and see if there's anything you can remember about any of 'em you might have been to with him."

Jimbo gave him a long look. "You think, maybe he went to all these places on calls? There must be thirty addresses here."

116

"Forty-one."

"Okay, forty-one addresses. I can look at the logs for when we worked together and see if there's any that match up. That's usually just addresses, too, but if I can come up with a name, I can see what the call was about."

"Good. How long do you think that might take?"

"Look, Mac, I got to go home and get some sleep." Jimbo sighed again. "Maybe at the start of my shift tonight. I'll go in a little early and see what I can turn up, okay?"

"Sure, that'd be fine."

"Because, otherwise, you're going to have to go to each of these addresses and get names. Maybe use a reverse directory, but I don't know if that's going to be much use either."

"Why not?"

"Well, for one thing, this address on Washington is a transient hotel. I'm pretty sure that's right. If it is then the reverse directory probably won't have the name that the report would be filed under."

"Yeah, I see your point."

"And I guess you want to see the report to find out if there's any similarity about the calls on the list, huh?"

"Sure."

"So, what's your theory?" Jimbo handed the notebook back to him.

Robert took it and sat looking at it, thinking. Finally, Jimbo leaned over and looked at him closely. "You don't have any theory, right?"

"Well, I don't really have any information . . ."

"It's all right, don't explain. I see what you're doing. You feel like there's some unexplained questions, like the gun and this list, and you just want to see if there's anything there that can tell you something, right?"

"Well, yeah, I guess that's right."

"Okay, Mac. I'll do what I can to help you out. But you

know this is likely to take you six months. The way you're doing it, it could take a year."

"Who's going to run the range?" Captain Bruce Kelly ran his hand over his face as though he had just been handed a stiff thirty-year sentence. "Dan Maguire?"

"He knows everything that has to be done. He can teach the shooting course as well as anybody." Robert waited patiently. He knew better than to try to argue his boss into anything. He never really had to. If he waited long enough for the logic of the situation to penetrate the hangover, Kelly could be counted on to give him whatever he wanted.

Kelly's expression was sour. "Dan Maguire is a twenty-eight-year-old kid."

"You might have to drop in on him once or twice to check out how he's doing." Robert agreed.

The captain leaned back in his chair and scratched his chin. Robert knew Kelly was allowing time for his second cup of coffee to hit bottom so his brain could begin to function. Robert waited with an expectant look on his face, thinking that he probably looked like one of Kelly's grandkids wanting the keys to his new T-Bird. Eventually, Kelly said, "You figure a month might do? I mean if I can talk . . . who the hell is captain at Southern Station now?"

"Captain Rolph."

"Oh yeah." Kelly scowled. Robert knew that Kelly thought John Rolph was an idiot. Rolph was chronically sober and intended to make deputy chief before Kelly.

Robert grinned helpfully. "Rolph will go along. He's always short of bodies and I know him from way back."

Kelly leaned forward, put an elbow on his desk, cradled his big chin in his palm and regarded MacDonald through bleary eyes. "Yeah, you would." Kelly was not a difficult man to figure out. Now he had to be thinking that if he didn't go along, let MacDonald take a month on temporary assignment to duties as a patrolman at Southern Station, the old guy might retire. Then Kelly would probably have to assign Dan Maguire to be the range officer. Robert deliberately put him in the dilemma because he knew that at this very moment Kelly couldn't picture a bleaker idea. "Yeah, okay. Maybe I could fix it up. Let me be the one to call Rolph, though. Has he been complaining about not having enough people?"

"Hasn't everybody?"

"Yeah, that's right." Robert knew Kelly was already thinking about how he could make it look like he was doing Rolph a favor. Kelly's face brightened a little. "And you don't mind going on graveyard?"

Robert shook his head enthusiastically. "Not at all. See, that was Terry's shift and . . ."

"Yeah, I got it." Kelly waved off the explanation. It didn't matter why he wanted graveyard. Nobody wanted graveyard and if he wanted it, no problem making Rolph think Kelly was doing him a huge favor. He looked at MacDonald again, thinking out loud. "If you just go over on a temporary assignment you don't have to get the medics involved, huh?"

"Pardon?"

"Your ears! You're deaf as a goddamn post!"

"I can hear all right."

"Right." Kelly rolled his eyes to heaven. "Okay, you got it. One month TA to Southern Station."

"As far as I'm concerned you can go back to patrol permanently. That's got nothing to do with me." Farrela's hostility broke through clearly. He had tried to sound like he was joking, but it was obvious he saw no humor in the situation.

Robert looked down at the little spiral notebook in his hand. When he looked up Farrela had walked off. He hadn't gone far, just two desks over to throw a file on a stack of "pendings" and grab another one. Robert followed him. "Look, Bill, I never said you overlooked anything."

119

"The hell you say. You went behind my fucking back and got Foster to give you my file so you could complete the investigation properly. Fine. Then you go do it."

"Bill . . ."

"I said, 'Fine.' You don't like our investigation, go ahead and do better. I'm not going to interfere and I can just about guarantee that Goldman's not going to bother you, either." He was breathing hard, hands on hips, glaring at the older man.

"Look, Bill, this isn't just any investigation."

Farrela's look softened a little. He turned away abruptly and looked at the file in his hand, ostensibly reading it while he walked back to his desk, Robert following. In a moment he looked up again. "Okay." He regarded Robert for a long moment. "I know Foster pretty damn well, and the only reason he'd let you go ahead with this is because he trusts you not to get all of us in a lot of trouble. Understand?"

"Sure."

"*Sure.* Well let me be positive sure. You can't go kicking up a bunch of shit without probable cause. You don't make an arrest in this case."

MacDonald just looked at him. Farrela had no business telling him anything about his powers of arrest and they both knew it.

"What I mean is, just because you might think you've figured something out, this is not an excuse for you to go looking for revenge." He was glaring again.

Robert looked shocked. "Revenge? Bill, I'm just trying to get some answers . . ."

"Yeah, okay. Look, Mac, I don't really blame you for wanting to do something, but you can't blame me for not wanting to help you very much, now can you?"

MacDonald regarded him for a moment, then turned on his heel and walked out of the office.

He walked across the street from the Hall of Justice with the energetic gait of a much younger man. He glared at traffic, daring anyone to come too close. When he reached his parked car he jerked open the door, got in, slammed it and twisted the key in the ignition. The engine roared as he brutally pushed the pedal to the floor. Then he stopped, his hand on the gearshift lever, and calmed himself down.

Why the hell should he be pissed off at Farrela? He had known that the inspector wouldn't be happy with somebody going through his file, wanting to redo his work. Hell, Farrela would have been pissed about another detective doing this, let alone a plain old street sergeant. No, Farrela's reaction wasn't unexpected, it was the fact that he had thought that he, Robert MacDonald, would be going after revenge. That was a crazy, reckless accusation. He couldn't remember the last time somebody in a fit of anger or drunkenness had accused him of anything like abusing his office or of dishonest motives. Jesus Christ, nobody could accuse him of that! Not the way he was, the way he had handled his entire career, refusing to be tainted, refusing to do anything that he couldn't show the whole world just to get promoted. After all that he thought he deserved better than to have somebody like Farrela accuse him of fucking revenge.

Immediately, he remembered what he had said to Jimbo the night they found Terry. He'd said he'd get whoever did this, hadn't he? Well, that was still true, that's what he intended to do, but it wasn't like it sounded. He wanted to show that Terry hadn't taken his own life, to vindicate his son's memory.

Robert put the car in gear and moved out into traffic. Even Kevin wanted him to give it up. Maybe it was because they just saw an old man refusing to give up on an idea because he was stubborn. He certainly had known old men like that, had to deal with the obstreperous ideas that seemed to come naturally to ossified brains. But that wasn't him, was it? It certainly was not. The red light was suddenly right in front of him and he had to slam on his brakes, putting the car into a shrieking slide over the crosswalk to avoid running right into the intersection. He sat sheepishly, looking at the light, now almost over his head, thinking maybe they were right, after all.

What the hell. He didn't really have to do this. The best people that he knew of had already investigated and they thought that they had come to the right conclusion. Why couldn't he just leave it at that? But they could be wrong. This wasn't physics, after all, this was a matter of gathering information, getting all of it together in one place and making a subjective evaluation, a hunch-laden judgment, and guessing at what happened sometime in the past. Of course they made mistakes.

It was just too bad if Farrela and Goldman got their feelings hurt because they thought nobody could make guesses as good as they could. Too fucking bad.

Robert pulled the Bronco up to the curb in front of his apartment and thought for about the millionth time that he should have tried harder to get a place that at least had a garage. This wasn't the worst neighborhood, but it wasn't all that great, either. He thought about the 30.06 Springfield, sitting in its wooden carrying case in the back of the Bronco, almost in plain view except for the old army blanket thrown over it. He kept it there because it was handy to try out new loads. It had a good four-power target scope and, sitting on a couple of sandbags, was very reliable. He just didn't want to carry it up and down the stairs all the time.

He looked up at the apartment building he lived in. It had been a nice enough residence at one time. But now it was just like the rest of this block, lived in by people that didn't own their homes. He lived like somebody right out of school, like the kids downstairs or somebody that couldn't hold a steady job for more than a couple of years at a time, like the guy across the street, not like somebody with a full career behind him. What the hell made him think he could investigate a murder case that other people had given up on, anyway?

Well, he decided, the honest truth was that he probably

couldn't. So why should he let Farrela get to him? Did he really care what Farrela thought? Well, yeah, he probably did.

Sitting in a seven-year-old Bronco covered with dents and scratches that he couldn't have afforded to fix, in front of the old house, past its prime, he had a revelation. He knew how he looked to Farrela. No, not to Farrela. It was how he looked to anybody with half a grain of sense. He was over the hill, a long way down the path to the end of it all and he didn't amount to very damn much.

Robert got out of the car, locked it out of habit and let himself in the house. He climbed the steps slowly, opened the door to his apartment and stood, looking around. There were boxes all over. Moving boxes that he and Kevin had never unpacked. Jesus Christ, they had been here more than two years and it looked like they had just stopped overnight. What in God's name had he been thinking about all this time? Did he think he was at a motel? Did he think that this was just a temporary stopping place that he would forget about as soon as he moved back into the house that he had sold to pay for Lorraine's medical bills? Did he think that at this stage he was going to save up again for another down payment and buy another goddamn house? Jesus H. Christ, just look at it! Who the hell was he kidding?

It was too much. Too much to think about for very long. He closed the door behind him and walked back to his bedroom. He had intended to try to sleep before turning his clock around and going to work at 11:00 P.M. Once he got to the bedroom, though, he realized that it was probably hopeless. He knew from old experience that changing shifts meant that he was going to have to put up with several days, at least, of misery and that there was no way that he could really prepare himself for it. You couldn't stockpile sleep.

He returned to the living room and tried to think of what he wanted to do, what he thought he was going to accomplish by going on patrol in the area where all these addresses were. During slow periods when they were just cruising, he could visit places on the list and try to see if there was anything peculiar, anything special that would link them together. He could at least satisfy himself that there wasn't anything there to be learned. Just doing that was worthwhile, wasn't it?

Probably.

But where was the gun? Terry's garage was closed, nothing was disturbed, nothing stolen. That didn't mean much. There were endless possible scenarios that would explain that away: if he had surprised a burglar, a car thief, maybe in the garage, and said he was a police officer. In that kind of situation somebody that was otherwise harmless might have panicked, shot him and then run away without stealing anything.

So, what else? Terry could have been involved in something illegal. He could have been cynical enough to decide that he could get away with something, drugs, gambling, it didn't matter what, just something attractive enough to suck in a young cop who didn't know any better, get him mixed up with people that were ruthless enough to kill him when he wasn't compliant enough to do what they wanted.

All of it was pure speculation. He just had to have more information or at least, finally, be satisfied that there was no more information to be had. You didn't have to be a trained investigator to do that. It was simple when you looked at it that way. Simple enough for an old man with nothing else on his mind, anyway.

THIRTEEN

Robert showed up at Southern Station wearing a blue police jumpsuit covered by an oversized pair of gray mechanic's overalls so he could drive to the station out of uniform and yet be dressed for work even if they didn't have a locker for him. He was carrying a flight bag with a change of civilian clothes, and in his car he had a hang-up bag with a more presentable short-sleeved uniform if that's what they wanted. He got to Southern about fifteen minutes early, talked to the swing shift supervisor and took a seat in the sergeant's office to wait for David Mallen. He hadn't talked to David yet and he didn't know what he might have in mind for him. He hoped Mallen didn't intend to sit him down at the sergeant's desk and have him act like another sergeant.

Through the open door Robert could see the people arriving to work graveyard. He was glad he had found a seat back out of the way because, as it was, several cops saw him and strolled in to say "Hi, what you doing here?" He joked that he had to qualify on the street and that got a laugh. Everybody knew him because everybody had to go to the range and had to go back periodically, but he was amazed how many people he couldn't recognize. He recognized Sheila Enderby and Judy Ramirez because they were among the first women in the department, but he wouldn't even have known half of the others were cops. Too bad. It was a small-town community of officers and one of the best things it had going for it was that everybody knew just about everybody else that was in it.

"I don't give a rat's ass what the mayor says!" He could hear a loud cop raising hell in the assembly area. "Tell her to come down and take a fucking look, if she thinks she can do better. But tell her she better not drive her own car if she doesn't have current plates because I'll fucking tag her, too!" MacDonald saw the big cop but couldn't put a name with him. He remembered him being at the range because of his size, maybe ten pounds bigger than Jimbo, and because he had a hell of a time hitting the backstop. He also remembered that he was loud.

"Hey, Dombrowski! Knock it off, will ya? Somebody on the moon's going to hear you bragging. Just try to act normal until you get on the street, huh?" Mallen sounded irritated. He walked into the little office carrying a folder with a lot of scraps of paper hanging out of it. He did a double take when he saw Robert. "Hey, Mac. What you doing here?"

"I'm assigned. Didn't anybody tell you?"

"No shit. No, why would anybody tell me who's working? What the hell. Am I working for you or the other way around?"

"No, I guess I'm supposed to go out on the street wherever you need me for a while. You probably got a message about it somewhere in there."

"No shit." Mallen seemed to half suspect that he was being watched and that Robert was sent there for that purpose. "Where you want to work?"

"Wherever you need the coverage. You got a car for me?"

"Really?" Mallen could smell trouble. Nobody gave him any free gifts like an extra sergeant and he was waiting for the explanation.

"I asked for it. I needed a change. This is just for a month."

"They send you over because of that meeting at the mayor's office this afternoon?"

"I don't know about any meeting." Robert was honestly puzzled.

"You know, the NAACP, and all that?"

"David, I don't know what you're talking about. I asked to come over because I wanted to look into a couple a things that have to do with Terry. You know, just work it in when things slow down."

Mallen nodded but continued to watch him, the mental wheels turning, wondering if there wasn't more. "You don't know about the meeting, huh?"

"I got no idea what you're talking about."

Mallen sat down behind his desk and ran his hand through his short hair. He held up the file. "Forty-seven tickets in a three-block area last night."

"Lotta parties?"

"Yeah, but not like what you mean. Had a narcotics guy get hit in the head at the Redstone Projects. He was serving a warrant and somebody got him with a two-by-four or some damn thing. Must have been about a thousand witnesses and not one of them can remember what the guy looked like."

"What did you expect?" Robert knew that the Redstone Projects were about 90 percent African-American and that the police were not particularly popular there. Either they hated you because you did too much or they hated you because you didn't do enough.

Mallen nodded agreement. "Yeah, surprise, surprise. So then last night we get forty-seven tickets for bad plates or no plates, white light on the rear, broken headlight, not coming to a complete stop, shit, everything."

"Putting the pressure on, huh?"

"No, goddamnit. It's nothing but strict enforcement. I'll bet two-thirds of those assholes complaining to the mayor been asking for more enforcement." Mallen put the file down and regarded Robert. Another problem. "You haven't been out here for a while. I'm going to stick you with another team for a few nights, just to get you acclimated, okay?"

"Sure. Whatever works best for you is fine with me."

"Good." Problem solved, Mallen threw back his head and bellowed. "Hey, Dombrowski!"

"How about sending me out with Jimbo? He was Terry's last partner, and I was hoping to get to talk to him, anyway."

Mallen looked at him, disappointed. "You don't want to baby-sit? Hell, I don't blame you."

Dombrowski stuck his head in the office. "Yeah?"

"Never mind, I couldn't get a sitter."

"What's that mean?"

"Never mind. Go to roll call, will you? And send in Jimbo if you see him."

It was Sheila's turn to drive and she seemed to be completely absorbed in the job. Jimbo sat in the front passenger seat and that left Robert in the cage, the back seat with no door handles and a wire-mesh screen between him and the front seat. Robert realized right off that he was going to have to be the one to get through Sheila's reserve. He decided that the best way was to pretend he didn't notice it.

"So, what's the drill, now?"

When Jimbo didn't say anything Sheila glanced over her shoulder as though to confirm that he was asking her. "Oh, we usually just drive down to the park, come back up Bankroft and if nothing else is going on, we roll through the projects and take a look."

"Been a while since I been out to the projects. Bet they haven't improved much."

"Probably a lot of things are a lot different from when you were on patrol."

Robert laughed easily. "Bet you're right about that. That's one neighborhood I never really minded, though. Lots of good people living there in spite of all the problems."

Sheila gave him a cool, deliberate look over her shoulder. "Right."

He laughed again. "Used to be, we had people that wouldn't even drive in there."

Then Sheila laughed. "Still do. I'm not saying who it is, though."

"No, don't tell me."

Jimbo looked over his shoulder, amazed. Robert didn't know very much about Sheila except that she was married to another cop who, as best he could remember, worked Juvenile, which meant days. He wondered how that worked. He wished that he had a daughter so he would know if it was all right to ask that kind of question now.

The patrol car was an old one, a clunker. All the equipment seemed to work, all right, but it was obviously not responding quickly when Sheila tried to accelerate. Robert decided that the rings were probably shot and it was losing compression. "We used to get better cars."

Sheila grinned, more relaxed now. "We lost the race tonight. Jimbo had to explain your little project to me."

Behind the mesh Robert nodded and glanced at Jimbo. "Hope that's okay with you."

Sheila threw up one hand. "Sure, what the hell. All we got is some assholes trying to start a war in the projects. There's four cars over there and that leaves the rest of the district to us. Might as well kill time that way, looking up addresses on a list, huh?"

"Well, we can see how it goes. Might have some time to check out a couple after the bars close."

Sheila nodded and glanced in the rearview mirror. She drove a few minutes, thinking, and then said over her shoulder, "That's true. Things'll be pretty quiet after about two-thirty." She thought some more. "You carrying around that notebook?"

"Yeah, I got it."

"Why don't you Xerox it? You don't want to get it all messed up carrying it around in your pocket. Suppose you have to use it in court?"

"You're right. I'll do that, first chance I get."

They took a complaint about a loud party. Turned out it was a bunch of high-school kids, parents out of town, so they stayed around until it looked like everybody had left. They checked out a report of a break-in, but it was a malfunctioning alarm. It was about midnight by the time they got back in the vicinity of the projects.

A block away they saw a black-and-white sitting in the driveway of a closed gas station, right behind a '72 Oldsmobile with rust all over it and broken taillights. The rear license plate was hanging by one fastener. The cop in the solo car was Hank Dombrowski and he was writing a ticket for an older black man sitting in the cage in the back of the police car. They waited until he was finished and the African-American man drove off before they got out in the empty parking lot of the gas station.

Dombrowski grinned at Jimbo. "That guy's having a good day. He didn't have his driver's license on him and I'm too busy to arrest him and take him in."

Jimbo didn't answer, but looked down the street in the direction of the projects. If they had arrested the man, they would have had to tow his car and the tow fee would have been worth more than the Olds. Sheila let Robert out of the back and he gratefully stretched.

Dombrowski saw him. "Hey, old man. What the hell you doing out here?"

"Thought I'd get a look at your modern police methodology."

"Hey, that's a good idea. But we call it fuck-over-ology." He started to say something else and then he saw Sheila. He hesitated just long enough for her to look off in the direction the old man had gone. He looked back at Jimbo. "You missing a good thing. I haven't had so much fun since I found that guy wrecked his motorcycle and his head popped off."

Jimbo nodded, without smiling. "Hard to top that one."

"That was number eleven, tonight."

Then Sheila did look at him. "You gave out eleven tickets on this corner tonight?"

"Well, it's been a little slow." He grinned at Jimbo again. "We'll get warmed up pretty soon, see if we can't beat last night."

Jimbo finally smiled. "That's a lotta tags."

"Fuckin' A, it is. Oh, 'scuse me, ma'am."

Sheila continued to glare off in the distance. She had gone to high school with Hank but he was five years senior to her in the department. You wouldn't think they had ever met to see them in the same room.

"Yessir. We gonna teach these people the true path to righteousness. Then, if we get the chance, we gonna think about some honest-to-God retribution."

Sheila was hot but she kept her voice calm. "You gave out eleven tickets already tonight?"

Hank addressed his answer to Jimbo. "We got to take breaks sometime. Union requires that, don't it?"

Another solo traffic car pulled into the lot. A thin cop with glasses and a mustache got out and leaned in the open doorway of the car, his elbows on the top of the door. He was chewing a toothpick, looking at Dombrowski. "I got eight movers. Where's that fuckin' tow truck?"

"I just gave him a load. He'll be back in a minute."

The thin cop looked at Phillips. "Hey, Jimbo." He looked around and saw Robert. "Mac! Decide to come out and shoot a couple for us?"

Dombrowski sat back against the fender of his car and crossed his arms, making the muscles bulge out of the short-sleeved uniform. "Better not be talking about shooting spooks. Some mush-hearted liberal might hear you and take it wrong. It's bad enough you insist they obey the fuckin' law."

Sheila drove out of the lot and slowly past the projects, then turned back toward town, taking the residential streets instead of where the traffic was. As they approached an all-night convenience store they saw a group of young men standing around the doorway. Sheila stopped in the street.

"I'm gonna clear these guys out."

Jimbo reached for his door handle. "I'll do it."

"No, I want to get some gum, anyway." Sheila put the car in park and got out. As she entered the store she nodded at the young men and they quietly walked off, disappearing down the darkened street.

She drove away again, going slowly in the narrow street. They saw a car coming toward them suddenly slow as the driver spotted them. As they passed, the cops saw two young men inside, Latin-looking with pomaded hair, staring at the cops with big, saucer-sized eyes. The passenger looked over his shoulder, still staring. Sheila watched in her mirror as they turned the corner at the end of the block. "I got to check that out."

Robert chuckled. "Did seem a little nervous, didn't they?"

Sheila stepped on it and took a left, paralleling the boys' course, then another left. They saw the car, a red Camaro, a block away. Sheila gunned it as best she could and finally got behind them. She switched on the lights on the overhead bar but the boys kept on going. She gave them a burst of the siren and they finally pulled over. Sheila got out while Jimbo sat in the open doorway, his foot on the ground, watching as Sheila approached the driver's side. Jimbo picked up the mike and spoke into the radio. "585 at Glencoe and Washington. I need a run on Texas number 405 SMP."

Sheila walked toward the driver's side of the Camaro. It took off: an abrupt roar from the engine, tires squealing, a puff of blue-black smoke out of the exhaust mixed with a spurt of gravel, and it was off and running.

Sheila jumped for the driver's seat and floored it while Jimbo was still closing his door, transmitting at the same time. "Code 33. They're heading west on Glencoe, now turning left onto Colfax!"

Pens, ticket books and an aluminum clipboard flew around the front of the car while Robert held on to the mesh with his fingers to keep from getting tossed against the door in the back. The siren drove sharp spikes into their heads. Robert jerked the hearing aid out of his ear and yelled at Jimbo. "Close the goddamn window!"

The Camaro, already a half block ahead of them, took a right on two wheels.

"Right off of Colfax onto . . . what the fuck street is this?"

Robert, his hearing aid reconnected yelled, "Andrews! He's going north on Andrews!"

The Camaro tried to take a left at the next corner and almost hit Dombrowski's car head-on as he came in from the side to join the chase. Dombrowski put the solo car into a four-wheel skid and stalled the engine while the Camaro swerved back in the direction he had been going, making for the intersection at Youree, two blocks ahead.

Sheila gripped the wheel so hard she rose off the seat. She let off the gas and coasted, still going about forty-plus miles an hour through the narrow residential street. Then she goosed it again, yelling, "Ambulance! Tell 'em . . ." But Jimbo was on the radio already. "We need a 408, code 3, maybe two or three of 'em. This is a bad accident up here."

The driver of the Camaro had run the red light at about

sixty. He hit a Toyota on the leading edge of the front passenger door without braking at all. The little car spun completely around in one direction while its engine, launched like a croquet ball, bounded up the street ahead of the still-moving Chevy. The Camaro turned a lazy arc sideways, sliding through the intersection, jumped the curb on the other side, rolled slowly, it seemed, onto its top and bounced while it continued to slide on the sidewalk and then stopped.

Sheila braked hard in the middle of the intersection. She ran for the Toyota as fast as she could while Jimbo ran across the street toward the Chevy. Robert was still locked in the back of the patrol car. He watched cars, all of them containing witnesses, pick their way around the wreckage and leave the scene, the occupants craning their necks to see as they left. Even from there, Robert could see gasoline leaking from the rear of the overturned Camaro. The patrol car's front doors were open so he started yelling through the mesh.

A pedestrian, a young black man, stopped next to the patrol car, staring at the accident in awe. He was holding a grocery bag in one hand and had a small child by the hand with the other. Robert was screaming at him by now. Finally he heard him.

He shifted the grocery bag to the ground and tried the door handle but, of course, it wouldn't open that way. Robert calmed himself down. "There's a latch on the doorjamb, next to the seat." He pointed. The man looked where he indicated and reached out. "Here?" The door sprang open and Robert ran for the Chevy. He forgot about the pedestrian.

When he got there Jimbo was trying to get the upside-down doors open. They had to lie on the pavement to see in. One of the occupants was on his hands and knees on the roof of the car; blood was coming out of the top of his head but he was awake and scared. The other occupant was hanging from his seat belt, working on the latch. He dropped in a heap on the roof and turned over and looked out. The front of the roof had collapsed and they could just move around in there a little. There wasn't room for them to squeeze out of the broken side windows and Robert could see that there was no way to get the doors open.

"Let's try the back!" Robert jerked at Jimbo's collar, then crawled under the upside-down trunk of the car. Gasoline was pooling on the pavement and still dripping. Amazingly, the rear window was intact. Robert turned around and used both feet to kick out the glass, then he and Jimbo tried to see in. The rear seat had fallen down and they couldn't get around it. One of them worked on each end until Jimbo's side came partially through. Robert pushed on his end of the seat to turn it while Jimbo pulled to get it out of the way. They could see the faces of the young men on the other side.

Suddenly, somebody had Robert by one ankle and was dragging him backward. He resisted for a second and then he heard the voices yelling, "Fire! Fire!" He saw Jimbo being dragged out the same way by Hank Dombrowski holding onto one ankle and running, dragging him along the pavement. Robert was still sliding and twisted around enough to get a glimpse of the black pedestrian that had freed him from the car, rescuing him again. Then the Chevy burst into a ball of flame in one big "poof," hiding the occupants.

Robert jumped to his feet and backpedaled away from the flames. He thought for just a second he could see fast, frantic movement through the flames in the interior of the Camaro. He could feel gasoline soaking the front of his jumpsuit and his heart leapt a moment and then settled down. Then he saw Sheila with a tiny fire extinguisher. She looked ridiculous, spraying foam at the huge fireball on the street with the scoop-shaped nozzle pushed out as far in front of her as she could get it.

Then there were firefighters all over. None of the cops had even seen the engine come up although now it blocked them off from the rest of the intersection. Robert saw Sheila drop her useless extinguisher on the street and run back around the fire engine. He followed her, feeling weak in the knees. When he caught up she was already inside the Toyota. He could see the two Asian front-seat occupants were unconscious. There was one person in the back lying on her side and crying out unintelligibly.

The whole car had bent from the impact and he could see that the driver's-side door no longer fit the frame. Jimbo grabbed the door handle and with a mighty heave, jerked it right off the door. Inside the car Sheila squeezed between the bucket seats and managed to get one leg between the steering wheel and the driver and kicked on the door. It opened enough for the cops on the outside to get their hands on the doorframe and pull it wide open.

A firefighter shoved his head in, helmet and all, and looked at the driver's face, nose to nose. He felt for a pulse on the neck and then backed out of the car, hauling the driver with him. Sheila crawled out and Jimbo pulled her out of the way of the rescue workers.

They knew from the way firefighters got the driver out that they thought he was dead. They strapped a cervical collar on the front-seat passenger in place and then turned him carefully and laid him on the pavement next to the driver. He didn't move either but one of the firefighters tipped his head back and carefully slid the plastic tubing in and got an airway established. They turned on positive pressure ventilation, the machine making a soft whoosh and pause. They began compressing his chest like there might be a chance. Gradually, Robert became aware that there was an extravagant amount of activity going on. A second fire engine had arrived and the first of the ambulances was just pulling in. There were police cars all over the place and nobody really seemed to be in charge.

He saw Sheila standing and staring, pale, with a red nose and a splotch of red on each cheek. Her mouth was open. The artificial lights and the strange colors, flashing amber, red, blue and white gave her face a carnival clown's mask of tragedy. Her pale thin lips turned down and she sniffled as though from the cold, still staring. Jimbo and Dombrowski were standing a little away from the Toyota and talking. They looked like they were discussing a football game, Hank grinning, his eyes lit up.

Robert pulled at the front of his uniform, feeling the gasoline sticking the shirt to his skin. David Mallen was standing next to him.

Robert glanced up at him. "Big mess, huh?"

"No fuckin' shit. I'll see what I can do to get you released so you can go change. Your brother's looking for you anyway, anybody tell you?"

"What are you talking about?"

"Your brother from Denver. He called earlier to find out what unit you were in."

"You sure he was asking for me? I don't have a brother."

"Cousin, whatever. He definitely was asking about you, personally. Wanted to know your unit, so we told him."

"I don't have a cousin or any kind of relative within eight hundred miles of here."

"Hey, Mac. Guy knew you and said he was your brother. What the hell, you'll figure it out when he finds you."

Robert walked over to where Jimbo and Hank were still talking.

"You wanta call off your code?"

Jimbo looked surprised. He hadn't even thought about it. "Oh, yeah."

"I hope you ain't thinkin' about havin' a cigarette, old man." Dombrowski's grin was full of meaning.

"What?"

"I said, I hope you ain't . . ."

"I heard what you said. What are you talking about?"

"You smell like you been drinking gasoline for years."

"Sorta feel like it."

"Hey!" Dombrowski ambled over to a fire captain, dwarfing the man. "How 'bout hosing down this guy before he turns into another torch?"

The captain turned around and looked at Robert to see what Hank was talking about. Then he actually looked at a firefighter who had a high-pressure hose going on the building next to the wrecked Camaro as though he was thinking about doing it. The captain looked at Hank seriously. "Better just take him in and let him change."

They had to find the four-boy who was taking the accident details down and stand in line to give him statements. When Jimbo was finished he had to go get Sheila so they could talk to her, too. She was still standing a few feet from the Toyota. She was holding her elbows in front of her and watching the firefighters work on the remains of the Chevy. She had started the night with her hair pinned up to go under her hat, but most of it had fallen down in back. Her mouth was open.

When Jimbo spoke to her she looked at him vacantly at first, finally closing her mouth and swallowing. Then she nodded quickly, impatient with herself, and started off with her two partners to find the four-boy.

"Hey, Sheila!" They saw a tall, elegant man with blond curls, creased jeans and a cashmere sweater approaching from the other side of the police line.

Sheila turned to Jimbo and Robert. "I got to talk to this guy." She walked quickly, even running a few steps toward the man. They talked intensely, Sheila apparently explaining something to him. Jimbo and Robert looked at each other.

Robert shook his head. "Must be IAD already, huh?"

Sheila's explanation went on and on. Jimbo scowled. "C'mon, we were in the fucking chase, too."

As they started toward Sheila they saw the elegant man suddenly put his arm around her and pull her toward him, her arms going around his waist. They stopped and Sheila turned her head and looked at them. "My husband, Jack Enderby."

Jack Enderby looked at them over her head. "You guys okay?"

Jimbo put on an agreeable grin. "Sure, no problem."

"Which one of you was he after?"

"Huh?"

"You got any idea who he was trying to get? Or was it just some maniac?"

Jimbo and Robert stopped in mid-step and turned around, speaking with one voice. "Who?"

"The guy that set the fire. Any idea who that might have been?"

Robert wasn't sure he heard right so he let Jimbo ask the next question. "What guy? You talking about the car, burned up?"

"Yeah. On the radio they say some guy set it, didn't you know? They even recovered the lighter."

Robert saw Sheila pull her head away from Jack's chest and lean back to look at him. Sheila said, "What the fuck you talking about?"

"On the radio. I take it you guys were underneath this car or something and this guy in a pickup truck stopped and threw a burning lighter onto the wreck, set it on fire. I guess Jerry Foster's on the way over here, now."

"All this is on the radio?" MacDonald still wasn't sure he was hearing it right.

Jack walked over to them, his arm still protectively around Sheila's shoulders. "They were trying to find somebody might've seen the pickup. Apparently it either didn't have any plates or nobody saw 'em. Just a beat-up old black pickup, and they were broadcasting around trying to see if anybody could spot it."

Sheila stopped and pulled back from her husband, both hands over her mouth, eyes wide. "Somebody set that fire?"

"Pretty sick, huh?"

"Jesus fucking Christ!"

"Just about turned you two into crispy critters, huh?" Jack was grinning. In a flash Robert wondered if this guy ever dealt with shit like this in Juvenile, decided he probably did. Then Robert thought about crispy critters. They had all seen them, fire victims turned to human-shaped charcoal, grotesque postures either from the action of the heat or from contortions caused by the pain, he didn't know. Absurd blackened grins where the thin flesh had burned away from the jaws. They always said death was from smoke inhalation, anyway. He saw, again, the fleeting jerking movements inside the car that he had thought he had seen through the flames.

"Jesus."

Foster met them at the Hall of Justice in the Homicide office. He still looked half-asleep, but not any more so for being called out at three in the morning. He had a cardboard box with him. MacDonald was in the clean uniform that he had brought with him but Jimbo hadn't changed. He looked disheveled and upset, his black hair curly with perspiration around the bald spot. He spoke first. "Find the pickup?"

Foster regarded him with sleepy eyes. "No. Not enough of a description to find shit." He quickly glanced up at Sheila, who was standing behind the chairs occupied by Jimbo and MacDonald, holding a coffee mug full of stuff that must have been made sometime the day before and left in the pot.

"How many beat-up old black pickups can there be down there?" She sipped, wide-eyed, not even grimacing.

"You'd be surprised. About five hundred if you drive through there and look in the driveways and see what's parked on the curb instead of out cruising around where y'all can see 'em."

Robert spoke up. "That the only description you got?"

"Yeah, 'fraid that's it unless y'all got any ideas." He reached in the box and pulled out a sealed plastic bag with something heavy and black in it and dropped it on the desk in front of them. It was a rectangular-shaped piece of blackened metal but it looked too big to be a lighter. Foster looked from one to the other. "You guys seen a Zippo lighter looks like that?"

"It's too big." Jimbo looked up at Foster's face, then back at the bag.

"Naw, it's an oversized Zippo. You can find 'em like that. Some people prefer 'em, I guess. The guy we looking for never got out of the pickup. He just pulled up next to the wreck while you guys were underneath and threw this thing out the window onto it. Must've started burning oil before it got the gasoline, or you two would've cooked." He watched them for a reaction but he didn't get one. "You never seen anybody you know using one like that, huh?" The two beat cops looked at each other and slowly shook their heads. Foster said, "Looks like you'd a remembered if you had, huh? Maybe not."

Sheila had leaned between the two chairs to get a look and now she straightened up and looked at Foster. "You know, that's the problem with starting a fucking war out there." Neither of the men had wanted to suggest a racial motivation to Foster. Sheila just went ahead, trying to sound tough although her voice was shaking. "You start antagonizing those people that live out there and you never know what the hell they're gonna do, you know?"

Foster leaned back in his chair and looked at her, a slow grin starting on his face. "You think this was a liberal?"

"What?"

"That's the other thing we got. The pickup truck was black but the guy in it was white. Both my witnesses seem to think that oughta be enough to catch him. They don't know how old he was, don't know what color hair, how tall. They just keep sayin', 'Hey, man, this dude was white!' Like that oughta clear it all up. Maybe if he keeps drivin' around out in that neighborhood, it will."

FOURTEEN

I don't understand. What is it this is supposed to show?" Jimbo was in the passenger seat of the patrol car with a Martin city map spread out in his lap, trying to look at it in the light from his flashlight.

"The addresses on the list are marked with a yellow Hi-Liter." Robert was driving. It was 3:00 A.M., and they had just completed the tedious process of booking a DUI, a guy that they were ready and willing to throw into the drunk tank without charges until he turned into a complete asshole in the parking lot. They had managed to get in a dinner break at the Silver Dime at two, so Jimbo was still in a relatively good mood. He didn't mind when Robert dragged out the map and told him to take a look.

"Why didn't you use green or something. I can hardly see this."

"That's the only color I had. Take a look at where that chase went on last Thursday."

"Where they had the wreck and the fire?"

"Yeah, take a look at where it started. See the yellow mark?"

Jimbo studied the map for a moment and then looked up. "So?"

"I'm not saying they're necessarily related. I just think it's worth thinking about."

Jimbo looked back at the map. "There's fuckin' yellow marks all over Southern district. No matter what, if it happened on our shift, it's gonna be near a yellow mark."

MacDonald frowned and leaned toward the map, peering through the bottom of his bifocals. "Naw . . . it's not that bad, is it?"

"Hey, just drive, okay? You can look at the map when we get to a light. And yeah, the answer's yes; all these marks are in Southern district, just like I thought. They're just places he stopped on calls or something, Mac."

Robert tried to look again as he drove slowly outbound, away from downtown in the early-morning stillness. Jimbo seemed so sure. How could it be that obvious? He could tell from the way that Jimbo looked up at him that Jimbo didn't believe that there was anything to it at all.

"Hey, Mac. I don't want to be the one to rain on your parade, all right? But just try to look at this like, say, Bill Farrela's gonna look at it. You think you got mysterious listings in the back of a notebook, Farrela's gonna see a bunch of addresses that the guy probably went to in the normal course of duty working Southern Station. He's gonna say, 'Who knows why he wrote 'em all down? Who cares?' See what I mean? You're gonna say, 'Well, what about these guys we were chasing coming from right near one of the addresses?' and he's gonna say, 'So? Where's the fuckin' connection?' Now what're you gonna say to that?"

Robert glanced over and saw Jimbo looking directly at him, trying to make the point. "Look at it, Mac. There's nothing there."

Robert drove slowly, thinking about what Jimbo was saying. "Okay, so why'd the guy try to torch us?"

"I don't know. Why does anybody do anything, huh? Hey, Mac, you been doing this a lot longer than I have. You ever see a requirement that somebody gotta have a reason to act like a piece a shit?"

Robert gave that some thought as they headed for the projects, taking his time. There were very few cars on the road so everybody they saw got the once-over. "I'd call a double homicide and attempted murder of police officers a little more than that."

Jimbo looked up from the map and studied Robert's face. "You agree with Sheila?"

Robert frowned. "I don't know what Sheila thinks."

"She thinks maybe they were after you. I don't know how she thinks somebody would know that was you under the car. All we know is that somebody called the station, claimed he was your brother and found out what patrol unit you were assigned to. Except he lied about being your brother, coulda been anybody trying to say 'hi,' you know?"

Robert nodded, thoughtful. "Sure."

Jimbo watched him for a moment. "Yeah, I don't know either. Spooky, huh?"

Robert grinned. "Sure as hell is." He thought for a moment, his face growing serious again. "I wouldn't have thought she would take so much time off."

Jimbo looked down at the map. "It's just for this week. Sheila can work if she has to. She told Mallen she could come back and he told her to take some more time. She'll be all right."

"Sure, she'll be fine." Robert thought that he would like to talk to her, make sure she wasn't still blaming herself.

Fog was coming off the river by the time they reached the projects. Most of the town was flat, spreading out from the banks of the Red on what had historically been a floodplain. Protected by dikes and the Army Corps of Engineers, now it only flooded about once every three years instead of every year. The low-lying ground, covered by development or not, still carried a swamp-like mantle of fog at dawn in the fall and early winter.

A loud noise, a sudden splat, hit the street in the quiet of the night. Robert sat forward and gripped the wheel, slowing the car down as Jimbo grabbed the radio microphone automatically. They both held their breath and stared out into the fog, eyes wide. Robert took a deep breath. "Not a gunshot."

"You sure?"

Robert nodded. "Just one sound. Somebody shooting down from the projects you get a double sound. The shot and then the impact when it hits the street or something. That wasn't a gun."

Jimbo relaxed a little but he still held on to the mike. "You say so." He looked out the side window and up. Robert leaned forward again and peered upward through the windshield. The twin towers of the projects loomed mostly dark in the fog. There were lights on in a few windows, making Robert wonder what they could be doing up at this hour. Maybe getting ready to go to an early job, maybe a sick kid. Hard to say.

"Is it time for coffee yet?" Jimbo kept looking up when he said it, not particularly serious about the suggestion, leaving it up to Robert.

Robert looked at his watch. "Let's give it another half hour, huh? We'll still be a little early."

Jimbo's gaze searched the upper stories of the projects as they passed them. "Sure. Just an idea."

The radio had been quiet, telling them that everybody else was having the same kind of night that they were. Nothing going on. Spooky. When the dispatcher finally said something they listened eagerly, hoping to find something to do.

"Nine-eighteen, four-nineteen Canby. Who's in the area?" A warm female voice. Consonants crisp, but otherwise, a familiar touch of friendly Southern womanhood.

Jimbo was on the mike immediately. "Five Charley three, we're on Livingston at the projects. We'll take a look."

"Okay, Charley three, go ahead."

Nine-eighteen was the radio code for "person screaming." It was almost a perfect call for 3:00 A.M. on a foggy night, except that it usually meant somebody was clowning around. The reason the cops normally found out it wasn't serious was that most of the time they could never find whoever was doing the screaming, if anybody was. They didn't hear it when they responded to the call and nobody ever turned up dead or injured in the morning to explain it. On a busy night, no cop wanted to bother with a 918 at all, but Robert thought it was fine for them under the circumstances. He did a U-turn in the street under the projects and headed back downtown. There was no real hurry.

"One of the addresses on the list is on Canby." Robert didn't look at Jimbo when he said it, just making a factual observation.

Jimbo sighed and looked at the map. "Four-eighteen. One off."

"You think it's all in my head."

"I didn't say anything."

Four-nineteen Canby was in an old warehouse district. When the river was a main line of transportation Martin, with a thriving dock industry, had been a collection point for cotton and rice heading north and a distribution center for retail goods heading south and out into the countryside. In the last forty years the river traffic had been taken over by the trucking lines and the Canby street commercial area had gradually collapsed. Now, several blocks of warehouses were mostly unused and ignored. The buildings were still sound for the most part. They seemed to be just waiting for a revival or for someone with a sound sense of hucksterism to think of a use for them or at least a use for the land that would make it worthwhile to tear the buildings down. There was occasional vandalism out here, but usually the Burglary guys got that when somebody noticed a broken door in the daylight. The few transients that borrowed the shelter of the buildings seldom left much of a mess to bother with.

The patrol car turned onto Canby and slowed down. They both rolled their windows down and listened for any sounds of a disturbance in the deserted neighborhood. The buildings were separated by parking and loading areas, expanses of asphalt, debris boxes and the odd rusted-out junker—brake drums sitting on the pavement, not even on blocks, long ago stripped of anything useful. Desultory security lights burned, automatically set to come on where power was still being supplied and somebody had the ingenuity to replace the bulbs. The lights served as a punctuation, an emphasis to the dark of the street and the fog made halos around them, isolating them further in their own spheres of impenetrable refraction.

Robert slowed the car even more, playing the car's side spotlight on the front of the buildings as they passed them. "She say four hundred block?"

"Four-nineteen."

The black-and-white was barely moving, the cops listening for any unusual sound and then, finally, for any sound at all. MacDonald stopped the car. "There isn't any four-nineteen."

"Sure?"

"Yeah." Robert used the spotlight to point. "That's four-fifteen and that's four-twenty-one." The car sat in the middle of the street, idling.

Jimbo turned on the spot on his side and scanned the building closest to them. "This one's four-eighteen. Maybe that's it, huh?"

"You hear anything?"

Jimbo reached down under the center of the dash and flicked the switch, turning off the radio to block out the occasional burst of static which was all they were getting on it.

They could hear the sticky valves of the car's engine. "Not a damn thing. Let's take a look."

Normally, downtown or even in most residential neighborhoods, they would have left the car running in the middle of the street, lights on and the radio turned up to hear any calls they might get. Now, however, since they were trying to listen for a sound that, presumably, somebody had complained about, and since Robert's hearing wasn't all that reliable, they shut off the car and doused the headlights. They stood for a moment, one on either side of the car, just listening. Robert touched his hearing aid lightly and the overblown thumping sound in his ear told him that it was working. He was still thinking, vaguely, about the address on the list, right across the street. He walked past the front of the car and crossed the street, walking toward a streetlight that he could see two hundred feet away at the next intersection.

He walked slowly, listening as best he could. He looked over his shoulder at the buildings behind him and saw that Jimbo had waited a moment, listening to the fog, and then started slowly after him. They were each carrying heavy flashlights. The department issue was worth about $6.95 and wouldn't work after you dropped it the first time. The ones they carried they bought out of their own pockets like all the cops in Martin and they cost $125. They weighed about four pounds and it was like carrying a piece of steel pipe in your hand, fourteen inches long and more useful than a nightstick. Robert saw Jimbo heft the familiar weight of the flashlight in his hand for reassurance.

Robert kept walking, scanning the buildings on both sides of the street, until he stood under the anemic light at the end of the block. He stared off into the fog all around him but could see little besides the periodic spots of light, emphasizing that the rest of the world around them was in shadow and darkness. Jimbo came up and stood a little behind him, back-to-back. Robert finally shook his head. "Nothing."

Jimbo turned to face him. "Wrong address or they went back to sleep." He grinned sheepishly at his own nervousness.

Robert started back toward their car. It seemed farther away than he thought it should be, but he knew that the night and the fog played those kinds of tricks on you. There were no sidewalks on this block. Robert walked on one side of the street and Jimbo on the other, both of them holding the flashlights loosely in both hands, walking quietly, still listening. When they reached the car they stood still a moment more, giving it one last chance before they gave up and admitted to the dispatcher that they couldn't locate the call. There was nothing.

Jimbo walked to the passenger side of the car, shrugged his shoulders and looked across the top of the car at Robert. He raised his eyebrows and his lips formed the word "Coffee?" What Robert heard, though, was a shriek out of nowhere. It was so sudden and unexpected that for just a second he thought that he was hearing Jimbo even though he knew that wasn't so. With only one ear hearing well with the aid, Robert couldn't tell the direction of the sound and he watched as Jimbo's face changed to astonishment and he raised his eyes to the building behind Robert. MacDonald spun around, but the sound had stopped.

He realized that his heart was pounding in his chest. The scream had started out high and come down slightly in pitch, lasting no more than a second before it stopped short. Then there was just the silence again and the fog and the dark. Robert spun back to look at Jimbo and see if he had identified where the sound had come from. Jimbo was staring up and down the block, looking up at the buildings on one side of the street. Clearly, the sound that had startled both of them had caught him by surprise, too short to get a fix on the direction with any certainty, even with his two good ears.

Jimbo took two steps to come around the car and froze in his tracks. Again the screech, sudden and violent, the voice suddenly loud in the stillness. It sounded almost like a horn blast, metallic although clearly human. Again, it was short, falling slightly in pitch and then shutting off as though the screamer had used every molecule of breath in his lungs. This was not somebody fooling around. The voice had the sound of terminal panic.

This time Jimbo had a fix on it, and he trotted toward the building closest to them, flashlight on the blank upper-story windows. He circled to his left, trying to see the windows on that side. Robert could see that the front door under one of the small security lights was solidly locked and, from the loose drift of garbage in front of it, hadn't been opened in months.

Robert walked around the side of the building to his left, looking for Jimbo. On that side there was a broad paved area and a loading dock that ran the length of the old warehouse. The dock, itself, was recessed into the building a good fifteen feet and on the back side was lined with a series of large roll-up doors. Jimbo had already reached the other end of the dock and started back toward Robert, walking more slowly, searching with his flashlight beam at the bottoms of the doors for an opening that would have admitted anyone.

They both saw it at the same time. One of the doors in about the middle of the dock had a small opening at the bottom; no more than eight or nine inches, but it was definitely open. Jimbo took two quick strides and vaulted onto the dock. Robert swept the flashlight back the way he had come around the building until he saw the steps. He trotted back to them and mounted the dock quickly, hurrying to try to catch up with Jimbo. Jimbo was on his back on the dock for leverage, both hands pushing up on the door until it gave. It rose no more than another two or three inches, resisting probably with the remains of the automatic inside lock, but it was open enough for Jimbo to shine his light inside and then slide under the door. Robert swiftly dropped onto his stomach on the dock and followed him.

Inside, they were in a relatively small room with concrete block walls and a steel door ajar in the back of it. Jimbo crept through the opening in the door without touching it and Robert again followed. Once inside the building they shut off their flashlights, agreeing without saying anything to kill their lights to see if they would see a light from anyone else. It was so dark Robert felt he was standing with his face to a black wall.

He switched his flashlight back on, pointing it at the floor so they could look around. They were at the end of a T-intersection of broad hallways. One hall extended on either side of them, running parallel to the dock. The other hall, the leg of the T, stretched out in front of them and Robert could see office doorways and glass windows on either side. He went down the hall, shining his light quickly into the offices, looking for signs of something being disturbed, although that would be hard to tell among the general detritus left by the departed company.

He glanced behind him and could see Jimbo walking softly down the center of the corridor, his head turning slowly from side to side, listening. Suddenly, the screech sounded again. Jimbo's head jerked upward involuntarily as though he could visualize what was making the sound through the ceiling above him. Robert swept the hallway with his flashlight until he spotted a broad staircase, the linoleum tile worn to black in the center from long use.

Both cops reached the bottom step at the same time and slowly, as quietly as possible, began their ascent. Robert turned off his light as they reached the first landing and stood still, feeling the grip of Jimbo's hand on his arm as they stood in the blackness and listened. Robert felt Jimbo's breath on his ear, his mouth almost against the hearing aid. "Smoke."

Then Robert smelled it, too, oily, acrid, but not strong. When they didn't hear anything else, Jimbo switched on his light, again, pointing it directly down to keep someone else from seeing it before they could see him. They went on up.

At the second landing there was another steel door standing open. Robert switched off his light as soon as he saw it and immediately Jimbo did the same. MacDonald thought he heard a metallic sound, almost a jingling. Then he heard what sounded to him like a series of rapid clicking noises, soft but getting a little louder as though whatever was making the noise was getting closer. He froze, one foot higher than the other on the steps and listened, trying to penetrate the inky darkness in front of his face.

Suddenly Jimbo switched on his light, trained on the doorway and Robert felt himself flinch as a dog appeared in front of them. A smallish mixture of shepherd and maybe half a dozen other breeds, danced on clicking claws in the hallway just on the other side of the door, wildly whipping its plumed tail back and forth at the sight of the cops, twisting and fawning in greeting.

They emerged from the staircase into a short hallway. To their left were more offices and to their right, about twenty feet down, the hall ended in a set of double doors. The dog thrashed its tail back and forth, eagerly watching them; then, getting no encouragement, trotted quickly to the double doors and pushed its way through, disappearing on the other side.

Again, they switched off the flashlights. There was a faint light on the other side of the double doors and they headed for it. Jimbo was in the lead and carefully cracked open the doors and peered in. He glanced over his shoulder at Robert and went on through, holding the door to indicate MacDonald should follow. On the other side of the doors they came out into a huge open warehouse area, windows high up along one wall showing the lighter sky. The floor space was dirty and empty, the flat expanse broken by pillars, a few empty cartons and a single forgotten handcart.

In a far corner, diagonally off to their left, they could see the source of the dim light and the smoke, a small bonfire, burning in a coffee can, apparently fueled by some kind of relatively clean-burning oil. A naked man was standing with his back to them, facing the fire. They swept the beams of their flashlights around the loft, checking out the far corners, but they couldn't see anyone else up there.

Robert could tell at the first glimpse of him that the man wasn't right. He had apparently claimed that corner of the warehouse as his camping area by stringing a line from the wall to one of the pillars and draping a blanket over it, creating a small three-sided room. Piles of garbage and old clothes showed he had been camped there for weeks. From where the cops stood it looked like he had something tied to his waist; a rope, thick as one of the ropes used to tie up large boats down at the docks, trailed from his middle to the floor. After Robert had taken a few steps toward the man he saw that it wasn't a rope and he stopped in shock. The man had a knife, a big, chrome-bladed hunting knife held in one hand out from his side, the blade catching the light of the fire.

The man moved then, staring at the flames on the floor in front of him, shifting his weight from one foot to the other in place, rocking gently from side to side, slow-dancing in the firelight. Robert took a couple of firm steps, deliberately making himself audible, but the man did not turn or acknowledge that he heard.

Robert took the microphone to his PIC radio off his belt and switched it on. "Five Charley three."

He hadn't tried to keep his voice down but the man still didn't seem to hear them. The dispatcher's female voice came back right away, loud in the silent loft until he got it turned down. "Charley three, go ahead."

"We're in a warehouse at, I think it's four-eighteen Canby." The radio's speaker was in the microphone so he held it up near his hearing aid to hear the response. He glanced around at Jimbo to get his agreement on the address, but Jimbo was standing about five paces back, staring, white-faced, watching the naked man. Robert looked back at the corner, but the man was still in the same place, rocking slowly from one foot to the other. The dog hung back from him, fawning, afraid.

"Go ahead, Charley three."

"We got a two-nineteen. Abdominal wound, looks bad. We gonna have to have a four-oh-eight, code three."

"Ten-four, Charley three. It's a stabbing? At four-eighteen Canby?"

"I think that's the right address. Real close, anyway."

"Ten-four, your ambulance is on the way now; ETA about four minutes, okay?"

"Okay, thanks." He clipped the microphone onto his collar so he could hear it better and circled to his right to approach the man from the side on which he held the knife. In his peripheral vision he was aware that Jimbo had gone to the left to come up on him from the other side. Robert could see the man in profile, then. The thick length of intestine trailed out from his stomach to the floor and seemed to contract, coil slightly as the man moved. Blood was trickling from the open abdomen, dripping off the end of his penis like red urine. The man's face was rapt, eyes bulging in horrified fascination at whatever he was seeing in the flame coming out of the coffee can. He was young. No more than twenty.

Suddenly, he screamed. It was the same blasting shriek that they had heard before, short and violent, the young man's body contorting, folding briefly in the middle with the effort of screaming and then straightening again to stand as before.

Robert reached out and gripped the arm of the hand that held the knife, slipping the handcuff around the wrist effortlessly and clicking the ratchet shut. The knife dropped and clattered on the floor. Jimbo grabbed the other arm and held it while Robert snapped the other cuff on behind the unresisting man's back. Robert brought one arm around the man's chest and gripped the opposite shoulder, then pushed with his leg against the back of the man's knees so he could force him backward and down, lowering him gently to the floor.

Finally, the man reacted. He struggled, kicking out with his bare feet until he could raise his head enough to see the fire in the can and then stopped, staring again into the flame. Robert had to look over at the can, just to be sure that there wasn't anything there to see. Then, impatient with himself, he looked around the area quickly for something to use and his eyes stopped on Jimbo. "Here! Hold him a minute, will you? Hold him like this with his head up."

Jimbo moved around behind the man and knelt, firmly putting his hands on the man's shoulders, using the crook of one massive forearm to brace his neck. Robert quickly stood up, snatched the blanket off the line and shook it, trying to knock the excess dust out of it, then dropped it on the floor next to Jimbo and the young man. Taking deep gulps of air, Robert stared for a second at the intestine. Then he bent over and began to pick it up gingerly, a loop at a time, cradling the thick coils in his arms against his chest, the mesentery bloody, sticking to his hands. He worked slowly until he had it all off the floor. As gently as he could he placed the whole pile on the man's chest, meticulously laying the draining distal stump off to one side so that it wouldn't accidentally empty back into the hole in the man's peritoneum. Then he covered him, exposed viscera and all, with the blanket, tucking the edges in carefully at the hips.

He looked at Jimbo's blasted expression, the chalky face with big black holes for eyes. "Here, I'll hold him. You better go downstairs and make sure the paramedics can find the place." Jimbo didn't immediately move, his mouth slack. Robert pushed on his hand, smearing the knuckles. "Come on, Jimbo, they never gonna find the goddamn place."

Jimbo looked at him. "Right. Okay, yeah, I'll meet 'em downstairs." He stared at Robert's blood-soaked uniform shirt. "Okay, I'm going."

Jimbo got up quickly then and crossed the empty warehouse floor, stumbling at first, then almost trotting. Robert watched him disappear through the double doors.

Alone then, with just the mutilated boy in the darkness of the loft, Robert could faintly hear the siren in the distance and decided that it was probably coming for them. He tried to lay the young man down. When he started to panic Robert raised him up again and supported his head so he could see the fire and whatever it was he saw in there that terrified and comforted him. The old cop sat on the floor with his legs pushed awkwardly in front of him and pulled the man's upper torso onto his lap putting his arms around his shoulders to hold him and laying the man's head on his chest so he could see the fire without effort.

The young man breathed rapidly as though he was about to scream again. Robert rocked him gently, rocking him back and forth, murmuring close to his ear. "There, there . . . There, there, now. It's okay, now . . . gonna be okay . . . Daddy's here."

FIFTEEN

I'm almost positive he was white."

"But you're not sure?"

"Well . . ." Mrs. Baccigalupe stood behind the wrought-iron gate that closed off the entrance to her building and looked between the two cops at the door to Terry's garage across the street. "I'm pretty sure he was white. I would've probably remembered if he wasn't."

"Mrs. Baccigalupe, this might be real important. I know it's a lot of bother, but if you could just try to picture what the car looked like." Robert was wearing his suit with a yellow shirt and a brown-striped tie. He looked like he might own a small hardware store. Jimbo, next to him on the sidewalk, was wearing Levi jeans, a long cardigan that didn't quite cover the holster on his hip and his badge, clipped on his belt in front. He looked like a clothes-conscious cop.

In the last two days, during their time off in the daylight hours, they had talked to all seven of Terry's neighbors who had been interviewed by Homicide plus another twelve that hadn't. No one but Mrs. Baccigalupe had seen or heard anything at all before the discovery of the body and she had forgotten to mention what she had heard and seen to Homicide.

Mrs. Baccigalupe was an unlikely rebel in miniature, standing defiantly on the other side of the gate. She was hornet-shaped, with thick black hair shot through with gray, oversized glasses and an authoritarian air. She hadn't said anything about inviting them in.

"Mister, it may be important to you, but I don't see how that makes much difference if I just can't remember the guy, do you?" She glanced up at Jimbo to see if he was going to dare to add anything. "Now I think I told you before that I don't want any part of this thing. It's none of my business and I'm going to stay out of it."

Robert looked down at his feet, then looked back at her as diffidently as possible. "Ma'am, there's no way we can just leave you out of it. See, you're a material witness. The DA might just have to come back with a subpoena and take you downtown to talk to you there. Now . . ."

"Bullshit."

"Ma'am?"

"Bullshit. All I heard was a noise that could've been anything and all I saw was somebody parked in a driveway and took off."

Jimbo tried to put on his nicest voice. "See, that's what might be important. You heard a shot and then you thought you heard another one."

"I said I heard a popping noise, like a car backfired or something. Then when I heard it again I looked out."

"And that's when you saw the guy get into the car in Mr. MacDonald's driveway."

"There's a liquor store right on the corner. People park in other people's driveways all the time. Now, that's it. Period. End of it. That's all I know and I don't have anything else to say."

Robert tried to be apologetic. "Mrs. Baccigalupe, I didn't mean . . ."

She turned her glare on him, a look that was intended to wither him on the spot. "I didn't see anything or hear anything that anybody's gonna get anything out of, so you can just go bother somebody else."

Jimbo thought he had been doing better than that so he tried again. "Mrs. Baccigalupe, we're really not trying to bother you. It's just that . . ." It was too late.

She stepped back inside the wooden door to the front of her house and hesitated just before she slammed it shut. "No, sir. I got company coming and I don't have any more time for this stuff. Talk to Mrs. Berdini."

"Who?"

"Mrs. Berdini, across the street. She's the one that talked to him."

From that point it took almost an hour to find Mrs. Berdini's address. None of the mailbox labels bore her name and there was no phone book in the liquor store. They called Southern Station and got somebody to help them look her up in the cross directory. She lived right next door to the building that Terry had lived in but had labeled her doorbell R. B. Smith.

Jimbo pushed the buzzer for her apartment and looked at his watch. Four o'clock. They were due to start their shift in seven hours and he was hoping to get home to get some more sleep before then.

The speaker over the door buzzer came on. "Yes? Who is it?"

Jimbo and Robert looked at each other. Neither one of them had ever seen one of those things work. Robert talked into the speaker instead of the perforations next to it for the microphone. "Robert MacDonald and James Phillips of the Martin Police Department, Mrs. Berdini. Could we talk to you for a minute?"

There was a long pause and then, "Did you say police?"

"Yes, ma'am."

"Oh, dear . . ."

Robert chuckled reassuringly into the speaker. "It's nothing to worry about, Mrs. Berdini. We just heard that you might have seen someone that we been trying to get in touch with and we wanted to ask you about it, all right?"

There was no answer.

"Mrs. Berdini?"

There was still no response from the speaker. Jimbo put his ear against it to try to see if he could tell if it was on. He pushed her buzzer again. "Mrs. Berdini?"

The door next to him opened suddenly and an elderly, heavy-set woman with parlor-curled white hair regarded them with an anxious frown. "You did say 'police' now, didn't you?"

Both of them fumbled out their ID cards and badges, smiling ingratiatingly. Robert said, "I hope you have just a few minutes. We were just talking to Mrs. Baccigalupe across the street? Well, it occurred to us that we hadn't talked to you yet about what you might have seen the night that fellow that lived next door to you got killed."

She watched him, expectantly, waiting for him to go on.

"Well, have you got a few minutes now?"

"Oh, I see. You want to talk to me."

"Yes, ma'am, if that would be all right."

"All right? Yes, of course it's all right. Do you want to come in? It's more comfortable upstairs."

"Yes, ma'am, thank you."

She turned and slowly worked her way back up the stairs. She inadvertently presented them with a large, cushioned bottom that undulated from side to side as she climbed. Jimbo looked at Robert, rolled his eyes and pantomimed giving her a push to help her on up. She suddenly turned on the steps and he had to pretend that he was just about to fix something on the front of his shirt.

"You know, I was wondering why you people didn't come by before. But I guess he did shoot himself in the head, so what's there to talk about, huh?"

"Really?" Jimbo acted interested in the question. Robert decided Jimbo was a lousy actor.

"Well, I'm sure *I* don't know; that's just what I heard that you people had decided. I was out of town to see my niece in Cincinnati for a month or so after it happened, but nobody ever came by that I know of to ask me anything about it, not that I know anything, really. I just knew him by sight. He never told me his troubles or anything." She turned and continued her quest for the top of the first landing.

"Well, you know how it is, Mrs. Berdini. We got busy and then just didn't get back around to talking to you."

When she reached the first landing she entered an open apartment doorway and continued on into her living room without looking around to see if they were following. Robert thought she must realize how slow she was. She went directly to a chair under a reading lamp and sat down heavily with a deep sigh of relief.

Robert walked over to her window and looked out. It opened onto a decent view of her neighbor's window, the one on the other side from Terry's building. He decided from the angle of the stairs that she wouldn't have a view of the street from anywhere in the apartment. He smiled down at her. "Mrs. Baccigalupe said you might've seen a guy that had his car parked next door on the night it happened."

She screwed up her face in concentration. "Well, I expect I did. If it was the same one that had been coming around."

"You saw him more than once?"

"Well, now I don't know if it's the same one or not. See, Mrs. Baccigalupe said that she saw a '71 Bel Air parked in that driveway. Now, myself, I can't picture that there might be two of those old things . . ."

"Wait a minute." Robert stopped her. "Mrs. Baccigalupe told you that she recognized the car as a '75 Bel Air?"

"Nineteen seventy-one. And no, she doesn't know a thing

about cars but she described it to me the next day and I know that's what she saw, because that's the same blue-and-white car that this fellow had that was asking questions about that MacDonald boy. He was a policeman, too, wasn't he?"

Robert didn't say anything. Jimbo nodded, trying to keep her going. "Yes, ma'am, he was. Did you know him?"

"Just to see him." Her expression was vaguely distasteful as though there was something about him that she didn't like.

Robert pretended he didn't notice. "This guy that had the Bel Air, did you talk to him?"

"Oh, he stopped me on the street twice. He seemed kind of dopey so I didn't want to talk to him, but he said he was looking for a friend's apartment and did I know Mr. MacDonald? I pointed it out to him and two days later he asked me the same thing, like he didn't remember talking to me the first time. If you ask me, the guy didn't have the brains to find his way home, let alone to somebody else's house." She thought about it a moment. "You know what I thought? I thought he was one of those narcotics cops."

Robert looked interested. "Why's that?"

"Well, he hadn't shaved in several days and his eyes were all watery like he hadn't slept. Looked just like a cop on TV."

Jimbo was trying not to be irritated. "Mrs. Berdini. How do you know it was a '71 Bel Air?"

"Oh, my husband was a nut about cars and all three of our boys are, too. I know all about 'em. My husband could take 'em apart and put 'em back together in no time. He could tear an engine out faster than you could think about it and before you know it he'd have the heads out, turn the crankshaft, grind the valves . . ."

"Mrs. Berdini, please. Could you describe this man for us?"

"Oh, I'm no good at descriptions. I never notice anything at all. My husband used to say . . ."

Jimbo sat down across from her on a worn couch. The apartment was stiflingly hot and Robert thought there was some danger that Jimbo would go to sleep right there. "How old would you say this man was?"

"Oh, I don't know. Maybe fifty, fifty-five, something like that."

"How tall?" Robert was trying not to sound eager.

She looked at him. "Well, taller than you." She turned to Jimbo. "Oh, say, you are a big one. He wasn't as tall as you. He was somewhere in the middle."

"Skinny or fat?"

"Medium."

"Race?"

"Oh, he was a white man, for sure." Her answer implied that she would have called them immediately if it had been otherwise.

"He didn't mention his name, did he? You know, introduce himself to you?"

"Oh, no. It wasn't that kind of conversation. It was just like he was asking directions, only he was already there."

Robert smiled at her. "Mrs. Berdini, you've been very helpful. Do you think you might be able to recognize this guy if he came back?"

"Well, yes, I think I would. He had a scar that came out from the corner of his mouth and went down, like this." She drew a line on her own face to demonstrate.

Jimbo and Robert looked at each other. Jimbo asked her, "Can you think of anything else that might be helpful to identify him?"

"You want the license number? I didn't like the look of him so I wrote that down."

SIXTEEN

Robert was exuberant, too excited, he could tell, the way he was accelerating. He glanced over and Jimbo had a half smile on his face, but his eyes, as he watched where Robert was driving, were not smiling. He turned his head and looked at Mac-Donald, behind the wheel of the Bronco. Robert was surprised to realize that Jimbo was faking it when he tried to sound like he was enthusiastic.

"We're taking this to Homicide, right?"

"You kidding?" Robert ran the tail end of a yellow light and, whipping the car through a left turn, headed down Campbell. He glanced over and saw Jimbo watching him, still trying to smile, but too serious.

"Where you going?"

"Southern, run the plate. What you think?" Robert couldn't believe Jimbo had even asked the question.

Jimbo tried a tentative chuckle that didn't fool anybody. "You got to take this to Homicide, Mac."

"Yeah, soon's I run the plate and . . ." He didn't finish the thought, but he was now passing all the other traffic on

Campbell. He was trying to think about what he was going to ask the guy with the scar when he talked to him and trying not to think about what Jimbo was saying.

"Hey, Mac, take it easy, okay?"

Robert glanced at his partner again and saw that Jimbo was still watching him but he wasn't even faking a grin now.

Jimbo said, "Foster trusted you, Mac, to take anything you found right straight back to him. Now, this might be nothing, right? But it is a piece of information that he doesn't know anything about and I think you got to take it right in."

Robert slowed the car, but not by much. He was thinking, "Screw that," but he didn't say it out loud. Foster *had* trusted him, damn him. He glanced back at Jimbo again and knew that he had given away his hesitation by the way Jimbo picked up the argument.

"Look, Mac, the lady could be right. You know, that this guy was a friend, some guy just trying to find him. And it might not have been the same car that the other lady says she saw in the driveway, anyway." Jimbo shook his head and looked through the windshield, not wanting to see MacDonald come down off his high. "No matter what, though, I got to get some more sleep before tonight and you got to take this shit in to Foster or Farrela or one of those guys and let 'em know what you found out."

Robert slowed the Bronco some more. He glanced at Jimbo twice, thinking about it and then heaved a huge sigh. "Maybe you're right."

"You know I am, Mac. Shit, I'll go with you up to Homicide, see what they say."

Robert braked hard at the next intersection, making up his mind, and headed for the Hall of Justice.

Foster was there, looking for all the world like somebody that had taken 100 cc's of Demerol, talking on the telephone as though it was about to put him to sleep. He negligently waved one hand at Robert, glanced at Jimbo, then looked back at Robert, his eyes opening wider. The person on the other end of the telephone must have been doing a lot of talking because Foster had time to look back and forth at the two beat cops, his glance going faster and faster and his eyes coming more and more awake. Finally, he cut his call short with a curt, "I'll have to call you later." Robert realized it must have been his wife.

Foster continued to look from one to the other, waiting as long as he could stand it. "Don't tell me you found the gun."

"Not yet." Robert hadn't realized that Jimbo was excited until he started talking. "You missed the lady that got the license number. She was out of town or something and her name's not on the mailbox downstairs. Anyway, she got a plate on the guy that was in the driveway when the lady across the street heard the shots."

Foster's eyes went back to looking sleepy. "Shots." He looked from one to the other, not getting it.

MacDonald was exasperated. "He's trying to tell you, the lady across the street heard two shots and saw this car in the driveway."

Foster woke up again. "Which lady across the street? She give you a description? You are talking about the night Terry was supposed to have done it, right?"

Now Jimbo was impatient. "We're way fuckin' ahead of you. This other lady lives next door to Terry, her husband used to run hot cars or something and she knows all about the damn things."

"So, what are you saying?"

"She got the plates." Robert shoved a pad under Foster's nose with the number written on it.

The computer showed that the plates belonged to a '71 Bel Air, which didn't surprise either street cop, but it was registered to Gretchen Nicholson at an address in Raimon City. They found her number in the cross directory and Foster called while the two of them did everything but sit in his lap. The phone was disconnected.

Jimbo looked at his watch as he got to his feet and then looked at his partner. It was a little after five. Foster pulled out a lower drawer in his desk and put his foot on it and leaned back, fingers laced behind his head, looking at the light fixtures. "Wait a minute, y'all. Just sit down a minute."

Jimbo pulled a chair over from a nearby desk and touched his butt on the very edge of it. MacDonald just stood there waiting, not very patient. Foster tipped his head forward a little and looked at him. "You got a description of this guy?" They gave it to him. They told him about the fact that he had been asking about Terry in the street and that there were two shots, not one, and where was the fucking gun, anyway?

"Okay, okay, slow down a minute. You got my file?"

Robert opened his briefcase and handed over the file. It didn't seem to be much thicker than when he had gotten it. Foster opened it on the desk in front of him and started reading from the beginning. Robert pulled up a chair and sat down, staring at the top of Foster's head. The detective reached across his desk and tore a page off a pad of investigative forms and wrote the file number and the description of the man on it. "I guess I better open this thing back up. I got the name of Mrs. Baccigalupe. Who's this other lady?"

They went over everything with him again. Finally, Foster shut the file and looked at Robert. "All you really got is this guy, driving his girlfriend's car, probably, was looking for Terry a few days before he got shot." He didn't say, "shot himself." "It may or may not have been that car in the driveway. There's a liquor store. People park in driveways all the time. Coulda been anybody, right?" He wasn't expecting an answer. "So we got reason to believe there mighta been two shots fired. I can check out who got treated for gunshot wounds around that time. I'll check with Raimon City police and the sheriff, too, all right? And I can check out this Nicholson lady, see if we can find her, okay? I can probably get started tomorrow or the day after. I promise you nothing, you understand? I'll just keep you informed as we go along and you can come down and check out the file anytime you want."

Robert turned his head to make sure he didn't miss anything. "Fine." He nodded, but he didn't look happy.

Jimbo looked at him like he could almost read Robert's mind.

Foster didn't seem to want to notice. "So. You ready to go back to the range before somebody shoots hisself in the ass?"

Robert tried to grin and added a compliant nod. "Fine. Whatever you think."

"You better give Mallen another night since he'll probably scream like hell if you don't give him at least a day's notice." Foster put the Homicide file on the stack in front of him. He looked at Robert once more. "I think the P.D. missed a bet somewhere with you. You done good work on this, but you shouldn't be working on your own case, okay?"

"Fine."

"Okay?"

"Sure."

As soon as they were on the elevator Robert pulled out his pad again and wrote down Gretchen Nicholson's name and the Raimon City address they had gotten from DMV. He looked up at Jimbo. "You wanted to get some sleep."

"You're going to Raimon City."

Robert looked down at the floor, waiting for the elevator to stop and the doors to open. He pursed his lips and looked up. "I guess I'm not supposed to, huh?"

"I guess not." Jimbo walked a little in front as they walked back toward the rear door of the building, heading for the Bronco. He didn't look directly at Robert. "You're not going now, are you?"

"I guess I got to work tonight."

"Mallen'd kill both of us, then Foster'd burn the bodies."

"Guess you're right."

The 909 call, "Report to the station," got to them about a quarter to twelve. They had just made one circuit, headed back toward downtown and stopped a speeder. It took them a few minutes to finish the ticket and figure out that there was nothing that they could say was so urgent that they couldn't go in. A 909 almost always meant that you had screwed up something on paper and they wanted you to come in and fix it up. Captains and lieutenants and even a few sergeants thought there was nothing in the world as important as paper and they would drive you nuts with it if you let them push you around about it.

"Five Charley seven"

They were in the "7" car and Jimbo was driving so Robert picked up the mike. "Charley seven."

"Sergeant Mallen needs to see Sergeant MacDonald right away. He says for you to come on in now." The dispatcher sounded like she was slightly scolding, teasing him.

"Charley seven, we're almost there, already."

"Does that mean ten-four, Charley seven?"

"Ten-four"

Jimbo laughed, suddenly in a good mood. "So it's your fault, huh? You're the one."

Robert grinned and rolled his eyes in mock resignation. "Looks like it."

Still, Jimbo took his time looking for a convenient parking space in the lot until they saw the back door to Southern Station open and saw the silhouette of Sergeant Mallen in the light from the inside. Robert could see the tension in Mallen's posture even though he couldn't see Mallen's face. He was already apprehensive when he opened the door and started across the lot, not even aware if Jimbo had gotten out of the car or not.

Mallen was scowling. "Better call Eastern. Talk to Harrington over there."

"Harrington?" Robert was trying to place the name.

"Yeah or Goldman or Farrela. They're over there, too."

He dialed Eastern Station from a number on a list taped to the wall over Mallen's desk.

"Eastern Station, Sergeant Harrington, may I help you?"

"Hi, this is Sergeant MacDonald."

There was a short pause as though Harrington couldn't think what to say and then, without preliminaries, came a voice that Robert barely recognized to be Eddie Goldman's. "Hey, Mac. Why don't you guys come on over here, can you? We got Kevin here."

"What . . . ?"

"I said, Kevin's here at Eastern. Come on over and I'll explain it to you."

"What . . . ? Kevin . . . ?"

"Hey, Mac, take it easy. He's all right."

Robert couldn't say anything, just hanging on to the phone for dear life. He could hear voices in the background at the other end of the line but he couldn't tell what they were saying. Then Kevin's voice. "That you, Dad?" Kevin did not sound all right.

There were four of them, counting Kevin and not counting the one that the coroner had—four students. Kevin and another boy were shaky and pale, but dry-eyed, trying to hold it together. The other boy and a girl were weeping openly. The four of them were huddled together in the only thing that could be called a sitting area at Eastern Station, the drunk tank, which just happened to be unoccupied except for them. When Robert saw them he assumed that Harrington had evicted whoever they had been holding so he could get the kids out of his office. Robert looked at Kevin a long time, making sure that it was him and that he was not hurt. Kevin had his arm around the girl and didn't get up when his father arrived, but Robert could see relief written all over his face.

Farrela was in Harrington's office with the door closed. "I got to get written statements. I'm just waiting for the typing, then they can go."

"What is it?"

"A fucking drive-by."

"A shooting?"

"A goddamn execution. Blew her fucking head off with a twelve-gauge. Fucking eighteen years old."

"Who?"

"The girl they killed. Here . . ." Farrela picked up a draft of his incident report. "Cynthia Ortez, eighteen-year-old freshman at State." Farrela bit his thumbnail, reading the report he had just written.

Goldman came into the office and closed the door behind him. It was too crowded for all three to be standing in the office so he went behind Harrington's desk and sat down in his chair. "I think it's mistaken identity."

"What'd you do, a polygraph on 'em?" Farrela was surly.

"Shit, they didn't know anything about it. Look at 'em."

"What are you guys talking about? Would somebody tell me what happened?"

Farrela gave him a black look as though he might be a suspect and went back to his report. Goldman leaned back in the chair and made a sweeping gesture with his arm. "Wasn't your kid, it wouldn't be such a big deal, Mac. Kevin and his friends had a hamburger down at Burgher Palace and when they came out some asshole drove by 'em in the parking lot and unloaded with a shotgun. Hit this Cynthia in the head and kept on going. We talked to all four of 'em and they don't know shit except what Cynthia looked like after she got shot. That seems to have made an impression."

Robert scowled. "Got a description?"

"We got shit." Farrela was fierce. "Girl says he was in a station wagon, one guy says a van, Kevin says a pickup and the other guy doesn't know. Coulda been a rocket ship as far as he knows."

"They see the guy doing the shooting?"

"Coulda been a Martian. Nobody saw anybody, just that fucking shotgun."

Other parents had arrived when Robert came out of the sergeant's office. One man was being quiet, a round, smooth-faced man who could have been an accountant or a lawyer with his chino slacks and loafers. He was staring wide-eyed at everybody who went by him. His red face was an open question, staring at each new cop that appeared, hoping that somebody would take the time to talk to him but not wanting to interfere, insert himself in some business that he didn't really understand and had the good sense to know it. Another parent, a strongly built man who had either been at home with his tie on this late or had decided to dress for the occasion, was under the impression that it was up to him to take charge. His wife had found a seat in one of the desk chairs and watched apprehensively as her husband tried raising his voice.

"I want to know if Billy's under arrest. Can you answer me one simple question and cut the bullshit? Is he under arrest or not?"

"He's not under arrest, Mr. Agnost. He's a witness. He's just waiting . . ."

"Well, if he's not under arrest, then he can just leave, am I right?"

"No."

"Well, goddammit!"

"Mr. Agnost, just give us a few minutes. It won't be more than ten minutes, okay?" Harrington had come out and rescue the patrol officer that had been stuck with him. "You don't want to be obstructing an investigation, do you?" He smiled.

The round man had worked his way through the desks to

the drunk tank and sat on a bench, taking over from Kevin with his arm around his daughter. "You okay? You weren't hit, were you?" Robert could see his concern with an ugly red splash that had gone across his daughter's white pants. When his daughter assured him she wasn't physically hurt he turned his concern to the boys in the cell. "How 'bout you guys? Y'all get hit? You okay?" He rolled his smooth concerned face back to look in the direction of the cops. "Nobody else got hurt but Cynthia?"

Farrela had walked into the tank, holding a typed statement. "You know Cynthia Ortez?"

"Her father works with me. He's a radiologist." His daughter opened her mouth and wailed, taking a moment to get her hand over her mouth to muffle herself and bury her face in her father's chest.

"You're a doctor?" Farrela ignored the wailing girl.

"Yes, yes I am. Is anybody else hurt?"

Farrela looked at him. *Not like that,* he was thinking. Out loud he said, "And Miss Ortez' father's a doctor, too, huh?"

"A very good one."

Farrela sat down next to him on the bench, elbows on his knees, looking sideways at the doctor. "Ever been any indication to either of you about drugs? You know, anything about any of the girls' friends or anything."

"Oh, Jesus fucking Christ!" One of the boys jumped up and spun around as though he was going to stomp out, but he didn't go anywhere. Robert guessed that would be Billy.

Farrela jerked his head in the boy's direction. "He doesn't seem to think so." And he smiled. Robert realized he hadn't seen Farrela smile in a while.

The doctor looked at him round-eyed. "I really don't think so, Lieutenant." He patted his daughter's shoulder. "I truly don't think so."

Farrela nodded, looked at the floor between his feet and

then back at the doctor. "Well, think about it. You have any thoughts about it, any ideas, give me a call, okay?" He handed the doctor a business card.

The doctor tucked it in his shirt pocket without reading it. "Oh, I certainly will. I . . . I just really don't think that's got anything to do with it, though. I mean, I guess you never know, but I know these kids pretty well, myself."

"What field of medicine are you in?"

"I'm an oncologist. You know, cancer? I know all about narcotics, I can guarantee you."

Farrela nodded, looked at the floor again, then looked back at him. "Yeah, I see what you mean. Guess you would."

"All about them."

"Okay."

Kevin was reading over his statement, pen in hand ready to sign. He looked pale and tired, taking the matter seriously. Goldman was standing next to Robert, outside the cell, watching Kevin. "I think they got the wrong group of kids." He said it quietly and Robert looked at him, not sure he heard him right. Goldman turned and led him back among the desks, away from the tank.

"This is the third drive-by in two weeks. It's a fuckin' epidemic."

"With a shotgun?"

Goldman shook his head. "No the others were thirty-eights or nine millimeters. Big stuff, you know? This is the only shotgun so far."

"So what do you guys think?"

"I'll tell you what I think about this one. I think somebody meant to get somebody else and these kids just happened to be there. If Kevin tells you anything makes you think different, I'd sure like to know, but I don't expect it."

"You said three murders in two weeks?"

Goldman nodded and raised his eyebrows. "Something, huh? Regular fuckin' big city."

Jimbo and Robert took one of the other boys and Kevin with them when they left. They dropped the other student at his dorm so he could go get on the telephone and scare his parents to death in nice safe New York City. He had been riding in front with Jimbo driving so then Jimbo was the acting chauffeur with Robert and Kevin MacDonald in the cage.

"He was stalking us, Dad."

"Who? The guy with the shotgun?"

"Yeah, the guy in the pickup."

Robert thought about what he was saying. "What makes you think that?"

"Well, Cynthia saw him before. She said something while we were eating about that truck going by."

"Going by the restaurant?"

Kevin screwed up his face in concentration, trying to remember. "I'm not sure. I thought at the time she was talking about over at the campus, over by the social sciences building because that's where we were before."

"Well, what did she say? She know the guy?"

"No . . . I wish I'd paid more attention, Dad. She said she'd seen this truck over by the parking lot at the social sciences building, but I thought she meant that she saw him again over there by the restaurant or something, the same truck."

"Did you see it?"

"No, I didn't know what she was talking about. Some dumb truck, who gives a shit, you know?"

Jimbo pulled up in front of their apartment and turned around in his seat to look at them in the back. "You saw this truck before? I couldn't hear."

Kevin made a face again. "I can't remember what it was she said about it."

Robert glanced at Jimbo, then back at his son. "Well try. She saw the same truck at the college campus where you were before, right?"

"I think she said something about this guy was following us or something."

"Following you or something."

Jimbo looked back and forth at Robert and Kevin. "You tell Farrela that?"

"I didn't think of it."

"Jesus."

"Dad, I was upset. I think she said she'd seen this truck over at the campus and then when we were sitting there she saw it again going by the restaurant. She wanted us to look at it, but nobody else saw it, you know, to get a look at what she was talking about. We weren't paying any attention."

"But you're sure it was a pickup and not a van or a station wagon or something, huh?"

"Yeah, I'm sure about that. I don't know what the others were looking at but in my mind I can see this old black pickup truck coming through the parking lot, moving kind of fast, and then this gun, seemed like it was pointed right at me, just the end of the barrel coming out of the passenger side and . . ."

"There were two guys in it?"

"Dad, I don't know. I don't think so, but I don't remember seeing anybody. That's just the impression I had that there was just the one guy in there and then this shotgun coming out and . . ."

"You see where he went?"

"Oh, man. Man, I couldn't see anything after that but I looked at Cynthia . . ." His voice caught. "She was right behind me. . . . Cynthia's head was just . . . like there was just this piece of it left, like . . ." The horror of it was in his eyes.

Jimbo opened his door and tugged at the release for the back in the doorframe. "Maybe we better go in with you, huh?"

Robert nodded vigorously. "Yeah, come on, we'll walk through the place, make sure you're settled down okay."

Upstairs, the apartment was dark. Robert flipped on the

light in the living room, looking around. Jimbo saw him acting cautious and shrugged his shoulders. "Nobody been in here."

Robert and Kevin both looked at him. He shrugged his shoulders again. "Okay, we'll make sure."

He strode into the kitchen, found the light switch and looked around for any signs of anything out of the ordinary. He checked the back door and found it locked with a chain across it. Robert saw him check it and went down the hallway to turn on the lights in the bathroom and the bedrooms, looking in closets and behind doors. He grinned sheepishly at Jimbo. "Looks okay, let's go." He turned to Kevin. "Just lock up behind us and go to bed, okay? You be all right?"

"Sure, Dad. I wasn't scared before."

"Okay, just lock up good."

SEVENTEEN

When Robert got home the next morning, the sun had already been up for half an hour. It seemed late to him, the rest of the world up and moving. If he wanted to get anything done he better be doing it. He knew, though, that the energy was an illusion, that he was bone tired and needed to get some sleep. The events of the night were jumbling in his mind so that the half-bagged kid that he and Jimbo had decided not to arrest because he was, after all, only walking home, and Kevin's gunman in the pickup were mixed up, the homeward-bound kid becoming a gang member, battling over turf, whatever that might mean in Martin, and thus in danger of shooting somebody or being shot himself before he could reach sanctuary. They had driven him home.

The shooting of Cynthia Ortez had started something new. The ordinary, quiet streets of Martin were almost threatening to Robert, occupied now by unfamiliar people, strange beings, aliens from another world, possibly Los Angeles. It didn't matter to him that other cops knew that this was something that was happening from Phoenix to Atlanta, another wrinkle in the evolution of social change. This was something personal

178

to him, to Robert MacDonald: like some just or unjust retribution. He realized that he was frightened and too exhausted to figure it out.

He opened the front door to the apartment, noting with some comfort that the dead bolt was locked. He stopped in the kitchen, thinking about breakfast, but he was too tired even for that. Before he went to bed he cracked open the door to Kevin's room and looked in, watching the tousled top of his son's head sticking out from under the covers and listening to try to hear him breathing. When he was satisfied, he went into his own room and closed the door, stripped off his clothes, dropping them on the floor, and fell into bed.

He got up at 2:00 P.M., feeling a little better, but not fully rested. He was anxious to be up and doing something, but once he was fully awake and on his feet, he realized that there was nothing that he needed to do. It was Thursday and he had already worked his shift. He only needed to be awake so that he might have a chance of sleeping tonight so he could go out to the range at his normal time on Friday. It seemed mundane, a return to the ordinary cycle.

At first he was surprised that Kevin had left the apartment. Robert thought that Kevin might have taken a day or two off from classes after what he had been through. After he thought about it, though, Robert realized that Kevin would want to be among his friends, not necessarily going to class but sitting around the Student Union coffee shop, probably, wide-eyed and horrified, a minor celebrity as an eyewitness, talking about it and trying to make sense of something so pointless.

He thought about calling Jimbo. Robert thought they ought to be feeling some self-satisfaction. He had spent all this time and effort, persisting in the belief that Terry had been murdered, no matter what the evidence seemed to show; and now, with the new information that he and Jimbo had come up with, it looked as though they might have been right all along. Well, no, Foster might say it didn't quite look like that yet. Robert considered running his ideas by Jimbo, just once more, because Jimbo had seemed as enthused as he was about finding some new "evidence." Maybe Jimbo would see the new information as a kind of vindication for looking foolish, for allowing the old man to talk him into chasing this down in the first place after Homicide . . .

What about Homicide? Wasn't there something funny there, too? Eight or nine guys assigned to that department normally, maybe a dozen right now, with everything else going on, and Bill Farrela had been personally assigned to everything Robert knew about. Farrela and Goldman investigating Terry's case, Farrela and Goldman showing up last night when this girl got killed standing in the wrong place at the wrong time, right next to Kevin. What? Why those two again? Could they think there might be a connection, too?

He called Jimbo at home, hating the telephone, but not wanting to just go over unannounced.

"Hello?" He sounded wide-awake.

"Hi, Jimbo, this is MacDonald."

"Hey, yeah, I been thinking about it, too. The fire?"

"What?"

"That car fire. You know, if a guy was trying to locate one of us when we were out on patrol and he had a scanner . . . all he'd need to know was what unit we were in and he could use a scanner to listen for a call of some kind on the police band that would give our location and he could just go to wherever we said we were, you know? I mean if a guy didn't have anything else to do, he could eventually catch up to us provided he knew what unit . . ."

"And some guy called and asked what car I was out in."

"Yeah, the guy that said he was your brother. You never found out who that was, did you?"

"No, never did." Robert was amazed that he hadn't thought of that, himself. He heard Jimbo's voice going on, sounding reasonable.

"You can buy a scanner in any Radio Shack, you know."

"Yeah, I think that's right. Get a hundred channels or something." Robert sat down at his kitchen table, staring at the tabletop, phone to his ear. "I was just thinking about this thing last night with Kevin."

"Me too."

"Seems like a pretty thin possibility that it's connected doesn't it? I mean, what's anybody got against all of us, anyway?"

"Yeah, yeah, I know. But a black pickup . . ."

"Yeah, that's what I mean. It seems like a hell of a coincidence, don't you think? Am I making something outa this?"

Jimbo didn't say anything for a long time. Robert was on the point of asking if he was still there when he heard his voice again. "Maybe . . . maybe you oughta come by and pick me up. We can go down and talk to Farrela again."

"Or Foster."

"Okay, Foster."

The receptionist that had worked at Homicide for ten years, at least, was sitting under grimy printed slogans and posters that adorned the wall behind her, reading *Vogue* when Robert and Jimbo breezed by her. She didn't bother looking up. "Nobody there."

They had to go in and look around, Jimbo craning his neck to see if anybody was hiding in the interrogation room, before they came back out and looked at her. She kept reading.

"Where is everybody?" Robert asked it apologetically, as though he hated to bother her.

"Either chasing killers or attending a retirement luncheon for Lieutenant Graham, depending."

"Depending on what?" Jimbo sounded very tired.

"Depending on who wants to know." She looked like she might have been reading her lines from the magazine. She finally made the effort to look up. "If you were witnesses or lawyers or a captain, they'd be in the field. Since you're plain old cops they're at Barney's out on Natchez Drive."

Robert stood there thinking for a moment, then moved toward the door. "Okay, thanks, Trudy."

"If you're going out there, take a bucket."

"What?"

"In case you need to pour one of 'em in it to give him a ride home."

In the hallway, Jimbo punched the elevator button with the bottom of his fist. "Now you going to Raimon City, huh?"

"Sure." Robert got on the elevator and faced the door, waiting until it had started down. "You don't have to go, though."

Robert could feel Jimbo scowling at the back of his head. The big cop sighed and looked at his watch. "Shouldn't really take that long. We ought to be able to get out there and back in plenty of time for me to get to work."

"You don't have to, Jimbo, if it bothers you."

Jimbo didn't answer right away, walking next to Robert back to his car. He got in, waited for Robert to start the engine. "Shit, I've gone this far."

Robert grinned and couldn't help glancing at him. "Got you hooked, huh?"

Jimbo shook his head, staring through the windshield. "Fuck."

Raimon City had once been a rural farm community, connected to Martin by a twenty-mile stretch of perfectly straight unpaved road, negotiable in the late fall mainly by mule. But the population of farmers had long ago been overshadowed, if not actually displaced by commuters who came for the less expensive housing, not for the rustic atmosphere.

The address Robert had from DMV was in an apartment complex, a group of buildings that, Jimbo remarked, only a developer could love, a "Raimon City Special," built free of the zoning and building standards imposed in the more cosmopolitan, larger city of Martin. Certainly, nobody who lived there would think that the apartments were much better than what they might expect from a relatively modest rent. The parking area was clearly marked off with reserved spaces for the tenants and a separate, unlabeled area for visitors. Her phone might be disconnected, but G. Nicholson still had her name on the mailbox, part of a bank of mailboxes, conveniently located at the entrance to the parking area.

They thumped their way up an open outside staircase to the second floor and entered the building, walking into a clean, characterless, carpeted hall. At the second door on the right they stopped and knocked. They could hear a stereo playing somewhere. No one answered the door so Jimbo knocked again. Still nothing.

Jimbo looked at his watch and said, "Listen. No children. Anyplace like this in Martin would have kids all over it, but there's no toys, nothing."

Robert nodded. "Probably, they don't allow 'em. Suppose that gives 'em status?"

Jimbo shrugged. "Sure quiet, though."

Robert looked up at him. "Let's wait outside a few minutes."

Jimbo nodded without saying anything out loud. The place was too quiet to talk comfortably.

When they reached the bottom of the steps Robert stepped off quickly and turned around, glancing up at the windows that faced over the parking area. He walked backward a few paces, glancing up again before he turned around and walked toward the car. When Jimbo caught up, Robert said, "Somebody is definitely home."

He turned the car around and backed into the stall, making no effort to conceal what he was doing: getting in position to watch the entrances to the building without having to turn around in the seat.

The windows on the second floor were not big and were placed high so that though almost none of them had curtains, you couldn't see much of what was inside. Robert didn't know the floor plans so he couldn't be positive about which windows belonged to the apartment they were watching, but one window that almost had to belong there had a shade over it with some kind of blue light on the other side.

Jimbo pointed to it. "Look at that, will ya? It's blue." Robert smiled.

Jimbo looked at him. "What did you see?"

"You see something?"

"No, a minute ago you said somebody was home. What did you see?"

"Oh. That shade moved, that's all. Somebody was looking to see who came outa the stairs."

Jimbo chuckled. "She's probably calling the cops."

A middle-aged man, portly in a business suit and no scar on his face, came down the stairs. He was blond and red-faced and in a hurry. He studiously ignored the Bronco and climbed into a BMW, accelerating out of the parking area. Robert looked at Jimbo. "She's not calling the cops."

"Dope house?"

"No."

A few minutes later a tall African-American woman in high heels delicately picked her way down the steps. She was dressed in Calvin Klein jeans and a bulky, bright green sweater. She walked directly toward their car with confident gentility. She did not seem to be the slightest bit perturbed.

"Hi." She acted genuinely friendly. "Somebody knocked at my door a few minutes ago. That wouldn't have been you gentlemen, would it?" She leaned forward next to the driver's door to bring her face down to the level of theirs.

Jimbo grinned across at her, apparently struck dumb by the sight of her. Robert said, "Yeah, actually we were looking for Gretchen Nicholson. Would that be you?"

She glanced a second time at Jimbo. "You guys have got to be cops, right?"

Robert laughed. "Right, Martin P.D. My name's MacDonald and my partner is Phillips. You Nicholson?"

"No, she's my roommate. She's not home, but I'll tell her you came by. You got a card? Like a business card or something with a telephone number on it she could call?"

Robert thought that she smelled nice, fresh, like she had just come out of the shower. He was mildly surprised when Jimbo produced a business card out of his wallet and passed it across. It didn't seem too badly shopworn.

She looked at the card, held in one ringed, enamel-tipped hand. "Can I tell her what this is about?"

"It's actually about her car."

The woman let her guard drop just enough to show that there had been one. "Her car?"

"An old Chevy?"

"Oh!" This time her smile was genuine. "That piece of shit!" She laughed out loud. "Pardon my language. I think she sold that old thing. What's the deal, did it have a bunch of tickets or something in the city?" Her grin was huge.

Robert laughed along with her. "Well, if she sold it, then it's probably the guy she sold it to that we want to see. He might've witnessed an accident, that's all. Any idea where we could find her now?"

The woman was still laughing, swaying with willowy grace on the tall heels. "Excuse me, I just thought she was in trouble, you know?" She made her face look serious. "I couldn't imagine why I thought that."

"Would you know where we can find her?"

"Sure, she's at work. Let me call her first and make sure it's all right if you go over there. She might rather meet you here or something." She trotted, as graceful as a dancer, across the parking lot and up the stairs. As soon as she entered the building they were both out of the car after her. When they got to her door, it was standing slightly open so they walked on in.

The whole place was dimly lit, with the shades down and heavy curtains over them on the inside. It was also warm and damp enough that Robert wanted to loosen his collar and tie, first thing. The woman was talking into an elaborately technical-looking telephone and smoking an ordinary cigarette. She smiled at them when they came in, listening to the phone. Then she frowned slightly. "No, they're cops from Martin, they're not from Raimon. . . . It's about her car, dummy." She rolled her eyes to the ceiling. "Okay. All right, I got it." She hung up the phone.

Robert had nudged open a door that he was standing next to. Inside the room he could see a king-sized mattress on the floor with rumpled white sheets and a towel on it. Next to the pad there was a low shelf with half a dozen bottles of oil and a container of talcum powder. There was also a stereo and a space heater and the blue light.

She dazzled them with her smile. "You guys are just looking for cars, right?"

Robert quickly closed the door. "Absolutely." He gave her a little-boy grin.

"Well, you can find Gretchen at the Pool Room. It's a bar just a block off Camino Real." She wrote on the back of Jimbo's card. "This is the address. She wasn't there when I called, but the guy that owns it says she'll be back any minute. She's a cocktail waitress there." Jimbo seemed a little disappointed that he was getting his card back as a piece of scrap paper. The high-tech telephone chirped and a machine clicked on, taking the call or transferring it, they couldn't tell.

EIGHTEEN

Hey, Greg?" Larry was a little out of breath. Greg didn't answer as he stood at the top of a small hill behind the trailer. He stared off across the low brush at the line of the forest about two hundred yards away. He had the shotgun in his hand.

"Hey, Greg, you ain't going hunting like that, are you?" Larry caught up to him and looked from the line of trees to his brother and back. "Nothing there but a few rabbits, anyway. You want some rabbit? Hey, that'd be good for dinner, anyway, huh?"

Greg didn't respond. He didn't seem to be aware of his brother's voice as he continued to stare at the trees, his knuckles white where he gripped the shotgun by the stock behind the trigger guard.

Larry looked at the gun, at the knuckles and then back at Greg's face. "Hey, Greg? You all right?" He looked at the gun, then the forest. "What you thinking about, Greg?" He stared anxiously at his brother's face.

Greg glanced at him and then looked back at the trees. "Nothing. I guess . . ." He stopped talking as though he forgot he was saying anything, absorbed in some inner idea. His eyes were thin, bloodshot slits. He seemed to remember Larry and glanced at him again. "Ain't you going to work?"

"Yeah. I got a couple a minutes. You all right?"

"Yeah."

"You don't look it. You look like you might be sick, Greg." Larry stared at the trees for something else to look at and then looked at Greg's face again, studying it. "Look . . . Why don't I go up to the house and call in?"

Greg turned to him and, this time, his voice sounded hoarse. "What?"

"I don't have to be there today. They could get by without me. Hell, they might not even notice I'm not there, you know?" He tried a weak chuckle.

"You got to go to work." Greg's voice was hoarse and unexpectedly gentle.

Larry's face was long and thoughtful, his mouth turned down in sympathy. "Hey, Greg? Why don't you give me the shotgun and come on in the house, get something on television? I need to call in."

"No, I'm all right. You go on to work."

"You ain't been yourself since you come out here with that trunk." When Greg didn't answer, Larry started to leave, stopped and then tried working up to the other side of him. "Hey, listen, Greg? I know I said I wouldn't bother you about whatever it is, but . . . Well, I think I figured it out. You're sick, aren't you? I mean, I can see that. Is it cancer?"

"What?"

"Look, I don't mean to stick my nose in it. I'm just worried about you. I mean, it's like I just found you again after all that time and now . . . Okay, I'll just ask you. You don't have AIDS, do you?"

"What? No, I don't have AIDS! What the hell . . . ?"

"Okay, I'm sorry, I just didn't know what was wrong with you."

"Well, I don't have AIDS."

"Greg, it wouldn't matter. I won't ask anything anymore. Look, I just wondered if I could get you anything, that's all."

"I'm all right. You go on to work."

"I don't know, Greg."

"I tell you what I need. I need some peace and quiet, some time to just get some rest."

Larry stared at him, not sure. "What, just to read them college newspapers?"

"I'll be all right, if I can get some time by myself."

Larry nodded. "You want me to find another place to stay for a while?" He seemed ready to cry, himself.

Greg shook his head quickly. "No. No, I don't mean anything like that. Just go on to work and maybe I'll get us a rabbit if I can just walk that far and then sit still and wait for one. Go on, I'll see you tonight."

"You sure?" Larry still hesitated, trying to see his brother's face without staring at him. "I know. I can start a subscription to the paper in the city. I can call 'em today and it'll probably start tomorrow. How would that be?"

"That'd be fine."

"Then you'd have the thing while it was still fresh in the morning. I don't know how to get that college paper but I could get the one from the city."

"Yeah, that'd be good."

With something to do now, Larry started to turn away, then stopped. "You not going to get any rabbits. You can't be quiet. They hear you coming ten miles, walkin' around like that."

"If I can get that far, I can just sit still."

"Yeah. Okay. Well . . . okay." This time he did start to leave.

Suddenly, Greg turned and called after him, "Thanks, Larry. I mean it, now."

Larry grinned and waved, almost laughing out loud in delight. "See you later!"

The tree line was no more than two hundred yards away,

but it seemed like a mile. The doctor had told him there was a hairline fracture at about mid-thigh and Greg pictured it when he tried to walk. It must be healing because it hurt less today than it did a few days ago in spite of the fact that he didn't give it any rest, didn't take it easy like he was supposed to.

The ground looked fairly level, fairly flat, if he'd had two good legs. In the cast, unable to bend at the ankle or the knee, it was impossibly irregular, with rises in the ground just where he had to swing the cast forward, depressions, just where he had to step down. In a few yards, he was sweating again, his face red with the effort.

It was ridiculous that the leg would heal like that, would just mend itself, go on doing it when there was no point, no future for it, whether it mended or not. It seemed to be a stupid waste of natural effort. It wasn't like Phil Blankenship at all.

Greg stopped. He was less than halfway to the trees, breathing hard, but that wasn't why he stopped. The name had just come to him all of a sudden. He had been thinking about Phil since he got hurt. Phil Blankenship was the guy's name but before, he could only picture him without the name. Phil had been shot through the leg on the side of a mountain and kept on going.

Greg remembered it in a clump, all of it together, that he hadn't knowingly thought about in maybe twenty years. A hundred-fifty marines, all of them kids, eighteen, nineteen years old, going up the Korean bluff like they were crossing the beach, no break, no pause, like bugs. They went over the top and found the Chinese, heavy artillery pounding at them before they got there. What they found were more kids, Chinese kids, this time, shooting back as though they thought they were bulletproof. Chinese kids were on the ground behind them, too, so they had to keep going whether they meant to or not.

Even when they could finally stop, the pass secure, Phil Blankenship would not go to get patched up. Other people got hurt, too, but Greg remembered Phil because he kept on going, hobbling for weeks, it seemed like, until he finally walked almost normally again. When he first got shot it looked like the hole was dead center in his thigh, another hole on the back side where it came out, and nobody could tell why it didn't hit the bone. One guy thought it did, but the bullet didn't break up or mushroom: just punched a hole through and kept on going.

Phil Blankenship kept saying, "Can't stop now. We're committed, now," as though he had gotten it from a poster somewhere.

When Greg got back and told the story, nobody got it. Nobody knew what he was talking about so he quit telling it. Now, because he hadn't told it in so long, maybe, it was all twisted, corrupted so that it came back at him now, with his own leg encased in plaster and he kept thinking, *I'm committed now,* because there just wasn't any way to go back.

The odd thing was the normalcy, the mundane, that occasionally crept into his attention. It was like he was steaming along at ninety miles an hour and all of a sudden he would see the whole world at a dead stop and it hadn't changed, didn't seem any different than it had just a month ago, two months ago, before it all started and he couldn't get off. When he saw others being normal, the world basically unchanged for all the changes that were going on in him, he had to shake his head, clear it of the deception, because once he had taken the first step all of that was behind him and he knew it; he knew it was going to be like that when he did it.

Now he knew the rest of it, had got the information, and he had to keep focused, not let himself get distracted if he was going to finish what he had to do. He blinked at the tree line.

Why the hell was he going out there with the shotgun, now? Because he didn't own a pistol. It would be easier with a pistol, but he could still do it if he used a stick to push the trigger while he held the muzzle braced against his forehead. He thought he should get a pistol.

Greg turned and looked at the house, the shack. He didn't want to go back there. He got physically sick at the idea of sitting there all day, unable to do what he had to do because of not being able to find who he had to find until he got a better idea. But he had to. He couldn't go on to the woods and find that stick, because he wasn't finished. He was committed now, and there was no way he could stop it unless he let her down, let himself down. He had to be stronger than that.

It seemed to Greg that he had been strong a long time, had managed to do things that others couldn't do, to make out when others couldn't have done it. It hadn't gotten him anywhere but here, but it seemed worthwhile when he was doing it and damn it! He didn't know how to do anything else now, but keep on going.

He started back for the shack, stumbling and sweating, clenching his teeth against the pain in his leg that now seemed a little worse than when he had started out. He had to remember that he was hurt. He had to take that into account or he wouldn't be able to do it. He would forget and then he would get stopped. They would figure it out and stop him just as he was getting the job done and it would be exactly as if he had pulled the trigger on himself, stopped himself by being ignorant and stupid.

He had to keep it in mind, to make allowances. Even though it seemed like a long time, like a gigantic struggle was going on, he knew that was probably wrong, that his judgment was gone. If he could just stay with it, keep his attention on what he was going to do next, instead of all the other goddamned crazy things that kept happening, getting in his way, the accidents . . . That thought stopped him. Why the hell did it have to involve these others?

He turned back around and considered the woods again. No, he had already decided. He only kept thinking about that because he was ignorant, stupid. It was because he was too eager, too angry to think anything through. He had to remember what he was doing and not get distracted anymore. He had to try to leave these other people out of it and just concentrate, stay focused, targeted on what he was after. And he couldn't go off into the trees and find a stick because then he would leave it unfinished. He could do that later, even buy a pistol, but not until he was finished with what he had started.

Until then, he had to try to protect himself, too. He had to try to make sure that he was all right, not because his own well-being had any value—it didn't, even to him—it was because he was the tool and he had to save, preserve himself as the tool until it was over: then he could quit.

But the worst part, the truly bad part, was the accidents. If he let himself think about that, he would go back out into the woods and get out of it, stop it, jump free of the maelstrom that had ripped him loose in the first place. Because it wasn't something that he had done that started it. It was something outside, somebody else that didn't give a shit and *they* had started the whole thing and he was just out to do a job; only trying to get it put back right so he could pause long enough to escape, to get out of it, himself.

He was doing it again, wasn't he? Just doing what he had done all his life. Just trying to do his best to do the right thing. It wasn't that he was too stupid and ignorant to know the right thing when it hit him up the side of the head, it was that he was not smart enough to do it, to do something completely foreign, completely alien, like this, and do it right the first time. He had to go against all of it, all his life, it seemed, just to do what he had always done and get the job done. Except now he had to concentrate and remember that he had to protect himself until it was done. Then he could stop. He could stop then, when it was done.

All in the world he wanted now, was just to see a way that he could make it all stop.

All his life, it seemed, he had been looking for a way to make things come out right. He'd thought he was doing everything he was supposed to do even though it was hard and no damn picnic sometimes, but all along he kept thinking that this was the way to do it and sooner or later everything would work out all right. But it never happened. It never did work out. He had kept on doing what he was supposed to do and still, every time he ran out of money, every time it seemed that he couldn't get up, his body desperate for more sleep, for rest; still, he thought that eventually, things would be different, would come out in the end, make it all worthwhile. But then it didn't. He never got there. These people came along and wrecked the whole thing; strangers came into it and ripped it apart before he could get there, before he could realize any of the rewards he was supposed to be working toward.

No, wait. That wasn't really true. There had been times, lots of times, times when it had come out right. Did he even know it when it did?

He stopped where he was, sweating, the shotgun gripped in his left hand, fingernails and knuckles white from the strength of his grip on the wooden stock of the gun, sweat running from under his callused hand and down his face, soaking his collar. He was partway turned, undecided whether he was going to the woods or back to the house. He tried to clear his head by taking deep breaths, opening his eyes and looking around. What the hell was he doing out here? He couldn't think in the little shack, that was the problem. Of course, there had been times when the world was right. Of course there had been or he wouldn't be out here now, half-crazy or completely crazy with the loss.

He took another deep breath.

Tears rolled down his face, streaking in the grime and the sweat, but he was hardly aware of them. He had to just keep going, now. No question, he was committed now. He just had to keep going until he was at a place where he could stop, when it was done.

NINETEEN

As he walked into the Pool Room, Robert noticed a small room just off the end of the bar. It held the same kind of high-tech telephone that he had just seen, sitting on a desk next to a huge Rolodex and a machine used to verify credit cards. A woman in her mid-thirties sat at the desk wearing a headset with a magazine open in front of her. This room was not part of the bar and the woman got up and closed the door.

The guy behind the bar looked cool, like he had been watching for them. He didn't smile at all and wore an open shirt with a heavy gold medallion on his chest and both a gold watch and a gold chain ID bracelet. He was clean-shaven and extremely neat, both of which were somewhat out of character for the rest of the bar.

It was a working man's establishment, undecorated pale brown walls yellow-streaked with old smoke, rising to shadowed, cobwebbed beams above thin metal light fixtures that hung down, suspended by their own conduits. The after-work crowd had already come and gone or else hadn't made it that day. The place was empty except for one table where three men in work clothes were ostensibly playing cards. The game stopped when Robert and Jimbo came in, the men at the table staring at them openly.

Jimbo stayed for a moment at the door and looked over the place while Robert, seeming to be as unaware of how he might look as he was about the hostility of the bartender and the card players, walked right up to the bar and edged between two empty stools. "Is Gretchen Nicholson here?"

The guy behind the bar kept scowling. "You the guys, talked to Nivedita?"

"Who?"

"Nivedita. The tall black girl."

"I guess so. Didn't get her name. What kind of a name is . . ."

"Gretchen's gone out. What you want with her?"

The question implied that Robert wouldn't be able to do much with her if he found her. The rudeness of it without a trace of kidding to soften it stiffened Jimbo's back but Robert didn't seem to notice.

"Oh, it's not a big deal. It's her car, actually, that we're interested in. Her car was at a place where whoever was in it might have been a witness to a burglary. We're just checking it out. No big deal."

The guy behind the bar just looked at him.

"Is she gonna be back?"

One of the men in the card game gave a loud cough and one of the others at the table laughed at him. All three of them were watching Jimbo and Robert, waiting for something to happen. The bartender glanced at the card players, apparently hesitant about whether to answer Robert's question.

"Maybe my partner and I will have a beer while we're waiting. You serve beer, don't you, asshole?"

A chair scraped back and Larry, one of the card players, stood up. His red hair and beard were covered with a powdering of concrete dust. The dust covered his T-shirt and arms down to the wrists as though he had been wearing gloves on the job. Robert saw a prodigious potbelly but the rest of him was big in proportion so that he didn't look particularly fat. He was bigger, heavier than Jimbo but not as hard. It was Jimbo that Larry was watching with little blue pig eyes, squinting through lids, puffy from beer. The other two at the table lounged back, watching and waiting.

The man behind the bar looked at Larry and quickly glanced at Jimbo, still standing near the door. Jimbo was watching him. "Okay, mister, don't get excited. What do you want?"

"Whatever you got on tap will be just fine."

Robert continued to look at him pleasantly, willing to pretend that he hadn't insulted him if the bartender was willing to pretend to be civil back. The bartender looked like the owner of a mastiff, not too sure he wanted his dog to get near another mastiff.

Robert leaned his elbows on the bar to bring his face closer to the bartender. "Look, I don't care what else you got going on here. All I want to do is find out about who's got this girl's car so we can talk to 'em, that's all."

A young woman breezed in the front door of the bar without paying any attention to Jimbo, heading for the door to the office. She was wearing Spandex bicycle pants and high heels with a tank top. She had a luxurious mane of black curls and oversized hoop earrings. She glanced in the direction of the bartender and stopped at some signal from him. Her face grew serious as she looked at Larry, who was still standing next to the table, and then she looked at Jimbo. "Oh. Ah, I'll talk to you later, Chuck."

She started to turn around but Robert called out to her. "You Gretchen?" He was relaxed and friendly.

She glanced at Chuck and looked again at the friendly old man. "No, but I'm sure she'll be right back." She beamed. Then she turned and bolted out of the door before anyone could say anything else to her.

Robert turned back to the bartender and spread his hands. "That's all I wanted to know."

"You want to know about Gretchen's car? I sold her the 280Z, myself. I can tell you about that."

"No, it's her old one. The old Bel Air."

"Hey." One of the card players, still leaning back in his chair, legs spraddled, called out. "Are you guys cops from Martin?"

Robert ignored him and continued to talk to the bartender. "Know who she sold her old car to?"

"Hey, Chuck. You said they were from Martin, right? You guys are outa your territory."

Another young woman came in the door, headed for the office. The bartender looked relieved when he saw her. "Hey, Gretchen. These guys are cops, asking about your old car."

She pulled up short, startled momentarily. She glanced at Robert and Jimbo and then gave Chuck a long look, wanting a signal of some sort on how to handle this. She had dark brown hair, pulled back in a low bun. She was wearing a short dress and, like any other woman with any connection to this place, high heels and oversized earrings. "My car?"

Robert smiled ingratiatingly. "Sorry to bother you about it, Miss Nicholson, but you didn't send in the change in registration to the DMV, and we thought you still owned it."

"What, did it finally die on the freeway or something?"

"We just want to talk to the owner, that's all. When did you sell it?"

"About two or three weeks ago, something like that, but it hadn't run for six months before that, before the guy that bought it got it started. What happened, did the guy get in trouble with it? Parked in a handicap zone, I bet." She tried to giggle, but her nervous glance at Chuck destroyed the effect.

"You know the name of the guy you sold it to?"

"Yeah, his name's Greg . . . Arnold? Something like that. You can ask this . . ." She started to point at the men at the card table.

"Hey! Fuck this shit!" Larry started across the room for her, his face beaming hostility and beer fumes. Jimbo stepped up in his way.

"Take it easy, now, just stop right there!"

But the guy'd had enough beer, he didn't even change directions. He charged straight at Jimbo, swinging and missing as he came. Jimbo grabbed him, but Larry was too big to take down easily. He turned furiously, trying to strike at Jimbo's head with his elbow until he broke free. He spun around to face Jimbo and crouched, red face glowing with malice and the exertion, looking for an opening. Then there was a knife in his hand, a carpenter's clasp knife that he had out and open. Jimbo faced him, hands up, ready for him to come again, circling to try to get Larry to back into a chair or table to throw him off, make him look away for a second.

Suddenly Robert was all over Larry. He seemed to climb the front of him, gripping him by the beard. He struck twice, forehand and backhand on the top of the red head with something that made a cracking sound, moving so fast the guy didn't even know it was coming. Larry jerked back and spun away from Robert, the knife scuttering across the floor. He was partly stunned and covering his head, bent over. Robert took a quick half step back and kicked him hard in the groin, then went right up his back before he could even fall, hitting him again in the back of the head as he went down.

Robert was straddling him as Larry hit the floor and he raised the sap again, but the big man was out. Robert jerked his gun out, on his knees, looking around. The other two card players had moved over to the bar and, seeing the way clear, darted through the door and disappeared. Gretchen was nowhere around, either.

Robert slid the sap into his jacket pocket. He looked up at Chuck, the bartender, who was standing with his mouth hanging open. Chuck gaped a couple of times. "Hey, I didn't have anything to do with that."

Robert holstered the gun, then sat back for a minute, trying to get his breath, too winded to say anything. Jimbo stepped over Larry's feet and got right in Chuck's face. "Now, who the fuck is this Greg guy?"

"She's talking about this one's brother." He indicated the man on the floor. "This guy's name is Larry Murray. But it's his half brother, really—different last name. I don't know what his name is but I don't think Arnold is right. I think she got that wrong. . . ."

"Where can we find him?"

"I think he moved into Larry's house with him." He looked from one cop to the other. "Oh, you want the address?" Robert got up, still breathing hard, and looked at him. Chuck started nodding like he was answering a question. "Okay, I know it. Here, I'll write it down for you."

He opened the office door with Jimbo moving right behind him to see what he was doing. The young woman with the headset was standing in the corner of the tiny office, terrified. Chuck didn't even glance at her. He picked up a notepad and a pen and came back to the bar. Jimbo spoke to the woman. "Step out here, please. It's all right, I just want you out here so I can see you, okay?" She nodded meekly, too scared to move. "It's all right, we're cops. Just step out here, please." He took her by one trembling elbow and steered her out of the office. Robert noticed that she didn't have on high heels. She had on running shoes. The cord to the headset dangled to her waist. She stared at Larry on the floor.

Robert was still gasping a little, but at least he could talk. "This guy work for you?"

"No." He looked from one to the other. "Well, he does odd jobs and things sometimes. He works for a construction company mostly."

"He do things like collections?"

"Hey, I don't need anything like that. I'm not a fucking mobster, man."

"How about his brother? He work for you?"

"No, look, I forgot that asshole even existed 'til a couple a weeks ago when he bought that car of Gretchen's. He works in Martin, never comes out here. You ask me, he's fucking crazy." The two cops stared at him. "Well, so's this guy. I'm not gonna let him back in here again, either." They looked at him and waited. He raised one hand over his head. "I swear to God. Look, I don't have anything to do with the brother. I just met him a couple of times and I told Larry to keep him outa here. I don't know what he got himself into with that car, but I don't have anything to do with that. Was it a hit-and-run?"

Robert glanced at Jimbo. The bartender really didn't seem to know anything, although it was hard to be sure. Jimbo picked up the pad from the bar and tore off the sheet with the address and looked at it. "Where is this?"

"It's on the way to Redding. You take 92 for about ten miles from Camino Real where it winds up in the hills. There's a Gulf station with a little store and the mailbox is about three miles on the other side of that. It's painted green for some reason. You can't miss it."

Robert watched him. "You go out there a lot?"

Larry turned over slowly and sat up, holding his head, leaning over with his elbows on his knees. Chuck peered at him over the bar. "Hey, Larry. You all right?"

Larry didn't answer, but he was at least sitting up. Chuck looked at Robert and grinned. "We went to school together." He looked at Jimbo and then at the young woman who hadn't moved at all except for the wobbling and shaking of the headset cord. Chuck seemed to think that explained the whole thing. "We knew each other in kindergarten."

TWENTY

As soon as they came out the door, headed for the Bronco, Robert made it clear that he wanted to say something to Jimbo, but Jimbo was too anxious to get out his own questions. "We just gonna leave him like that?"

"We don't have any authority down here."

"How about a felony in our presence? We don't have to be in the city to . . ."

"Look, we don't have time for that. It'd take us two hours to explain everything and get him booked. Somebody could be calling this Greg asshole before we get a chance to get out there and pick him up. Let me tell you something . . ."

"Mac, we ought to be calling Homicide anyway, tell 'em what we got, let them go out there and pick him up."

"I know that. Listen a minute . . ."

"Well, what are we going to tell 'em when they want to know . . ." Robert's jaw tightened. "All right, tell me what you were going to say."

"Don't ever spar."

"What?"

"Don't spar. Not ever, you understand? This ain't the Marquis of Queensberry, for Christ's sake. You don't dance around and spar like that. You get in a fight with a suspect, you hurt him as often and as much as you can until he can't think of anything else and then you arrest him and you stop. You don't fucking spar."

Jimbo slumped back in his seat. "I'll try to remember."

"Don't try—remember. Now, I don't know what connection this all has. Somebody that was somehow tied up to this hooker business was asking about Terry, trying to find him."

"Is that what that was all about?"

"What did you think Nivedita was, a chiropractor?"

"Oh, yeah." Jimbo smiled. Thinking of Nivedita as a hooker seemed to put a whole new light on the business of vice. "What about the bar?"

"I bet it was outcall massage."

"They just run it like that, in the open down here?"

"I knew about a case once. They had a hooker ready to testify against the guy that set the thing up. Vice put her in Dallas to keep and they still killed her before the trial. Who gives a shit about hookers? I never thought the whole prosecution was worth it."

"Maybe Terry was a customer?"

"I don't know. It's possible Terry had something else to do with 'em, too, got mixed up in it some way. It might have something to do with that list."

"What?"

Robert took a deep breath and blew it out, thinking. "I don't know. Maybe not."

"You know something, Mac? We don't even have probable cause to make an arrest. Let's just suppose this guy matches the description. Middle-aged white man with a scar. We got a witness says he was asking about the victim, asking where he lived and maybe his car was blocking the driveway or in the driveway when the shot was fired. Maybe not. Your witness won't be able to say that was the car."

"What?"

Jimbo took a breath and spoke up over the noise of the Bronco. "I said, Mrs. Baccigalupe is not going to be the greatest about identifying the car."

"I know."

"So what else you got? You going to make an illegal search of the guy's house for a gun?"

"What gun?"

"I said, are you going to search for a gun?"

"Based on what?"

"That's what I'm talking about. There's no probable cause!" He nearly shouted the last into Robert's hearing aid.

"So? I guess we'll just go talk to him, then."

Jimbo sat back in the seat. He raised his eyebrows. "Oh." He thought about it a minute. "You're not going to try and bring him in?"

"Of course I'm going to bring his ass in. What the hell do you think we're going all the way out there for, the drive?"

"What's the basis for the arrest?"

"I don't know, I haven't written the report yet."

Jimbo had to think it over again. "What would Homicide do?"

"I don't know. I never worked Homicide."

Jimbo sat up again and leaned forward to make sure Robert heard. "See, that's the trouble. Neither one of us knows what the fuck we're doing. Foster, Goldman and Farrela. Those guys would know how to handle it so they got a good arrest on him."

Robert took his eyes off the road long enough to give Jimbo a serious look. "I been doing what I'm supposed to do all my life. I been following all the goddamn rules. As far as I can tell just about nobody else bothers with 'em, not at all. I am just not going to call Homicide right now. By the time Homicide sobered up and got around to this guy he'd be in Mexico, and with no more of a case on him than we got they'd quit think-

205

ing about him in about six months. Right now, it seems to me that the iron is hot and I'm going to go get him first and tell Homicide about it later. Besides, I'm still not breaking any rules, am I?"

Jimbo sat and looked at Robert a minute. "I'm supposed to be at work in three and a half hours."

Robert looked at his watch. "You'll make it."

"He might not even be the one that did it. Did you think of that?"

"What?"

"That Greg Arnold or whatever the fuck his name is might not be the guy that shot Terry."

"Yeah, I thought of that. Right now, though, he's the only one we got."

"You agree, it could have been somebody else?"

"Still might've been a suicide."

"Well, it might."

"Okay, where's the gun?"

"Yeah, okay." Jimbo leaned forward in the seat and looked through the windshield. "That must be the mailbox."

There was a standard metal mailbox on a post, both box and post painted an aggressive green color, probably left over from some farm equipment. Robert drove right past it. "That's not it. We still got a ways to go."

"I hope everybody out here didn't paint their mailbox green."

Robert didn't seem to hear. The woods on either side of the highway were getting thicker and dusk was coming up on them quickly, made even darker by the shade of the trees. Robert looked at his watch, then looked through the trees to try to see where the sun was. He had no idea when sunset would normally be. He had worked days for many years and the nighttime didn't interfere with working at the range except in December and January a little at the end of the day. Working nights, lately, he had lost all track of the normal cycles and had to think about it. This was October, so the days were getting shorter. He couldn't think when sundown was supposed to be in October, but he thought they must be close to it, even if they had been out in the open, away from the hills and trees.

Jimbo was staring out of his side of the car, not paying any attention to the road. When the Gulf station and store appeared, the exterior lights were already on. Robert said, "Now, start looking for a green mailbox."

Jimbo nodded and looked to the front, frowning. He definitely looked uncomfortable. When the odometer indicated that they had gone two miles past the Gulf station Robert slowed down. He switched on the lights and put on the high beams so they could see the mailboxes better as they passed. They needn't have worried about the color of the mailbox. The one they were looking for had been painted the color of AstroTurf and the name "Murray" was on the post in reflective tape. The box had once been mounted on a post like the others that they had passed, but now it dangled from one of its supports with the door pointed at the ground. It had also been shot a number of times. Robert decided that they didn't get much important mail. He supposed if they were expecting relief checks, the box would have been new.

He turned the Bronco into a country lane next to the mailbox. It suddenly seemed to be dark, as though he were driving into a tunnel made by the narrow roadway, with the trees arching overhead. The dirt road went gradually uphill for about a mile, then became very steep. The road twisted back and forth in switchbacks going up the side of the hill and its condition got worse as they went. Robert ardently wished they had been doing this a few hours earlier with at least some sunlight to help him keep from driving through the fringe of trees next to the road and plunging straight down the side of the hill.

Finally, they came over the top of the ridge and started

down the other side. Within a half mile, the trees thinned and Robert could see the remains of bright sunshine on the hills in the distance. The roadway opened up and they were driving into a long narrow valley with the house right there at the near end of it. He realized he must have lost his direction in the switchbacks because they were coming into the valley from the west. The shadow of the ridge they had come over filled the basin of the valley and climbed partway up the face of the hills on the other side. Above the shadow line the hills were brilliant where the golden alpenglow mixed with the brown leaves of early autumn, splotches of color mixed into the prevailing growth of pine.

Jimbo yawned in the seat next to him. Next he would be complaining about being hungry.

As they got nearer to it, the house looked worse. It had once been a small ranch style but someone had attached a big house trailer to one end to expand it instead of just building more house. The trailer was a gray-blue that wouldn't have looked too bad, clean, but the house was a putrid-looking yellow. Even that paint was peeling off the weathered siding in big flaked patches. There was a wooden porch attached to the front as an afterthought. The posts on the porch sagged to the left as though barely held up by the remnants of wire screen that were still attached to them. The door was closed but two windows that they could see were dark and open. A pair of sizable dogs came from the back of the house and greeted them with a rush of barking ferocity and tail-wagging, fiercely protective but delighted at having the car to chase.

Robert smirked when he saw Jimbo regarding the dogs with some trepidation. "Just country dogs . . ."

He felt the spatter of glass beads from the windshield against his face before he saw the hole or heard the gun. It seemed to take him forever to connect the sensations and by that time a second bullet had punctured the top of the windshield in front of Jimbo. "Shit!" Jimbo doubled over, his hands grasping the top of his head. Robert spun the wheel to the right and stomped on the gas. As the Bronco lazily responded another bullet hit it somewhere in the door and Robert put his nose down on the top of the steering wheel, thinking, somehow, that might make him a smaller target.

The road continued past the house and the Bronco picked up speed as it went, bouncing over the uneven surface. Jimbo straightened up and leaned out the window with his gun and fired three times at the house as they went past, firing past the wrecked windshield and turning until Robert thought Jimbo was going to shoot right past his nose and pulled it back. Robert steered past the house but couldn't see any obvious cover ahead of him. The firing continued to come from the back of the house as he sped off. He tried zigzagging and then thought that he was losing too much time and just floored it, trying to find the road in front of him by the relative scarcity of weeds in the two wheel ruts that the road turned into.

Jimbo was on his knees in the passenger seat with his left arm out the window, firing spasmodically with no hope of even hitting the house. Robert could see that the road was going up a slight incline and that it topped out somewhere about fifty yards ahead. He hoped that it would drop off sharply and give them enough cover to get stopped and get out to be ready for whatever was going to come next. It turned into a gentle crest that gradually descended on the far side. Robert used the grade to pick up speed and searched on either side of the road for cover he could turn into. Everything seemed to be flat. Then briefly they were flying. He had driven off the road at an angle into a drainage ditch hidden by the brush that grew at an almost uniform height across the entire area. The ditch was only a couple of feet deep, but hitting it at an angle, it was enough to turn over the Bronco. It seemed like they had gone several revolutions but when it stopped they were on the roof. Jimbo's head was between his knees and he struggled to get himself upright. Robert was somehow lying prone on the inside of the roof.

He took long enough to just glance at Jimbo and see that he was awake and operating. Jimbo's eyes were huge and he lunged from window to window on the upside-down roof of the car, trying to see out to find out who was following them. Blood covered his face. Robert shoved him toward the window. "Cover for a minute, 'til I can get the Springfield out." All they could see through the back window was brush. Somebody could walk right up to them and they wouldn't know the difference.

Jimbo wriggled out quickly and then stuck his head back in. "I'm out of bullets." Robert got his own gun out of his holster and passed it over. He knew he didn't have any extra .38 or .357 ammunition in his pockets and he wasn't sure about what was in the back. Upside down, the usually orderly collection of equipment and junk was a mess. He grabbed the wooden case for the Springfield and shoved it out through Jimbo's window. He grabbed the ammunition box and tried, wildly, to remember how many rounds he might have in there. Maybe seventy-five or a hundred by the feel of it. He shoved the box out and crawled out after it.

Jimbo was crouched behind the front bumper of the Bronco, Robert's Smith & Wesson gripped in both hands, leveled at the high ground they had just come over. He looked calmer than he had a moment ago, but he had a lot of blood on him. Robert brought his stuff around to the front next to him and opened the box. The bolt was removed from the Springfield and wrapped in a grease-coated hand towel, testament to the calm, unhurried atmosphere he expected to have when he opened it. He ripped the towel off and snapped in the bolt, already frantically looking for the clip in the box. No clip. He didn't hesitate once he realized it wasn't there, but dove back through the window to retrieve the "junk box."

Along with the patches and stapler there were two unloaded clips. He jammed these in his pocket, frantically scanned the wreckage for any sign of forgotten pistol ammunition and then went back out the window.

Next to Jimbo again, he loaded one clip and snapped it into place and then raised up next to his partner, finally ready. Nobody was coming. He tried to calculate how far they were from the house and how long it would take somebody to get there on foot. He might not be able to hear a quiet vehicle coming toward them on the other side of the rise. . . . Wait a minute. He couldn't hear a goddamn thing. He put his hand to his ear. It was empty. Miraculously, he still had his glasses on but he could feel the plastic end of the hearing aid, broken off. He glanced at Jimbo and wondered if he had been trying to say anything to him. He would probably be able to hear him okay, up close, but that was about all.

He glanced up at Jimbo. "Hear anything?" Jimbo shook his head without taking his eyes off the horizon, close in front of them. "How's your head?" Jimbo answered something. He could see his lips move and hear his voice but couldn't make out what he said. He was talking quietly. Robert patted him on the arm and pointed at his own ear.

Jimbo glanced at him long enough to see that the hearing aid was gone and then kept his eyes on the hill but leaned his head close to Robert's ear. "I said it feels like I been hit with a hammer. It's okay, though."

Robert straightened up and looked at the top of Jimbo's head. He parted the hair in front and saw an elongated furrow. It wasn't actively bleeding any longer. He got back into firing position and then said over his shoulder. "Bounced off."

"Good."

Jimbo had turned his head to make sure Robert heard the response so he must be thinking all right. That was reassuring. Robert thought that Jimbo must have been wondering if there was a hole in his head and a bullet in his brain. They had both heard of people who had survived, briefly, with a bullet in the head, unaware of how seriously they were hurt. Robert remembered guys in the war, shot through the chest, that didn't know they had been hit. He leaned back and checked himself, but there wasn't any blood and he didn't feel anything. He decided he wasn't hurt.

He looked at Jimbo quickly. "He's had time to get up here if he's coming." Jimbo nodded and said something that he couldn't hear. Then he realized it and leaned closer.

"You got four-wheel drive?"

Robert nodded vigorously. "Haven't used it in a while but it probably still works." He hadn't used it in five or six years. "Think we can turn it over?"

Jimbo nodded. "I think so."

The car had almost cleared the ditch when it came off the road. The ground sloped sharply for a foot or two near the roadway, but then leveled off on the other side. The top of the Bronco was out of the ditch away from the road and the ground sloped on down from there toward the woods, about a hundred yards away. It looked like it might be possible to roll it downhill to turn it back over.

Robert left the cover of the vehicle and crept through the weeds to the top of the rise, keeping his head down so far he looked like he was trying to retract it into his shoulders. The landscape was empty all the way to the house, about a half a mile away. For whatever reason, whoever had been shooting was not following them from this direction. Robert ran upright back to the car. He was suddenly aware that anyone who knew the country would be able to get a lot closer to them behind cover without coming up the open road. He could come up to within a hundred yards by circling through the trees.

Jimbo handed Robert's pistol back to him and he holstered it. He laid the Springfield down and braced his back against the side of the Bronco gripping what would have normally been the bottom window sill in the door. Jimbo looked it over and then took it head on, bracing his feet and putting his hands against the top of the side, what was normally the bottom of the door.

Suddenly, Jimbo's face screwed up with effort as he gave a tremendous shove. With surprising ease the car rolled and Jimbo caught the roof as it came up and kept it moving. The Bronco bounced on its springs and remained upright, looking normal except for the windshield. Jimbo grinned like a little boy and then winced as the effort caught up with him. A fresh trickle of blood ran down the center of his forehead and dripped off the end of his nose. He negligently brushed it off with his sleeve and looked at Robert. Jimbo was saying something, talking rapidly.

Robert didn't hear at all. He touched Jimbo's shoulder and got him to repeat it in his ear. "I'll cover. See if it'll start. No, wait a minute." He picked up the Springfield and handed it to Robert. "You cover. Give me . . . " This time Robert understood and pointed to the keys, still in the ignition.

The electricity to the starter was okay. It turned over vigorously, but the engine wouldn't fire. Robert turned his head, vainly trying to hear what was going on under the hood. Finally, after four or five attempts he waved to Jimbo to stop. He got out of the car, keeping low, and crept around to where Robert was crouching. Robert said, "Might just be flooded. It might start later if you don't run down the battery."

Jimbo nodded and looked around at where they were. Robert asked quickly "Hear anything?" Jimbo shook his head. Robert scrambled back to the top of the rise in the road and took another look. It was still empty. The ground was dry and rocky and the brush and weeds that he saw were brittle and dusty. There were incongruous patches of green weeds sticking up here and there away from the road. His brain barely registered the fact that the green patches were marijuana.

He sat down and looked around and tried to think about it. The best way for somebody to stalk them would be to come up through the woods. If they did that they would be in the trees, effectively hidden, while they sighted at their leisure at the men in the open next to the car. He made up his mind rapidly that the woods was the place to be if they could get there before the other guy. The problem was that he didn't want to just run right at them if they were already at the edge of the trees watching. He looked at Jimbo, crouching beside the car with the pistol in his hand and blood all over his face, smeared from where he had wiped at it with his sleeve. Probably the only reason nobody was shooting at them was because it was getting dark. He glanced up at the side of the valley and the alpenglow was gone, displaced by deep shadow. They would soon have stars.

He crept back to Jimbo and told him to try the engine again. Jimbo opened the passenger door because that was the side away from the edge of the trees. He got behind the wheel and then stared at the dash. He looked up at Robert, confusion in his face. Then he seemed to make up his mind and tried the key again. It didn't work. By holding his head close to the hood Robert could hear the starter turn it over, but no spark. The starter motor was slowing perceptibly. He motioned for Jimbo to stop again.

Jimbo crawled out of the passenger door and then immediately dropped to his hands and knees and vomited. He retched several more times, but his stomach was empty. He sat back against the wheel of the car and tipped his head back, gulping air. Robert could see he was saying something so he leaned his ear close. "Head feels about three feet across."

"Are you dizzy?"

"I don't know."

"Can you stand up?"

Jimbo forced himself to sit straighter and then to rise to his knees. He looked over the hood of the car at the woods and then turned back to Robert. "It's okay. I feel better now." He didn't look like he felt much better.

Robert glanced at the trees, but the shadow was already so deep that he realized that somebody could be standing in the brush and he probably wouldn't see the guy.

"You stay in front of the car and watch the woods," he told Jimbo, "You can listen for anything that you can't see over there. I'll take the back and watch the road. When it gets full dark we'll try the car again and if it doesn't work we'll sneak back toward the house."

Jimbo nodded his understanding. Robert couldn't make out his face well anymore. He went back to the squared off rear end of the Bronco and squatted next to the bumper. He tried looking at the top of the rise through the scope on the Springfield. The damn thing was going to be about useless in the dark. A hunting scope with a broad range of vision might have been all right, at least usable in the dark, but the target scope gave him a field about four feet across at a hundred yards, and without daylight to find landmarks he wouldn't even be able to find a person moving over the top of the rise, let alone shoot him.

He turned his head, trying to see if he could make out any sounds at all. There was a sound, but it was the white noise that his own head made when he didn't have the hearing aid in to drown it out. He had gotten used to wearing the hearing aid all the time except when they were actually shooting at the range. He had forgotten how deaf he really was.

He started, realizing that his concentration had wandered dangerously. He strained his eyes, but could see nothing moving that he could identify as alarming. Were these guys seriously trying to grow marijuana this close to populated areas? It seemed incongruous that they would be so haphazard about growing dope and then so murderous about protecting it. Maybe there was more to it and he just didn't see it yet.

Robert remembered to watch. He strained his eyes and stared into the darkness until he was convinced that there wasn't anything to see. If somebody was still trying to shoot

215

them, the guy was being awfully cautious about it. In the dark he could walk right up to within a few yards of them and stand there undetected if Jimbo didn't hear him. He could just wait for one of them to move and then shoot him in the dark or put a light on them that would blind them and then shoot them.

No way could they just sit here in the dark. They would have to get going one way or the other. He turned and, crouching with the rifle across his chest, moved forward along the side of the car. He whispered, "Jimbo, let's try this damn thing again." He was more concerned about letting Jimbo know not to shoot him than he was about telling him anything.

Jimbo didn't come around to him. He whispered louder. "Jimbo, come on!" He opened the passenger door and jumped into the car quickly to turn off the dome light. The window was down on the driver's side of the car and he stuck his head out. "Jimbo!" He turned the key in the ignition and could feel the car shake as the starter motor turned the engine over. He could hear that a little. It turned over quickly but then just as he was having hope for it, the motor slowed down and stopped. Now the battery was about dead. He thought the battery was at least four years old.

He pulled the keys out of the dash and opened the door quietly and got out. He could see Jimbo lying on the ground in front of the front tire. He could see his outline against the lighter color of the ground, on his side as though asleep. Robert bent down and picked up the Smith & Wesson and put it back in his holster. He shook Jimbo's shoulder and bent down near his head. "Jimbo, come on."

"Okay."

The voice was weak but at least he was awake. "Let's get moving." Jimbo just lay there. "Jimbo!"

"What?"

"Jimbo, can you stand up?"

"Okay."

But he lay still for a minute before he tried anything. Then he rolled partially to his hands and knees before his arm gave way. He would have rolled back onto the ground if Robert hadn't been holding him. Robert forced him backward until he was sitting up and leaned him against the tire. "Jimbo, come on. I need your ears."

"Okay."

"Okay. Can you just sit here a minute?"

"Yeah."

Robert patted him on the shoulder and then stood up. The stars were out now. Maybe in a little while there would be a moon, a little better light. He could see a lot better now than he could have just a few minutes before. Maybe it was being scared or maybe it was doing something other than just crouching, waiting to get shot. Never mind. He could see better. He felt with his hand under the seat of the Bronco. There was usually a flashlight down there but it had probably become dislodged in the wreck. It took him several minutes, feeling the sticky debris under the seat and on the floor of the car before he finally found the flashlight in the back. He shut the car door before he thought about it and jumped when he heard the noise. He paused and searched with his eyes for any sign of movement, but he didn't see any.

He squatted in front of Jimbo who was still leaned against the tire, but with his head hanging down. Robert tipped his head up and looked into his eyes with the flashlight. "Jimbo, wake up." He could see the eyebrows go up with the effort and then the eyes opened a little.

"Okay."

"Let me take a look at you, here. Hold your head up so I can see your eyes."

"Okay." Jimbo raised his head a little and struggled to keep his eyes open. One pupil looked bigger than the other, but Robert couldn't be sure. There were pools of purple discoloration now under both eyes and he could see the beginning of swelling at the top of Jimbo's forehead, the knot disappearing into the hair on the front of his head.

He heard the bullet hit the car before he heard the shot. Jimbo's eyes opened fully before Robert switched off the light and jerked him violently away from the car by one arm. He pulled him, half-dragging him away from the tire and heard another round go off somewhere in the dark. It was coming from up on the road, not in the woods. Without the hearing aid he could at least tell direction again if a sound was loud enough for him to hear it at all.

Jimbo got to his hands and knees and crawled laboriously forward. He understood that much, that they had to move. Robert got out the pistol and pointed it up at the road, watching for a movement. He didn't want to fire blindly and give away his location. He didn't know if the guy up there could see him, but he didn't think so. Jimbo continued to crawl so Robert backed up on his elbows and knees, dragging the rifle in one hand, the pistol in the other, watching for any movement that he could shoot at. Whoever was up there could surely hear them. If he fired again in the dark Robert wanted to be sure and see it this time so he could shoot back at the flash.

Instead of a man he saw a dog. The goddamn dogs. There was no way those dogs wouldn't find him in an instant. He raised the pistol, tempted to shoot the animal, thinking about the trade-off of giving himself away. Then he remembered this wasn't the only one. At least two dogs, maybe three had come running out at the car when they had pulled in. He only had five rounds in the pistol and he would probably miss a few times.

The dog, though, wasn't hunting. Robert could see it faintly as it trotted down to the car and sniffed around. It paused and he could imagine it pissing against the tire. Then it turned and trotted over to where he was, wagging its tail. The dog was a moron. Robert lay flat on the ground under the thin brush while the dog sniffed at him curiously from about five feet away. He put his hand out toward the dog and whispered as quietly as he could, "Good boy."

The dog fawned and came up and sniffed his hand. Then cocked its head low to have its ears scratched. The man on the road must have said something because the dog suddenly turned its head in that direction and listened. Then it broke into a gamboling run back the way it had come. Whatever this game was, at least *the dog* was having fun.

Robert crawled back to where Jimbo had finally collapsed. One of the other dogs was there, but showed no more understanding of what it was supposed to be doing than the other one had. It backed away from Robert and stood there watching. When Robert tried extending his hand again the dog sniffed but kept its distance, not sure what was going on but not so confident that it wanted to get within reach. The dog circled around and sniffed from the other side. "Good boy." This dog wasn't buying it. It woofed once, halfheartedly. Then it turned back to the road, ears cocked, listening.

No question, the man was still up there somewhere, but Robert couldn't see any movement. He lay still and watched. The dog trotted back to the road and disappeared from his sight in the direction of the car.

Then he saw something. It took him a minute to figure it out. Someone had raised the hood of the Bronco. The guy was disabling the car for sure. Robert lay prone, holding the pistol in both hands, trying to sight at the front of the hood. When he thought he had it about right he fired.

The man answered, firing back at Robert three times from different spots over and around the car. He was shooting wild in the dark, shooting by sound alone since he probably hadn't been looking Robert's way to see the muzzle flash. Robert held his fire, hoping to get a look at the guy. That first shot had been foolish with no clear target. Now the guy was peppering the countryside and he might get lucky and hit one of them.

Robert felt around near him on the ground and came up

with a fairly hefty rock. He rolled onto his back so that he could throw without rising and heaved it about fifteen yards. The guy fired again at the noise, but he was behind the car and Robert knew he couldn't have gotten a clear shot at him even in daylight. When he held the gun up, trying to sight, he could see it shake. He swore silently, feeling the sweat sticking his shirt to his back.

He maneuvered the rifle up into place against his shoulder, thinking that with his elbows braced against the ground he could hold it steadier. He tried looking through the scope again but all he could see were dim outlines bouncing every-where with his shaking hands. He lowered the rifle and took a deep breath, trying for calm. He could hear his own pulse if he let himself listen to it.

He cradled the rifle in his arms and concentrated on watch-ing. He realized that he had dropped the flashlight at some point. That was just as well. That's what the guy had fired at when Robert tried to get a look into Jimbo's eyes. If the guy found it and turned the light on, Robert thought, he could shoot him.

He tried to make himself more comfortable. He couldn't fully extend his legs because brush was in his way and there was a buried rock or hard piece of dirt under his chest and he couldn't seem to move off of it. He could see pretty well. His glasses were okay and he could hear a little. Not a whole lot, but a little. That was better than not hearing at all. Okay, if it just took waiting it out until dawn, he could manage that. He would have to stay awake and watch carefully. . . .

Suddenly light flooded his sight as the shadow of the hills passed off him. The moon had come up. For a moment the moonlight was so bright he thought he was exposed, but then he realized that he would not be seen from as close as the car, even. He looked up and saw it was a half moon. It looked like it was sitting on the top of the ridge line of the hills.

He wondered about Jimbo. He might be dead. He certainly

seemed to be on the way. The bullet might have broken his skull and he might be bleeding inside, blood running free over his brain. He better try not to think too much about that. He had to get Jimbo out of here as soon as possible, but for now he couldn't do any more about that than what he was doing.

He eased his way backward, trying not to disturb the brush too much. He came even with Jimbo's head and felt for his pulse. It was strong. The guy's neck was huge, maybe his heart was big too and would keep beating a long time. Maybe he would even wake up. Not likely. He wasn't just sleeping. He tried to turn his watch so that he could see it with the help of the moon. Eleven-thirty already. Jimbo was late for work.

TWENTY-ONE

Hour after hour dragged by, the stars rotating as they always had, the breeze picking up as it did every night, toward morning, the moon tracking, mocking him by its normalcy, Robert afraid, even to move.

He raised his head above the level of the surrounding brush to make sure that there was nothing to be seen. Not that there was nothing there, because he had no way to know that, just that he couldn't see anything.

But this time he saw movement.

Something moved near the road on the top of the rise against the sky. Robert rose up too quickly, reaching for the rifle in front of him. He had to be careful to move slowly, even hidden partially by the brush and maybe totally by the dark he didn't want to give away his best advantage, being hidden. He crawled, as low as he could get and still watch the spot where he had seen something, to a place where he could sit up with his back to the brush to break his silhouette. He felt unjustifiably sure that somebody was there.

He had only seen a movement for a second or two. He hadn't clearly seen the outline of a man, but he was sure that

that's what it was. Still moving slowly and without taking his eyes from the top of the road, Robert dug his heels into the hard clay of the ground. He carefully braced his arms, his elbows over the tops of his knees, and raised the rifle. He got into position to fire and held his head a little away from the scope so that he could see clearly around it to the area where he expected the man to appear.

For a long moment nothing happened. Then a light came on quickly and then off again. It was a strong flashlight beam that focused on the car just the briefest moment and then went out. Robert tried to mark the spot that he had seen the light with landmarks in the skyline of the hills behind him. He rotated the rifle to where it snuggled into his shoulder and laid his cheek on the stock. He looked through the scope and carefully scanned. He thought he saw something and held the rifle still.

Then he had a terrible thought. He couldn't tell who he was looking at. Suppose somebody heard the shooting earlier? Suppose the sheriff had been out and they just now found out there were some men down in the valley with a wrecked car. A deputy sheriff might very well come out here cautiously, being careful to look over the situation before he came strolling into a bullet. He could be up there now, calling out and Robert wouldn't know the difference.

He saw movement again. He looked through the scope and this time he was positive he was looking at a man, squatting just off the side of the road, just his head and shoulders visible above the brush. He was sitting still, watching, just like Robert was. He might even be watching him.

What if it was another lawman?

Robert wasn't ready for this. He wasn't prepared to have to make a decision about whether to blow somebody's lungs out or give up the advantage of his hidden location to identify who he was shooting. The unfairness struck him and he wanted to stand up and just call out, call off the game of hide-and-seek and just do something sensible like call a fucking ambulance, get the rescue guys out here to pick up the wounded man. He felt his muscles tense with the urgency of his need to stand up and put a stop to all of this; it was too much.

He settled his head against the rifle stock and looked again through the scope. He checked with his finger and the safety was off. He centered the head in the scope and held it there. He took a breath and held it, bringing his finger down to the trigger, feeling it lightly, making sure that he had it in his grip. He let out the air and watched. He took another and suddenly called out: "Police! Stand up right there and show your hands!"

Before he could finish the sentence the view in the scope blurred with the motion of the man leaping up. In the very top of the scope's field he saw the bright orange blossom of firing and Robert raised the sight and fired back, almost before he heard the sound of the shotgun. He felt a thump in his shoulder but he kept his face down on the stock, still holding onto the vision through the scope while his hand worked the bolt, rapidly ejecting the spent brass and slamming the new round into the chamber. The scope's field had gone gray. He could see nothing identifiable but the top of the brush where the man had been sitting. The field cleared. Smoke. He had been seeing smoke.

Robert couldn't see the man. He knew he had been hit, he had felt the thump. Couldn't be bad, it hadn't even knocked him off the target. How could it not be bad? No time for that.

Movement. The head again, just the top of it this time, moving to Robert's left, toward the center of the road and then gone, down below the line of the brush. Robert found the trigger again and stroked it gently with his finger to make sure he had it. He watched for movement in the brush, thinking of shooting under what was moving, shoot through the brush and finish him. All the guy had to do was crawl ten feet one way or the other without stirring up a lot of movement and he would be out of the field of view.

Robert held tight to the spot he had seen him last. A drop of sweat dripped into the corner of his eye, the one staring through the scope; he was afraid to blink. He had to. He squeezed his eyelid down and opened it. The stinging drop of sweat was worse. He ignored it.

Nothing moved.

Robert let out his breath and felt the shuddering unsteadiness of it, of his control of his own chest. Pain shot through him so fast and harsh he couldn't tell at first what hurt. It wasn't his shoulder; it was up high in the side of his chest. He couldn't feel pain in his shoulder at all, just a point that felt like somebody was holding a pencil against it, pushing a little. That was a lucky hit. Probably a single pellet. Just dumb luck at this distance with a shotgun with no target but a voice in the dark. Goddamn the bad luck!

Robert was still in a classic sitting position, the rifle at his shoulder, only his head raised a little to see over the scope.

Nothing moved.

Robert tried to take deeper breaths and hold them longer, control his breathing so he could control the motion of his chest and the pain. It made it worse.

The sky seemed lighter. He wasn't sure, but it seemed a little lighter. Some of the stars might have faded a little, but just a little. He couldn't see his watch here in the shadow but he thought he was beginning to see a little of the predawn.

Robert thought he'd better try to get himself to an unexpected position so that as the daylight came up he would know where the other guy was, approximately, but the guy wouldn't know where Robert was. If he thought about what he was doing, concentrated on moving slowly so that he didn't create a lot of movement in the brush, concentrate on that, he wouldn't feel the pain so much. Okay.

He raised his head and looked, holding as still as he could while he stared. He was as high as he needed to be. The spot he had moved to was only slightly elevated from the road, but it was enough; better than being below it.

Robert looked back at the road where he thought the man should be. It took him a long time to see him. The man had to move before he was visible. He was hunched over, seated, with his legs crossed in front of him. His body was facing toward Robert and his head turned to look at where Robert had been before he started his crawl. It had worked. He didn't know why, exactly, he was surprised, but he was.

He could see clearly now that it was Red Beard, the guy from the bar, the brother of the guy with the scar. What was Red Beard's name? He had to think, to try to remember before he shot him because this time it was going to be a clean shot in cold blood. Oh yeah. Larry.

Okay. He brought the stock to his shoulder and laid his armpit over his knee to brace. It hurt. He was leaning right on the wound in the top of the side of his chest. He concentrated on the target through the scope. He centered the scope as though the man's upper torso was the bull. He thought, *Okay, Larry.* He tightened on the trigger, squeezed his whole hand steadily until he knew it was too much. The safety. He took the safety off and settled back down on his knee. He took a breath, let it partway out and held it. He squeezed again.

In a split second he saw the arms fly out, spread-eagled as the big body flopped back. It didn't fly or jump, it just flopped over backward, arms out, legs still crossed.

Robert jerked the bolt open and closed in one motion, ready to shoot again. He waited but Red Beard didn't move. He looked dead, and Robert was as sure of that as he had ever been of anything. He couldn't hear his own pulse now. His ears were ringing, from the sound of the shot. He could hear the shot all right. The one bit of aural information that he didn't need, he had in abundance.

Robert lowered the stock of the rifle to the ground and sat back to wait. Red Beard wasn't going to move. He could practically smell it from the way he had gone backward. Robert watched for whoever else might be there. Where was the guy that got Larry into all this? The brother was probably home in bed, the son of a bitch.

Finally, Robert thought about Jimbo and although he would have liked to just sit still for a while to see if anything else developed, he knew he better push it a little. He better push it a lot.

He stood up and walked rapidly downhill toward the body. He came over the rise and saw that there was a pickup truck, not thirty yards from the top of the rise. The asshole had *driven* down here from the house. He might have kept the lights off, but he had driven down here where just about anybody else would have heard him. The dumb son of a bitch deserved to be shot just for that.

He walked over and looked down at Larry. The bullet hole was just to the left of the center of Larry's chest. Automatically, Robert thought, *Ten ring, nine o'clock.*

TWENTY-TWO

Robert looked back up toward the house and saw the man standing still, staring back at him. The dogs had come partway down to the pickup and were standing off, not sure what to do. Robert used the scope of the rifle to see the guy better. He couldn't have shot at him, that far away. *What the hell is he doing?* Robert thought.

When the man finally moved Robert saw he was wearing a cast. He seemed, even at the distance of a half a mile or so, to have a huge cast on his right leg and swung it awkwardly, with a great effort, to one side when he walked. Robert could see that he had a pistol of some kind in his hand. He shoved it in his belt as he hopped-walked.

Robert ran a few steps toward him and realized it was hopeless to try to do anything. He was too weak and it was just too far. Then he saw the Bel Air. The man went straight to it, threw the gun in and then had to work to get the cast into the car. He took off immediately, throwing dirt out behind the car in a cloud.

Jimbo. Oh, shit. Robert ran down to the pickup. The keys

were in it so he started it and drove down and parked even with where the Bronco sat in the brush to one side of the road. He walked down, looking carefully, but it took him a few minutes to find him. He thought they had been a long way toward the forest but they were never very far from the road at all. He must have shot at the guy that first time from about a hundred feet away in the dark.

Jimbo had turned over on his back. It took Robert a minute to realize that he'd moved and then the first thing he thought of was that something, an animal maybe, had moved him. But Jimbo was breathing in deep, steady respirations. His left arm was turned back under his body. Robert was elated.

"Hey, Jimbo." He thought he saw the eyelids flicker.

"Jimbo, can you hear me?" This time the eyes partly opened and then closed and his lips moved. "Jimbo, can you help me? I got to get you into the truck. Can you help?"

Jimbo opened his eyes and raised his head enough to look at the truck. He sighed deeply and closed his eyes again, letting his head drop back to the ground.

Robert thought for a minute, looking at the sheer bulk of his partner and the height of the bed of the pickup. He untangled his jacket from Jimbo and laid it over the top of a bush to have a marker that he could see from the cab and then backed the pickup down to it. Now all he had to do was lift him into the truck.

First, he got behind him and sat him up by grasping him under the arms and heaving, bracing him with his knee and then heaving again. Jimbo seemed to understand, all right. His eyes opened and he reached forward with his right arm to hold on to his leg and help himself sit there. His left arm hung down ominously. His head wobbled from side to side as though it had become too heavy for the huge neck to support.

Robert was sure that he couldn't do it and then just did. He turned purple with the effort but squatted to get under him and then hoisted Jimbo into the bed of the truck. Jimbo opened his eyes momentarily, but then he seemed to lose interest in what was going on and closed them again.

Robert drove slowly back up the road to the house, trying to feel the ground with the tires to avoid bouncing his cargo. He thought about driving on out with Jimbo in the back, to save time, but he didn't like the idea of getting on the freeway with Jimbo unconscious or confused in the open rear end. Besides, the gas gauge on the truck was indicating empty. The dogs greeted the truck, friendly at first and then startled that somebody strange was driving. They set off a confused barking racket that even Robert could hear. He found some shade to stop in and made sure that the tailgate was up before he went into the house and dialed 911.

He could hear a distant burr sound that he took to be the phone ringing. When it stopped he spoke without waiting to hear anything. "Listen, buddy, I'm very hard of hearing and my hearing aid's broke so you got to shout, understand?" He thought he heard an answer. "I said you got to speak up or I can't hear you! Anybody there?"

"I understand. Do you have an emergency that we can help you with?" The woman on the line pitched her voice as low as possible and spoke loudly, slowly and distinctly. Robert closed his eyes in gratitude. He could have kissed her trainer.

"I'm a Martin police officer. I have a one eighty-seven and a four-oh-six." Those were the codes for a homicide and "officer needs emergency help."

"All right." She shouted back. There was a short hesitation. "Ten-four. Are you hurt?"

"My partner's been shot in the head." He had forgotten his own wound. It took him a minute to give directions and then he went outside and checked on Jimbo. He seemed to be sleeping but didn't respond this time when Robert tried to rouse him. He realized that emergency services, even the Highway Patrol, would take a while to respond out here. The two dogs hung back at the door, one of them periodically deciding to bark, confused at being ignored. The other one, the moron that had come up to him in the dark, followed him around, apparently hoping for some food.

The dog's attitude reminded Robert that he hadn't eaten in a long time and he went back into the house to see what might be there. He pushed on the door with his left arm and pain shot through the shoulder and down through his chest. He was surprised. He hadn't even looked. He tried then to find the entrance wound through his shirt. He could just feel it, a tiny hole in the back of his shoulder. The real pain was coming from his upper side and he could tell that the pellet had passed through the muscle of the shoulder and hit him there. He couldn't tell for sure, but with his fingers it felt like the hole under his armpit was between the ribs. He took a deep breath and that worked all right. His lungs must be okay.

He was light-headed and groggy, but he had been up all night and was hungry so that didn't tell him anything. He decided he wasn't hurt bad.

The inside of the house looked to Robert like a chaotic portrait of poverty. Floorboards were weakened and sagged under him. There were two metal folding chairs and an ancient Formica table to one side when he walked in. There was no other real furniture. The kitchen sink was next to the table and over that there was a window through which the morning sun flowed in abundance. Somebody had designed that cheerful opening, but it wasn't either of the current occupants. MacDonald took a deep drink of water, cupping his hand under the faucet, and then found a cup and carried some out to Jimbo. He was still unconscious so he didn't try to pour it down him. Somebody would be here soon.

When Robert went back into the house the first thing he saw was a half-empty box of 9 mm ammunition. Live rounds were scattered on the tabletop as though somebody had grabbed a handful and fled. He decided he better look for the

9 mm weapon so he could tell the other cops that the man was armed for sure. He assumed that he wouldn't find it.

He opened the door that led to the tacked-on trailer but it was full of boxes of junk, broken furniture and even a couple of old bicycles. Other than that there was only one bedroom with two mattresses on the floor and an old sleeping bag thrown in another corner. There was an ancient bureau, with splitting veneer and a footlocker.

Robert opened the bureau, one drawer at a time. There was old laundry, maybe twenty or twenty-five T-shirts and several old pairs of jeans, but nothing that struck Robert as unusual or particularly enlightening.

He reached down and flipped open the top to the footlocker. He froze, staring inside and then he slowly knelt down, staring into the stacks of folded clothes and cardboard cartons. He could see the butt of a pistol, sticking up between two cartons. He used his shirttail to keep his fingerprints off of it and gingerly lifted it between his thumb and forefinger. He held it up, stared at it and then sat down next to the footlocker on the floor.

He was holding a Colt Cobra. He didn't know the serial number from memory, but even without looking at it there wasn't the slightest question in his mind that this was Terry's gun. He turned it over and stared at it as though it might tell him something.

He carefully replaced it in the footlocker, trying to get it as nearly in the same position that it had been in as he could. Then he thought better of it and carried it back to the front of the house and placed it on the table next to the 9 mm ammunition. He went back to the footlocker and lifted the lid to the box nearest where he had found the gun. There was a newspaper clipping on top and he caught the headline: "FIERY CRASH ENDS POLICE CHASE." He recognized it as the article about Sheila's chase where the two boys had burned up in the wreck. He pulled out the clipping, careful not to tear it, and laid it on the floor next to him. In ballpoint somebody had scrawled "Missed!" across the top. He stared, thinking about it. Out loud he said, "Goddamn."

He pulled out another newspaper clipping that he didn't see any significance to and laid it aside to look at later. Under the clipping he immediately recognized a police Incident Report. He lifted the whole box out then and stared at the report that was now on the top, trying to tell why it was so familiar.

Robert's scalp felt prickly, his cheeks felt like they were weighted down and his eyes blurred momentarily. Out loud he said, "Who the fuck is this guy?" He rubbed his hand over his face and tried to clear his head. It was the police Incident Report about Melody Arneson's death. He hadn't seen the report before, but it was Farrela's handwriting and that was what had looked so familiar.

He was suddenly too agitated to sit still and stood up to go outside again. As soon as he stood he felt like he might fall back down to the floor. He waited until his head cleared, then walked out to the back of the pickup and checked on Jimbo. He didn't seem to have moved in the time that Robert was inside the house. Jimbo was still breathing deeply and regularly and the pulse was still pounding in his neck. There just didn't seem to be anything else that Robert could do for him until the paramedics got there. Robert stood next to him and wished that he could talk, tell him what he thought about all this. What the hell was going on, anyway?

Robert went back into the house and returned to the open footlocker. He took the lid off another carton and looked in. Inside, there was a smaller box from a bank, with several new books of checks. The name printed on them was Gregory Arneson, with an address in Martin. Under the box of checks was a bundle of pay stubs from Rickenhauer's Cadillac, a big agency in downtown Martin. The pay stubs were also made out to Greg Arneson.

Robert lifted out the carton and rummaged quickly in the

footlocker until he found what he was looking for. It was in a padded jewelry box from which the inside partitions had been removed. There were several photographs and a stack of report cards from a high school in Martin, tied up with a rubber band. The top report card was more than a year old and it was for a senior, Melody Arneson. Then there were the photographs.

Robert didn't want to let himself dwell on these for longer than it took him to see what they were. They seemed to all be snapshots of a young girl. In the pictures, as he flipped through them, she was laughing, hugging a dog, pouring something out of a pan in the kitchen with her hair hanging down in her face, spraying at the camera with a garden hose. Then Robert's hands stopped. It was a photograph of the girl in the cap and gown of her high school graduation, standing next to a beaming, proud man in his mid-fifties. Robert took off his glasses and brought the photograph close to his eyes. He could see the scar that ran from the corner of the man's grinning mouth down his chin. He quickly put the pictures down and pushed the footlocker away from him.

Farrela's report was dog-eared, as though Greg Arneson had studied it over and over. As the father of the victim, Arneson would have been entitled to a copy of the Incident Report, just by asking for it. Holding it, though, Robert thought that it was too heavy, too bulky for what it was. He turned to the back of it and saw that somebody, maybe Trudy, maybe another cop, had accidentally copied more than they were supposed to out of the Homicide file that this report would have been kept in. It was Farrela's and Goldman's memorandum of speculation about the case, not even an official document. It was just their rambling notes to themselves or any other Homicide detective that might pick up the file and want to know what was really going on, what they really thought.

In this memo Terry was clearly identified as the one most

likely to have hit her, but that was no surprise. Robert was identified by name. What for? Just to mention that he was Terry's father? What did they think, that he could cover something up? Apparently Arneson thought there was something significant about it because he had underlined Robert's name so hard that the pen had broken through the paper.

Then toward the end, there was a whole paragraph dedicated to Kevin. The cops hadn't believed his story. Just as Kevin had thought, they speculated that he was the one that had sex with the victim. They speculated, as Kevin had said, that it could have been after she was unconscious. Obviously the detectives thought that nobody outside the department would see this memo and then some idiot had copied it without reading it and handed it out with the Report of Incident.

Even though there was nothing new in the documents, Robert found himself shocked, seeing them the way the girl's father must have seen them. It looked like a callous, cynical conspiracy to hide the facts of a rape and murder with the whole damned MacDonald family involved.

He didn't want to, but he reached over and picked up the photographs again. The man looked tired. There were deep lines in his cheeks and around his eyes, but he looked happy and the way his mouth was open as he was smiling, he might have been saying something just as the picture was taken. His arm was tight around the girl's waist, her arm around his.

Robert put the photographs down and picked up the clipping that he hadn't read yet. It was recent, just last Thursday's campus newspaper. It was about one of Kevin's teachers, probably one of Melody's teachers too, Robert thought. The professor, Cortland Peterson, had acted in New York on the stage and had written poetry, published in *The New Yorker.* That was apparently why they had hired him at State and why the paper had done the article. Since Peterson didn't have seniority with the rest of the faculty, he got stuck with an eight o'clock class three days a week that most of the students would usually be expected just to skip, except the article said that Peterson had standing room only.

Robert carried the clipping into the kitchen, sat in one of the folding chairs and held his head between his hands. What had the guy been looking for in this stuff? He looked back at the article and his eye fell on Kevin MacDonald's name and an innocuous quote about how great he thought Professor Peterson was. Robert's hand dropped away from his face and he stared. His mind racing, he scanned back to the spot in the middle of the article where they talked about the schedule. The class was Monday, Wednesday, and Friday, 8:00 A.M. What the fuck day was this? Thursday? No they came out here last night, Thursday, late afternoon. Today would be Friday. He looked at his watch and it showed 7:35 A.M.

Robert walked out to check on Jimbo again. His breathing was unchanged and he still wasn't responding, not even as well as he had when Robert loaded him onto the truck. Robert thought he might be hearing a siren. Normally, he couldn't hear anything in the upper registers. High-pitched noises were hard for him, even with the hearing aid. Once in a while, though, for no rational reason that he could identify, he would hear something. An electronic beep or a child's whistle, something that by rights he shouldn't hear at all. He listened, trying to tell if he was imagining it or if there was a siren out there, just at the edge of his hearing.

He looked at his watch—7:39. As the sun rose, the shade that Jimbo was in was moving and he would have to move the truck pretty soon to keep him out of the direct sun. He got behind the wheel and started the truck. He looked around the yard for more shade, but didn't move for a while. He sat there thinking, without moving. Finally, he backed it to the door of the house.

He got down from the cab and stared in the direction of the driveway and the highway out beyond, out of his vision. He couldn't wait. He opened the tailgate and pulled Jimbo as gently as he could to the edge and then lifted him and half dragged him inside the house. Quickly, beginning to hurry now that he knew he was going to do it, he chased the dogs out of the house, made sure the door wasn't locked and then closed it behind him. He stopped then, trying to think, trying to make his fatigued brain come awake, goddammit. He went back inside and, using his shirttail again, brought the Colt out and put it down near Jimbo along with the police report with its damning memorandum attached, the checkbooks and the articles about the car fire and the English teacher. Surely, anybody that came along would find these things and figure out what he, MacDonald, was doing. He thought about leaving a note but when he couldn't immediately find a pen to write with he dropped the idea and went back outside.

The pickup was a black Dodge, ten or fifteen years old and several years older than that in abuse. The seats were torn and the passenger door was wired shut. It had been recently jury-rigged with a hand control for the throttle, no doubt so the one with the broken leg could operate it. Still, it managed to accelerate reasonably well and Robert had to fight to keep from bouncing right off the narrow lane that served as a driveway. He reached the mailbox and searched rapidly for an opening in traffic so that he could keep going without stopping. He saw the Highway Patrol coming and had to brake hard to get stopped. He got his wallet out and waved his badge out the window, sticking his head and shoulders out. When the patrol car came even and stopped, he shouted, knowing that he wouldn't hear a reply.

"My partner's wounded bad in the house there at the end of the drive."

The county ambulance was right behind the Highway Patrol so the officers waved and shot into the driveway, the ambulance bouncing in behind them.

As soon as he picked up speed on the highway, Robert

checked the gas gauge. The needle was so far down that it wasn't even moving. He pulled off at the Gulf station and had removed the nozzle from the pump before he thought about how he looked.

He knew he had blood on his shirt but he hadn't bothered to try to pull it around so that he could see. He was also wearing his gun. He shoved the nozzle in and started pumping gas, glancing around to see who was watching. There was nobody outside the little store so he would have to go inside to pay. He had barely pumped in two dollars' worth when the pump shut off. Of course. The fucking gauge was broken. Had plenty of gas.

Robert walked into the store feeling more self-conscious than he had in years. There was a young woman behind the register with hoop earrings that looked to be about four inches across. She was reading a magazine and chewing gum like it might be the most important thing she did all day. She gave him a bored glance when he came in and looked at the console that told her what to charge. She never looked at him again, directly, so she didn't notice what he looked like at all. He had counted out his change as he walked up so he could just set it on the counter, turn and go back out without saying anything.

A station wagon had pulled up to the pump on the side opposite the truck. The two men inside stared at him openly. He thought they probably knew that truck and were trying to place him. He ignored them and got back in the cab and sped off. He glanced in the mirror and saw one of them standing next to the pump, watching him as he went off down the highway.

He tried to think what he was worried about. All they would do would be to call the sheriff or Highway Patrol to stop him and check it out. He thought that might be better, anyway. If they stopped him he would just tell them to call ahead to Campus Security or Martin P.D. to watch for this guy coming to Kevin's eight o'clock class with this guy Peterson.

If they believed that that's what he was doing. He was sure they would believe him, eventually, but they would be hesitant, want to make sure this guy wasn't some old nut, out of his head from the wound and being out all night in the brush. At first, they wouldn't want to alarm the city cops until they were pretty solid that this was a legitimate concern. It might work out all right, but he thought he just couldn't take the chance of their being too slow. He figured he could be at the campus in half an hour if he pushed it and he better just go there first.

His vision blurred briefly and he wiped his face with his hand, trying to clear it. For a split second he couldn't remember what he was trying to do and then he was okay again, coming into the edge of Martin already. He was surprised at how fast he got there and wondered for a wild second if he had slept at the wheel on the way in. He realized that his hands ached from gripping it so tightly, that his teeth were clenched and he was leaning so far forward that his chin was almost on the wheel.

He leaned back, trying to make himself relax, settle down. He still had a ways to go and through traffic. "Goddamn," he said out loud, "you are getting old." He woke himself up trying to watch in all directions at once, hoping to see a familiar face in a patrol car and get immediate help. Then he was wishing for any patrol car, even one with some snotty kid that would be hard to convince. It was 8:10.

He got off the freeway at the downtown exit and then accelerated out Folsum. Speeding up to fifty on a main artery, he was hoping that he would attract attention. As he went through the tunnel at the Demming overpass he realized that at fifty he was only holding his own with the rest of the traffic.

He turned left on Twenty-seventh Avenue and floored it, looking simultaneously in his mirror, out the windshield and up every side street, looking for a black-and-white. Of course, nothing. It was 8:20.

When he got to the other side of the park he was close enough to the school that he no longer wanted to be pulled over. He shot through a red light at Kirby and kept going. He tore past the traffic waiting to turn into the shopping center at Stonestown, using the old streetcar tracks' raised right of way, and then bore down on the entrance of the university, tantalizingly close ahead.

He knew exactly where he was going. Andrews Hall, the English Department's building, was at the other end of the block, past Administration and this time he wasn't looking for parking. He slid the pickup to a stop in the street in front of the building and jumped out without shutting it off. It rolled slowly forward by itself as he ran around the back and into the building, drawing his gun as he ran.

He slid on the polished wooden floor inside and crashed into a wall. He could hear screams, sounding like they came from a long way off. He knew, though, that they had to be close for him to hear them. He ran down the hall, hearing more voices yelling, not able to make out what they said. He saw the sign next to the door that said "Cortland Peterson, Visiting Professor," heard more young voices screaming and crashed through it without stopping.

Inside, the classroom was not in chaos. The students were all at their desks and the teacher at the front. Everything was normal except that they were staring at him, at Robert, *startled and frightened half out of their wits by him.* His knees buckled and he tried to catch the side of a student desk. He held onto the edge and fought to look around, but the student stood up and the desk turned over in Robert's hand. He saw the floor coming right up at him until it hit him, hard.

Robert tried to rise, but could tell that he wasn't getting up, his eyes closed. He felt someone grab his wrist and pull the gun out of his hand. Kevin's voice, close to him, said, "Dad?"

TWENTY-THREE

Sheila gave Hank a warning look. She was good at those. The look showed no overt hostility, but no real amiability, either. It was a look that should have told him volumes: "Don't fuck around here, I'm serious about this, I'll explain it all in a minute, just chill out until I'm ready and we'll go." The whole message was delivered with the slightest beginning of a smile that wasn't really smiling, added to the cold, steady look of the eye, making direct eye contact.

Dombrowski missed it all because he was staring at her tits.

Sheila thought she couldn't hit him yet because she had only just now been assigned to work with him and she was determined to prove that she could work with *anybody.* "Hank, just a minute, okay? Aren't you even a little curious?"

"So, a couple a guys are late for roll call. Big deal."

"Neither one of 'em's ever late for anything, Hank."

"Big fuckin' deal." In fact, he knew she was right and he was plenty curious as to what excuse they would have for both of them being late. But Dombrowski had decided as soon as Ryan told him he would be partnered with her that he had to establish who was boss. They were the same age, but he had five years seniority on her at the department and she better not forget it. Jesus, though, what a rack!

Sheila dumped her equipment on top of the paper debris that already covered the sergeant's desk and picked up Ryan's phone. She used Ryan's phone list and punched out the number. No answer at MacDonald's house. She punched out Jimbo's number. Nothing. She let it ring.

Ryan walked up, looking at her equipment on his desk. "You calling Jimbo?"

She nodded and continued to let it ring.

"I already tried both of 'em. They probably went to dinner together and lost track of the time or had a flat or something. They'll be here."

"They would have called."

"They'll be here. Look, the only reason I asked at roll call is that Foster, from Homicide, wants to talk to one of 'em. Come on, Sheila, we got three house fires out here already tonight, and I'm one car short. We need everybody out. I'm even going out myself in a few minutes."

"No!"

"Come on, Sheila, it's gonna be a long night anyway."

"Okay, just one more number." She punched out Martha Mease's number from memory. Martha was a friend of Sheila's, a nurse, who had dated Jimbo a few times and who Sheila kept hoping would latch onto him. In a few rings she got Martha's answering machine so she hung up without leaving a message and punched out the number of the nurse's desk at Mission Emergency.

Sergeant Ryan looked dismayed. "Sheila, will you let me do that?"

"Okay, this'll just take a second."

Dombrowski had already put his gear in the car and he came back in with his hat on. He looked at Ryan. "Who's she calling?"

"Hello, Martha? Oh, could I speak to Martha Mease, please?"

"Jesus Christ, Sheila, are you calling your friends?"

"I'm trying to locate my partner. Do you mind? . . . Martha?"

Dombrowski looked at Ryan again. "She's calling one of her friends at the hospital."

"Will you fucking back off a minute! Sorry, hey, you heard from Jimbo? He hasn't shown up at the station yet."

Dombrowski turned his back on her. He was three times her size and had seniority on her and here she was cursing him in front of everybody. And at the beginning of the goddamn shift. Out loud, he said, "Cunts," and looked knowingly at Ryan, who decided it would be better all around not to hear.

Sheila was still talking into the phone. "Okay. No . . . they probably had a flat or something. No, I'm sure he's fine. I'll let you know . . . sure." She hung up the phone.

Ryan was standing right next to her, watching. "She know anything?"

"Not a damn thing!"

"Hey, don't blame me."

Sheila closed her eyes and shook her head. "Sorry." She looked at him, trying to impress him with her seriousness. "It's just not like either one of 'em to be late, not to anything."

Ryan dropped his voice low and leaned toward her. "You sure you don't need a couple more days off?"

"No, I'm fine. I thought you were short."

"Well, I am, but . . ."

"Well, that's why I'm here. I'm fine."

"Great! Let's get this show on the road!" Dombrowski seemed to be trying to make peace, grinning at her. He looked at Ryan. "That's what MacDonald says when he thinks it's time to go somewhere. 'Let's get this show on the road!' just like that."

Sheila picked up her equipment and Ryan busied himself, seeing to it that his papers had not been badly disturbed. Sheila breezed past, heading for the door. "I'm driving."

"Wait a minute, I drive."

"I called it first."

"I always drive." He was beginning to get pissed about it. Sheila turned around in the parking lot, teasing. "I'll flip ya for it."

"I always drive."

"Me too. You wanta flip?"

Art Kennedy and George Simon pulled up next to their car on the way out of the lot. "Hey, Sheila, where's Jimbo?"

She shrugged. "Got me."

Dombrowski opened the trunk and took the shotgun out to put it in the rack. "What's the matter, he owe you money?"

George ignored him. "He just didn't show up?"

"Guess not."

"Did anybody call his house?"

"Yeah. MacDonald's not here either."

"You gotta be kidding!"

"He owe you money, too?"

Art Kennedy leaned over from the driver's side. "You mean you two are working partners tonight?"

Sheila laughed and rolled her eyes to indicate it was all right. Dombrowski stared at him. "What's that mean?"

Art chuckled. "Nothing. See ya later." They took off.

Dombrowski looked at Sheila. "What'd he mean by that?"

"Nothing, Hank. You want to flip a coin, see who drives?"

"No, what the fuck. You drive." Anyway, he thought, if he was nice to her, this could be interesting.

She jumped into the car with enthusiasm. "Redstone?"

He grinned. "Redstone." That meant they would cruise through the projects before they did anything else. They weren't particularly looking for anything, just being visible and available. After that the routine was to cover the whole district once and then, if nothing was going on, back to the projects for another drive through and then maybe a cruise down Third, looking for drunks on the road.

They were halfway through their second drive through at Redstone when it occurred to Sheila that Hank Dombrowski was being unusually agreeable. He was letting her pick their routes, not arguing about anything.

He smiled at her from the passenger side. "Where would you like to eat, later on?"

She thought, *oh-oh.* She said, "I don't care, you name it."

"It doesn't have to be the Silver Dime, if you want to go someplace else." He was using his soft, solicitous voice, the one reserved for good-looking young "girls" that he liked to pull over to get a better look at.

Sheila thought, *Okay, here it comes.* Out loud she said, "I like the Silver Dime. That's fine with me."

"Well, I thought you might like to go to Stars or something."

"It closes at two." She tried to imagine if any cop in uniform would inflict himself on Stars even if he could afford it. Besides, cops went to the Silver Dime, especially ones like Dombrowski. The chief had sent out an order that nobody could accept gratuities of any kind and everybody knew that meant the Silver Dime. Before the order the owner would try to feed the entire night watch in there because it made him feel safer. Now, the hamburgers weren't free, but if you were in uniform, they were huge and the fries were piled on. Pie managed to make it to you and get accidentally left off the tab. It was a very popular place for the cops at night. "You want to take dinner break, now?" It was only two-thirty and they had a long way to go to the end of the shift.

He looked at his watch, wisely. "Well, it is a little early. We could take a cruise through Amherst Park first."

That was outside their sector and outside the whole Southern district.

"Actually, I am hungry. Let's go ahead and eat early."

He sighed and looked out his window.

They were taking it easy, rolling out an empty Folsum Boulevard, when the radio dispatcher said, "Four-nineteen at

One-oh-two Grambling at Folsum, anybody in the area to respond, please."

That was a fight with weapons *at the Silver Dime.* Hank was on the radio immediately. "Five Charley four, we got it!" He screamed at Sheila, "Hit it, goddammit!"

They were only two blocks away, but there was already one patrol car ahead of them. Sheila jerked to a halt right in front of one of the entrances. They could see an officer going in the far side of the dining room and a young Vietnamese man standing in the middle of the aisle between the tables, furious, yelling his head off, in his hand a dull table knife that he was waving around, threateningly. He didn't look like he could weigh more than ninety pounds or so.

Dombrowski was out of the car before it stopped and crashed through the door like he was after a mass murderer. More patrol cars were pouring into the small parking lot and more cops pounded for the doors while Sheila sat there and watched. The first cop to reach the little Vietnamese snatched the hand that held the knife and jerked the man completely off his feet. Dombrowski made a leaping tackle that looked like a rhinoceros hitting a pygmy, his momentum taking the other cop down, too. The slower cops made dramatic-looking dives, piling on until there was a jumble of flying arms, legs and handcuffs in all directions. If they had been in the NFL, the cops would have been penalized about three hundred yards. It was a clear error in judgment to create a disturbance in the Silver Dime.

Sheila sat in the car and watched, waiting to let things calm down. Now, besides having to arrest what was left of the guy that started it all, the cops were dealing with two irate women who had seen the whole thing and were trying to get everybody's badge numbers. A couple of older-looking cops pulled out their pads and listened to the women, nodding in sympathetic agreement and offering to get the badge numbers for them. One of the waitresses was trying to get a plate of eggs and sausage off the floor and another was offering anybody she could distract free coffee. Patrol cars continued to come into the lot, but when they realized that they were too late and saw the mob of police in the dining room, the angry women, they turned around and drove out, hoping not to be identified.

Sheila picked up the Auto hot sheet and added a car that had just come over the radio, a blue '71 Bel Air, and the license number. Homicide wanted to know about it if anybody saw it. Sheila raised her eyebrows. *Homicide?*

Not knowing there might be a connection, she went to a pay phone and called Southern Station. Nobody knew anything about MacDonald or Phillips. Foster came on the line. "They say anything to you about where they might be going?"

Sheila was surprised that Foster was even down there. "Not a thing. I haven't even talked to them in several days."

"Okay, thanks." The detective hung up without saying anything about why he wanted the Bel Air or even that it had anything to do with the missing cops. Sheila had forgotten about the car already. She called Mission Emergency but Martha couldn't come to the phone. No, there was no way to call back, she said, she would call her again, later.

Two hours after the incident at the Silver Dime Dombrowski got Sheila to pull into an alley so he could piss. He did it right beside the car while Sheila wondered why in the hell some men thought it was sexy to piss in front of a woman. She had thought he would at least walk off a few feet into the dark. When he suggested, again, that they check out the park, she told him to fucking knock it off and pay attention to what they were supposed to be doing.

It took him a few minutes to get over his huff and after that he was all right. She decided that he wasn't all that bad for somebody with all the subtlety and mental acuity of a Brahma bull. She decided to try to be civil, at least until the end of the watch. They transported a pair of juveniles from Company C to Juvenile Hall. Then, since it was close to the end of the shift and nothing was going on, decided to go back to the Silver Dime and have some almost-free coffee. It was full light by then.

Back on Folsum, anticipating the coffee, they got behind the Bel Air about the time they passed Webster. If the guy hadn't made a right turn out of the wrong lane, Sheila might not have even noticed him.

By that time traffic had already picked up on Folsum so Sheila had to reach down and flick on the overhead light bar and even touch the siren a couple of times to get across traffic and take off after him. Dombrowski shook his head. "Big deal, Sheila."

"That car was added to the hot sheet."

"Yeah?" That woke him up. You never knew what might happen when you pulled over a stolen car. You might get the owner, all pissed off because the cops hadn't figured out that he got the car back, but you might actually catch the car thief or something even more fun.

The Bel Air turned left a block ahead of them and Sheila followed, hesitant to make a chase out of it. The Bel Air was making jerky movements whenever he had to use the brake and slow down so Sheila and Hank were both becoming convinced that the driver was intoxicated and probably dangerous. When she made the turn, though, it was clear that he was trying to avoid them and she goosed it. He turned back toward Folsum. This time, when she made the turn after him, she put on the siren and went after him more seriously. A half a block ahead, he didn't even slow down. He gunned it down to the corner and ran the light, turning right into the flow of traffic out Folsum.

When they turned the corner, coming onto Folsum after him, they were in all-out pursuit, Hank on the radio calling the code and the car's description. The Bel Air was going full-out, too, smoke puffing out of the exhaust as he raced the engine, squeezed by the right side of an empty school bus and tore up the exit ramp at Grambling. The school bus pulled its front end to the curb and momentarily blocked the ramp to the patrol car, the driver blissfully unaware of anything going on around him. Hank turned on the switch to the Public Address mode. "Get your ass over! Turn to your right! I said to your right! Your *right,* dummy!" The bus driver finally woke up, pulled sharply to his right and stopped on the ramp without going far enough to bring the bus parallel with the edge of the road. The bus completely blocked the ramp for the patrol car and sat there while Hank put the driver into a deeper state of paralysis. "You dumb son of a bitch! You idiot! Pull up! Move! Move! Move! I said *move,* goddammit!" The driver of the school bus sat there and looked around, unable to see the patrol car directly behind the bus and bewildered by the obscenities. He was even more startled to hear a female voice, Sheila's, on the same PA mike. "Please move your bus forward. Move the bus forward, you are blocking the road." He jammed the gears. He double-clutched and finally got it right, slowly easing the bus forward until the released patrol car shot by him.

Sheila ran through the stop sign at the top of the ramp and then immediately slowed down. No Bel Air. He was gone and they had no idea which way. To their right Grambling ran past the Muni main offices. To their left was a possibility of a U-turn or the entrance to the Sears parking lot. A block ahead was the Silver Dime and another major intersection where the side road rejoined Folsum, so Sheila rolled up that way, switching off the siren and overhead flashers. No Bel Air.

Sheila rolled the patrol car into the middle of the intersection and the two of them swiveled their necks in all directions, trying vainly to see the car. A block ahead of them, to the west, there was a little boy jumping up and down on the sidewalk, waving his arms and legs frantically, trying to get their attention. They ignored him. They didn't have time for public relations at the moment. The boy began to run toward them and then stopped, jumped up in the air again and made a sweeping gesture over his head with his arm, beckoning them toward him. They sat there and looked around. Another schoolboy came running out of the side street and joined the first. Soon they were yelling in unison to magnify their voices. *"Po-lice-man! Po-lice-man! Acc-i-dent!"*

That got them. They decided to give up the Bel Air and see what was going on. Hank called off the code. The next intersection was with a dead-end street to the right. The Bel Air had made it three-quarters of the length of the block before he realized it. He had tried to do something that the Chevy couldn't do and wound up hitting a parked car and going out of control. The Bel Air was stopped across the sidewalk, the front end accordioned into the side of an apartment building.

Sheila was in no hurry now. She casually drove up to within twenty-five feet of the car. They could see the driver, upright with the back of his head to them, doing something with whatever was on the seat next to him. Sheila got out and stood for a moment next to the patrol car, hitching her utility belt and stretching. Then she searched her back pockets for her ticket book and notepad.

Hank dutifully reported the accident and called for a four-boy to do the report since there was probably enough damage to the building to justify it. Then it occurred to him to call for a tow truck to haul away the car after they arrested the scuzz-ball at the wheel.

When he got around to it he looked through the windshield and his eyes popped wide open. Sheila was standing just outside the wrecked car, her feet braced wide apart and her gun in both hands pointed at the driver's head. Dombrowski snatched the shotgun out of the brackets and raced up to her. The driver, an older white man with a scar running down from the corner of his mouth, held both hands up where they could see them. He had a Luger in one hand. While Hank held the shotgun's muzzle in his ear Sheila reached in and disarmed him.

TWENTY-FOUR

The first thing that MacDonald was fully aware of was that somebody had a grip on his hand. He tried to pull it away, but he could tell that his effort was no more than a feeble tug so he quit trying. He tried to open his eyes, but when his lids came up, even a little, the light was too much and he scrunched them closed again. He could not hear much, but he thought he faintly heard a female voice.

It seemed to him that some amount of time passed, and then he tried to retrieve his hand again. It was still confined. His eyelids arched and strained as he tried to open his eyes. This time when he got them open a little he saw a woman's face, close to his and coming right at him. He closed his eyes again and something pressed wetly on his mouth. He was aware that there was a papery feeling to it and there was something hard that pressed into his lip, but on the corner of his mouth he felt the contact of flesh. He lay there for a while thinking about it. He realized that he had been kissed. His eyes opened.

He was on his back on a bed. There was a woman sitting next to the bed with his hand trapped in both of hers, the fingers intertwined with his, pressing the back of his hand to her chest between her breasts. She gave him a huge, showy smile. "How you feeling?" He could just hear her. She kissed the back of his hand and laughed for no apparent reason. His eyes closed.

Robert thought he must be dreaming because it was Suzanne Lynch. Then he thought, *Shit! It's Suzanne Lynch!* He opened his eyes and she was still beaming at him, tears beginning to pool but not quite falling yet, her mouth looking twisty like she was about to let go and just barely holding it back. She said something else but she was whispering and he couldn't hear it. He closed his eyes again.

He was vaguely aware that some amount of time had passed and that Suzanne had his hand in hers. No, someone had his wrist. He opened his eyes and the nurse looked at him. "How you doin', cowboy? You finally gonna wake up?" He looked around but Suzanne, if she had ever been there, was gone.

The nurse bent over the bed, bringing her head close to his. "You are in Kettering Memorial Hospital. You're in the PAR."

He smiled. "What's par around here?"

"It's P-A-R. Post Anesthetic Recovery. You've been in surgery."

"Okay, fine." He closed his eyes again for a moment, trying to orient. He remembered being in the classroom at State and falling down. He felt the nurse move whatever covering had been on him and press a cold stethoscope against his skin. She moved it several times, then wrapped a blood pressure cuff around his upper arm and inflated it. He thought she should let him alone for a few minutes, anyway. He opened his eyes suddenly. "There was another guy, another cop, a great big guy . . ."

The nurse smiled. "I don't know about that. I just know about you, cowboy, and you look like you're doin' pretty good, considering."

Before he could get any more explanation than that, another woman came. The nurse gave her room so she could get to the bed. This one exposed his upper torso and he could see that his left side was taped up to his armpit. When this one prodded him it hurt. She slid one hand under him and rolled him toward her so that she could get to his back, holding the stethoscope low against his ribs. "Take a deep breath slowly and then let it out." He complied but he was beginning to feel irritable.

"I'm Dr. Donna Trunkey. I'm your surgeon, you understand?"

He was surprised, but he said he understood. "You have to speak up."

The doctor pulled a chair up to the edge of the bed and straddled it backwards, like a man. "You got shot, right? You remember that?"

"It's a little hard to forget a thing like that."

"Right. Well, I guess it was a shotgun pellet, buckshot. Just one of them hit you."

"Did you save it?"

"What?"

"Did you save the shotgun pellet?"

"It's in a plastic bag, labeled with my initials and passed on to a cop. There's cops all over the place, wanted to come right in and take it out themselves because they didn't think I'd remember to save it. Don't you guys trust anybody?" She laughed as though that were a good joke.

He smiled and closed his eyes. They weren't going to get much out of a shotgun pellet for ballistics. He could imagine the disappointment on Farrela's face when he saw that it was just a piece of buckshot.

"Sergeant MacDonald, let me just tell you what's going on with you, then you can go back to sleep, okay?"

"Okay." He opened his eyes again.

"The pellet passed through this muscle here"—she pinched the corner of his shoulder on the good side—"and went into your chest right here." She dug the tip of her finger between his ribs, but it didn't convey much information to him. She saw his puzzled look and raised her jacket to show her own underarm. She was wearing a sleeveless blouse and he could see the rounded softness of the edge of her breast above and behind her bra. She seemed oblivious to that part of her anatomy and pointed to the interstitial space just below the armpit. "Right here. Understand?"

He nodded mutely.

"Now, you've got a lot of important structures inside here, understand? You've got a sort of network of nerves that supply your arms and there are some big blood vessels that go right through here." Still using the tip of her finger, she was rapidly diagramming across the top of his pectoral on the un-injured side. "Now one of these is the subclavian vein. That's a great big vein that takes all the blood that's been circulating through your arm and returns it right here and dumps it into the superior vena cava that goes directly into your heart. Can you sort of picture that?"

"Sort of."

"Well, I'll get somebody to bring you a diagram of what it looks like if you want, but here's the thing. This pellet took a little piece out of the subclavian vein right where it comes into this larger vessel, the vena cava. When you got here you just about didn't have any pulse at all because you had been bleeding into the inside of your chest, understand? I don't know, I think you must have just been bleeding off and on, not continuously or you wouldn't have been able to drive in from wherever you were out in the sticks."

"Raimon City."

"Jesus! You drove from Raimon City like that?"

"I guess I was lucky, huh?"

She shook her head as though to say that she was always having to clean up messes that bad little boys made of themselves. But out loud she said, "Now, what the surgery was for, was that I had to open up your chest under the side here and stitch up this little hole I told you about that was in the vein.

You took a lot of blood. You took . . ." she referred to his chart in her hand, "you took sixteen units of blood." She looked at him, impressed.

"Is that a lot?"

"The total capacity of the human body is less than that. Your whole chest cavity was full of blood. We were ankle deep by the time we got you cleaned out. Yeah, that's a lot."

"Well . . ." He didn't know what to say. Was he supposed to thank her at this point or what? He was still confused and his side was seriously beginning to hurt.

"Now, the reason I'm telling you all this is that there were a couple of things that happened in surgery that I need to tell you about, okay?"

"Okay." He couldn't imagine why this couldn't wait. Breast or no breast, he was getting a little tired of this woman. He wanted to be left alone to sort out what he was thinking about Suzanne Lynch. She couldn't have really been here, could she?

"Now, here's the important part. During surgery you arrested. In fact you arrested twice. I guess it was because you had already lost so much blood. . . ."

He lost the thread of what she was saying. She kept talking but all he could hear was the thudding of his own pulse in his ears. His face felt suddenly hot and he was wide awake. "Wait a minute, slow down a second. I can't hear very well, I . . . I . . . what did you say about an arrest?" He knew perfectly well what she had said. He knew it the moment she said it, but he wasn't buying it.

Dr. Trunkey wasn't going to give him time. "You had a cardiac arrest, your heart stopped for just a few seconds. It actually doesn't stop; it goes into what we call ventricular fibrillation, where it sort of flutters and doesn't pump, but it's called an arrest." She was talking fast, rushing it, nervous now. She seemed vaguely aware that she wasn't handling this exactly right. "We gave you an electrical shock and it started right up again, but then a few minutes later it did it again and we had to shock you again. We kept you in there another hour, just watching, but your blood pressure's been real good since then and everything seems to be working fine." She stopped and took a breath, pleased with herself that everything seemed to be working fine. "Now, we have to monitor you closely, so you are going to go from here to the ICU, okay?" She stood. Abruptly, she was finished. He was speechless, staring up at her with his mouth open. She looked around for the nurse, then looked back at him. "Now, are you in any pain?"

He stared at her, then managed to close his mouth, realizing that he was supposed to respond. "No. I mean I guess I am a little, but not bad." He stopped his voice, not trusting it. His mouth was suddenly dry and his voice sounded shaky, not at all what he wanted.

"Okay. Well, if you need any pain medication, I've left orders for you to go ahead and get what you want. We've got you on morphine to help keep your heart calm, so if you need more, just ask the nurse." She seemed to be out of words. "All right?" She asked it brightly.

"All right."

"Okay, I'll be by and check on you later." She abruptly patted him on the good shoulder and turned to walk out. Then she turned to the nurse as a sort of afterthought. "I guess I'm going to let one of these cops out here talk to him but just for a couple of minutes. If he starts having pain or gets to looking too tired, just tell 'em I said time's up."

Before she went out the door she looked at Robert, a quick look, making sure he was still there, maybe, then left hurriedly.

The nurse patted his hand to get his attention. "She's a good surgeon, but she thinks everybody's a potential cadaver. She doesn't mean to be so callous. She's just always in a hurry."

Robert looked at her. *How could that possibly matter?*

Bill Farrela must have been right outside the doorway. He crept in with such a big grin on his face that Robert almost didn't know who this was, creeping in as though afraid to wake him up too much. Farrela turned the chair around that the doctor had dragged over and sat down. "How you doing, old man? Get some more gray hairs?"

Robert looked at him without seeing him.

Farrela reached in his shirt pocket and fished around with two fingers. "Kevin said I was to give you this, first thing." He came up with a hearing aid. It was the older one that tucked behind the ear instead of attaching to his glasses. It looked bulky and clumsy compared to the one he had lost but he was grateful to see it. He plugged it in his ear and was immediately annoyed with it, hearing all of the sounds in the room simultaneously, at the same level. He heard a toilet flushing down the hall as though it were in the same room with him. Everything was amplified to the same volume.

Farrela looked at him a long time as though he didn't know where or whether to begin. Finally, he said, "You want me to say you were right before I ask you any questions?"

It took Robert a minute to remember what he was talking about. He had almost forgotten that they'd ever had any disagreement. "Forget it, Bill. That doesn't matter."

Farrela reached over and gave his shoulder a squeeze with one hand. "You asshole. I knew you'd say that."

"How's Jimbo?"

Farrela's face froze. He didn't change expressions, his features just immobilized. It was enough to tell Robert the answer but he had to have Farrela say it. "Is he at least alive?"

Farrela's mouth formed a flat thin line across the lower part of his face and he shook his head in the negative. "He didn't even get to the hospital."

Robert thought about Jimbo wanting to bring in Farrela, wanting to call these guys before they even went out there. He tried to quit thinking about it but he couldn't for a minute, hearing Jimbo's voice, arguing with him in the car. He could see Jimbo's face above the huge neck, the tentative, suspicious smile. "You're going to call Homicide, right?"

Farrela opened the briefcase he had brought in and pulled out a tape recorder. While he was still looking down he said, "How'd you get all the way into the fuckin' campus without any blood in you? The pickup you stole had more blood in it than you did."

Robert looked away, suddenly embarrassed, remembering the frightened looks of the students in the classroom where he had collapsed. "That guy . . . that guy Greg Arneson never went to the school, did he? He wasn't even there, huh?"

"Well, he didn't make it, but he was on his way when he got picked up. Foster knew you guys were looking for that car so he put out a call on it when Jimbo didn't show up for work and nobody could locate either one of you." He grinned, quick and easy, more relaxed now. "It's complicated, but I'll fill you in when you feeling better. Listen, I'm sorry, but I got to ask you about all this. There was that other guy that got killed." He held up the small tape recorder.

"Okay."

"You feeling up to it?"

"Go ahead." He wanted to get it over with, get everybody out of here or go to the next room they were going to take him to or do whatever they were going to make him do next. He just wanted to be left alone and he knew that wasn't going to happen until he said something about killing this guy. He tried to lift his left arm, taped to a splint with an IV line in the back of his hand. Pain woke up from wherever it had been. At first it was unfocused, nauseating pain and then it settled down under his arm and dug in. He waited for it to quiet before he could say anything.

"You all right?"

"Yeah, go ahead."

Farrela asked questions, stopping Robert's explanations every few seconds, it seemed, to make him backtrack and explain details. Robert started with their search for Gretchen

Nicholson and, with Farrela prodding and questioning, went through the whole thing. When he got to the point where he had realized that Jimbo was shot he stopped and waited a minute, Farrela giving him time, until he was ready to go on.

He told Farrela about Jimbo and the shooting in the night. When he got to the part about sighting on the guy in the dawn, he stopped and thought about it.

Farrela prompted. "So by then there was enough light you could identify him as the same guy that was in the bar earlier?"

"That's right."

"So then what happened?"

"I shot him."

"Wait a minute, I got to get this in detail, here. Did he look up and see you, make a move like he was going to point the shotgun at you?"

Robert just looked at him, for once not answering.

Farrela looked at him narrowly and seemed to think about what to say. "All right, let me get it straight. You had already given a warning, and identified yourself as a police officer, and the guy still looked like he was trying to shoot you and so you fired one round into his chest, is that about it?"

Robert looked at him. That sounded pretty good and actually, none of it was a lie, the way he put it. "That's right."

"All right. For the benefit of the record, I can see that you are tired and that you are in some—that you're in *considerable* pain, so I'm going to terminate the interview at this point." He switched off the tape recorder and looked around, troubled. "You better not make me eat this goddamn tape, you understand?"

"I understand."

"You going to remember that last part?"

"I'll remember." He wasn't sure why Farrela was bothered by the final shooting episode. He couldn't have said, for that matter, why he had hesitated to tell him about it.

Farrela put down his briefcase and snapped open the tape

recorder to show that it was off before he set it on the edge of the bed. He clasped his hands, leaning forward so that he wouldn't have to talk so loud to be heard. "They caught that Arneson guy, the one that shot at you first. Terry must have shot him in the leg, broke his thigh." He looked up suddenly with a tired grin. "They actually stopped the asshole because he couldn't drive worth a shit with his right leg in a cast. They got him stopped about two miles from Kevin's classroom." Farrela looked around for the nurse. He went on when he didn't see her. "Listen, Mac, I saw the stuff, the pistol and the newspaper clippings and stuff that was next to Jimbo when they found him. You put that stuff there?"

"Yeah, that's why I figured out he was going to the school."

"You thought he was going to go after Kevin at that guy's class, the guy that the article was about?"

"Yeah, that's what it looked like to me."

"I'm going to have to go over that with you on tape, how you happened to find that stuff. You had it figured out all right. You just read that newspaper clipping about the teacher and figured that's where he was going?"

"Yeah, it seemed pretty obvious."

"Listen, Mac. How did you happen to find that stuff?"

MacDonald stared at him for a minute without answering.

"You didn't go digging around in anything, did you?"

"Did Arneson say anything?"

"No, he's not saying shit. He just fuckin' sits there. So how did you happen to find that shit? Was it out in plain sight some-where, I hope?"

Robert stared at him.

A little while after Farrela left there was a brief commo-tion while they transferred Robert to another gurney, rolled him down the hall, and then put him on another bed that was standing between an assortment of monitors and lights. This, he understood, was the ICU. He didn't want inten-sive care. He didn't want anything to do with any of them, but he couldn't think of any way out of it. He went to sleep.

Abruptly, he snapped awake. Still in the ICU. It seemed to him that he hadn't been asleep more than a few seconds. The ICU nurse, a male this time, was in the same position he had seen him last, making notes in a chart with his back partially turned. Robert closed his eyes and took a deep breath, wanting sleep. His side was hurting bad now. It hurt to breathe. It hadn't been hurting before but now, when he wanted to sleep, when he had the chance to sleep, it hurt. He closed his eyes tighter and thought it wasn't so bad. He would be able to sleep.

His eyes snapped open. Sweat was soaking the bed. He hadn't realized that he was that scared. He had taken out the hearing aid and without it he wasn't bothered by noises outside his head but he was afraid to go to sleep.

His eyes took in the monitor screens, the ventilator crouching next to the bed, ready for him in case he should falter. He could remember the ventilator from when Lorraine had needed one. He wasn't sure what most of the other machinery was. The IV line stuck in the back of his hand curved up and behind him so that he couldn't see where it ended. The plastic tubing had various ports and valves attached along it, ready to medicate him, pump him up if he should suddenly start to deflate again, he supposed. Maybe this time, though it wouldn't work. Maybe this time they wouldn't be able to just jump-start him, goose the heart back to life once it stopped. Twice? It had stopped twice?

Irrationally, he thought about Suzanne Lynch, sitting next to his bed. He wondered why he would have a dream about her when . . . well, he could have been a lot better with her. He could have let her down more gently than he had. He had just been worried about his own situation when Terry had caught him and then he had dumped her as though she hadn't meant anything at all to him. He groaned out loud at the thought and the nurse looked around at him.

"Hi, Sergeant MacDonald. Are you feeling pain? I can give

you some more morphine now, if you like. Can you hear me okay?"

"I can hear you."

"Do you want some more morphine?"

"I don't know. How long do I have to stay here?"

"In the ICU? That depends on how things go. If you don't have any complications, you can probably go to the ward in a day or . . ."

"No, how long do I have to be in the hospital?" There was an idea, less than half-formed, that it was important to get out of the hospital. There was something urgent about that, but Robert couldn't have said why.

The nurse laughed. It was a professional laugh, designed to minimize the drudgery, like the word "complications" was used to minimize the idea of sudden death. "I wouldn't worry about that yet. You just got out of surgery. It won't be long, though. They don't have enough beds so they'll fix you up as fast as they can."

Robert closed his eyes so that he couldn't see the nurse going through his routines. He immediately thought of Jimbo and regretted it. He had been thinking more about his own fuckin' skin than about his partner, his son's partner, a decent goddamn human being. Robert realized he was even feeling sorry for himself for not having enough character to face Suzanne Lynch, even in a goddamn dream. He groaned out loud before he knew he was going to and could stop it.

The nurse patted him on his good shoulder. "Sergeant Mac-Donald?" He opened his eyes. "Sergeant MacDonald, now I know you have *got* to be feeling some pain, am I right?"

"I guess so."

"You ready for a shot? My name is Randy and I'm your pusher for this evening. Legal dope is our special for today. Are you ready? I'm going to give it to you through the IV line so I don't have to poke any more holes in you than you've already got. Look. Sergeant MacDonald? Take a look at how this works, it's pretty interesting. At least I think so. See?"

In spite of himself, Robert opened his eyes and watched as the nurse picked up a prefilled syringe and plugged the outlet into one of the ports in the IV line. "Ready or not, here I come." He elaborately pushed the plunger, disconnected and covered the port. "That'll hit you pretty fast, I guess. Don't worry about the dope. They switch you to Demerol tomorrow and in a few days you might not even need anything. Don't let it bother you, if that's something you worry about. How you feel?"

"No pain now."

"Well, the medication hasn't had time to work, yet. Shows you what your brain'll do for you all by itself when you're convinced. You just need to get comfortable and you'll sleep like a baby. You won't even know you're in here pretty soon and then you can relax. That's why you got me here. I just have one patient and that's you, so you don't have to worry about anything, okay? Everybody that comes into the ICU is nervous about it if he's awake. That's another thing that the morphine sulphate takes care of. It doesn't cure anything, but pretty soon you don't give a shit. That's why there's such a great market for it. People will pay anything to not give a shit."

Robert realized that his nurse was chattering. It was just noise, a stream of soothing, distracting noise that was almost meaningless when you realized that he probably said the same thing, a sort of routine, with every patient he had. Robert realized that he didn't feel the pain and that he was smiling.

"Now you got it." The nurse laughed, a deep-throated chuckle like he was holding his voice down on purpose. "That's what I wanted to see. Feel better?"

"Yes, definitely."

"Okay, go to sleep now, if you want." He patted Robert's shoulder and stood up. Robert had not realized that he was seated until he stood up and went back to his charting. Could the nurse have been right about people wanting not to give a shit? He smelled antiseptic.

Jimbo was leaning against the tire in the dark, his head tipped back, gasping for air and talking to him, but Robert couldn't hear what he said. He was stuck on his hands and knees a few feet from Jimbo and couldn't crawl over to where he was so that he could hear what Jimbo was trying to say. Jimbo's eyes were closed and he looked asleep, but his mouth was moving. Robert couldn't hear it.

Then Red Beard sat up. He still had his ankles crossed and the shotgun across his lap but he didn't grab for it. He sat up and looked right at Robert for a minute, fiercely angry. Suddenly, Red Beard threw his arms out again and flopped backward and lay there. Robert crept up to him and watched in horror. Red Beard's eyes were half-open, his face the slack pallor of death, a hole in his chest. Then Red Beard sat up, glared at Robert a moment and then flopped backward again as though to demonstrate how to do it, all you had to do.

"Hello, Mr. MacDonald? Bob? Does everybody call you Bob? Hey, can I wake you up for just a second?" A very young-looking man was standing over the bed. He had a trim beard and bright, cheerful eyes. "Hi, I'm Dr. Friedman. You can call me Michael, though, if you don't tell the chief resident on me. I have to check you over, okay?" He didn't wait for permission. He rolled Robert onto his good side and listened to his back with the stethoscope. "Deep breaths. Again. Again. Does that hurt?"

"No."

"Good. Any particular pain? Do you hurt anywhere?"

"I don't know."

The doctor laughed. "Well, then it must not be too bad." His breath smelled like cloves. "Did they tell you your son, Kevin, was here? He can't come into the ICU but he's been in the hallway all night."

Robert looked around. His view was blocked in all directions by curtains behind the machinery. He wondered what time it was. What did "all night" mean, anyway? He couldn't think to ask. The doctor had rolled him onto his back again. He threw the sheets off of him and hoisted one leg and then the other, testing his reflexes, rapping with his knuckles on the patellar tendons. "You're a policeman, aren't you? How do they let you be a policeman when you're so deaf?"

"Waivers." He wasn't irritated. The question would have irritated him any other time, but the way the doctor asked it, the circumstances, maybe, it didn't bother him.

"I see. You got a job where it doesn't matter so they just waive that problem, huh?"

"Right."

"That makes sense. You seem to be pretty healthy other than your ears and getting shot, huh? No other problems?" The doctor was grinning down at him.

"No. No other problems."

"Okay, you need anything else, or are they taking care of you all right?"

"No, they're . . ."

"Good." The doctor patted him brusquely on the good arm and strode off, looking for the nurse. Robert was alone for a minute so he closed his eyes, vaguely hoping to go back to sleep. His eyes popped open.

He tried turning onto the uninjured side but the weight of his arm came against the operation site and he had to roll onto his back again. The doctor had pulled the sheet over his legs but he felt exposed. He was cold and the hospital gown was sticking to him with sweat. He was sweating heavily, suddenly aware of it. A nurse put a basin of water on the table next to the bed. This one was black.

"I'm just going to rinse you off a little. Closest thing to a shower you gonna get in this unit." From his voice Robert could tell he was the same nurse that had been here before. He hadn't noticed that he was black before. Why hadn't he noticed? He couldn't think. He closed his eyes and felt the warm wet cloth on his skin. . . .

TWENTY-FIVE

After thirty-six hours in the ICU Robert was looking forward to being left alone. The double room they rolled him into already had one tenant, an older Asian man who was visiting with his family as Robert's gurney was rolled in past them. The old patient looked up, over the heads of the visitors drawn around his bed and saw Robert. The patient raised a hand in greeting to his new roommate. The gesture was feeble, but there was nothing weak about the old man's welcoming smile. Robert guessed that they were Vietnamese since Martin seemed to have a fair-sized population of them now. An older woman, one of the old man's visitors, turned a tear-streaked face shyly toward the intruders, Robert and the battery of nurses who came in with him, then looked away.

Robert raised his usable hand to return the old man's greeting, trying to be at least as friendly as his new roommate. "How ya doin'?"

The nurse at his head bent down toward him. "I don't think any of them speak English." She drew the curtain between the beds before they unloaded Robert at his new berth.

This time he left his hearing aid in place. He lay back, alone at last, and closed his eyes, hoping that he could just sink back into oblivion.

He could hear the voices of the family on the other side of the curtain. He thought about pulling out the hearing aid then, but decided that the voices didn't bother him that much. He wished that he understood some of the language, then realized that he didn't wish that at all. This way they could each talk to their respective visitors and still have a private room for all that the other could understand. He closed his eyes and smiled at the idea until he heard the break of a sob from next door.

It was the voice of the woman. She was crying quietly, unable to stop in spite of the consoling sounds from the young men who were with her. Then the patient's voice, weak with age or with illness, but rich in confidence. The old patient laughed and his visitors laughed with him at something he had said. His voice then went on for a while by itself, the others obviously listening. A rush of language and again, the laughter, louder this time, while the old man kept on talking and then another peal of laughter. The woman answered something back, her voice whining. The old man's consoling answer was joined by reassuring clucks and murmurs from the young men.

Robert didn't need to know Vietnamese for this. The woman was the wife of the patient, obviously, and these were their sons. She was upset about something that the old husband thought was trivial and he was kidding her about it.

Kevin strolled in, his blond head towering, looming suddenly in the opening of the curtain. He looked terrible. There were circles under his eyes that could have been penciled in, they were so well defined. He was wearing a grin that looked painful. "Hey, Dad. I went downstairs to get coffee and when I got back they let me sit in the hall for another ten minutes before they bothered to tell me you'd been moved. I wanted to see you, first thing. Did you think I wasn't there? Does it hurt a lot?"

"Not so bad."

There was a long pause while neither of them said anything, then Kevin pulled a chair up next to the bed. "Did you see Mrs. Lynch?"

Robert stared at his son. *She had really been there? Suzanne?*

Kevin chuckled. "You probably don't remember. She said you opened your eyes for a minute but she didn't know if you were awake enough to recognize her. She is something! The nurses told me I couldn't go in because you couldn't have any visitors yet but Mrs. Lynch just sailed on in like she knew what she was doing and nobody said anything to her. She told me she was visiting somebody downstairs and she heard on the television that you were in the hospital so she came up to see if she could see you."

"Television?"

"Yeah, Dad, you were a big star for about twenty seconds. You know, 'policemen ambushed' kind of thing. I'm waiting for contract offers, but nothing yet." He laughed.

They thought about that for a moment.

"How do you feel?"

"Just groggy."

"Yeah, still getting a lot of dope, huh?"

"I guess so." Robert cleared his throat. "Sorry about busting into your class like that."

Kevin broke into a big, unfeigned grin at the remembrance. "Are you putting me on? That's the most dramatic thing that class has seen all year. No kidding, Dad, the theatricality of that entrance surpassed anything I've ever seen in my life. It was just . . . great!" He indicated the state of dramatic perfection with his circled thumb and forefinger.

Robert chuckled and shook his head, but he had to look down to cover his chagrin at the memory. "They must have thought it was some crazy street person or something. I must have looked . . ." To his utter humiliation, a tear coursed down his cheek.

"Dad."

Kevin was whispering but his voice was urgent. "Dad, for Christ's sake, who gives a damn about that? How could that possibly matter, what you looked like?"

"Sorry." Robert kept his head turned away, wiping his face. "It must be the narcotics."

"Sure, come on, don't worry about stuff like that. Hey, Dad? Foster told me all about the whole thing." He put his hand on his father's arm. He was on the left side of the bed and the contact on the wounded side hurt, but Robert, with an act of will, didn't let him know. "I just want to say thanks, Dad."

Robert had to think for a moment to realize what he was talking about. "The guy didn't even make it there. I should've known I wouldn't make it in time if he didn't get stopped, I was too slow getting started, then I just couldn't get there any faster. . . ."

"Dad. You got there. I don't care if it was wasted or anything about that. You got there, okay?" Kevin squeezed his arm, seemed ready to say more and then couldn't. They heard a nurse come into the room and stop at the other bed.

"How you doin', Mr. Leung?" She had raised her voice as though the increase in decibels would penetrate the language barrier.

Robert stared out the window for a long moment. All he could see because of his angle lying in the bed, was the sky.

Kevin said, "You up for talking to Foster? He's in the hallway, waiting for me to leave."

Robert looked at his son. "Don't you have classes or something?"

"Yeah, but it's all right."

"You should go to class."

"You tired? Want to sleep some more?"

"Yeah, I think I'll go back to sleep after I talk to Jerry."

"Okay, Dad. It looks like you're doing pretty good. I mean, considering. You want anything?"

"No, I don't need anything. You go ahead."

"I'll come back later, okay?"

"All right, see you later."

When Kevin had gone Robert realized he didn't even know what time it was. He should have asked him for his watch. He couldn't think what possible use he had for knowing the time, he just didn't want to feel like he was left out of the train of things going by. He felt disconnected. He supposed that his drugged state had something to do with it and speculated that he was coming out of it more than he had in the last two days. But there was more to it than that. There was some urgency about it that he kept forgetting.

Jerry Foster had had a couple. He wasn't drunk by any means, maybe he never was truly drunk, but he'd definitely had a couple or three of some strong beverage. When he came in and looked at Robert, though, he didn't seem to have any problem taking care of business. At least no problem that was being caused by the booze.

He pulled up the chair, close beside Robert's bed but he didn't sit in it. He put one big foot on it and leaned on his knee with his crossed elbows, his thick, blunt-fingered hands hanging down. "This is the goddamnedest case!"

He stared over the top of Robert's bed, looking out the window. His comment didn't seem to invite any response so Robert just waited for him to go on.

Foster kept staring out the window. "Farrela brings me this chicken-shit piece of tape and then tries to tell me that you were on drugs or some goddamned thing or other, like that's gonna explain the fuckin' tape away. Now how the fuck do you know that the guy you shot was the one that was shooting at you?" He rotated his big, sleepy-looking head and looked down at Robert. He kept his voice low, quietly conversational.

"Like, f'rinstance. How long was it between the time you got shot and the time you could actually see the guy to identify him?"

Robert stared back at him, trying to think.

Foster didn't want him to think too much. "Come on, I haven't read you your rights or anything, I just want to know."

"I'm not sure. Maybe half an hour."

"There, see what I mean? It may seem obvious to you, but you couldn't hear nothing and you couldn't see nothing. You can't say who shot at you or when or if there was one guy or sixteen guys doing the shooting, now can you? For sure, now?"

"He had the shotgun in his lap!" Robert was incredulous.

Foster turned his head to look back out the window again, musing. "Yeah, okay, that's something. You know . . . or I guess I should tell you, that his brother, Gregory Arneson, had an oversized Zippo lighter on him when we picked him up. Brand-new." He rotated his big head around to look directly at Robert. "You know, like maybe he had to replace one that maybe he lost recently?" He let that sink in a moment and then looked back out the window. "Trouble is, we got a record for this other guy, Larry Murray. He been in a few fights, one burglary about twenty years ago, but nothing like murder. And nothing at all against him in about fifteen years. Usually, they mellow out, they don't get worse."

"Maybe, because of his brother . . ."

"Now, that's another one. This guy, Arneson, never been in trouble in his whole fuckin' life. You know what he's been doin'? Gregory Arneson been workin'. He worked the same goddamned job, twenty-some-odd years, at two or three different places and half the time, he still be moonlightin' to pay his bills."

"Must have had a lot of expenses, huh? He tell you this?"

Foster looked back at Robert. He looked at the IV line in his arm, glanced up at the plastic bag hanging on a pole next to the bed as though to remind himself that this man was in the hospital. "No, he's not sayin' a thing. He don't ask for a lawyer, he don't say nothin'.

"No, I take it back! He made 'em take off that cast in the jail. He wouldn't stay still until they did that and then he shut up. Oh yeah, and one of the jail inmates musta bothered him a little too much 'cause Arneson busted his nose into about a million pieces. He won't even tell anybody his side o' that. He just sits there." The big detective stared out the window, his black face glistening, thinking about it.

"I talked to a guy worked for him. Arneson was the foreman at the service department at that Cadillac dealership . . ."

"Rickenhauer's?"

Foster turned his head back to look directly at Robert, making sure he had eye contact. "I don't want to know anything else you might have found, looking through that goddamned shack." He stared back out the window as though looking for his train of thought. "Anyway, I guess this guy's wife split on him right after that girl was born. He raised her, himself, never even got a divorce that I can find out. He sent this kid to piano, dance lessons, horseback riding, anything she wanted. That's why he had to work two jobs, sometimes."

Foster's voice was low, making it a little hard for Robert to hear, but he was getting most of it and didn't want to interrupt him. The captain's face looked haggard more than sleepy, now that Robert thought about it.

Foster said, "I guess he went over the edge when she got killed. He never even called the car agency. Never even called in and said, 'Fuck you.' He just never went back anymore. And you wanta know something?" He turned and looked at Robert and then looked away again. "They never reported him missing. The guy worked for 'em, for Rickenhauer's, for ten or fifteen years or something, I forget which . . . He doesn't come to work. They call his house and nobody answers. They musta known about his daughter, every goddamn TV reporter within six hundred miles was tryin' to burn our ass on that. . . . But fuckin' Rickenhauer's, they just go on about their business, maybe even drawing straws or kissing ass or something to see who's gonna be the new foreman. Never once tried to find out what happened to the son of a bitch."

Robert waited, but the detective didn't go on. He stared out the window, apparently wondering if white people could really be human, after all.

Robert waited. He wanted to ask what was going to happen next, but Foster would know that. He would tell him when he was ready. "Judge appointed that little shithead in the Public Defender's Office, Ferguson, to represent him. He don't need no fuckin' lawyer, he keeps just sittin' there like he doin'. Anybody that watches *L.A. Law* can tell you we can't use the stuff you found on that goddamn, fuckin' illegal search. Now, how am I supposed to prove it was him and not his fuckin' half brother that was goin' around shootin' people up?"

"How about a skin test? He must have had powder on his hands, huh?"

Foster shook his head, looking at the floor. "Hate to tell you, but nobody thought about that. Maybe I was just thinking about you and Jimbo or . . . no excuses, we just didn't do it. Looks like we can't really prove anybody but Murray fired any shots although, to tell you the truth, I'm not sure about whether he did or not."

"What do you mean you're not sure . . . ?"

"Look, Mac. I know it sounds like I'm bein' hard on you. Believe me, I understand you were doin' the best you could in a bad situation. But what I got now, I only know one thing for sure. And that's that I got one of the most dangerous men I ever seen in jail right now, and I don't see how I can keep him there."

Long after Foster was gone, Robert rolled over gingerly and tried putting the weight of his arm in front of him to make it possible to lie on his side, facing the wall. He closed his eyes. Why had Suzanne come? He thought that he had treated her so shabbily, he didn't see why she would want to come see him. After Lorraine had died he had heard Suzanne was divorced and still hadn't called her. Maybe she *was* just accidentally in the hospital anyway, but he doubted it. Maybe she thought it evened out. With her, he had treated everybody else in his life shabbily, so maybe she hadn't expected any better from him.

Robert gradually became aware that now there was a male Anglo with the family of the Vietnamese patient, evidently the doctor. He could hear their conversation clearly through the curtain.

"The primary tumor was in the liver, does he understand that?"

There was a cadenced murmuring, then one of the sons: "He says he was never a heavy drinker. And that's true, he never really liked the stuff that much. . . ."

"No, this is different. This isn't caused by drinking. I wish . . . We don't really know what causes this kind of liver cancer. But let me explain, okay? There's a large artery that supplies the liver with blood and that was mostly blocked by the tumor. We cleared that, but there was . . . there were little tumors all through the liver and in the other organs as well."

The son translated and then the mother's voice and then the translation again. "She wants to know if he can come home or will there be more surgery now?"

"No, no more surgery. Make sure she understands that more surgery would not do any good. There isn't anything else that we could do with surgery."

Then, without waiting for the translation, the mother's voice in Vietnamese, a little louder this time. "She understands. She understands that you can't do anything else. She wants to know if she can take him home pretty soon." The mother's voice again, insistent. "She says to tell you there are lots of people, family members, live right in the same block and they can help her take care of him better than here." The boy hesitated, probably thinking about how that sounded. "She's not being critical, it's just . . ."

"I understand. . . ."

"See, I got two cousins and their families, they live right there within a block of the house. . . . See, he's their favorite uncle. . . ."

The doctor was momentarily stumped. "I . . . I think he can go home in a few days. We want to make sure the incision is healing all right."

The mother was talking at the same time the son tried to translate. "She says she can watch him all the time or one of my cousins could . . ."

Robert stared at the ceiling. The demon was out in the open, right next door. Random firing into the brush, the same thing as the seeds growing, the random invasive destruction of tiny integral cells, parts of essential organs, eating him, wasting him away. It was just like Lorraine: for nothing, no reason at all that he could see.

The guy that had been shooting at Robert didn't even know who he was. The guy probably just thought that the Homicide cops in Martin were figuring it out and found him and he wasn't ready to get arrested and that's why he was shooting. But the cops could have been anybody; it was random happenstance that it was him they were shooting at. And they got Jimbo first, who didn't have anything to do with any of it. Jimbo.

It made no sense at all, the utterly random destruction of the innocent. The Vietnamese man nurturing in his own body, like Lorraine had, the aggressive, punitive little invaders that had nothing whatever to do with him, nothing that he had done or not done but grown by him nevertheless, out of his own genes and protoplasm, the beads of death spreading in random splotches everywhere he could look with his inward eye.

It was the goddamn war all over again, the troop carrier forty-five years ago, going into the beach at Oran. Kids, boys, had been joking while they were pissing their pants; vitality existing in the same instant with annihilation and oblivion; youth with nothingness, a void for a quick trade; the random falling of shells half as big as a car, and bullets, fired from too far away to be aimed on purpose, random selection of meaningless choices, meaningless victims, none of them counting for anything in the thrall of the chance of numbers, falling without order or direction or any sense of justice, any sense of any kind at all.

He must have slept for a while because when he awoke the visitors next door had left. He heard his roommate clear his throat periodically and heard rustling paper. He wondered if the old man could read English or if he was catching up on political events on the other side of the world, events that could have no more meaning for him now than they would have for Robert.

He heard the bed creak and then noticed that the curtain between them was jerking. Robert looked over and saw a small hand, spindly fingers, working to grasp and move the curtain. Robert reached over and pulled it back. The Vietnamese man was leaning perilously far out from his bed, caught in the act of trying to reach the curtain. He had to work at it to retrieve his balance but he smiled a big, toothy grin when he saw Robert's face.

His head looked much too big for his body. He was skinny to the point of emaciation, with hollow cheeks and huge dark eyes. The whites of his eyes were slightly yellow, surrounding big dark brown irises. The yellow eyes, Robert understood, were the surface evidence of the liver's ultimate betrayal within. Mr. Leung was wearing a clean, dark blue pajama jacket that hung off him in folds of excess material. Robert wondered if it had fit him before. The old Vietnamese grinned and nodded, the big head bobbing on the skinny remnant of his neck, staring at Robert. Then he had to lie back against his pillows to recover from the effort. The head of his bed was raised so he could sit up.

He pointed to the visitor's chair on Robert's side of the curtain, still grinning. "You . . . you san?"

Robert had to smile back at him. "Yes. That was my son." He noticed that he, too, had raised his voice to be better understood in Vietnamese and that he was nodding vigorously to take the place of words.

Mr. Leung pointed at his own chest. "My . . . my . . . I" He held up two fingers. "Two sans." He grinned, proud of his accomplishment, and nodded vigorously to elicit a corresponding nod from Robert to show that he understood. "You?" He pointed the finger back at Robert, interrogation written all over his face, lost for English words, but communicating nevertheless.

Robert hesitated, then held up one finger. "Just one. I have just one son."

His neighbor nodded vigorously to show that he understood and, with a lingering smile on his face, stared off into the middle distance. He lay there, apparently relaxed and smiling for a moment, then looked back at Robert, gearing up for another effort. "I two sans." He thought about that for a minute. "You san . . ." He was making a tremendous mental effort here. "You san bed taw." Robert was puzzled. His neighbor thought for a moment, licking his lips in concentration. Then he raised his hand as high as it would reach, brought it down and thought again. "I two sans"—a pause, then pointing at Robert—"you san bed taw!" waving his hand high up in the air.

Robert laughed at his roommate's antics, in spite of himself. "Yes, my son's very tall."

His neighbor nodded vigorously, grinning in that skeleton face, full of good humor and yellow eyes. "Bed taw!" He laughed and waved his fingers at the tallest he could reach. "Bed taw!" Robert laughed, too, nodding his head up and down to show that he understood. He wanted to say something back but he had to think of something he could communicate with sign language.

He pointed to the empty visitors' chairs on his roommate's side. "You have two fine boys."

His neighbor quit laughing although his eyes retained the crinkled good nature of smiling. He looked at the empty chairs, searching for the meaning, then looked back at Robert. MacDonald pointed at the chairs and tried again. "You . . . have two fine sons."

The neighbor's quick grin showed he got the gist of it. "Two sans . . ." he agreed, then grew silent as his store of English seemed to be played out. He seemed resigned and pointed to his chest. "I . . ." but he couldn't think of the word. He put his hand next to his head and closed his eyes. Robert couldn't tell if he meant he wanted to sleep or he was going to die. The man grinned to show his good humor and then dropped his hands next to his sides and let his head sag, his face miming utter fatigue. Then he quickly laughed again and put his hand next to his face and shut his eyes. Then he made a snoring noise.

Robert laughed and thought that the man didn't need words. "You want to sleep?"

"Sleep." He gave the "sl" a liquid quality that Robert could not have imitated.

"I'll pull the curtain, then." Robert reached out and showed him what he was going to do. Mr. Leung nodded agreement so Robert waved good night and pulled the material across between the beds. Each had his privacy again.

TWENTY-SIX

Robert weighed out the powder carefully, sixty grains of standard 4895 powder to load behind a 180-grain, copper-jacketed bullet, and dumped it into the case. Then he put the bullet on top of the case and crimped it down with the long handle of the reloading tool. He wished that he had been able to get Stuart to build a four-hundred-yard range. He wished he could practice with this big load before he needed it. He was used to using forty-five grains of powder behind a 165-grain bullet and this new load would behave differently over a long distance. He had only been out of the hospital a week but Arneson's preliminary hearing was tomorrow and he wasn't ready. The guy was going to get out. Everybody seemed to think there was no question.

"What the hell you doing, going hunting?" Stuart was standing behind him, looking at the scale. He was letting Robert use his shop at the range for his reloading since there was no real setup in Robert's apartment.

Robert hadn't heard him come into the shop, but he didn't mind. He had to talk to Stuart about this thing tomorrow and now was as good a time as any.

Robert looked over his shoulder at Stuart. "You got a few minutes, we could talk?"

Stuart looked at him curiously but then had an idea. "Bet your ass I do. I want to know if you're finally going to retire and if you can come to work out here and give me a break." This was not the first time Stuart had had this idea.

Robert put the lid back on the powder can and looked at the fifty rounds of new loads that he had lined up in his ammunition block. Set the primers and they'd be ready to try out.

Stuart came in the door to the shop with two glasses and a bottle of Jack Daniel's under his arm. Robert didn't have to look to know that it must be five o'clock. Stuart was grinning, the hundreds of lines that made up his face crinkling into a cheerful mask that could have been drawn on a walnut. He stopped grinning and looked at Robert. "What's the matter with you?"

"There's some chance that Arneson's going to get out tomorrow."

"That's the guy that shot you."

"His brother."

"Oh yeah, okay. This is the dangerous one, huh?"

Robert wished Stuart would take it more seriously. "The way I understand it, the judge might not rule in court so it may be a few days off, but he could just say the word and he'd be processed out by the afternoon sometime. He could come out here. It's possible, that's all."

Stuart shook his head. "Even if the son of a bitch knows where you are, you think he's gonna want to come out here where everybody around has got a gun in his hand? I thought you said he wasn't crazy." Stuart kicked a stool out from under the nearest workbench and sat on it, while he went about the serious business of pouring the whiskey.

Robert watched him, his mind miles away. "I don't think it's too likely he'd come here. I just don't know."

Stuart set one glass in front of Robert and sipped from the other. "What about Kevin? Where you puttin' him?"

Robert didn't pick up his glass. "I been talking to Linda Durham, Lorraine's cousin. I'll probably get him to go up there for a while."

"Where's that?"

"New Mexico. Up near Los Alamos."

Stuart nodded but, clearly, the specific location didn't mean a thing to him. "Sounds good. How long you think you can store him up there?"

"I don't know. Until something happens, I guess."

"You mean like until this guy shoots you in your bed and they can get a case against him that's gonna stick?"

"Stuart . . ."

"Okay, I didn't mean to butt in. I just thought maybe, since you're out here most of the time anyway, you could just put a cot in here for a while. You can use my shower when you want, my trailer's not more than half a mile up the road. Take you five minutes to walk it with rocks in your boots."

"Well, thanks, Stuart, but I don't think I . . ."

"Got a sleeping bag? I can loan you a sleeping bag if you need one."

"Well, I might decide to do that. I don't think so, but I'll keep it in mind and maybe I'll call you about it."

"Okay. You can leave word on my answering machine at home if I'm not around." He thought a minute, swirling the whiskey in his glass, then tossed it back. "If it was me, I think I'd get out of my house for a while, see what happens. I've thought about what I'd do if some husband got after me. I think that's what I'd do. Just lay low and let some time go by, see what happens."

Robert got to the Hall of Justice a half hour early. If he had to guess, he would guess that he had probably testified more than a hundred times in criminal cases, once even in a civil case where somebody was suing the city over an intersection accident. He kept telling himself that it was silly for him to be nervous about testifying but it didn't do any good. His stomach was in knots, refusing to hold coffee, which was all he was offering it. He hadn't intended to get there early. He had picked up his car from the garage when it first opened that morning and then thought, *What if there's problems with traffic,* and the next thing he knew he was rushing downtown.

He knew that the main thing he was going to do this morning was to wait around. If he was lucky, he could wait in the prosecutor's office but, more likely, he would have to sit in the courtroom, waiting for their turn, their case to be called. Arneson's case.

Robert was carrying a wrinkled manila envelope with copies of the statements he had given to Homicide and IAD and then another one to Homicide. He had been over and over these statements with the prosecutor, mapping out the danger areas where the prosecutor thought Ferguson would try to trap him. They had talked about what they would want the judge to pay the most attention to. The lawyer had even suggested that Robert rethink his motivation in looking around the shack but that didn't matter now; the evidence that Robert had found had already been thrown out. What mattered now was what Robert had seen and when.

The prosecutor would have been delighted if Robert had a sudden memory of catching a glimpse of Arneson through one of the shack's windows when Jimbo was shot. Robert thought that idea was stupid and anyway, he'd been over that point on the tape with Homicide in the second interview and he'd have to be an idiot not to realize what a huge contradiction that would be. No question in Robert's mind, he would have to tell the story as best he could remember it, without adding anything or embellishing. He just didn't know any other way to testify.

Robert could see the doorway to Department 3, the court-room where they were to hold the hearing. It was nearly at the other end of the hall. He looked hard at the ebb and flow of foot traffic in the hallway and then realized that Arneson would be coming from the jail, entering the courtroom from a side door accompanied by a deputy sheriff, not from the hall-way. That was it.

It wasn't the courtroom testimony that had him nervous. It was seeing Arneson. He realized that he'd never seen the man. He knew the description of him that he had from one witness, the photograph and the glimpse that he had gotten through the telescope over a long distance, but that didn't show any detail of what he looked like. He had never seen him up close, had never looked at his face.

Robert walked down the hall, thinking about what it would be like to see him. He wondered if he would have a sudden flash of the old anger, the hatred that he had felt because this was the man who had shot Terry. No, he decided, probably not. So much had happened since then that he didn't feel any hatred directed at an individual anymore. Somehow in all the work, the effort that he and Jimbo had put into finding out who he was, the vengeful spirit had quieted and left him with determination to finish it, to find him and prove, somehow, that he had done it. Well, that part was over. It didn't matter that they wouldn't be able to convict him, couldn't use the Cobra that he'd found in the shack to prove that he was the one that shot Terry. At least he had proved that Terry didn't do it himself and that was what was important about that.

The problem was that now it had changed. He had been the hunter, the motivator for the action up to the point that he shot Larry Murray and now, after all the waiting and the pain of being in the hospital, after being told that he had had a car-diac arrest, after all of that . . . it was out of his hands. He wasn't in control. And he was scared. More than that, he real-ized, he was terrified of this man with the scar that could burn up people that he didn't know because they happened to be close to his target. What about Kevin? How in the hell could he be sure that Kevin was going to make it through all of this?

The prosecutor stepped out of the door to Department 3 and looked directly at Robert, grinning. "You're early."

"Didn't want to miss anything. Is he in there yet?"

"The judge?"

"Arneson."

"No, they won't bring him up for this. He's still not talking to his lawyer so there's no point. The sheriff's got him upstairs but I told 'em you couldn't identify him if you saw him, so they're just going to take him back to the County Jail."

TWENTY-SEVEN

Robert emerged from the air-conditioned cool of the airport terminal and stood for a moment on the sidewalk, looking over the parking lot. He took a deep breath and blew it out through pursed lips, relieved. It had been more of an effort than he had counted on to get Kevin on that plane and headed for New Mexico, a place the poor kid had never seen and had no particular desire to see.

When the judge had ruled from the bench that there was no probable cause to hold the defendant for trial, Robert had been out of the courtroom in a second. He had tried to make sure that they wouldn't let Arneson out of jail for several hours. The sheriff, a shooting buddy, would take his time with the paperwork, stall overnight if it was possible, although Robert didn't think he could manage that much delay if the public defender got on his ass about it.

It didn't take long to get Kevin's clothes packed, considering his wardrobe, but Kevin, the optimist, hadn't made any advance preparation at the school about what to do about his classes. Robert patrolled the front of the apartment, looking out the window every few seconds, even though he knew Arneson couldn't be on the street yet, while Kevin got on the telephone and talked to his teachers. Kevin set it up so that his professors would leave his written assignments in a box at the English Department office's front desk for Robert to pick up. They were even going to put the mailing label on it with the address in New Mexico so all Robert would have to do would be to pick up the box the next day, take it to the UPS office and pay for the shipping. It was going to cost a bit because they were including a number of books or they would have mailed it themselves.

The Martin Municipal Airport did not have any direct flights to anywhere, it seemed, except Dallas or Atlanta. Robert had stood at the counter, checkbook in hand and had grown almost frantic with the methodical nonspeed of the process of getting Kevin booked, his bags tagged and then seeing him safely, finally, aboard the plane. Kevin had almost made him feel like a kidnapper, but now it was done. Robert stood on the sidewalk and took another deep breath and let it out before heading for his car. Nothing else for him to do, really, until he picked up the package and mailed it the next day.

Robert was momentarily lost, time on his hands. It was four-thirty.

The lock on the front of Robert's building was not a good one. He had never been particularly concerned about it because it only let somebody into the stairwell and he had a good lock on the front door of the apartment. When Robert got back from the airport the downstairs door didn't look like it had been forced, but it was standing slightly ajar. He pushed the door open without going in and looked up the stairs. There was a man, visible against Robert's white front door, sitting at the top of the steps. Robert flipped on the light switch, ready to dive back away from the door if the man moved.

Farrela grinned down at him. "What's a matter, scare you?"

"Jesus Christ."

"Sorry, I shoulda thought about that. It didn't seem that dark when I came in."

"Jesus Christ Almighty, Bill. Suppose I'd been armed?"

"Yeah. Well, you're right, I won't do that again. I didn't think you'd be coming back here. Why aren't you armed?"

"Come on in and have a beer, anyway. You on duty?"

Farrela stood up. "No."

Robert opened the front door and let them in. He got out two beers and opened one, trying to relax. "So, what are you doing here, then?"

"Arneson caught a cab. Must have called it from inside the sheriff's office because when the cab drove up, he came out and jumped right in."

"You were following him?"

"Yeah, well, that was the idea. The cab went straight to Sears and let him out. By the time I got inside the store he was just gone, disappeared. I guess he went in one door and out another. Could've caught another cab or a bus or something. I don't know where the hell he went."

"Maybe he was just inside the store, somewhere."

"Mac, take my word for it. He was not inside that fuckin' store."

MacDonald took a sip from his beer and studied the label, thinking about what Farrela was saying. He looked up at him, took a breath as though he was going to say something and then changed his mind. He wasn't sure he wanted to ask Farrela anything about what he was doing.

Maybe the detective just wanted to be a good guy. Maybe, and this seemed more likely to Robert, he felt guilty about dropping the investigation in Terry's case too soon, not talking to enough neighbors or not talking to them long enough to get to the same place that Robert had, just by stumbling along. Robert thought about telling Farrela that he shouldn't feel guilty about it. These things just happen and you can't go around thinking too much about what you should have done or shouldn't have done when things work out the way they do. He wanted to say all this to Bill Farrela but he couldn't think of a way to say it that wouldn't embarrass both of them.

When he looked up, Farrela met his eyes. "You know what I'm thinking?" The detective didn't mean it as a question. He seemed to think that Robert knew. When Robert didn't answer he said, "Arneson evaded me on purpose. I should have thought it through better."

"How you mean?"

"Somebody spends nineteen days in jail and doesn't talk to hardly anybody the whole time, he's got a lot a time to think."

"Yeah, I guess he would."

"Mac, this guy wasn't just making up poetry in his head. He was making plans, Mac, about what he was going to do as soon as he got out."

"You think he knew he was gonna get out?"

"Just because Ferguson said he wasn't talking doesn't mean he wasn't listening. I checked. Ferguson was out to see him three times in nineteen days. You think they just stared at each other? He must have told Arneson something, right?"

Robert nodded his head in agreement and took another pull on his beer. "You're probably right."

"Well, what are you gonna do?"

Robert shrugged.

"What about Kevin?"

"I got Kevin out of state." He took a final sip and crushed the can in his hand.

Farrela sat back and looked at him. "Well . . . okay, that's something. You think I'm right, huh? You already thought about all this."

"Sure, of course I thought about it."

"Well?"

"Well, what the hell do you have in mind, Farrela? Join the foreign legion?"

Farrela grinned and then looked away. He took a long pull that finished his own beer and crushed the can, putting it on the table next to Robert's.

"Hey, anybody here?" They both jumped. The voice was right outside MacDonald's apartment door. Robert started to rise, trying to remember if they had even closed the door when they came in. He looked down and saw Farrela starting to laugh.

"It's Eddie Goldman. I told him to meet me here."

They both walked out of the kitchen to the front door. Robert looked at Farrela sideways. "You jumped as much as I did."

"Hell I did! But you gonna have to clean up that chair I was in."

They opened the door. Goldman looked past them and saw the crushed beer cans. "Got any left?" He walked between them to go look for himself. "I went all the way around the block on foot and didn't see anything funny. You got any idea what kind a car this guy might have? I know that old Chevy's junk, still out at the police yard, I think. What about the old pickup?"

Farrela looked down at the floor. "I checked at the jail and they had his home address listed as that place out by Raimon City. I went out there just to take a look and the pickup's sitting in the yard on blocks. I guess he must've had somebody come get it but I didn't check out who did it for him. Shit, that's at least one person he must've talked to. I shoulda checked that out."

Goldman opened a beer and looked at his watch. "Police lot is closed. I'll check it out in the morning, okay?" He looked at Farrela. "That be okay?"

"Sure, okay." Farrela seemed embarrassed. He looked around the apartment as though trying to think of something to suggest. "You got someplace else you could stay? You wanta come over to my place?"

Robert laughed. "No, I got a place I can go to if I decide not to stay here."

Goldman and Farrela looked at each other, then both of them looked at Robert. Farrela said, "That's a pretty good idea. Give us a couple a days, see which way he goes."

Robert shook his head and looked away. "I don't . . . I don't think you guys need to do all this. I mean, I do appreciate it, but I don't know. Seems like it's really my problem, not the police department's right now, huh?"

"You gonna wait until it's Homicide's problem?" Goldman was not kidding.

"Well . . . maybe it won't come to that, huh?"

"Right. What you gonna do, he shows up here? Talk to him?"

Robert realized that that was what he had been thinking. He had half entertained the idea that he could talk to the man, reason with him—a man who had sat for nineteen days in jail without saying shit. The way Goldman put it, it seemed a little stupid. Goldman and Farrela were still looking at him. "Okay. I'll get my stuff together and go out to the range. I can stay out there for a while."

Farrela grinned again, with relief this time. "That's better."

Goldman looked at his watch. "We'll wait for you to get packed and on your way, huh?"

"That's okay. I can do that without a baby-sitter."

Farrela turned toward the door, suddenly decisive. "Yeah, shit. I guess you can pack your own goddamn toothbrush. You know how to call me, right? Anything suspicious goes on, you call right away and let me take care of it even if it's on the other side of the river, okay?"

"Sure, Bill. I'm damn near retired already."

Robert watched the two detectives go down the stairs and out the front door. Then he heard one of them shake the door to make sure that it was locked. Robert wandered back into the kitchen, threw away the empty beer cans, opened the refrigerator door to get himself another, then thought better of it and closed the door. He stood still and listened. The new hearing aids were good on both sides, letting him in on more of the world than he had thought he was missing. He could hear traffic, an occasional car outside in front of his building. He could tell just by listening that the people downstairs were not at home or at least that they had turned off their television, a rare occurrence. He'd only noticed that he could hear their television with the new aids.

He meant to go get his things together but instead he sat down at the kitchen table. He stared at the wall opposite him, a blank wall that he had never gotten around to putting anything on. The whole damn place looked more like an institution than a home. No wonder Kevin didn't like to spend time here. Neither did Robert.

He looked around the kitchen. There were no hanging pots, no pottery jar of long-handled utensils, no hot pads, hanging on little hooks, no evidence that anybody considered this a kitchen where food was to be prepared for anybody to eat. He reached out with the toe of his work boot and kicked open the nearest cabinet. Inside, there was a box that had never been unpacked in the almost three years since he had moved into this place. That was where the pots, the utensils, things like that were. They were still in boxes, in temporary containers waiting for him to decide that he really did live here, or at least that he wasn't going to move anywhere else soon. The whole thing was temporary.

He thought about Stuart's house trailer. It sat on a small hill on a concrete slab, an inexpensive house, no more a mobile home than this building where Robert's apartment was could be called mobile. But it was not like this. Several times, Stuart had invited Robert over for a drink after he shut down the range, so Robert was familiar with it. Stuart, seventy-five years old and a bachelor for at least the last forty, lived in a kind of permanent solitary encampment. He had his cooking things out, burnt and dented with use, his clothes hung in their proper places, magazines sitting out in his little living room. Next to Stuart's front door there was a huge bag of "horse candy," nuggets of compressed oats and molasses, that Stuart would drop in his pockets on the way out to his corral, a galvanized metal structure a hundred yards from the trailer. Stuart's place was lived in.

Robert got up and walked down the hall back to his bedroom. He opened a grocery bag and put in several changes of underwear and work clothes. Then, with the bag sitting on his bed, he got his utility belt out of the closet, strapped it on, and made sure that the Smith & Wesson was loaded. He got out a box of .357 ammunition from a bureau drawer and put it in the bag with the clothes. He looked at the bag a minute.

Then he unlocked the gun cabinet, took down the M1 and laid it next to the bag of clothes on the bed. He opened the wooden carrying case that he had hand-made to carry the M1, checked it to make sure that the slide was in there, extra ammunition clips, the sling. He put the gun in and closed it.

He carried everything to his front door and paused, looking around. On impulse, he walked back into the kitchen and opened the cabinet that he had kicked open earlier. He put the cardboard box on the counter and took out the contents.

There was a pressure cooker, yellowed and streaked with old use, looking very much as if Lorraine had had it out the day before. Under that was an aluminum skillet, black on the bottom, shiny and scratched on the inside. The empty spaces in the box were full of wooden mixing spoons, metal measuring spoons, a salt and pepper shaker that he had long ago replaced, knives. He laid everything out on the counter and looked around for places to hang things or put things away. No hooks. He wondered if he had hooks around somewhere that he could screw into the walls.

He shook his head, laughing at himself. What the hell, he'd be back in a few days at the most. He could fix things up then.

He carried the empty box downstairs with him when he left, then stomped it flat and stuffed it in the garbage can. There were a lot more boxes upstairs that he would have to get rid of more efficiently than that.

Robert drove over to Jackson and made a right turn, headed toward downtown to take River Road over the bridge. He had gone several blocks on Jackson before he saw the pickup in his rearview mirror. It was an old, beat-up black truck, a Dodge? He couldn't tell at night. As he drove he kept trying to see if he could get a glimpse of the driver as they passed under streetlights, but all he saw was the reflection off the windshield and then a lone silhouette in the cab.

He felt the Smith & Wesson, then took it out of the holster and set it on the car seat next to him. He jerked the Bronco around a corner and stopped. The pickup kept going on Jackson and as it passed Robert could see that there was a woman behind the wheel.

Robert sat a moment, thinking that he had to make a U-turn and keep going. But his hands felt weak, his arms achy and heavy. He was going to have to settle down. He couldn't very well go on like this indefinitely. Something was going to have to happen or he thought he was going to completely come apart through sheer fright, even if Arneson didn't do anything at all. He reholstered the pistol, shifted into first gear and spun the Bronco around, headed for the range.

The last two miles to Stuart's place were over a blacktop county road that served no purpose except to connect two larger county roads and give access to half a dozen farms on the way. The countryside was open, cultivated land with stands of trees left in long strips of the original forest to serve as windbreaks and as shelter for rabbits, raccoons and an astonishing number of wild turkeys, considering the way they were hunted.

On impulse, Robert pulled to the side of the road and switched off his headlights. There was a quarter moon that gave him a fair amount of light to see over the cotton fields to the next stand of trees. He rolled down his window and shut off the car engine to listen. If he listened a long time he thought he might be able to make out the sound of crickets although that was pretty high up in the register. He could sit and remember what they used to sound like before the war. He could hear frogs. That probably meant there was a stock tank somewhere around that he couldn't see, an artificial pond scooped out of the earth, overgrown with algae and water weeds where the cattle hadn't trampled it into a quagmire. He could picture it in his mind's eye, the lily pads and the splash in the dark.

He wondered how much it would cost to buy a couple of acres out here and put an old mobile home on it. He would talk to Stuart about it. Maybe he would wait a few months, then ask him so it wouldn't seem so much like a pipe dream. No, he would ask him about it tomorrow. See what he thought about it. If he went to work for him, Stuart might be willing to help out with the financing. Robert would need the help, he thought. What the hell, no harm in thinking about it.

He saw the headlights in his side mirror and stared at them, watching them get larger behind him. They were high off the ground, more like a pickup than a car. As they got closer he could tell that they were round, old-fashioned, not like the newer square, halogen headlights, and coming right for him. No they weren't. They were in the middle of the road, going past. He took a deep breath and let it out. Something was going to have to happen.

Stuart saw the Bronco in the morning and brought him down a bag of rolls and a thermos of coffee. Robert helped him open the place for the day and set up the coffee in the snack shop. At noontime he took a turn in the control tower to give Stuart a break and then went up the road to Stuart's trailer to shower before heading into town. He was in a good mood, not nearly as jumpy as he had been the night before. Maybe this would all work out okay and he could just bring Kevin back in a week. He would give it a few more days before he tried to decide that.

No real hurry, now, since Lorraine's cousin, Linda Durham, had a daughter, Jody, who was eighteen years old and that Robert had completely forgotten existed. Kevin was delighted and somewhat curious as to what the actual status of a second cousin was. Robert had talked to them on the phone that morning. Kevin had said that the Durhams thought the whole business that sent him up there was exciting, "Pure television, Dad." So there was no hurry to decide on when Kevin had to be back as long as he could do his schoolwork at a distance. Robert hoped that most of the schoolwork was to be in writing since Kevin had made it clear to him that he would have to confer with the professors, billing it to Robert's home phone.

It wasn't until he walked from the public parking area near the Student Union to the front of Andrews Hall, that he suddenly remembered the last time he had been there. He stopped cold. He had to think about it for a minute before he realized, convinced himself, that very few people could have actually seen him make that melodramatic entrance, waving a gun. Based on his experience with eyewitnesses, Robert guessed that the chances of someone remembering him well enough from that one episode to recognize him were about zero.

He walked in and consulted the directory board to find the English Department office. He sneaked looks at the students that he passed in the hallway but nobody seemed to notice him. A young woman leaned against the wall, just outside one of the doorways. She glanced up at Robert as he walked past, then looked back down at the notebook in her hand, earnestly chewing the end of a pen. The thought suddenly struck Robert that Melody Arneson had been an English major, too.

The girl in the photographs must have hung out here like the rest of them. Like Kevin, she probably centered her social life around this place. Talked about it at home.

He wasn't so cocky as he walked into the office. He waited patiently until the student-receptionist decided that he had been waiting long enough to establish her position of importance. She looked at him as though he was another bothersome interruption, but not as though she was personally put out with him. "May I help you with something?"

"I'm Robert MacDonald. I think you're supposed to have a package here for me?"

She raised her eyebrows and shrugged. "I'll look." She half-heartedly rummaged under the counter.

"I'm Kevin MacDonald's dad."

"Oh, you are?" Her smile came up over the top of the counter different, more genuine, seeing that he was a parent and not just an ordinary deliveryperson. She searched a little harder. "What does it look like?"

"I don't know, exactly. He had to go out of town for a while and his teachers said they were going to put his assignments and some books in a package here for me to pick up."

"Bet they forgot."

Robert smiled, trying to be agreeable. "You might be right. Could you check and find out if anybody's seen it?"

"Sure. Tell you what. I'll see whose classes he's taking and see if they might be around. If they forgot to do it, they can take care of it while you're here." She disappeared into an inner office.

In about ten seconds an older woman came sailing out of the same door and bore down on him, all flags flying. She was clearly angry. Her artificially red hair stood stiffly out on the sides of her head as though bristling, her face tilted slightly down so that she could peer over the top of half glasses and give him her most intimidating glare. "Excuse me, sir. Would you mind identifying yourself?" She continued to relentlessly advance on him.

Robert was startled by the overt hostility. "Well . . . Sure, I'm Robert MacDonald, Kevin's father."

When she saw his reaction the woman softened from the "all flags flying" to the "approach with caution" phase. "You mind showing me some ID?"

Robert stared at her, wide-eyed. It was so clearly an honest expression of surprise that the woman lowered her battle flags the rest of the way. "I'm sorry. There were some test papers in that package that haven't gone out to the rest of the students and something funny's going on here." She looked at Robert's driver's license, looked back at his face. She was puzzled and turned to yell over her shoulder. "Well then, who was that other guy?" She turned back to Robert. "Kevin was supposed to be going to Arizona or something, right?"

"New Mexico."

"Oh! That's right! I typed the address on the label, myself."

"Did you give the package to an older guy?"

"Well . . . maybe a little younger than you. He came up and asked something about Kevin and I thought it *was* you."

"Scar on his face?" Tentatively, Robert put his fingers next to his chin.

"Oh!" The woman beamed. "I guess it's all right, then. You obviously know him."

TWENTY-EIGHT

In the shop at Stuart's range, Robert pulled his shooting block down from its shelf and put it under the light. He searched around the bench until he came up with two boxes that were the right size and began packing them with the 180-grain monster loads from the block. He was wearing a loose-fitting, brown-canvas shooting jacket with a leather patch in front of the right shoulder and oversized pockets with button-down flaps at the sides. Concentrating hard to make sure he packed everything he needed, he didn't hear the sound of footsteps on the stairs until they almost reached the door. He put his hand on the Smith & Wesson and stepped rapidly backward, almost falling over one of the stools. Stuart walked in and looked around. If it had been Greg Arneson, Robert would have been dead already.

Robert had stuffed a small zippered bag with the clothes he had brought from home and set it by the door next to the wooden case holding his M1. Stuart looked at the case steadily and then at Robert. "Missed him, did you?"

Robert continued loading the two boxes as though it was something he did habitually at this time of evening. "Guess so."

"You think he found out where Kevin went?"

Robert finished packing one of the boxes, closed it and put it in his jacket pocket. "Looks like it."

"Called Kevin and warned him, didn't you?"

"Sure, as soon as I found out."

Stuart pulled a stool over, out of Robert's way, and sat on it to watch. "So now you gonna go to New Mexico, huh?"

Robert paused in what he was doing to look over at Stuart. "Is this a quiz show or something?"

Stuart used one fingertip to push the cowboy hat up off his forehead. His glasses glinted in the light, hiding his eyes. He might have been smiling. Robert looked around the shop, saw a pair of field glasses and stuffed them in the bag with his clothes. Stuart walked across the landing to the control tower and came back in a minute carrying a holstered .44 Colt. With the gun belt, Stuart looked for all the world like a real cowboy. He set the gun down deliberately on the workbench. "Be glad to help you out. You could probably use the help, you know."

Robert opened his old junk box, pulled out three empty M1 clips and dropped them in his other pocket. "Help what?"

Stuart tipped his head back and scratched under his chin, the light catching on the lenses of his glasses again, hiding him. "All right." He reached into his hip pocket and from his wallet extracted an oil-company credit card. "I been meaning to give you this if you going to go to work for me. Use it for business stuff, it'll help me with the books."

Robert took it and put it in his shirt pocket. "Okay."

Branson stood up and started to walk out, then seemed to change his mind and turned back. "You probably gonna need this." He took off his hat and put it on Robert's head.

Robert tugged it down and nodded. "Just about fits." He grinned at Stuart, a short flash that was gone in an instant. "I'll bring it back."

Stuart sat down again under the harsh light, his wispy white hair, a sparse damp tangle over his shiny scalp. He looked naked and obscenely old without the cowboy hat. "I know where you can get an M16."

Robert looked at him to see if he was kidding. He didn't think so. Robert nodded, a curt, "That's okay." He picked up the box with the M1 in one hand, took the bag with his clothes in the other and went down the stairs.

Robert stopped to fill the Bronco's tank for the second time near Wichita Falls. The sun was coming up behind him where he was leaving the country of green lush growth, coming onto a landscape that was changing gradually to higher, flatter, drier country, the bare beginnings of a great desert that stretched all the way to the Sierras in California.

It was all lost on Robert MacDonald, who marked distance in ciphers of time, ticking off the names on a map, as marks on a rule, measuring the continuum to where he should be now, should have been last night. He conquered the distance by the length of time he sat, immobile, tense and fatigued, enclosed in a hurtling machine that, as long as it was in motion on the road, took him nearer.

In Robert's mind there was little enough excuse for what had happened to Terry. The signs had been there for someone more perceptive, less self-involved than Robert had been, to see. As long as Lorraine had been alive and healthy, he had left all that to her. Left it to her to tell him what he needed to do, to temper his own sometimes harsh ideas, mold him to reality about the boys. She's the one who got him to buy the shoes, the endless succession of blue jeans and shirts and jackets and socks. All the little things that made up a continuity of caring, of attention to the details of living and connecting.

When Robert grew up there had been a larger body of people, even though they lived in a smaller, poorer part of the country where the boundaries of human experience could be marked almost by geography, county lines. But there were more people that counted. There were uncles and aunts and people who were related through some strange almost-forgotten connection of marriage and name. And the others, the nonrelatives, were familiar, orderly categories of people that you knew by sight and who knew you and your family by sight and name and history for generations past.

All of that had disappeared after the war. He couldn't have said why because it hadn't been just for him that it was gone. For Robert there was just the need to find and impose order again, to stop the chaos, dig in his heels and say, "Now, here, this is how we're going to do it. This is how it's done right. This is what a man is supposed to do." And for the next forty years he had stayed steadily in that track like a man he had seen behind a mule in his youth, keeping the furrow straight, not looking to the side or any further ahead than he needed to, to keep the thing going straight.

Except for Suzanne. He couldn't have explained Suzanne to Terry. He couldn't explain the whole thing to his own bitterly complaining conscience. Only Suzanne seemed to understand what it was and she never explained it to him. Probably he would not have understood if she had tried. The explanation wouldn't have fit with the rest of the forty years any more than his actions with her had. It didn't fit. He couldn't live with it if he thought about it and so he assumed that Terry couldn't live with the knowledge of it either.

Even so, he thought, he should have seen; he should have seen the darkly troubled man that other people saw so readily, without any apparent difficulty. Somehow, there should have been a way for him to see it and stop it, impose the old order before the chaos caught up and killed him. He'd had plenty of opportunity and he had missed it. He hadn't seen it. He didn't know the clues, the danger signals that were there to be seen if he had been the man to look.

This time was different. This time, he had kept going and figured it out. Maybe it wasn't any great feat of intellectual cunning or even investigative skill, but there it was in front of him.

This time the facts were all there for him to consciously pass by if that was what he was going to do or to move ahead, in spite of the fear and the deviation of the furrow, to look ahead and take whatever steps he had to take to stave off . . . What? The inevitable, relentless march of accident; the random falling of shells wiping out generations of descendants in the smoky pulverization of a few thousandths of a second; the overwhelming, primal, driving urge of his own organ to force him—no, deliver him—into the hot sweet darkness of chaos; the misdirected swing of a riot baton; the unspoken word, the neglected kindness of a word that might have, could have been said. If he thought about it, and he might not let himself think that much about it, Gregory Arneson could be thinking the same thing.

But after all this time, after all of this. Surely, somewhere, there had to be, at the very least, substantial order. Surely there had to be that left at the end.

In the north Texas dawn Robert replaced the gasoline nozzle in the receptacle on the side of the pump, the metal cold, chilling his bare hand. He was giddy, his head skidding along with lack of sleep and hunger. The station had vending machines inside and Robert emptied his pockets of change, buying prepackaged food that he could open and eat as he drove. He kept going.

Maybe he could just arrest Arneson if he found him.

Actually, he could. He could make a citizen's arrest, even using force. For what? For attempted murder. He was so tired, he thought, that his mind was wandering.

Robert thought about Terry, of his head as he lay on the concrete floor of his garage, then of his feet sticking out from under the yellow tarp. Any thought of making a clean, sanitary arrest of Arneson evaporated in that image. He had to think about Kevin, now. He had no right to rely on anything less than a certainty. Anything else was just stupidity and simple cowardice.

He stopped and called the Durhams.

"Everybody okay?"

"Of course, Robert, everything's fine."

"Linda, this is serious."

"I'm sure it is, Robert. Where you calling from?"

"I'm in Santa Fe. Has anybody been around? Anybody you don't know?"

"Really, Robert, you worry too much. You've been a policeman too long, Lorraine always said that . . ."

"You . . ." He made himself control his voice. "You're probably right, but I wish you would be extra cautious right now."

"Robert you come on out to the house and have some dinner and a good stiff drink. You'll feel a lot better. The kids are fine out where they are."

"Where are they?"

"A whole bunch of 'em went camping up on Table Mesa. I'm not sure they're supposed to do that because it's either on an Indian reservation, or real close to one but they been getting away with it for years . . ."

"They went camping?"

"Robert, they're all kids that have been Jody's friends for . . . oh, since she was in first grade, practically. Three of 'em live within a hundred yards of here, the Johnson kids. They just live right . . . Why don't you come on out to the house? You're only about a half hour away."

"Sure, okay. I'm sorry, Linda, I'm a little tired. It's just that this guy seems to be a lot smarter than I thought before. The way he found the address and everything, I don't know if it was just the off chance that he went up to the department and asked for Kevin or . . ."

"Robert, for heaven's sake!"

He hesitated, realizing suddenly what he must sound like. "I guess I'm pretty tired."

"I should say! Come on up here before you worry yourself into a heart attack or something. You want me to send Ben down there to get you?"

"No, I'm okay. Be there in about a half hour."

When he got back in the Bronco, though, exhaustion swept over him in a wave of nausea. His head suddenly ached and his arms were weak. He realized he was relieved. He didn't know what he had expected to find when he got to the Durham's, but he thought he probably expected a bunch of people huddled under the beds with the lights out. Linda's reassuring authority and the news that Kevin had gone off with a bunch of kids away from the house, away from the address that Arneson had, brought the immediate emergency to a sudden stop.

Okay, Kevin was safe. That didn't mean that Robert could relax, though. Arneson could very well be waiting near the house, watching, and he would probably remember the Bronco after shooting at it. Robert would have to be careful how he approached. He stopped in Los Alamos and got a local city map and an Indian Country map so he could locate Table Mesa. After studying the map of Los Alamos, he circled around several blocks in the Durhams' neighborhood, gradually closing in on their house, looking for the pickup.

The fact that he didn't see it wasn't particularly reassuring. The guy might not have made it in the old truck, no matter how much work he did on it, but if he did make it, he sure didn't come all this way to take a room in the Holiday Inn. Sooner or later he would show up.

When Robert pulled up in front of the Durham's house he saw Linda throw the front door wide and come down the front walk.

"For heaven's sake, Robert! What took you so long?"

He glanced at his watch. "I wasn't that long, I stopped to get a map in town is all."

"Twenty minutes from Santa Fe to Los Alamos and another twenty minutes to get the last block to this house? Did you get lost between the Johnson's and here?"

Robert got out and walked around the front of the Bronco. He could see a man approaching on the sidewalk and immediately tensed, not listening to Linda carefully.

She raised her voice to yell toward the approaching man. "It's okay now, Pete. Here he is, finally. Robert MacDonald, I want you to meet Peter Johnson, he's the fa . . ."

"That's not him." Pete Johnson stopped on the sidewalk and stared at Robert.

Linda said, "What?"

Robert was too tired to catch on quickly. "Not who?"

Peter stared at him and then at Linda. "That's not the man I was talking to in front of my house. Besides, he had an old pickup truck . . ."

"Did you tell him where the kids are?" Robert's fatigue disappeared.

Peter looked slightly offended. "I . . . I might have. I don't know exactly what I said, I thought he was you." He turned to look at Linda who was turning white, clasping her hands in front of her stomach. Peter stared at her. "Is there a problem?"

"Peter, what did you say?" Linda's voice was rising in pitch.

He turned his attention to Robert, apparently hoping to talk to someone rational. "I knew you were coming from what Linda said earlier and when this guy stopped and asked did I know Kevin MacDonald, I just thought he must be . . ."

"Did you say where they went? Did you tell him that?" Now she was screaming.

Peter hesitated, apologetic, although he clearly thought he was being unjustly accused of something. "I said they went camping . . . but I don't know if I said Table Mesa."

Hysteria came into Linda's voice with a shrilling crack. "Peter! For God's sake, think! Did you say it or didn't you?"

Robert was already back behind the wheel, trying frantically to open the Indian Country map as the Bronco fishtailed and took off down the block.

TWENTY-NINE

Robert allowed the Bronco to roll along the shoulder of the highway, going slowly past what had to be Table Mesa. It stood out by itself, isolated, smaller than the vast mesas that he had been driving past all day, but strikingly majestic, all by itself, standing up out of the desert floor. He could see a fence about fifty feet off the shoulder, running parallel to the highway. He hadn't seen any roads leading into the mesa or breaks in the fence. He didn't know if there might be another approach but the map didn't show one. On the other side of the butte was the reservation. Robert didn't see the pickup although he looked for it carefully. He decided that if the neighbor had inadvertently told Arneson where the campers were, Greg hadn't found the place yet. Maybe he had to go back into town and find a map.

Robert formed the vague idea that he had to get close to the kids, to Kevin, to be able to see Arneson coming to them. He didn't know of any other way to find the man other than to sit by the bait and watch for him, watch for the truck. With any luck, Linda would have called the local police and sent them out to bring the kids back. He could sit and watch and wait for the highway patrol or whoever had authority out here.

He rolled slowly past the mesa, looking for whatever might be there, something to present an idea of how to approach. The Rio Grande flowed right by the base of the thing. Most of the country was barren of what Robert would call real trees but there were juniper bushes, shrubs, everywhere. The only trees were along the banks of the river where there were cottonwoods growing thickly, a long narrow strip of forest in the middle of the desert, the beginning of the mountains.

A mile past the butte he pulled off the highway. He saw headlights in his mirror and stopped, leaving his engine running, lights on as though just looking at a map. The car went past and he was alone again. He waited until the taillights disappeared over the next hill and then pulled off the shoulder, across a shallow depression and stopped next to the barbed wire fence on the other side. Then he shut off the engine for good and turned off the lights. He sat for a minute, trying to think what he was going to do next. He was brutally exhausted but exhilarated, too. A truck passed on the highway, headed back the way he had come and Robert felt exposed, sitting in the Bronco.

He got out of the car and pulled out his jacket and put it on. He set Stuart's hat on his head, pulled out his utility belt with the Smith & Wesson in the holster and buckled it around his waist. Then he went to the back, lifted the tailgate and pulled out the Garand. He removed it from the case, threw the box back into the Bronco, took out the binoculars and closed the tailgate. He locked it, automatically, without thinking about what he was doing and dropped the keys in his pocket, hearing them clank against the ammunition clips in there. At the side of the car away from the highway he sat down and loaded the three clips, working by feel in the dark.

He climbed through the fence and strode quickly in the direction of the cottonwoods by the river, his back turned irrevocably to the highway, his last chance of innocent explanation gone as he walked away from his car with the guns.

He knew he was on an Indian reservation, but had only the vaguest notion of what that meant. He had a simplistic mental picture of Redskins in breechclouts and feathers and he knew that wasn't right. He didn't know what was right. Maybe they all dressed like farmers now or all had jobs in town. He thought it was possible that Indians hunted out of season, legally, on their own reservation and from a distance, with the hat, it might be possible that he could be mistaken for an Indian. He knew all of that was the rankest, dumbest form of speculation. He knew that he would have to start being extra careful because it was obvious that he wasn't thinking right. He was too tired.

The cottonwoods were a lot farther off than they appeared from the highway. Just to his left, in front, he could see a low, small building, a hovel. It was dark, but he didn't even know if they used electricity here. He walked slowly for a while, watching and listening for dogs, wanting to avoid any commotion. Then beyond the building in front of him he saw a house, the distant square of a lighted window, maybe a mile away. It had lights all right and it looked like it was right down near the riverbank among the trees.

He walked faster again, going on past the darkened building. He turned when he was past it and looked, just wanting to be sure. He was walking slightly downhill so when he turned around he could see the building outlined against the sky, a framework of some kind on top of it and something going off to one side. He realized it was a cross, the framework was the remains of a shoddy steeple and a cross, tilted at a crazy angle away from it, as though it was about to fall to the ground. It was an abandoned church that in its heyday could not have held more than ten or twelve worshipers at once. He turned and walked on down toward the river.

When he got to the cottonwoods he walked right in among

them and then stopped. He leaned against a tree to break his outline and stared back the way he had come. He could make out the Bronco, sitting up there, so close to the road and he wondered that he did not have the urge to go back, to retrace his steps to try to regain the safety, the inconspicuous, anonymous honesty of the road. Honesty was not the word he wanted. It was legality. What he was doing might be illegal but it was not, he decided, dishonest.

But he didn't want to go back. He was ready to keep going. It seemed as though at some point between the car and the trees he had crossed a line where it was all right to do it. Not all right, exactly, but he was committed. Now that he was started, he knew that he would keep on going.

Up through the ribbon of trees was the butte, Kevin and probably, at some point anyway, Greg Arneson and whatever was going to happen was just going to happen, because back there, back in the "safe" car on the "safe" highway were Terry and Lorraine—not Lorraine, what was he thinking? Even thinking that way was chaos, random notions that would not make sense.

He turned abruptly and walked toward the butte. He better quit thinking. He was getting more tired and making less sense and he better stop it now. He had taken too long to get this far.

For a second his heart thudded, a sudden spasm of fear. How did it come to this? Everything he had always done was done by the rules. He had to quit thinking. Ahead was order, not chaos. The rules had to matter.

Arneson must be trying to get Kevin isolated, to try to shoot him when there were no immediate witnesses. He had thought about this before. There was a long gap. What was it, six weeks? Anyway, there was plenty of time between when Arneson shot Terry and when they finally got the guy. He knew where Kevin was in school, where to find him. He must not have done it then because part of the whole point was to get away with it, to not get caught until he had the chance to get Robert, too.

The only thing that didn't fit was burning that car. But that was probably a random opportunity that he just couldn't pass up. It was a chance to *burn* Robert.

It was just past midnight when Robert reached the foot of the butte. He regretted the time that he lost in going so far up the road and then having to walk back, but Arneson knew his Bronco so Robert had to at least make some attempt to conceal it, do something besides just leave it next to where he was going, on the shoulder of the highway.

Up close, standing at the foot of the mesa, the physical characteristics of it were formidable. It was at least two hundred feet straight up, Robert thought. Maybe twice that; he didn't have any way to tell. The night was clear. With more than a quarter moon there was some light, but he couldn't see any way to get up to the top. He decided to walk around it, going along the side away from the highway since he had already determined that there wasn't a road coming in from that direction.

Robert was wearing good, practical workboots, prepared to have to do some hiking. The river didn't come right up against Table Mesa. It may have at one time, a few thousand years ago, maybe, but now it was a good two hundred yards off. He discovered he could walk out a little away from the cliff, away from the debris that had fallen over time, the boulders, smaller rock slides that were against the base of the cliff. Out away from it he had easier walking but no concealment at all. He thought about going all the way down to the river and following that, staying back in the trees until he got to the other end of the butte. Then he might miss whatever path or track there might be that let people get up to where the kids were camping, so he better stay close to the face of the cliff and look for what might be available.

Walking out in the open, even in the dark, he was uncomfortable. If Arneson didn't see him, somebody else might. Somebody might want to know what kind of business brought a man out wandering around an Indian reservation after midnight with a sidearm and an M1. He slowed down. He walked carefully, trying to be silent, as silent as he could be in the dark.

He saw movement in front of him. It was bigger than a jackrabbit but not a man. It ran directly away from him, broke into the clear and then stopped and turned. It was dog-like with big ears. A coyote? He supposed so. At least it didn't bark.

He found the road. It was little more than a dirt track, but it was a road, graded at some time by somebody. From his perspective at the bottom Robert couldn't tell where the road went except up. It angled out of his sight and probably doubled back to get up there, but he couldn't tell. He started walking up.

The sides of the mesa were relatively soft, available for someone determined enough to dig caves, to make dwellings out of them, protected, ultimately, by the cap rock. Here, they had cut out this road, borrowing dirt and rock to pile up where they needed it and grading and smoothing the surface to make it more usable for something so unadaptable as a man. On the cliff side it went down, sheer to the bottom. On the other side of the road, up against the mesa, itself, there were cliffs going up and crevices, small canyons and big rocks, debris from the road-making and from the simple continuation of the course of nature, fallen from above. There were places to hide, but not much of any place to run.

Robert's new hearing aids were a little better protected, inside his own ears, so he didn't have as much trouble with the wind noise as before, but there was still some interference from the wind blowing across them. It took him a little time, then, to sort out the voices he heard coming from up on top, but by the time he was three quarters of the way there he was sure that he heard them. They were laughing, young teen-agers, older teenagers, laughing. At least they were still up there.

He sat down when he heard the voices, to take a rest and let his heart slow a little and catch his breath. The land beneath the surface projections like the one he was on was not flat but it wasn't as hilly as he had thought. There were huge domes and giant depressions, a rolling landscape, something like the plains that he had crossed in western Nebraska and eastern Colorado a long time ago.

He could see lights, a town. He was disoriented and didn't know what town it might be, but he wasn't particularly curi-ous to know. There were roads, visible from where he was by the headlight beams of individual travelers, out there in the distance going somewhere deliberately, maybe going home, somewhere in the midst of all this.

He stood up again and kept climbing.

When he got to the top he could see a campfire and a camp lantern not too far away, the light confined to a small space, cocooned against the night.

Robert circled the lights, staying away, keeping his head low at the level of the juniper that was growing up there on top. The campsite was near enough to one side of the top that he was relatively sure no one could be concealed over on the other slope. It would be up to him to go around the rest of the perimeter and see if it was clear, to try to make sure.

He went all the way around the camp once, not seeing any-thing suspicious. The problem was that there were plenty of opportunities for concealment. Making one slow pass around the edge, just out of the light, left a lot of ground that he hadn't been able to see. He went back to the road and looked at where it led away from the area where the campers were. He decided to follow it a way to see if there was an obvious place for an ambush of some sort.

Robert started to worry. What if Arneson didn't come up

here? If he wasn't here by now, what if he wasn't coming? What if Arneson decided to stake out the house and wait for an opportunity there? He didn't have to think, just because Robert thought he ought to, that it was better here, away from town. And where were the local cops? They might not take it too seriously at first, but surely they would come up here and check it out after they talked to Linda. If Arneson wasn't here and Robert had to wait until dawn, or if the cops didn't get here until it was light then Robert was stuck. He didn't see any way he could just walk back, walk out of the trees carrying his M1, he would have to . . . Hold it!

The truck. The pickup. The fucking pickup was right in front of him, maybe a hundred yards from where he was crouched. He dropped to one knee and froze. He stayed still, not moving an eyelash, not twitching a hair for what seemed to him like hours, but he knew was only minutes, seconds maybe. He allowed himself to breathe, but only slowly, listening for any sound he might make. His heart was pounding as hard as it had at any point in the long climb up there, but he didn't pay any attention to that. Then there was the sound of laughter at the campsite a quarter of a mile from where Robert was crouching; they were laughing and laughing. Then the explosion of a shot from a high-powered rifle.

Robert, already tense with waiting and watching, erupted, sprinting toward the sound of screaming, hearing the shot in his head over and over. He ran, stretching his legs in long strides, holding his rifle in two hands, swinging it back and forth in front of him, running as hard and straight as he could around the junipers, across the top of the butte toward the spot where he could see the lantern. He heard a second shot and more screaming.

Robert strained to tell where the sound of gunfire had come from, slowing his running because it seemed as if it was off to his right, not in front as he had thought. He hesitated and then ran in that direction, more cautiously, listening, trying to figure out where the son of a bitch was so he could get in his own shot, ready now to shoot, sick that it was too late. Terrified and furious, he listened and watched for any sign that would give Arneson away.

Then the truck started. The pickup seemed to start moving, lights on, as soon as Robert heard the starter. Arneson had planned it and Robert wasn't thinking. He had been fooled good and he wasn't thinking yet. He ran toward the truck a few steps before he realized it was headed down toward the road, escaping down the road that it had driven up on, the only way up there.

Robert fired from 150 yards away, standing off-hand, trying not to breathe because he was badly winded and shaking with rage. He fired the whole clip, practically in a single burst, almost as fast as a machine gun. The pickup disappeared down the road, below the edge of the top of the butte.

Robert ran after it, torn by the futile chase on foot drawing him away from finding out if Kevin was dead. He stopped then and turned the binoculars on the campsite. He could see Kevin standing, tall and excited, his shirtfront covered with blood, but standing and shouting, pointing toward where he, Robert, had been when he was shooting.

Robert turned and ran, skidding near the cliff edge when he cut to his right to head down the road. He was running downhill then, picking up speed, going too fast to control. Oil! There was oil all over the road. He had to slow down but oil, gravel and dust skidded beneath his feet as he tried to control his speed. He ran slower then, carrying the rifle in his left hand, feeling for a new clip in his pocket with the right. He pulled it out and dropped it on the road. The heavy, loaded clip bounced and slid to the end of the switchback and went on over the edge. Robert stopped, cursing the delay but carefully removed the empty clip from the gun and inserted the remaining loaded one. He started down again.

Then there were pieces of tire in the road and no more oil.

Robert guessed that he had hit the engine and, a wild shot, since he was trying to hit the driver, one of the tires. He could hear the engine of the truck and saw it emerge from the road at the bottom of the butte, bouncing, limping, running on one rim, dragging the front bumper without the tire to hold it up. Still it went on, heading, Robert was sure, for another road, one that would lead out of here, where he could put on the spare and run at least until the engine finally froze.

Robert sat on the edge of the road, trying to brace the M1's forestock across a rock on the cliff side. Arneson was a long way off, too far. Robert fired all seven rounds, shooting at the cab, but not hopeful that he would hit anything at that distance. The truck stopped. He could see Arneson emerge from the cab. In the dark and at that distance he couldn't see his face, but Arneson stood for a second in the light from the cab and then ran, apparently unhurt, for the trees near the river. He was carrying his rifle.

Robert didn't know if he had hit the truck again or if it had finally succumbed to the bullet he had hit it with earlier. He didn't puzzle over it, but reloaded the empty clips rapidly, then started after Arneson.

When he reached the bottom of the road Robert could see the pickup, a dirty metallic sheen in the moonlight, and he tried to judge the nearest point in the trees down by the river that Arneson would run for. Robert started running to head him off, to cut directly across country, although, with the lead Arneson had, he would definitely reach the trees first. Robert was running, watching the tops of the trees, all he could see clearly, trying to get a fix, a landmark of any kind. His foot struck a rock in the dark and he fell, his mouth hitting the rear sight of the gun as he landed on his elbows. He was up again immediately, running and running, only spitting out the blood when it filled his mouth and he noticed it. It did not hurt.

He saw a muzzle flash in the dark, and knew that Arneson was just shooting at the sound he made, running. He shifted the M1 to his left hand and drew the Smith & Wesson, still running, right at where he saw the flash, now firing with the pistol as he ran.

He fired all six rounds, shooting fast, not even breaking stride and then he was there. He was in the edge of the trees with the empty pistol in one hand, the M1 in the other. He kept running a few steps, expecting to see Arneson fire or rise up, but nothing happened.

Robert stopped, trying to see into the dark under the trees, the empty pistol upraised so he could swing it, or throw it. He thought he was that close.

He heard splashing and just glimpsed a flash of water on the other side of the river. He fired once with the M1, trying to draw an answering shot that he could see, but there was nothing else.

Robert started forward again, but stiff-legged, unable to command his legs to run. His chest seemed to freeze, spasmed and then he made a horrendous sound, sucking in air. He tried to stop it, hearing it loud, but he couldn't. His chest seemed to go on its own, sucking in air and blowing it out, taking control away from him. His legs gave and he went to his knees, still staring across the river at the last spot he had been able to see anything.

His mind, reason, came back before he could rise. He was on both knees and one hand, still in the trees where he had fallen, his back convulsing, bucking with the effort to draw breath, but he was thinking: *The son of a bitch had panicked. He ran! Where the fuck did he think there was to run? What for? There wasn't any good reason for him to run, to go anywhere. He had to know that it was him, MacDonald, after him. Wait! No, he didn't.*

Robert rose to his knees and bellowed as loud as he could. He caught his breath, sucking as deep as he could, drawing it in with the aid of the panting and yelled again. "It's me! MacDonald! Mac . . . Don . . . Ald!" His hearing aids picked up the echo, coming back at him from the far mesa wall, bouncing inside the canyon and coming back. Almost immediately Arneson fired. Too far away, too quick but firing one, two, three times, the rounds evenly spaced, the speed of a man working rapidly with a lever action and a magazine.

Still panting, Robert got to his feet. "All right, asshole. Now you know. Just stay there." He said it out loud, but to himself, no longer yelling. His hands were shaking while he was trying to reload the revolver, though he settled right down. It was not fear. Robert didn't think about that at all, now. He was excited, tired maybe, but not scared now. He thought he might be a little crazy. If he didn't use more caution he was going to give the game away right now, a default for overeagerness. He forced himself to slow down. Now they were each hunting the other. Arneson would draw him away from the trees, work to set an ambush, equally confident that Robert would keep coming after him. Now they each knew the game plan, each knowing precisely what was driving the other on.

He splashed into the Rio Grande and looked at it in the dark. It was shallow, sandy where he was standing. Was there quicksand? Probably. He stepped quickly, trusting to luck and plunged into the channel over his head. He pushed off the bottom. It was only about six feet deep and he caught and clawed his way up the sand and gravel on the other side. It was hard work with the M1 and the heavy boots, but he crawled out of the water. He was only on a sandbar. It looked like he was in midstream. He stepped carefully then, trying to sense if he was sinking too fast in the sand so he could fall forward if he had to. He realized in mid-step that he still had Stuart's hat on. The rest of the crossing, though, was no more than two feet deep and he splashed over easily.

Arneson did not fire again.

Robert tried to remember where the firing had come from. He should have fixed the place in his mind, using some spot on the landscape that he could see, like the top of the line of the mountains or, better, some feature that was visible on the mesa or canyon mouth nearer to him. He decided to stop, squat down where he was and try to figure it out. He didn't think that Arneson would run from him now. He would try to ambush him instead. Arneson was the quarry, he could sit still and wait. Robert would have to go to him.

Robert turned and looked back at the mesa he had just left, on the other side of the river now. He could see flashing lights and hear, faintly, the siren of another vehicle coming. Maybe an ambulance. Maybe just another police car, he couldn't tell. He was mildly surprised that the hearing aids still worked. He hadn't thought they were waterproof, but maybe they were because he could hear.

Whether he had heard an ambulance or a police siren didn't matter. It meant they could get an ambulance there soon. Kevin had been on his feet and Robert had seen him; clearly Kevin had been standing and shouting. There had been blood on him but was it his own? Was somebody else hit? Robert didn't have any way to tell. He would have to assume that Kevin was not hit or, if he was, that it was superficial and that the ambulance that was coming would take care of him. He had to just trust that he was right. He had to.

The sheriff's posse or somebody would be coming after him soon, he knew. They would be down here where he was with all-terrain vehicles and floodlights to search them out, put a stop to this business. He thought of going through it all again, the arrest, the wait, the possible release because of something that he, Robert, couldn't control, some legal maneuver that would put them right back where they were. He wasn't going to risk it again.

He turned and looked over the ground in front of him, between him and roughly where he thought Arneson must be. He moved up, keeping low. He stayed in a crouch until he was right up against a juniper bush and then knelt, listening and watching for any sound, any movement that would give Arneson away. Nothing.

Robert moved only through where the brush, the sage, but especially the taller juniper, was thickest. Robert tried not to allow himself to go through a spot where his outline would be clear even though he thought it was still too dark for anybody to shoot him, looking down into the brush and the dark ground. He worked his way toward the canyon wall on his right, picking it at random because it was nearer than the other side.

Then he heard the stones falling. Nothing big, just a few pebbles maybe; maybe something the size of a baseball, falling from a spot on the wall of the canyon that he was headed for, bouncing and dislodging more stones as it came down. It was a small sound, nothing major. Just enough to tell Robert what he needed to know.

He moved toward the opposite wall. He would have to cross a flat open space of light-colored sand. He paused and thought about it. The sandy space was about fifty yards across, out in the open. If he could quietly get into a position on the other side of the canyon, climb silently, he might be able to look down on Arneson when the sun came.

He stayed in the crouch and started across the open sand. He was halfway across when he heard the shot and right behind it the harsh flat sound of the bullet striking rock. Robert sprinted, running straight up and then zigged just before the second shot, and dove into the brush as soon as he reached it.

Son of a bitch wasn't up there. Arneson was at the bottom of the canyon, behind a boulder practically in the center of the wash. He must have thrown a rock up on the wall to draw Robert in and then sat there chuckling when he fell for it. Not so stupid, after all.

Robert sat still. If he had set up this spot as an ambush, Arneson might think it worked and he would have to come down to look. Robert decided he could wait him out right here, force him to come out in the open.

Arneson didn't come. Robert was not aware how much time had passed, but he knew it was too long. Arneson was not stupid at all and he wasn't going to make mistakes this easily. It seemed to Robert that he had just blinked his eyes but, suddenly, he knew it had been too long by far. He raised up, his legs aching with the effort, and watched, wondering if he had slept.

Robert saw him, just glimpsed him climbing up into the canyon on the same side Robert was on. He realized that he could see the crevices and he would have to go after him as the first gray light of dawn threatened to reveal each to the other.

Robert climbed, moving awkwardly up the slope when the ground permitted it, scrambling between or even over boulders when it didn't. He saw Arneson again, even farther in front of him. Robert knew he wasn't trying to get away, but he was having a lot of trouble getting the time to set up his ambush.

By the time the sun was fully up neither of them had fired in at least two hours, probably longer. Robert sat, his back against the canyon wall, rocks on both sides of him. He could, by stretching his neck, see behind him, the way he had come. There were people down in the trees by the river with vehicles. He saw one man on horseback, trotting along the edge of the tree line.

Getting up, Robert started moving into the canyon again. He couldn't get very high on the wall before his way would be blocked and he would have to descend to the bottom to make forward progress. He was trying to hide his movements from both directions now, and it was slower going. All Arneson had to worry about was what was behind him, so Robert was afraid that he might be going pretty fast, by now.

But when he caught another glimpse of Arneson, he saw he

had gained ground on him. Arneson was still clambering over rocks moving away from him, but he seemed to be going slower, more awkwardly. Robert didn't know what advantage he might have gained, but thought maybe that leg wasn't holding up to the effort.

Robert moved faster. He dropped down the canyon wall to the floor and ran for a space in the open and then jumped back into the rocks. He was taking a chance, he knew, but he was getting closer, now. He was almost in range.

By ten o'clock it was already blisteringly hot. The rocks were hot to the touch and Robert could feel the sun baking his back through the heavy canvas jacket.

He didn't know where Arneson had gone, except in the roughest approximation. He concentrated on hearing the wind, listening for any sound of falling rock that might tell him where his prey was at the moment. Arneson would have to come back for him, for Robert, because there wasn't anything else left for him.

Robert looked at the trees at the bottom of the canyon again. He would be able to see much better from there if he could make it. He decided to risk it.

When he tried to stand, his legs wouldn't straighten. Blood was caked around his mouth where his lip had split on his own gun sight. It had dried and blackened, big flakes stuck on the three days' growth of stubble on his face. His hands and knees were bloody from the rocks, his pants hung in tatters on his raw, scraped legs. He forced his legs to move as he would have forced a rusted piece of equipment, knowing that once it moved a little it would go easier from there. He stumbled upright out into the open and then had to run again, making for the trees.

Arneson's shot was too slow, striking the rocks at least fifteen or twenty feet away, behind and above Robert. The twin sounds of the rifle and the ricochet redoubled again, the sounds bouncing off the canyon walls and coming at him from every direction until it was impossible for him to tell where the first sound had come from.

Robert's hips and knees stiffened as he came under the trees and hit soft ground. He couldn't make his joints bend and lift his feet fast enough and so he fell headlong, sliding on his chest in sandy mud. Arneson fired again before he could get up and again before Robert had dragged himself to the opposite side of the canyon. Running in mud, staggering as he came out onto rocky ground again, Robert scrambled into the rocks. He immediately turned around and leveled the M1 over the boulder he was crouched behind. Arneson didn't fire right away so Robert figured he wasn't behind him. Other than that he had no idea where the man might be.

Robert waited. He held his breath until he realized that he was doing it and then he found that he couldn't breathe normally. His breath was coming in huge pants, blowing in and out on its own, beyond anything he could control except to stop it, hold it and then he would have to blow and pant some more.

For an hour Robert sat with his back twisted awkwardly so that he could brace his butt on the rock next to him and lay the fore stock of the rifle in a small crack in the rock in front of him to steady it, ready to pivot and fire, the safety off. Sweat soaked all the way through the jacket, the dark spots under his arms and across his back, finally joining to make a band of sweat that circled his whole body. His mouth was dry and his nose filled with dried mucous and dust.

In the second hour Robert saw the stones fall. Small ones, a pebble or two and some sand was all, but the movement was enough to catch his eye.

The place where they had fallen was diagonally across the main canyon and just into the mouth of one of its tributaries. It was right out in the sun, just like Robert's position. MacDonald moved very slowly to bring the binoculars up and look. Above and to the left of the place he had seen the rocks fall, he could see a hole big enough for a man. Robert couldn't tell how deep the depression was. It might be deep enough for some temporary shade only or it might be deep enough to hide in. Arneson, being right there next to it, would know.

Robert couldn't see any other spot that looked shady so he shifted his body a little and swung his gun to sight on the spot between where he had seen the stones fall and the shade.

It had been at least two hours, maybe two and a half, since Arneson had fired. Robert's eyes swam and he began to see spots, tiny amoebic flashes of light, swimming, rotating in his field of vision. He blinked hard, opened his mouth and tried to stretch his face, feeling the stiffness of the dried salt and blood around his mouth and eyes. Under the brim of the borrowed hat his eyes were watery, bloodshot slits in his grimed face. Still, he didn't move.

Three Appaloosas worked their way slowly into the convergence of canyons, nibbling the growth along the way and pawing at the sand, looking for water. Periodically one of them would shove its nose into the damp ground and snort. The horses weren't in any particular hurry. They paused for long periods, munching lazily and swishing their tails in the sun. They appeared to be impervious to the heat.

Robert watched them but not because he was distracted. He knew he had to look away from the bright face of the wall he had been staring at or he wouldn't be able to see anything at all. He watched the horses' ears. If there was a sound of movement they would hear it first. He didn't expect much reaction, they weren't wild horses, so he had to watch them carefully. There. Finally, a quick glance, the sharp pointing of the second horse's ears.

When he looked back up the face of the wall opposite him, Robert could see Arneson on his hands and feet almost spread-eagled, trying to work his way up to the shade. His right thigh was dark with blood and Robert instantly thought that the broken bone, barely healed, must have given way. Arneson was right out in the open, maybe figuring that Robert had gotten away, maybe trying to prevent it. Except the man didn't even have his rifle. Robert had the fleeting thought that maybe he was out of ammunition and had thrown it away.

Robert settled his cheek against the stock of the M1, checked the safety with his forefinger and then wrapped it around the trigger. He let out his breath gently, drew it partway in and then held it. The explosion rang in his head so loud that he couldn't hear the rocks falling, crumbling, sliding under Arneson's body as he fell.

Arneson slid about twenty feet and then thumped to a stop on top of a boulder. He didn't move. Robert shifted, raised himself slightly so that the gun's muzzle came down and the front blade sight rested once again on Arneson's body. This time when Robert fired, the body did not move. Robert looked through the binoculars, but they were not strong enough to allow him to see a bullet hole.

He heard, vaguely, someone calling him. He ignored it, concentrating, focusing everything on the next shot. This time he settled the blade under the head. He squeezed and with the sound of the explosion, saw a pale pink spray fly up around the head.

"Sergeant MacDonald! Robert MacDonald, stop where you are. Your son's all right and we have everything under control!" It was the loudspeaker in a helicopter, hovering over the ridge behind him. Robert hadn't even heard the engine as it approached. "MacDonald! We have you in sight! MacDonald!"

Robert tried to stand but at first he couldn't do it. Then he made a tremendous effort and lurched to his feet, stumbling forward down toward the bottom of the canyon. Then he was on level ground, the sandy wash. He noticed that the horses were gone. Maybe they were there and he couldn't see them anymore. He started walking out, walking in the center of the wash, out in the open. He didn't think there was enough room between the trees for the helicopter to land here and he didn't even look up, acknowledge that they were up there.

He stumbled in the sand but didn't fall. He just kept walking until he heard the siren. He stopped walking, looked up ahead and saw a white Jeep headed his way up the wash, siren whooping and the lights on the overhead bar going like mad. He realized that he was still armed. He took out the Smith & Wesson and held it and the M1 at arms' length on either side of him but he couldn't bring himself to drop either one. He bent over and gently laid them on the ground.

He stood up and started to put his hands in his jacket pockets as he walked towards the patrol car. He realized what he was doing and held his hands out to show that they were empty. He walked on like that, his hands out to either side, walking toward the approaching policemen, his head up to see them. *Okay,* he thought. *All right. Order.*